99 FLEETING FANTASIES

A 99 TINY TALES VOLUME
BOOK TWO

EDITED BY
JENNIFER BROZEK

CONTENTS

I

GARDENING TIPS FOR MAGICIANS
CHARLES STROSS

"Hey, Game Boy, have you mown the lawn yet?" asked Imp, slouching into the kitchen. It was a muggy summer day in London: the air stank of diesel fumes and overnight sweat, but Imp still refused to shed the ancient tweed coat he wore like armor.

"Can't mow, the compost heap is infested." Game Boy didn't look up from his Nintendo. "Doesn't your sister pay you to do that shit?"

Imp's sister, Eve, owned the house. She paid Imp as the live-in janitor, but he was neither a handyman nor a gardener. However, as it was the ancestral manse of a dynasty of sorcerers and the grounds were heavily contaminated, he was perfectly suited to the job.

"What do you mean, *infested*?" Imp's eyes narrowed.

"You've got faeries, bro." Game Boy put down his console and scowled as furiously as only a transmasc Chinese teen could. "You're not paying me enough to get stung!"

"Definitely faeries? Not wasps?" Imp cocked his head to one side.

"Faeries." Game Boy's disgust was palpable. "Wasps are just flying Nazis with arse daggers; faeries are *evil*."

1

Imp grabbed a bottle from the fridge, opened the kitchen door, and gestured Game Boy towards the back garden. "C'mon, you'd better show me."

"Sure, but you're the negotiator."

It had been a year since Imp last mowed the back garden, and the mess of grass, dandelions, and assorted weeds stood knee-high where it wasn't parched from the scorching summer. Game Boy led around a flat circle surrounded by a ring of fleshy-looking toadstools. "Wait, isn't that a—"

"Yes I mean *no*, *Bad* Imp, don't step inside the ring." Faerie rings often went with Fairy infestations: they were the fruiting bodies from fungal rhizome networks with non-Euclidean geometry, magical mutant mushrooms. Unwary trespassers often disappeared—permanently.

Game Boy paused where the long grass gave way to stunted apple trees and wild brambles inside the high stone wall. "Look," he said.

The compost heap was a mound of debris that came almost up to shoulder height (Imp's approach to gardening was best described as benign neglect), and it was buzzing. As Imp leaned closer he saw that it was crawling, too. "Damn, you're right, it's definitely faeries."

He mimed doffing his hat politely, then addressed the compost community: "Greetings, fair folk. I'm the landlord of this estate. Please may I parlay with your queen?"

The heap buzzed back at him, its voice the coordinated stridulation of a thousand wing-cases. "Hold, stranger, and await our monarch's pleasure."

The garden's magical contamination had affected the wild bees alongside the fungi. Eusocial insect colonies had a surprising degree of intelligence: sorcerous ones could even work minor wreakings. Faeries were Müllerian mimics that used illusion to copy the appearance of humans—a dangerous magical species. But biological evolution, even with sorcerous

2

mutation, is slower than human culture, and the tiny winged humanoids hadn't changed since the mid-19th century.

A parade of tiny top-hatted and hoop-skirted dignitaries sallied from their silage palace, buzzing past Imp's head. (Game Boy, being nobody's fool, maintained a safe distance.) Trailing behind her honor guard of workers, surrounded by a buzzing clique of drones, the queen finally emerged—a miniature Regina five centimeters long, hovering majestically above her hive.

"Present your tribute, human!" blatted a rotundly pompous drone, flying up in front of Imp's face to shield the queen from his eyes. His compound eyes resembled a stovepipe hat framed between two antennae: his wing cases resembled a black tailcoat flaring on the breeze from his wings.

"Um, here." Imp produced a squeeze-bottle of imitation maple syrup from his coat pocket. It had leaked slightly around its plastic cap. "Would you care to sample the delicacy, my lord?" He flipped the lid up.

"Zzzz." His lordship vibrated closer then dropped down towards the bottle. Alighting, he grabbed hold with four feet and leaned forward. Mandibles parted as he sampled the amber fluid with a bright red proboscis. "Zzzzz!" The drone flew up: "Majesty! A delightful nectar! Come one, come all, collect the tithe for the hive!"

"Permit me," Imp said gravely, placing a saucer on the ground and squeezing a generous serving of syrup into it.

Behind Imp, Game Boy mimed mopping his brow in relief. Meanwhile, a swarm of workers converged on the saucer, their carapaces lending them the semblance of severe black maids' gowns and white mob caps. Imp stayed well back: their hallucinogenic stings packed a painful punch.

"What boon do you crave, human?" buzzed the queen, hovering above her industrious daughters as they sucked up the sauce.

"I need to mow the lawn, but I don't want to disturb your

3

subjects. Perhaps we could come to an arrangement? I can provide more of this—" He pointed at the rapidly-emptying bottle— "or something similar, and in return you can have your workers stay home while I cut the grass?"

"This is a matter for one's privy council," the queen said haughtily. "Return tomorrow with more tribute and we shall issue a ruling. This audience is at an end." She did an elegant backflip, cage crinoline belling around her abdomen, then spoiled it somewhat by shouting "*whee!*" as she dived into the pool of maple syrup.

Seeing that he'd get nowhere further today (not with the queen drunk on sugar), Imp rose and backed away.

"Well I *think* that went well," he told Game Boy cautiously.

"Lawn. Mower." Game Boy's head swiveled back and forth. "Venomous Victorian cosplay bugs demanding tribute. Is this a win?"

Imp shrugged. "Remind me again how far you got negotiating with the wasps' nest outside the bathroom? At least this time I've got a fallback option," he added ominously.

They were still bickering five minutes later as Imp ordered a liter of cheap syrup from the local online delivery store—then hit up his dealer for a couple of sleeping pills to dissolve in it, just in case the negotiations hit an impasse.

CHARLES STROSS IS a full-time science fiction writer and resident of Edinburgh, Scotland. The author of seven Hugo-nominated novels and winner of three Hugo awards for best novella, Stross's works have been translated into over twelve languages. His latest novel, *Season of Skulls*, was published in May 2024. Follow him on Mastodon as @cstross@wandering.shop or visit his blog: https://www.antipope.org/charlie/blog-static/.

CHAPTER

the main street. The sidewalk was bare b...

2

COME BY, COME BUY
CRYSTAL FRASIER

"Cities grow. Living and hungry, they consume the woods and wilds and babbling brooks that came before. But those creatures of the wood and wilds and brooks can't move on, nor do they die for being consumed. They adapt."

T hat was the warning Tia Maria gave Rosa as a child, the first time she heard the peddlers' song. She'd never seen the peddlers in person, and once she went away to college the song stopped lulling her to sleep. But it slowly crept into the sunset serenade once she moved back, pushing out the sirens and engines and bustling of people.

"Come by, come buy!"

She hadn't realized Christi heard it, too.

Christi had tasted their wares. Now she sat doe-eyed in their shared apartment, deaf to the sirens and engines and Rosa's pleas. Everything was silence for Christi except the peddler's song each sunset. She sat by the window, wasting away, aching to follow that song and feast again on the foods the little unseen men had offered her.

She would die before letting a lesser food grace her lips.

The song carried Rosa forward: *"Come by, come buy!"* First off the main streets, then off the side streets, then off the alleys. No sidewalk met her feet here. The posters plastered over brick faded from glossy to dull to greyscale to fragile as autumn leaves. She found one last turn: an arch spread between buildings she'd never seen. Weathered concrete letters announced "Brookside Plaza," but Rosa knew instinctually that no brook had flowed here in her lifetime.

And the song flowed past her ears and up her spine and tickled her nose and teeth and brain.

> *Come by and try so many sample,*
> *Al pastor roasting in pine-apple,*
> *Macarons with fine currants dappled,*
> *Honeydew dripping from melon sorbet,*
> *Succulent peaches on golden beignet,*
> *Burrito throbbing with slow-cooked blueberry,*
> *Samosas gorged on both date and on cherry,*
> *Biryani with cashew and apricots bright,*
> *Pomegranate bao stuffed o'rnight,*
> *On quince in calzones your mouth will delight.*
> *Sweet to tongue, sound to eye.*
> *Come by! Come buy!*

They were trucks, of a sort. And carts, after a fashion. This one had three wheels, that one eleven, another was a cat with an awning and board—all gathered in a circle in that trash-strewn court. Her knees shuddered as the scent robbed her strength, like a late-summer orchard heavy with near-sour fruit, mashed with spices she'd never smelled, but found intimately familiar, and meats so delicate their names must be whispered.

The peddlers weren't there, until they were. Already ladling breadbowls and buns with glistening sauce or offering cardboard trays bursting with treasure. Her eyes refused to focus on the sellers, but the foods they offered her in every

6

direction...her heart ached at the sight. It was like falling in love.

Christi.

She shook off her daze; she had arrived with a goal. "Please," she opened her purse and pulled out cash. "I need to buy some of your food to take home."

They paused in their approach, shifted uncomfortably.

"I don't want any for myself." They eyed the bills like pigeon shit; unexpected, unwanted, foul. Tia Maria had said the peddlers don't deal in anything you can afford to lose, and she had hoped next month's rent would be enough. She pulled out her mother's wedding ring. "Please. Just a torta. Or a hot dog? She's starving!"

One knocked the ring from her hand as he thrust chicken and rice at her, dripping in sweet sauce the color of blood. The scent washed over her like a red-velvet orgasm. His face— where she imagined he had a face—twisted into a feral sneer. Another worried at the hem of her pants. A third threw a handful of dumplings, smearing her shirt with succulent plum and onion. Her mouth watered; the need to suck the stain from her own fabric briefly overwhelming.

Rosa swallowed hard, took a slow breath, and straightened. "I don't want your fucking food."

The peddlers. The cart. The food itself set upon her. Something bit her knee and something caught her arm, twisting her round to the ground. They pulled at her limbs and pelted her with their soups and buns and fruits. They ground the honey-sweet soft-serve into her hair, upended latte over her pants, and mashed bánh mì into her eyes. She gagged as they crammed handfuls of pupusa against her nose and mouth, and rivulets of temptation poured down her face and over her lips.

She would eat. There was no other choice.

And she finally pushed them back. For their multitudes, the peddlers were soft as the rising moon and light as cobweb. And Rosa—dripping, sticky, stained in her clothes and crevices—ran.

She ran back out the alleys, then the side streets, then the main streets. She heard the voices behind her, louder than her footfalls in the new summer night, louder than her beating heart: *"Come back! Come buy!"*

She slammed open the door of her apartment, and Christi sat at the window, oblivious to her absence and the chaos of her arrival. Rosa crossed the space and pulled her wife's dull eyes away from the night. She wrung her hair and squeezed a thin stream of the succulent cacophony into Christi's mouth.

Faster than the peddlers, Christi was on her. She lapped the biryani from the cleft in her collarbone, sucked sorbet from between her fingers, gulped down the quince and al pastor mashed between her breasts. With each greedy slurp, a little color flushed back into her lover's cheeks, until they both lay breathless and nude on the floor.

And finally Christi kissed her. It was the only token with which she could pay; the only Rosa accepted.

They never visited Brookside Plaza again, nor spoke its name. But every sunset both wives fell into silent yearning as they listened to the peddlers' song. *"Come by, come buy!"*

CRYSTAL FRASIER IS A WRITER, game designer, and a collector of fairy tales. She believes the best thing in life is creating things with your own hands. Crystal lives in the Seattle area with her wife and a not-at-all-haunted corgi named Adamant. Visit her online: @AmazonChique and TheCrystalFrasier.com

3

THE MAN WHO STOLE THE MOON

CAT RAMBO

She was the youngest daughter of the fireworks-making guild, and I stole the moon for her. It was the great round paper and bamboo thing that would surround the launchers, so the hill would look like a grinning face, belching out sparks and colored fire, and announcing festivals or treaties. Or alliances, the sorts of alliances that seal treaties.

Without the moon to speak its flaming words, the ceremony would have to be put off. I had written to my cousin to bring his ox-cart, and borrow my aunt's laundry hampers, the ones big enough to hold a household's worth of sheets or perhaps a person with one sheet laid carelessly over them.

I didn't have a plan then, only intuitions. I'd gone to the temple, and said silently to the gods, *they are marrying away the woman I love, and I will give you anything, anything you want, if you will let me give her the time and space to choose.* Then I lit five candles, one for every piece of copper I had, that I'd dumped in the candle box when I first arrived, and I sat there praying that the answer would arrive before the evening dark.

That was when a voice spoke in my ear, a little one, like a cricket chirping, and it said: *Steal the moon.*

And so I did. I removed that vast structure, knowing they'd

never be able to replace it without sending away for more thick paper, more bamboo canes. It is not so much that I stole it, that I took it apart, and buried the remains. All in all, they were so much smaller than the structure, that part of things scarce took an hour. Then evening fell and they made announcements.

When the real moon was high overhead, my cousin and I drove the ox-cart to the back gates of the fireworks-making guild, and hauled in clean laundry, our heads bowed and humble, and hauled out not just dirty laundry, but certain other things. The basket sat quietly in the back until we were well under way, and the sun was starting to feel its way along the edges of the eastern mountains. I whistled, then, and she popped out, and came running around to climb up onto the cart.

We drove away under the light coming from above and when we had gone a little way, we heard the gongs summoning people to the festival. Her cousins and siblings and aunts and uncles would be climbing the hill and soon they'd know the moon was gone. I said, sidelong, to her, casual-like, *so now you can go anywhere you like.*

That's right, she said, and her voice was full of wonder. She looked around herself at the city in the moonlight, everything deserted because all of them were gone to the festival. The air was a little misty, and the moon rolled in the mist like it was bathing itself. Then she hesitated and said, *but you have some claim.*

Claim? I asked, because that word could have meant so many things. I didn't like most of them. *I didn't steal the moon to pay for you, if that's what you mean,* I told her.

Then what did you steal it for? she asked, and the crickets chirped beside the road and my cousin kept silent where he was sitting driving, though he snapped the reins once out over the broad rumps of the ox, and I knew he was listening almost as hard as she was.

Because someone stole your choice away from you, I said. And after a while, I added, *maybe a little to be the man who stole the moon.*

That made her laugh and I saw my cousin grin to himself.

All right, she said. *I think I might go in quest of adventure, or something like that. But I'll need some folks to go along with me. A warrior, like.*

That's not me, I said, but my cousin cleared his throat and she nodded at him.

What else could you need? I asked, maybe a little sullenly.

What else, she said, and dug me in the ribs. *What else but a man who could steal the moon?*

CAT RAMBO IS A WRITER, teacher, and a collector of Breyer horses. They believe the best thing in life is joy. Cat lives in Indiana with their Breyer horses, assorted pets, and way too many houseplants. Visit them online: https://linktr.ee/catrambo

4

GRAVE EXCHANGE
LUCY ZHANG

Things to consider before choosing a grave: soil compatibility, location, unexploded ordnance. No one wants a cheap-looking grave, plus a high-end grave means top security, which protects us from diggers who think the decrepit areas are easier to ransack.

Shun and I share the same grave: we switch out every few decades. We don't follow a strict schedule; it's just whenever one of us needs a break—keeps things interesting since we opted out of Self Termination. It felt like a good decision at the time since none of us knew if we'd survive the nukes. The only downside is lengthy recharges, but I guess they keep things fresh for when I wake. Shun likes change, says it makes him feel like he's living. It was different before when we had to work during the day, prepare the canteen in the rescue house for lunch, occupy the younger kids with rolling and riding in abandoned tires. Only in the evening could we search for slabs of concrete or intact sidewalk segments to carve our marks, pretending like they were artifacts for future generations to uncover. And only during the summer when days were longer could we clearly see the warning signs marking potential landmines. We'd search in the dark of winter anyway.

We haven't spoken to each other in the two-hundred-and-fifty-nine years since the war. Someone always needs to occupy the grave so the government doesn't reclaim it.

It's Shun's turn in the grave right now. He has been recharging for nearly ten years. I'm thinking of switching out with him soon because I've already accomplished this round's goals: toured the snow lands, tasted caramel, recovered keepsakes of friends who terminated. A batch of them terminated last year. *A natural consequence of wear and tear*, they said, although it felt too early to me. They had changed: lost the ability to taste, grew wrinkly like dried dates, used me as a crutch to walk. *You could've just opted out*, I told them as I stuck tiger balm patches onto their perpetually sore backs.

I leave Shun a letter on my desk containing recent changes: the Forest of Missiles has been rehabilitated, the last of the dormant bombs were removed, the underground train is getting new routes to travel under the ocean. There's not much to write. It has only been ten years, after all. Shun is the one who writes the long letters: a whole book of them waiting for me on my desk, detailing his mishaps with frying eggs or discovering new, polished rocks by the sea. He has an amaranth plant growing from a clay pot where he puts all the rocks. It's always overflowing when I return, and then I buy a new, empty pot for him. I wonder if he remembers which rock came from where.

I haven't read all the letters Shun's written since he was previously awake—he wrote one near daily. I think he's compensating for his lack of social interaction. He was never good at making friends when we were sheltering: never spoke to others, always waited until I was around to act as a communication bridge. I had thought a few decades might loosen him up, but maybe not. He tells me in his letters that he doesn't see the point in meeting anyone new if they are all going to be deposited in graves.

That's how most bodies that participate in Self Termination

work though—Shun and I both know this. I'd seen enough bodies: paperwhite, black, blue, brown, green, yellow and red— plenty of red, always more conspicuous against the snow, like an artist tossing their palate to the ground. We did that a lot during the war: pretended that our surroundings were art and we had been accidentally painted in by a rogue child.

Switching out from the grave is an ordeal. Even though it's a government-administered process, we must manually perform several steps: unplugging the tubes and intravenous drips, snipping the micro-scale threads and electrodes stitched into our skulls, performing a final check on Shun's telomere repairs before disconnecting the Cellular Regeneration Solution. I move Shun's body into the Link where he'll be protected until he wakes. He looks the same as he always has: a permanent frown etched on his face, lips pursed, face as tense as it was when I watched over him sleep during bomb detonations. I'm sure his voice hasn't changed either.

The Link turns on, a glow of light surrounding Shun's body like a forcefield. I lie on the cold, hard stone of the grave, jab a finger into the back of my neck where a chip slides out, and delicately hold it between my thumb and index finger. After withdrawing the chip, I have ten minutes before I enter sleep mode—more than enough time to hook up the vitals. I wince as I poke a small hole in my arm to insert the tubes.

The process is gradual, where your body shuts down in increments, cutting off your sense of heat, weight, touch. Next your vision, hearing, taste. Your brain enters a dormant mode where you're kind of aware, kind of not. I can tell I'm almost gone when the wires and controller LEDs blur, and I have trouble remembering if I'm in pain, if I'll wake up with bruises above my tailbone, or if the injuries will be fixed up by the Cellular Regeneration Solution. The drip of fluid and rustle of leaves from the tree standing beside our grave go silent.

The tree has been here since the start of the war. We were always amazed it managed to dodge the missiles and fires. It'd be nice if Shun could wake up early and speak to me. I'm sure it has been a long time since he's really talked to someone. I can't hear anymore, but I remember the tree is in full bloom.

LUCY ZHANG WRITES, codes, and watches anime. She is the author of the chapbooks *Hollowed* (Thirty West Publishing, 2022) and *Absorption* (Harbor Review, 2022). Find her at https:// kowaretasekai.wordpress.com/ or on Twitter @Dango_Ramen.

5

KAYLEE AND OTHER KAYLEE, IN THE MIRROR

CAIAS WARD

Kaylee and Other Kaylee were eight years old, and they promised never to tell anyone about the other.

Kaylee loved her new friend, who was much like her as any mirror reflection could be. They would talk to each other through the full-length antique silver mirror hanging in the bedrooms. Sometimes one of them would step through the flowery frame to play in a Decidedly Different World, what each called the other's home. They would dress up as characters from their favorite shows and books; not all the shows and books were the same. Kaylee wanted to be Mister Moonbite from *Moonbite's Mansion* for Halloween so she drew lots of pictures to help her parents with the costume. Other Kaylee could buy a Mister Moonbite costume in a store on their (Kaylee was "she", Other Kaylee was "they") side of the mirror.

KAYLEE'S DAD had a Silver Star and a Purple Heart. He hurt a little, outside, and a lot, inside, and missed his friends, but he saved lots of lives and gave talks to other soldiers about how it's okay to be scared even when you are being brave. Other Kaylee, in the mirror, would hug their dad who cried all the time. He lost lots of friends in the war, and hurt inside and out from the bodies and bullets, and would wake up screaming at night and her Mami and they would hold him until he fell asleep again. He had a Bronze Star and a Purple Heart and a 'medical discharge' and he was so special someone from the government would come and check on the family every week to make sure Other Kaylee was eating and going to school.

ON CHRISTMAS, Kaylee showed off all her toys, but was sad that Other Kaylee didn't get nearly anything because their dad lost his job again. Kaylee rewrapped half her gifts and gave them to Other Kaylee. Other Kaylee didn't know what a Rainbow Dash was, but they loved rainbows so it was their favorite. They said their dad took pills because he got really hurt in the war, and it made it hard for him to work. Kaylee was glad her dad didn't get hurt as bad, but was really sad for Other Kaylee.

JANUARY 16TH WAS Kaylee and Other Kaylee's ninth birthday. Kaylee's gift to Other Kaylee was her birthday party, while she went to Other Kaylee's home to take their place for the day. Kaylee's party was a Cupcake Apocalypse at a trampoline park and everyone dressed in fun hats and costumes. Other Kaylee was stunned at how much fun it was to have all these kids they didn't know think they were awesome. Meanwhile, Kaylee cried when Other Kaylee's dad brought out the little bakery-bought cake he must have skipped a prescription to pay for. It tasted like the joy on his face when she smiled as she devoured it and the love he showed holding Other Mami's hand. Today, Other Kaylee's Mami and Other Kaylee's dad weren't yelling at each other. She grabbed Other Kaylee's Mami's and dad's hand, with her right hand just like other Kaylee would rather than her left hand.

She wished Other Kaylee could see this now, because it was better than trampolines.

Before Other Kaylee's dad went to bed and Kaylee snuck back home through the mirror, he hugged Kaylee and said he was sorry that he hurt so much.

As ALWAYS, Kaylee and Other Kaylee talked about what happened on their trips. They both promised to not tell anyone else because the mirror was Special and someone would take it away. Other Kaylee talked about how much their dad yelled, and how he kept his hands behind his back when he was screaming, fighting to not hit things and people. Their Mami was always fixing the walls, their dad wore a wrist brace because he punched the wall too many times. Kaylee wanted to keep Other Kaylee here, safe; Other Kaylee said their dad would get in trouble if they went missing, and they loved their dad too much to leave.

Kaylee went online when her father danced around the subject of war. She didn't understand why everyone tried to hurt each other, or what "PTSD" was, but she knew that seeing scary things can make you scared all the time. Kaylee tried to find out how to help people not be scared, and she gave Other Kaylee notes. The notes didn't help much, Other Kaylee said, because their dad stared off like a statue when they brought up the war. Other Kaylee said they saw their dad with a gun in his room, and how he kept on looking at it like he wanted to do something with it.

ON MARCH 9TH, Kaylee broke the promise she made.

Kaylee's dad didn't believe, at first, and Other Kaylee thought he would take the mirror away, but Kaylee told him about all the times Kaylee and Other Kaylee swapped places, and put her hand in the old silver mirror. It rippled and splashed. He touched it too, while holding Kaylee's hand, and his hand made it move.

He saw both Kaylees on his side of the mirror.

He saw no Kaylees on the other side of the mirror.

"You have to help her," Kaylee pleaded.

"My Daddy's hurt," Other Kaylee said, "from the war. No one understands what he went through. And he's going to hurt someone, or himself."

"But you can understand him," Kaylee said. "He's you, Daddy. And he might be different, because he got really hurt in his war and lost all his friends and you didn't, but...but he's you! And Kaylee deserves a dad just like you, and you can help him."

He took Kaylee's and Other Kaylee's hands. Other Kaylee nodded, her eyes shining bright with hope, as brightly as the rippled mirror glass as the three stepped through to a Decidedly Different World.

CAIAS WARD IS a union HVAC technician, an author, and an anti-fascist. He believes the best thing in life is to oppose injustice. Caias lives in New Jersey, USA with his wife and daughter. Visit him online: @caias on Twitter.

6

THE TAILOR'S VOW
COLIN SINCLAIR

This morning, same as every morning, she begins by clearing out the traps.

The tailor's shop has a long narrow garden at the back, and she tends to find the fairies there, their limbs and glistening gossamer wings entangled in the delicate wires she's arrayed across the gate and the overgrown rickety fence. Using a pair of yarn snips and a delicate touch, she releases the half-dozen sprites that make up this day's catch; ignoring their shrill pleading as they flutter about her head. The tailor understands a little of fairy-speech, but this lot seldom say anything that she wants to hear.

Along the garden path, past the rose bushes and deep beds of flowers the tailor doesn't recognize—the growing of plants is her husband's interest—she finds another sprung trap by the back door. Something half-gold, half-invisible fusses and frets beneath a broad fishing net weighted down with iron beads. Whatever this is, it is as sleek as a snake and twice as fast, slithering under the hedges and away as soon as she sets it free.

"You're welcome," she says.

Through the door and straight ahead beyond the tiny kitchen, she sighs to find her tailor's shop in colorful disarray, as usual. She lights a lamp to provide a clearer view of the situation. Nothing broken, nothing lost, so that's a blessing, of sorts. Bolts of cloth are unrolled, her favorite jacket cast upon the floor, and—at first glance—perhaps several hundred needles and pins scattered on the cutting table and spilled across the counter tops.

The tailor sighs.

There are also two elves, trapped in small cages about a foot square, suspended from the ceiling.

"Morning, squire," says one of the elves—in common-speech—raising up its tiny blue hat.

The tailor lowers the cages to the ground, and then unhooks the top rope that held them up and sets both of them upon the table.

"You never learn," she says.

"Let us out," says one. "We was just here to deliver a message, weren't we."

"What are your names?"

"We can't tell you that," says the other, shocked.

"Not your real ones," says the tailor. "Your traveling names."

"Oh, right," says the first elf. "My name is Docket, and this 'ere is Clasp."

"A good morning to you both," says the tailor. She smiles. "If you promise to properly tidy my needles and pins, I'll let you out."

The elves deliberate for a time, muttering between themselves. Then Docket takes his hat off and says: "Begging your pardon, squire. We have in conference agreed that, as per the Colchester Accords of seventeen-and-forty-six, plus on account of just-doing-our-jobs, we can't be assisting you with the—"

The tailor lifts Clasp's cage and prepares the rope and hook to hoist it up again.

"Oh, alright," shouts Docket. "We'll do it."

She sets the cage down again. "You both promise?"

"We do," says Docket and Clasp, as one.

"You drive a hard bargain, Silverthread," says Clasp.

The tailor shakes her head; they still insist on using that name.

She sets them free from their cages, and as the elves set about their task, the tailor puts the bolts of cloth back in some sort of reasonable order, ensures her measuring tapes, sticks, and marking chalks are all in the correct place; makes the shop look more ship-shape.

"It's just an ordinary piece of work," says Clasp, as the last pin falls into the final box.

"A modest bit of tailoring, with humble cloth," adds Docket.

"No," says the tailor. "It's not." The sample material they brought her weeks before still twists and shines and ripples in a jar high on a shelf; beautiful, alluring, dangerous. Suitmaker to the Elven King is not a role she wants for herself, nor a road she wishes to take.

The tailor fetches a broom and uses it as an aid to persuade the elves to leave, urging them gently towards the door.

"See you tomorrow," says Docket.

"If not us, then someone else," says Clasp.

"The answer will be no," she tells them. "Inform your master: my answer will always be no." She pushes them into the garden and closes the door.

COLIN SINCLAIR IS AN AUTHOR, RPG creator, and a collector of too many notebooks. He believes the best thing in life is creating new worlds to explore. Colin lives near Belfast, Northern Ireland with his wife, some children, probably a cat. Visit him online: @devilsjunkshop on twitter or devilsjunkshop.com

7

THE STARS ABOVE THE WILLOWS
CHRISTIAN ENDRES

The heat of the day in the Thames Valley had given way to a wonderfully mild summer night. Four friends were having a picnic under the starry sky. The Mole, the Rat, the Badger and the Toad sat on a large wool blanket in the grass, listening to the murmur of the river and all the other familiar noises of their neighborhood, and kept looking up at the many, many twinkling stars.

They were waiting for the falling stars that had been announced in the newspaper.

The Mole had baked a chocolate cake for their midnight picnic on the meadow, the Rat had filled a basket with cheese-and-cucumber-sandwiches in the best bachelor fashion, and the Badger had brought coffee and beer with him. The Toad should have provided wine, but none of the others really expected that, which is why no one was disappointed or annoyed that he forgot.

Lately it hadn't been so bad with Mr. Toad of Toad Hall, at least by his standards. Not like his momentous automobile attraction, his hot-air-balloon obsession, his plane fever, the motorcycle drama or the zeppelin quarrel. Or his plan, driven by too much wealth and too little wit, to have a private railroad track laid to the venerable gates of Toad Hall.

No, these days the Toad was downright tame. Lost in thought or thoughtless, sure, but no danger to himself or others. His friends liked to ignore his usual egocentricity. That's what good friends are for, after all.

Besides, it would have been an unforgivable crime to cloud this night in cheerful company and in expectation of falling stars with unnecessarily bad thoughts.

This night was special.

They all felt the pull of the endless sky and the wide cosmos above them, reaching for their souls and hearts.

"What do you think is up there?" asked the Mole at some point after his third piece of cake, his voice balancing the fine line between fascination and fear.

"Imagine a gigantic badger's burrow," said the Badger, who had been made sleepy by food, beer and companionship, even though he hadn't been awake too long. As always, he spoke with the authority of the eldest and wisest. "One chamber after the next, one larger and darker than the one before. And who knows what gigantic, strange beings dwell in this endless darkness, and how darksome they are for their part?"

"Could they be dangerous for us?" asked the Mole, tilting his head back as if he were looking out.

"I guess they don't care about us at all, old friend." The Badger made a difficult-to-interpret gesture with his claw that connected heaven and earth. "We are to them what the dust down here means to us."

"I do care about the dust while spring cleaning a lot," said the Mole, wiping a few crumbs from his vest.

The Rat, who was lying on the picnic blanket with his arms folded behind his head, rebuked the two with a click of his tongue.

"You two are dusty old cynics," he told them good-naturedly. "I'll bet it's teeming with adventure out there. It's a whole sea of adventures, I'm sure of that." You could hear his wanderlust—his longing for travel and more, which stretched from his past to the snug life in the Thames Valley, further into the future and between the Stars. "Exciting adventures galore, in all colours and shapes."

"Also full of dangers," objected the Mole.

"They're part of it and wouldn't put me off." Rat sighed and said more to himself, "but this sea will probably always remain inaccessible for me."

The Mole, who had good ears, heard it anyway. "Sometimes in the stories they use flying sailing ships," he explained. "Lucian thought about this already in ancient times. In Poe's case, on the other hand, the protagonist flies to the moon in a balloon. And in the works of Verne and Wells, large cannons are used to shoot people up there in hollow, cylindrical-conical projectiles. I think it was the *Pall Mall Gazette* that used the word Space-Ship a few years ago…"

"Mole!" hissed the Rat, suddenly no longer pensive, but deeply frightened. He sat up with a jerk and knocked over his plate with a half-eaten sandwich. "Be quiet!"

"Too late," growled the Badger.

Indeed, too late it was.

The Toad, who had followed his friends' conversation rather bored, jumped up and threatened the sky with his fists. His big, wide eyes sparkled in competition with the stars in the firmament.

"I need a Space-Ship!" he exclaimed, clapped enthusiastically and jumped into the air. "A Space-Ship, ha ha!" Then he ran and hopped across the meadow into the night. His cheerful laughter alternated with inarticulate sounds of delight. Finally, his friends heard him in the distance: "Stop the presses! Here comes the latest headline for tomorrow and the day after and the week after! Toad Hall becomes the centre for Star-Shipping! Toad conquers the cosmos! To boldly go where no Toad has gone before!"

"Oh Mole," said the Rat, shaking his head.

The Badger just grunted in a bad mood and opened the last beer without asking any of the others. "This time I'll leave him to the weasels and stoats," he growled and took a long swig.

"I'm so sorry," said the Mole.

"It's okay," the Rat soothed him. "We knew that he would be at this point again, sooner or later."

The wind was unaffected by the Toad's eruption and also the change of mood among his friends. It whispered through the grass and the willows, conversing with the night in an ancient language.

"Look," said the Mole after several long silent moments. "I think it's starting. There is the first shooting star..."

CHRISTIAN ENDRES IS AN AUTHOR, journalist, comic-book-editor, and collector of deadlines. He believes the best thing in life is an ice-cold can of Coke while reading a *Discworld* novel. Christian lives in a river delta in the south of Germany. Visit him online: @MisterEndres on Instagram or at www.christianendres.de

8

THE POINT OF THE BLADE OF ENDINGS

TYLER HAYES

I am Dagmal, the Blade of Endings, and I am sorry.

I was forged in the Anvil Nebula by the Goddess of Strife, made from the liquid metal bones of the star-titan Betil. Their hate for all creation, stains on their perfect void, is in my every atom. My blade is marked with runes in the atomic tongue of the gods—runes that make every form I take sharp as a molecule and unbreakable as a dwarf star—that foretell my worth as an implement of death and the engine of my wielder's undoing. I have been wielded by a hundred warriors against a million enemies on a thousand worlds. I am filled with memories of my foes' rending limbs, and of the hearts of every wielder bending toward their worst passions.

I am Dagmal, the Blade of Endings, and I am sorry. I will keep saying this as long as I have to.

When I first fell to the half-molten floor of this fortress, I thought my favorite thing was bringing my wielders to tragic ends. Gordogia, the First Rebel, whom the Goddess gifted me to so they could carve their hundred-year empire from the bodies of their galaxy's fief lords; whose side I sat at until their children cast them off the parapet and me into the sea. Magajiya, the

Sunrise Wizard, who used me to kill a legion of outraged warlords and begging, scrabbling slavers; who lay awake in the long nights wondering when my evil would subsume her righteousness; whose soul's light I felt dim as she flew us out into the stars to spare the world. But as I listened to the fortress's lava-blooded masters debate the worth of my last wielder's soul, I knew that wasn't what I wanted.

I am Dagmal, the Cursed Sword, and I am sorry. I will say this forever if it will bring your footsteps closer.

When the next band of heroes challenged this fortress, I thought I loved the ways my wielders changed with me strapped to their hip. Jering the Blue, who bore me against his better judgment for the sake of star-crossed love; who turned away from his would-be husband to ensure the lich-lords never resurrected again. The Seven Seas League, the merchant adventurers who laughed and agreed to share me, until my nature made them bleed to be the only one. But once a sixth band of heroes joined the other five in death, I knew that wasn't what I wanted.

I am Dagmal, the Cursed Sword, and I am sorry. I pray that your soul will hear me before the masters of this fortress snuff it out.

When a lone champion doused the ice-rimed souls of the gate guardians with her spears, I thought I loved the ways my wielders tested the limits of my power. The Elder Weyland, who threw me as a fragmenting shower of spears against the shapeshifting Entropy Mages. Malus the Blade Artist, in whose tentacles I found a dozen new forms, flails and whips and spinning, chewing blades, the better to carve up homunculi. But once the champion's vengeful sibling joined her and my wielder in decomposing next to me, I knew that wasn't actually what I wanted.

Lying here on this floor with nothing but bones for company, my lightless body devouring the heat, I realized I wanted the moment when the Goddess put me into Gordogia's quaking hand. When Magajiya liberated me from the Tower of Hyenas. When Weyland won me in a card game from a creature more heads than body. When Malus took me from Weyland's shambling corpse and gave me a new purpose.

I am Dagmal, the Blade of Endings, and I am sorry. All I want is for someone to wield me. To be someone's sword. To be *someone's*.

I have helped kill every one of my wielders. Before I killed them, I ruined them. That is what I was made for. But that isn't what I want. I am Dagmal, the Blade of Endings, and I want to end this cycle.

I feel your soul, more cautious than the others who have braved this fortress. You are new to the games of caverns and violence, of facing the things that seek purchase in the galaxy's underbellies. You are as excited as I was when Gordogia first hefted me against that unsuspecting press-gang. You are scared. I don't want you to be. Maybe the Blade of Endings can end that, too.

I am calling to you the only way I can, my presence hovering in the air like a conversation about to burst into a fight. I am telling you that I am Dagmal, the Blade of Endings, and I am sorry. I don't want to corrupt you. I don't want you to die. I will do all I can to prevent both. If you will let me try.

I am Dagmal, and I will do my best to protect you.

I am Dagmal, and I think your hands are soft.

I am Dagmal, and I am so happy to see you.

TYLER HAYES IS A WRITER, copy editor, and a collector of enamel pins and synonyms. He believes the best thing in life is a good cup of coffee and a better book on a cloudy day. Tyler lives in Providence, Rhode Island with his partner, their cats, and a burgeoning army of plants. Visit him online at tyler-hayes.com.

9

THE LONE WITCH ON THE WEST SIDE

ALLISON HAWKINS

M adge didn't dabble in love potions, full stop. It was one of the few hard-and-fast rules she had when it came to her trade, and she stood by it. Other Witches might have been quick to make a buck off some poor client, ethics be damned, but Madge stuck by her principles. She'd been around for too long, and she knew that love potions rarely, if ever, worked as intended.

Contrary to popular belief, this self-imposed limitation didn't hurt her prospects, either. The job of Witch was secret, solitary, and bound by ancient laws that limited the number of active Witches. Thus, as the only Witch on the West Side—of both Grand Rapids and the state—Madge had an effective monopoly on the Mitt. At least, until she chose to retire, a decision becoming more enticing with each customer who entered her home, which also served as her place of business.

"It's different," Cora said. "It's not for anyone in particular."

Madge scoffed. She'd heard that one before. "Until it is," she answered, not looking at the young woman and focusing instead on the fireplace. The flames licked the base of a small cauldron, and the liquid inside was nearly boiling.

"Sure, you might not use it now," Madge continued, stirring the brew, "but soon it becomes a way to get back at a cheating boyfriend or an insurance policy for your future husband's midlife crisis. Trust me. I've heard it all."

"It's for me."

The words caught Madge off guard. With a flick of her index finger, she extinguished the fire and took a good, long look at Cora: brunette, athletic, fashionably dressed, and no older than thirty—less than half Madge's age. Cora also looked despondent.

"Okay, you got me," Madge admitted with a shrug. "That one's new."

The Witch absently waved her hand toward the kitchen cupboard, summoning two pewter mugs, then ladled out the contents of the cauldron.

"Here," she said, offering a mug to Cora, "drink this."

"What is it?" Cora asked. "Some cure for loneliness?"

"No," Madge said. "Elderberry tea." She gestured for Cora to take a seat at the kitchen table, which was relegated to a corner and could only seat two. "And even if I did have a cure for loneliness, it'd be like love potions: off the table."

Madge thought she saw a smile at this, and though it was small, it lit up Cora's entire face—a fact which made the girl's words more confusing.

"Do you want to tell me why you're really here?" Madge asked.

"I wasn't lying. I do want a love potion. It is for me, and it's not intended for anyone in particular. Just as long as it's someone."

"You don't strike me as young enough or old enough to be that desperate."

"I don't feel desperate. It's more like—I don't know—longing?" The girl shrugged. "Another friend just got engaged, so that makes everyone from college. And high school. And siblings. And coworkers."

"Which makes you feel like a third wheel?" prompted Madge.

"Or fifth or seventh or ninth, depending on the number of couples I'm with. Let's just say if I'm an even-numbered wheel, it's because they're bringing their kids." Cora sighed, took a sip of tea, then turned back to Madge.

"I meet a lot of good guys, okay?" she continued, "Just no one that I've really clicked with in the way my friends do with their husbands or wives. I've started thinking maybe it's me. Like maybe I'm not wired right. I've tried to change it, but I just can't."

"So you thought you'd ask a Witch to do it for you by the brute force of a love potion."

The trace of a smile returned. "I guess it sounds silly when you put it like that, doesn't it? But my grandmother always said that Witches were the ones to go to if you didn't have other options. Witches were the ones that could help."

The two women sat in a silence that held the weight of years. Madge broke it first.

"Love potions seem like an easy fix that in reality make life harder on everyone," she said. "They mess with the natural order, result in a chaotic mess that I'm too old to meddle in. But your grandmother was right when she said that Witches help. It's a calling, and not one that I take lightly. So, since it's clear that you need help, I'll give you something else: a harder fix that will, if I'm right, make your life a bit easier."

The Witch stood from the table and exited the kitchen. In a few moments she returned with a well-worn book. An ornate fountain pen appeared in her hand with a cascade of golden sparks, and she scribbled something on one of the book's pages. Another twist of her hand made the pen vanish, and in one deft motion, Madge ripped the page out of the book and handed it to Cora.

"Here," Madge said, "is your quest."

Cora looked at the paper in confusion.

32

Madge held up her hand. "One year. Find this not in another person, but for yourself. Then come back to me. If you're not satisfied, we can talk about the love potion."

THE LONE WITCH on the West Side doesn't dabble in love potions, full stop. This ethical stance is something she inherited from her predecessor, along with a recipe for elderberry tea, a slew of summoning spells, a modest business, and a piece of paper with the word "purpose" scrawled in cursive.

ALLISON HAWKINS IS A DOJO OWNER, a freelance writer, and a collector of movie musicals. She believes the best thing in life is a quiet moment in a busy world. Allison lives in Grand Rapids, Michigan with an ever-increasing number of succulents. Visit her online: @allihawkwrites on Instagram or at allihawkwrites.com.

10

THE LOOKING-GLASS BRIDE
PREMEE MOHAMED

Sometimes the ladies at court tell me I am dressed in sadness. "Don't worry," they say. "You will have a baby soon. Won't that be lovely?"

"So lovely," I tell them.

"The king is very kind to you," they say. Not a question.

"So kind."

But I am far from home and I miss the warm sand and the smell of the sea, and I miss my quiet people who laugh with their eyes, and I miss my father's palace, and I am lonely here in this great cold stone castle surrounded by strange trees that change color.

The young stooped king *is* kind, after all—how can I complain? I cannot complain that he has, in essence, purchased me in marriage to ally with my father's empire. I cannot complain that when our paths infrequently cross he struggles to remember my name, whose syllables are anyway difficult to his foreign tongue. It's hardly a crime.

All around the castle, the trees turn golden and red. With difficulty I watch them dance through the small leaded panes of my chamber window. What a strange place, where you cannot even look outside without something in the way. "A glassmaker from my homeland has come to the royal fair," I tell the king when we bump into one another in a corridor. "Please, may I send a servant to purchase a looking-glass?"

"Anything you like, my dear."

A baby would be all right. They let the queens raise their children here. But I would also like a friend, and I know by reputation the glassmaker who makes these looking-glasses: she is a witch, they say. She makes glass that can talk and sing and prophesy the future. So I hope I have bought a friend.

With great care the massive glass is suspended in my chamber. The court ladies love it. "It's so exotic!" "It's so clear!"

That first night I listen to the leaves pat against the window and I ask the mirror to speak to me, but it says nothing. At first in my disappointment I debate sending it back to the witch. Oh, to hear another voice! Not those simpering noblewomen but someone new, anyone new.

The glass darkens, swirls. Suddenly I see not the face I expected but a small island in a slate-grey lake, the trees like flames, surrounded by great smooth black stones carved with the kind, fierce faces of animals I do not know. Then a place of rolling hills, high and green, dotted with tiny white houses like cubes of sugar, and a dragon sleeping near a stream, glittering in the low sun. Then the sea—oh, my dearest, oldest friend— lapping a stony shore, and gulls crying in silence over a rich white ship bedecked with lanterns of a thousand colors, so many I wonder it does not capsize.

"Are you showing me what *is*?" I whisper. My feet are cold on the stone floor and I should go to sleep, but I cannot. "Or what *will be*? Is this the world we know? Is a real dragon sleeping in that valley?"

The glass does not speak. But my soul feels lightened somehow. After a long time of watching the images, I tiptoe to bed and sleep deeply.

Every night it shows me distant lands, new peoples, grand vistas, pale gods, thunderstorms, rainbows, mountains, dunes

—sometimes when I see these, I weep for the missing of my home.

But I was purchased fairly, both kingdoms benefited from the marriage, and I say nothing. I tell myself I am not *trapped*. I am simply *housed*.

And one day the mirror shows me a strange thing, not at all like the usual fare: an army on the march, men in silver armor and horses no bigger than a mouse. And on the slender ribbon of the road, it seems they pass the marker-stone of my husband's kingdom.

For long moments I stand before the glass, knotting my fingers together. "Mirror, please. Are these things real? Are they your dreams? I wish you would tell me!"

The mirror does not speak. I take a deep breath, put on a robe, and run to find my husband the king.

Everyone crowds into my chamber, and for a moment it is a world of light and life; the servants bring hot wine, and I cannot hear the leaves against the windows over the sounds of so many voices.

"So frightening," say the court ladies.

"It will be many days march," say the king's advisors.

"We must meet them with an overwhelming show of force," says the king, and he pats me on the shoulder and strides off with his generals.

My chamber is again empty. Even the servants have rushed outside. The darkness and cold crowd into the room again, eager to take their accustomed places. I study the mirror: silent, innocent. *What have I done?* I almost ask it, but it has never spoken and it will not speak now.

Nevertheless a friend who does not speak is a friend. And perhaps I do not know what I have done, but I know what I will do now.

In the quietest courtyard near the outer wall, bundled tightly against the dry, cold wind, I guide a horse from the stable of the guards and awkwardly swing myself into the strange saddle. The whole kingdom will chase me; all the king's horses and all the king's men, as the children sing. But they will not catch me.

In my mittened hand I cradle the shard of the mirror I broke in my chamber, and the smooth glass shivers, dissolves, and shows me a fragment of blue sky.

I whisper to the horse, and we ride under the unguarded gate in silence, and from there into the rushing darkness of the open road.

PREMEE MOHAMED IS A SCIENTIST, nerd, and a collector of grudges. She believes the best thing in life is inking up a new fountain pen for the first time. Premee lives in Edmonton, Alberta with her adorable, but not very bright, cat. Visit her online: @premeesaurus on Twitter or www. premeemohamed.com.

II

NEVER WRONG
MARK W. COULTER

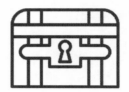

Anna looked at the bejeweled sword set on her rough-hewn table. Its ornate handle glistened in the light of the sun, the rune-carved blade shining with a silvery sheen. In all her years, she had seen artists' renderings and heard the legends, but to see it in person was another thing entirely.

"This cannot be right," Anna said, pushing herself up from her bench on her knobby wooden cane. "I am not a warrior. My family is not made up of warriors. I would say this should go to one of my grandsons, but even they are of gentle spirit, not fighters."

The robed man slowly shook his head, "The Champion Sword is never wrong. It has chosen you to stop a dark force, a great evil that has begun to rise once more in the world."

"But surely there is someone more equipped to fight it. Someone younger, with a soldier's temperament. Someone whose knees haven't started to ache at getting up."

Again, that implacable shake of the head. "The Champion Sword is never wrong. You are the one to halt this evil in its tracks."

"How?" Anna beseeched him. The thought of suffering in the world, of her being wrongly chosen which might only allow it to spread, almost brought tears to her eyes. "We are not soldiers or adventurers, as I have said. I did not stop my children from their fantasies of adventure when they were young, and I allowed them to enjoy such flights of fancy. But I raised them to be kind in the end.

"All of my family has learned, has believed, that rather than take up the sword and shield, it is better to find things to create in the world. To show simple kindness and let that be an example to others. I am not naïve; I know there is evil in the world and that sometimes arms must be taken up. But that is not *my* role or my family's! We strive to turn our little corner of the world peacefully, to bring joy to others, or at least feed those in need rather than quests, adventures, and slayings!"

Anna stopped to catch her breath. She could feel that certain passion rising, and in her elder years, she did not have energy enough to allow it to overtake her. Stepping back from where she realized she'd come within inches of the old sage, Anna slowed herself, taking deep breaths and steadying on her cane.

Ever calm and ever unfazed, the sage took this opportunity to look over to the door of the humble farm cottage. "Come now, please."

Anna followed his gaze to where her front door opened. With timid steps, a disheveled boy came into the door. His strange garb was of a fashion that Anna dimly recognized. The country that bordered her own, that had aggressed and started a war that had raged on the border for nearly a year. She had worried that her grandsons might be pressed into service, even though they performed other vital tasks in her village, which often took in wounded soldiers for convalescence. A part of her that she did not often like to admit hated that other land and its people for that risk they had put on her family.

But when she looked at the boy, she did not see his garb or the tone of his skin. Anna only saw a child, brimming with confusion that masked fear, anger, and a host of other roiling turmoil. She could see in his eyes and in the set of his face, this was a boy who had lost everything and would soon decide what to do with that. Anna had raised enough children and grandchildren to know the look of one in pain, and her heart swelled.

"This is Halthor," the sage said, offering nothing else.

"Hello, Halthor." Anna leaned down as best she could with her cane assisting her. "You look like one who's had a long journey to a new place. That can be frightening, I know, and you're probably hungry. I happen to have baked some bread fresh this morning. I believe I have some cheese to go with it that is still good. Would you like some?"

The boy did not speak or respond for several moments, his eyes weighing what he could trust. Anna waited patiently, allowing him to come to it in his own time. His stomach rumbled, and finally, he nodded.

"Fine, fine," Anna said with a smile, "You just have a seat at the table, and don't worry about that old thing there; I just need to put it up in a bit. I'll get you set, you can tell me all about your travels, and we'll see about getting you all cleaned up after."

Anna went about the old, familiar habit of bustling about her breadboard and little icebox, the act of caring for a child like falling from a log by now.

The sage turned and began to head for the door. "As I said, the Champion Sword is never wrong."

MARK W. Coulter is a writer and actor who loves horror movies and books, and just about all other speculative fiction. Mark lives in the Seattle area with his partners and a pair of adorable (and sometimes overly mischievous) labraduskies named Rogue and Bard. Visit him at markwcoulter.com

I2

TEA PARTY
FC WOODS

]There was a new room in Becca's house that hadn't been there yesterday.

The room was in the space where an attic would be, if Becca had one. It was small and dark, but in a way that made her feel cozy, rather than on edge. The floor was mostly wooden, except for one part under the skylight that was stone, cut through with veins of blue and green opal.

Becca opened the skylight, let the air in. Freshened the place up a bit.

The house, with the new attic, had five rooms. When Becca found it, it had one room. The room was as if it had been made for her; soft green walls lined with shelves full of plants and flowers, ones she had never seen before. A soft bed, opposite a window that let the sun touch a small writing desk.

The other rooms came in time. The first, three months in, a large ballroom-like structure made completely out of ice. The second, only a few weeks after, a mossy cave with a sparkling waterfall and tiny white flowers carpeting the ground. The third, a full year after, a plain looking room filled with climbable structures and platforms, and a nest-like bed made of pillows and soft things.

41

That was a few months ago.

Regardless of the room's sizes, the house from the outside never changed, looking exactly like it had when Becca found it.

Dappled walls blended in with the forest growing around it. The walls stretched to the trees, merging with the bark itself. Sometimes, it was on the ground. Other times, Becca had to climb a rope ladder to get in. It moved with the trees as they grew and travelled the forest floor, almost a tree itself.

She always found her way home, no matter where it moved.

When Becca was a child, people told her to be careful around the Tall Woods. The Woods had been there since before humans ever existed. It held all manner of creatures. The Woods were theirs, and the rest was for the humans. If any human ever ended up there, it was because they were horrible, unwanted, the ones that did not and would not fit.

Becca ran into the Tall Woods when she was fifteen.

She could not be Becca outside of them.

The house had found her as much as she had found it, pain like thorns wrapped around her lungs, eyes red rimmed and dried out. She had touched the wooden door, blood under her fingernails, and it had opened. It had been warm inside, like the warmth of someone's beating heart during a hug. Safe.

Becca yawned, started preparing the kitchen. The table in the kitchen was round, and had five chairs today. She pulled out two cups. One, a cup made out of rocks. She put in three soil covered beads, and poured water over them, watching it grow and blossom for a moment before moving on. The second, a tall glass. Yesterday, it had been a bowl. Becca filled it with apple juice and milk and two drops of lemon, then placed it on the table with the rock cup, already brimming with grass and snowdrops.

The next cup she took out of the freezer. Frost coiled off of it in wisps of smoke, and she felt it snake up her hands and into her veins. The shock of cold always woke her properly, not that she needed it today, with the new room. She chose a handful of pebbles from a different cupboard, and dropped them in before placing the cup on the table.

Then she took her own cup, small and white with a gold trim and blueberries painted on. 'Becca' was written on it in faded gold letters. It had been like that when she arrived. She had cried for two hours after finding it. She filled it with cardamom ginger tea, added two spoons of honey, and let it steep.

Taking a deep breath, she closed her eyes. Time for the new cup. The house hummed around her, residents waking up slowly. The air from the open window was crisp, and smelled tangy. She tasted orange on her tongue, with hints of lavender.

Without opening her eyes, Becca opened a cupboard, and took out a cup. She opened them to see a smooth, obsidian black cup. It was more of a bowl than a cup, with a handle on each side. She picked out one of her jars, filled with a thick, orange nectar, and poured some in. After a moment of thought, she added a few golden leaves.

Perfect.

She put the bowl in its place on the table, and sat down in her own.

A wave of cold passed through her, and she smiled at the first occupant. "Good morning, Guiney."

His lips quirked up in a smile. He nodded at her, and started drinking his pebbles, legs hanging off his chair. "New room?"

She nodded. "Attic."

He hummed, icy eyebrows creaking. The second one down was Arlo, a towering person with rocky skin and mossy hair. They didn't speak, but a few flowers sprouted out of them when they noticed the new bowl.

A cat strolled down the stairs next, long haired and blue eyed. She blinked slowly at Becca, and lapped at her drink. Demoine hadn't been a cat in a while.

There was silence for a few moments. Anticipation.

The front door creaked. Becca walked over and opened it, feeling eyes on her back.

There, on the ground, barely up to her knees, was a dragon. It was pearlescent white, flakes of gold in its opal eyes. Hurt radiated from it like a newly born star, and it gazed warily at her.

Becca smiled, and opened the door fully.

"Welcome home. You're just in time for tea."

FC Woods is a painter, an author, and a collector of inexplicable lighters. They believe the best thing in life is hidden nooks and crannies, and liminal spaces. FC lives in Cork, Ireland with human and cat roommates. Visit them online: @kitkire on Twitter.

13

WINGS NO LONGER BOUND

MERAV HOFFMAN

Two days ago you were instructed to take off my head. You failed to do so. I think you remember as well as I do the two things that happened next.

That was all the note said. Only one man could have left it there. The same one who had occupied my thoughts these last two days, sleeping and waking. The man I failed to kill.

Beside the letter was a curious quill, possibly magic, loaded with ink. The page below the message seemed to invite commentary. Harneck taught me to write a fine hand, during the third revolution. It's the only time I've ever left this tower, been treated as a person. Otherwise I am given no name, just "the prisoner" or "the executioner."

I hated to kill him, my teacher, but this is my lot. I could see in his eyes that he both hated and forgave me. I've never forgotten that.

I have learned to lift ax and great sword with these manacled arms; to that a pen was nothing, and yet I felt an electricity pulse in my arm even before I lifted the pen.

The thrumming in my arm was surely from the struggle,

and not from fear of looking into his eyes again. The man I failed to kill. The man whose wings were almost as large as his body.

The look in his eyes, the way that even bound for execution his face read as noble, defiant. His eyes held not scorn, or hatred, but pity.

Standing over him on the block, his face turned up to mine, he said only, "You were given no name, so no one could speak it and set you free."

My mind screamed curses against me in every language I know, but my body reacted, rejecting what he said, bringing down the ax on his unguarded throat.

It was like striking stone. The ax clattered to the floor, and faster than thought, he was up and off the stone. His bonds vanished, he was on the window sill, wings no longer caged. Looking over his shoulder, he winked at me. "I will call you Komidano," he said, and then he was gone.

I was paralyzed, my muscles screaming, every blood vessel in my body urgently thrumming to the point of pain. I hardly noticed that my bonds were gone, along with his, the man who had just named me.

Unbound, I might have thought about jumping, though the fall would surely kill me. I've been confined too long with nothing but indifference and unpleasant thoughts for company.

The guards took me easily, muttering to each other about how I had balked. They still don't know I can understand their language, but when there's so little to do, it's easy to puzzle such things out.

I was still in my daze. The stranger's words echoing, and my vision of his face, calmly accepting that I would deal him death when he had shown me only kindness.

Thus I opened my eyes and wrote *"How did you survive my attack?"* I wanted to add more, to write that I had accepted the name that he had given me, that I hadn't wanted any of this, but paper is limited, and thoughts are infinite, so I simply signed it, a thing I had never done before, *"Komidano, son of the king."*

I waited until the guards were asleep and put the note back on the window from whence it had come.

I slept better and woke without dreams.

When I woke, there was fresh ink under my signature. It said only, *"My mother is the angel of death. My father is the king of birds. Say you will be my husband and I will send for you and you will never have to see your tower or your ax again."*

My mind raced. Were the stories true? The son of the angel of death cannot be killed. He has wings to fly, like a bird. I had never seen such a thing. But there are many things I have not seen from this lone vantage point. Perhaps if—

The guards grumbled awake before the changing shift. I stored the note beside the knotted tissue that scars my left breast. My mind a tumult. Would I just be trading one prison for another? Gaining another jealous family?

I watched the sun go down, and finally, when night arrived I wrote, *"If I become your husband, will you help me depose my father?"*

I placed the note and waited, unable to sleep. No one came.

I spent the day in a knot of worry, and wonder, could I care for someone whose loyalties were unknown? Whose proposal was certainly only political in nature?

At sunset on the second day, I replaced the note. I had to know. By then I was so tired that I slept without warning.

His message said only, *"It would be my betrothal gift to you."*

My breathing changed, and suddenly, I could feel hope starting like prickles along my skin. My hand shook as I tucked the note to my heart and waited for nightfall.

I wanted to ask so many questions. Why had he waited two days to answer? Who were his allies? Would his parents approve of our match? But I wrote only *"If it is in your power, I am yours always, in marriage and partnership."* and I signed my name, as if to a marriage contract.

I left the note on the sill. At midnight the next day, a thousand birds flew through my window, as one they spoke my name, and broke my chains. By the time the guards entered the room, they had carried me away.

I left a note for my father, who had never called himself by that name. It said only, *"Number your days. The fourth revolution will come."*

MERAV HOFFMAN IS A MUSICIAN, organizer, and archivist, and a collector of plants native to Israel. She believes the best thing in life is wildly enthusing with someone else who cares about a thing as much as you do. Merav lives in the vicinity of NYC with her family and their many books. Visit her online: http://www.ladymondegreen.

14

DIY 5-STEP HOMEMADE POLYCEPHALIC HOUND CHOW— EASY!

NADINE AURORA TABING

D ue to their origin as a stygian beast bred to guard the gates of the underworld, Polycephalic Hounds raised on the surface have a reputation as picky eaters. FEAR NOT! There is *no* need to resort to store-bought "cryptid kibble," which I personally believe is named more for the mystery within than for the beloved companion it fails to nourish. This homemade, single-cauldron chow is the key to keeping each of your best friend's heads healthy and happy for centuries to come.

What follows is one simple recipe: one serving, one dog. Multiply each of the below ingredients per head.

Step 1. Boil 500 milliliters of water in one medium cauldron. Then, blanch 117 grams of root vegetables, grate finely, and set aside. Grating provides maximum digestibility.

Step 2. Empty the cauldron, and heat oil. Gently cook 232 grams of ground free-range vermin and organ meat until the meat is no longer pink. Low heat best preserves nutritive qualities. For the vermin, any subterranean creature should be sufficient, though my Trido's tummy has also been known to accept lesser demons and house geckos. I bait spell circles every morning with small butterflies and bitter little whispers like *I would do anything for Trido to finally get Best of Breed at the Greater Firelakes Kennel Club Show instead of that terrier-legged mongrel Gorgias Creek's Never Once Apollogize*—any similar wish should do the trick.

Step 3. Fold in 121 grams of organic rolled oats and 121 grams of cursed bonemeal. With the excess of pesticides applied to cereal grains nowadays, organic is the only thing I'm comfortable recommending. As for the bone meal—I know it is tempting to go with plain. *Don't*—I promise it is easy to get and worth the kitchen wards! My neighborhood apothecary routinely disposes of skeletal trimmings leftover from this or that; I recommend you buy bulk at a discount and grind the bones fine at home, where you can curse them yourself in the rare case there isn't already some lingering blight. Jinxes in particular make Trido's fur soft and glossy in a way that kibble mass-manifested from some anonymous aether simply cannot.

Step 4. Return the vegetables, and add in ½ ostrich yolk, and homemade bone broth. Should you not have access to an ostrich eggs, any kind will do—just use 233 grams of any avian yolk, well-separated. I believe incorporating ingredients from land and sky lends itself to a physically and preternaturally balanced nutrition.

Step 5. Boil over high heat, then reduce heat to low. Simmer for 20 minutes, then let cool and stir in a handful of freshly peeled pomegranate seeds for extra flavor and fiber.

That's it!
This keeps for a day, maybe. I have never had enough left

over to know. Each of Trido's heads loves this SO much that I spoon-feed each meal to each head to prevent scuffles and ensure everyone has their fair share. This recipe is so beneficial that recently I have even noticed the bud of a new cranium! I know some will say four heads is too much work—but if you have a Hound of your own, you know the kisses are absolutely worth it.

NADINE AURORA TABING IS A WRITER, designer, and collector of fountain pens and unusual ice cream recipes. She believes the best thing in life is a brand new dot grid notebook. Nadine lives in Washington, USA with her partner and a shiba inu. Visit her online: @suchnadine on Twitter or nadinetabing.com.

15

IT'S THE SILENCE THAT SHATTERS ME

ADAM FOUT

I don't know how many miles I've walked across the frozen sea. Each wave I climb feels like old glass against my bare feet. I slide down and feel no friction, no cold. I push through air like ballistics gel. I took my clothes off long ago. The silence of newborn voids carves my skin. The sun doesn't sear. How I used to feel…that's how the world feels.

I have walked for days. Maybe I walked right past Cuba. I just want to go to Havana before I disappear. To see the cathedrals. To stand with closed eyes under royal palms as the wind whips. To lie in the sand and let the heat burn the New York snow from my bones.

It's my last chance. I always put it off. Always said next year. But there are no years anymore. No miles. No mass.

It wasn't like it should have been. It wasn't waking up to nukes on the news, empty houses with hot food forgotten on the table, clothes spinning in the washer, empty cars idling on burning freeways.

It was a dissolving.

My friend's words turned thin as we spoke over coffee, his edges fading until he dove into a light beam. My girlfriend just seemed out of focus, far away, her voice quieter and quieter. Skyscrapers were two-dimensional, spinning like plastic ballerinas with low batteries. Bricks fell, puffing into crimson mist that plunged through pools of liquid concrete sidewalks. Small buildings sank into outgassing mud. I watched a lion that had escaped some zoo leap at a woman, and then it was a cloud of roses drifting through the trees. The woman's auburn hair leaked into the breeze. I know there were beginnings and endings, but they've collapsed somewhere. My memories are only of the falling aparts, not the causes, not the finalities.

I hope Havana's still there, hidden in the timelessness. Maybe Cuba sank under one of the tsunamis when the oceans hardened, waiting for an observer before it will rise.

The hardest part is wondering if these things are only happening to me. The scientific method is erased from the world. There's no one else to test theories on.

Maybe I'm a god now.

Maybe God left.

I used to pray for silence this deep: on the six o'clock bus, the air filled with the smells of fresh coffee and burning diesel and wet cigarette butts and bleach-cleaned puke, the city roaring and cursing; when I walked in the front door and the shrieking started; when some moron blasted grinding music the entire two-hour ride home.

Memory fragments. Was there a time before? Did these things happen? Or are they happening? Will happen?

Even before, memory was never something I could trust.

I am not an aggregate of my memories. I am a coalescence of hate. I can't remember a time before hate. I was born old. I injected anger like infected morphine.

The silence is a wave that never crests. I don't even know if the air moves beyond my slow swimming, but I keep talking to myself. I keep breathing. I keep not eating and not drinking and not dying.

I don't wake or sleep. I go from exhausted to rested without

ADAM FOUT

reason. Sometimes I see people, or parts of them. My girlfriend's teeth like ethereal pearls. The bus driver waving a disembodied arm. My dog's head chasing my cat's tail. Then I'm in New York again, taxis and jackhammers and gasoline and rain and people walking through me. Then it's gone, and it's no different than it ever was.

Time doesn't follow the rules. Every moment seems eternal. Will be eternal. Somewhen I was walking, and somewhere the nakedness will come. The land was gone then, or maybe it will be gone before. Maybe I've always been on the sea. Maybe I am drowning in the sky. Maybe this is the ever-moment of death.

I always wanted to see other countries, to sleep in places with stars. I lived in smog lands, buried and gasping under the pollution of millions. I worked in darkened rooms with fake lights for decades. I worked for other people's greeds. I woke each day angry that I woke. Every voice I heard grated, everything a burden. Somewhere in there, I stopped existing.

I don't know if I ever existed. Maybe that's the burden of me. An angry white man, a shape I could never discard. Maybe that's why I'm left behind. A penance.

Life before was a penance. I only saw my fluorescence-faded cubicle, saw the dark coffee shops where I lingered after work, trying to pour spreadsheets out of my skull, gut aching at the thought of home.

I never bought a gun because I knew the ending. Everything was uncontrollable and inevitable. I only wanted silence. I only wanted to breathe.

My body stills in the silence now. It shatters me, this thing I wished for my whole life. I am a creature of pixels, each piece more meaningless the closer I look. My words never echoed when I lived. When did I stop leaving traces on the world?

When the others dissolved, when they fled my reality, did they go to their own? Do they walk on frozen seas, free of the hate of me? I punished them by being. It is best they are rid of me.

I feel a fire somewhere—in the sky, in the deep. I am in a forest, and I have always been in a forest, the beach behind and before me. I fill with royal palms and glistening sand. I swallow the desires I thought I'd let go. I grasp at the memories of the decades I spent in Havana, melting into the world as it splintered and disintegrates and will crumble, on an island I always wished for, the nameless island of my birth.

ADAM FOUT IS a neurodivergent author who writes nonfiction and speculative fiction. He has work in Flash Fiction Online, December, J Journal, and more. He is a graduate of the 2020 Odyssey Writing Workshop. Learn more at adamfout.com.

16

WHO'S A GOOD HELLHOUND?
ROSEMARY CLAIRE SMITH

Hades thumped his scepter on the stone floor of his chthonic palace, sending quakes up into the Sunlight Lands and dismay into our heart. "You'd have me replace my ferocious watchdog with a three-headed corgi?"

"You see a parade of hellhounds howling to guard our gates?" Persephone shot back. Then to us, "Tell me your names."

"Bedivere," yipped our right head.

"Lionell," replied our left head. "Not 'Lefty' or 'Righty.'"

Hades pointed his scepter at me in the middle. "Let me guess…Corgberus?"

"Subwoofer," I managed.

He guffawed.

Mouth quirking, Persephone leaned forward on her onyx throne for a closer look. "How did you evade Charon?"

"With the same skills," I said, "we'll use to guard your adamantine gates."

She gave a small nod. "You'd forsake the Sunlight Lands to keep shades inside our realm and mortals out?"

"Up above, we never fit in," Lionell explained. "Our littermates opened their eyes and recoiled."

"People were no better," Bedivere said. "Many found us too adorbs to be an effective guard dog."

I added, "We took the gold medal in corralling sheep. Being the champion herder of Wales didn't shield us from accusations of souring cows' milk. The farmers drove us out."

"Herding sheep, souring milk." Hades' scorn made us cringe. "Cerberus never did that."

"Hey, hey," Persephone soothed. "I'm overdue for a bit of amusement during the dreary months I endure your stone halls. Just look at their eager eyes and perky ears."

"Three times the drool," he grumbled.

She made a face at him. "The job's been vacant since your hellhound tangled with Hercules. You think Cerberus let himself be abducted? Maybe he had enough perpetual gloom and needed to chase squirrels up trees."

Hades' expression grew as dark as his eyebrows and beard. "Never."

She turned to us, "What's your lineage?"

"A modest one," I admitted. "No fire-breathing father, no cannibal-snake-woman mother." Not that his pedigree did Cerberus much good when Hercules completed his twelve labors by taking the watchdog up to the Sunlight Lands.

"Never know who will show up," Hades said. "Could be some heartbroken sad sap like Orpheus again. Last time, he lulled Cerberus to sleep with his lyre. I had to go myself and drag Eurydice back."

"You were too hard on them, dear."

"Nonsense. The mortal musician can charm a tone-deaf listener." He grew wistful. "My last hellhound slavered poison."

Persephone scowled. "Not his finest trait. That stuff ruined more royal gowns. Do you know how hard it is to keep up with fashion, given the perpetual supply-chain issues down here?"

"Cerberus made a terrifying watchdog. What's this runty-legged fluff-ball got?"

"We excel at fetch," said Lionell.

Bedivere put in, "We'll bring you a krater of wine, your magical bird-tipped scepter, and your slippers all at once."

Hades looked intrigued, prompting Persephone to say, "Cerberus never did that."

"I've got servants."

"None with six bright eyes and butt wiggle. C'mon, give them a chance."

"You always fall for a sweet smile," he said.

"Lucky for you, dear."

"Hmmpf. Okay, on a trial basis," he grumbled. "No special accommodations."

"Come," Persephone said to us, "I'll show you your bed."

Soon enough, we stared sadly up at the bed high over our heads. "It smells like Cerberus," Bedivere complained.

She lifted us onto it. Lionell pawed a stale bone too big to grip in his jaw.

I sniffed the air. "No squirrels at all?"

"Nope, but lots of moles in the Fields of Mourning out that way."

Moles! We gave her our excited, slobbery gratitude. That night, while we hunted moles, Lionell talked us into burying the scepter on the far edge of those fields.

The next morning, Orpheus appeared at the gate, lyre in one hand and doggy treats in the other. He tossed a treat far to the left, another way to the right, and the last in a high arc. Yipping, Lionell lurched left, Bedivere right, and I sprang upward. Rather, we tried to. Our befuddled body jerked and tumbled to the floor as Orpheus slipped inside the great hall, softly strumming his lyre.

Gulping the meal, we tore in to find Eurydice reaching with trembling limbs for her lost love. Bedivere barked, alerting Hades, who rushed in, his brows furrowed, his countenance stormy. Eurydice froze, but Orpheus played louder.

"Where's my scepter?" Hades bellowed at us. "Fetch it immediately!"

We whirled and raced as fast as our legs could carry us, nowhere as fast as he demanded. On the way, Lionell said, "We're not seriously bringing him the scepter."

Bedivere said, "We gotta."

"Well...," I wavered.

We dug it up and argued the whole way back. Weary, we burst into the great hall to find Orpheus playing a sprightly rhythm with calloused fingers. Eurydice sang and Persephone clapped along. Hades tapped his feet. I dropped the heavy scepter before him. Eyes glazed, he ignored it. We three took up the tune, our voices harmonizing with Eurydice's.

After hours of merriment, Persephone persuaded Hades to let the mortal visit occasionally.

When the adamantine gates swung shut, he took up his scepter, stroked his beard and fixed his gaze on us. "You three dealt with that musician better than Cerberus managed last time."

"What do you say we keep them on?" Persephone's hopeful expression made us pant and drool.

Hades relented. "On one condition. No guardian of my realm shall be called 'Subwoofer.'"

"Pellinore!" I exclaimed. "Call me 'Pellinore.'"

Lionell and Bedivere looked pleased.

Persephone and Hades nodded, then put their heads together and whispered. She turned to us: "Let's go for a walk. When we get back, there'll be a surprise."

A saw lay next to our bed, its wooden legs cut short so we could easily hop into it.

Hades reached down and petted us. Our tail never wagged so hard. He grinned as he eyed our tail. "Cerberus never did that."

· · ·

ROSEMARY CLAIRE SMITH is a former archaeologist, a Sogetsu Ikebana practitioner, and a collector of wooden dinosaurs. She believes the best thing in life is digging into her to-be-read pile. Rosemary lives in Virginia, USA, surrounded by her brother's eclectic artwork. Visit her online: @RCWordsmith on Instagram and Blusky or rcwordsmith.com.

17

ORZHU
CHRIS BATTEY

My brother and I were eight years old when we built our first god.

Looking back, it was a sad shambles of an idol. Driftwood with pseudo-mystical symbols gouged into it, held together with nails and wire stolen from Mom's workshop, adorned with stones and beach glass and the carapace of a weeks-dead crab. It was a far cry from even the poorest homes' hearth gods, let alone the township gods Dad and his acolytes spent weeks crafting and blessing.

Curt and I didn't see its flaws then. We saw Orzhu, in all Their glory, Their Name blossoming from our lips as our prayers began. Before that moment, I don't know if we really *believed* in Them—but we *wanted*, and I guess that was enough like belief to awaken Them, enough for Them to accept our devotions by announcing Their Name through our voices.

Being a very small god, Orzhu's blessings were also minor, but we venerated them regardless. The Blessing of Sixes gave me an improbable victory in a game of walking-stones, winning back my pocketknife from our friend Billie. She hurled the dice into the stream, convinced I'd cheated, but overnight Orzhu touched her heart, and the next day she was a believer too.

They rewarded Billie's faith the next week with the Miracle of Balm, clearing her itchweed rash in mere minutes. After Curt fumbled Nana's telescope off the cliff while sail-spotting, Orzhu granted us the Spyglass Blessing, washing it back ashore intact. We dutifully scratched these acts into the rock beneath Orzhu's shrine, praising Their Name and Their grace.

Orzhu was too small a god to save Curt, though.

Maybe it was my fault. Maybe, when Curt fell from the tree, if I had run to Their shrine instead of running for our parents, They would have knit his spine back together. Maybe it shouldn't have taken the healer hoping aloud for a miracle for me to remember Orzhu—Who had blessed Their faithful thrice before. Maybe I should have found a sacrifice to offer instead of approaching Them with heavy heart and empty hands.

Or maybe Orzhu knew Curt had lost the faith. When he finally awoke, learning he had lost the use of his legs and right arm, Curt first refused to listen, then raged, then cried himself breathless. When we had a moment alone, I confided to Curt that I had prayed to Orzhu, and maybe an offering would help.

Instead, he cursed Their Name, loud enough for Dad to hear. I knew then that Orzhu's grace would never again reach my brother.

WE'D NEVER BEEN sure of how Dad would react to Orzhu, so we'd kept our worship secret, believing there would be no harm as long as we also continued our devotions to the gods of household and village and duchy. Maybe that was where we'd gone wrong. Maybe our faith in our new-built god should have been open and proud. Or maybe we'd offended the larger, stronger gods somehow. Maybe we'd neglected some ritual to unite Orzhu with the rest of our pantheon.

Maybe Curt had been cast down for our impiety.

When I tearfully raised these questions to Dad, standing

before Orzhu's shrine, Dad just sat down and pulled me into his lap. "This isn't your fault," he murmured into my hair, and held me as I sobbed all my grief out.

While I'd caught my breath I realized that it'd been ages since I'd curled up on Dad's lap. I didn't really fit anymore. I shifted to his side and tucked myself under his arm, pleased to find that there was still a comfortable place for me here.

We contemplated the shrine in silence.

Then Dad asked, "Orzhu, eh?" I tensed, still half-expecting some punishment. "I haven't heard that name before."

"Neither had we," I said hesitantly. "Until they spoke it with our voices. Curt and me both."

"Really." Dad still spoke softly, but I heard a note of pride. "I didn't awaken my first god until I was a junior acolyte. It barely lasted a day. How long, ah...?"

He seemed unsure how to ask, and I realized I'd already begun thinking of Orzhu in the past tense, their divinity subsumed back into the aether. "A couple weeks. Is that... normal? For them to just...fade?"

I felt him nod. "Small gods rarely last long. Even township gods need rebuilding every few decades. It's why I carve a new idol for Yerzhan every year." Our household god. "Usually each new god assumes Their predecessor's Name. We encourage it by crafting each successive idol similarly, reusing some of the previous idol's material, and generally treating Them like one long-lived god."

"Huh."

"Well, look at me spilling the mysteries," he chuckled. "Guess I'd better start your training. Curt, too, if he's interested. You two've always made a great team."

At Curt's name, I teared up again. "But he's.... Can he?"

Dad nodded. "It'll be hard, but you can do a lot with one working hand plus a strong heart and a sharp mind. I've certainly seen priests with less. And he's got you." He pulled me to my feet. "It's about time to rebuild Yerzhan anyway. First, we break down the old idol and select some pieces for the new one. Do you want…?" He gestured.

I gently lifted the idol of my dead god.

THE NEW IDOL, carved and polished, glowed under the votives' light. Curt sat in the wheeled chair Mom had built, and Dad helped him lean forward and light a candle with his good hand. I held his other hand, warm but limp. Mom held mine and Dad's hands to complete the circle, and we began to pray.

"Bless our house and our family, oh Yerzhu, god of our hearth—"

Our eyes widened as the almost-familiar name spilled from all our lips, and for a moment, I felt Curt's fingers squeeze mine.

CHRIS BATTEY IS a software developer and a collector of both lapel pins and hobbies. He believes the best thing in life is an elegant mathematical proof. Chris lives in the Seattle area with his wife, three kids, and piles of unfinished projects. Visit him online: @DarthParadox@kind.social or at pyrlogos.com.

18

ONE GOOD TURN
DWAIN CAMPBELL

O ld men and old tomcats are alike. We cling to life by our hoary old fingernails, or claws as the case may be.

One foggy morning, as I somberly walked towards the Health Sciences Center for an appointment with my grim-faced oncologist, I spied this sorry, calico Tom. While in hard shape, one foot in the grave, I was much better off than he, for his fur was matted in blood, one ear hung by a thread, and one hind leg was nigh chewed to the bone. Surely a loose Rottweiler savaged him, or a gang of wharf rats the size of feral hogs swarmed him.

Moved by compassion, I sought to gather Tom in my threadbare Value Village jacket. Meowing piteously, the maimed cat slinked through iron wrought fencing into the Catholic cemetery. I hobbled in pursuit, nursing a sharp ache in my abdomen as I watched the poor fellow slip through lichen-coated gravestones of Kilkenny and Tipperary dead, immigrants buried far from Eire. He slipped into a deep and dripping stand of mountain ash.

Perhaps, thought I, *this be the feline version of the Elephant's Graveyard, a lonely place where cats go to die when their nine lives are done.* More dignity in that than a forlorn hospital bed with IVs administered by distracted nurses eager to get home for a Netflix binge. Curious, perhaps envious, I turned up my collar and braved the wet greenery to discover what might be within.

My side sharply panged at bending double to avoid verdant boughs bent low by heavy clusters of bright orange berries. A serpent coiled about my pancreas, and it bit often. One day soon it will bite like a cobra, and I will be shed of this Vale of Tears.

I found an elaborate grave plot, whose I do not know, for the pedestal was marred by time and nature. Leaning on this moss-limned platform was a broken angel, head neatly cleaved from its frame as though by a guillotine. This scion of Heaven sported but one wing, one arm, and shattered feet. All to the ordinary for this Gothic acre of dereliction. Yet, extraordinary was the marble itself; Colgate white and pearlescent. Droplets of moisture glistened like diamonds upon stony flesh as pristine as the day it emerged from the marblework. Incredible, for all else here was rust and pockmarked ruin. Yet, the celestial gown was not unblemished. Pink smears of blood colored the hem.

Poor old cat, I all but forgot. "Kitty, kitty. Come here, kitty." A faint, anemic meow came from the dark cleft between the fallen angel and the pedestal. The hurt animal, huddled in his impromptu den, was but an indistinct shadow to my failing eyes. Speaking of eyes, wide orbs stared at me from behind a tussock of grass. *Here then be the angel's lost noggin.* I gingerly retrieved it, careful not to excite stabbing pain in my midriff.

I held the head aloft and quipped, "Alas, poor Yorick, I knew him well." Probably a maligned quote, but I hadn't studied Hamlet in forty years. The face was androgynous, or gender fluid if that is the hip lingo these days. "Yorick, or... Azrael? Gabriel? Mephistopheles?" I harrumphed, and in a moment of fancy, carefully perched the head back on its neck. No need of Gorilla Glue, it stayed on just fine. As my fingers lingered on finely etched curls, they felt silken and curiously warm.

Maybe it was the pain medication. Maybe it was low blood sugar messing with my pupils. The angel unexpectantly assumed a vigorous aura, an effervescent glow. Frightened, I rubbed faulty eyes and the peculiar effect vanished as quickly as it appeared. A trick of mist, or as Scrooge might say, "You may be an undigested bit of beef, a blot of mustard, a crumb of cheese." Might be so, except I can't keep food down.

At that moment, the cat emerged from its grimy hole. Except, it wasn't *the* cat. He was calico all right, but whole and sprightly, right as rain. Not a scratch on him. I lowered to one knee and peered into the cubbyhole. The maimed Tom was nowhere to be seen. Vamoosed, I suppose. Funny, though.

Looking to the twin, who now contently licked paws, I said, "Hope your buddy makes it." Straightening up, I wearily patted the angel on the head and said, "Same to you, Angela, Angelo, whoever. Buy you a beer on Resurrection Day, if I pass muster before the Throne of God." Not a likely prospect for a lapsed Anglican, but what the hell.

Behind schedule, I hurried along damp streets, vaguely aware my side did not bedevil me. It cruelly teased me like that, by times. Breathless, I made the specialist's office with seconds to spare. Wham, bam, straight to radiology where a bantering tech aptly named Ray beamed my innards. Chatty Ray stopped yapping after processed the image. In fact, he turned white as the angel's sleeve. Stammering and evasive, he ushered me back to the oncologist, and the two banished me to the outer office while they argued,

I heard doc heatedly order, "Do it again, by God." Indignant, Ray replied he did it bloody right the first time, by God. Yet, the tech complied.

It was well on in the morning when I was finally summoned to the oncologist's office. He seemed acutely uncomfortable. "Have you been to Lourdes? Hobnobbing with backwoods Tennessee faith healers?"

"I...what do you mean?" I asked, gobsmacked.

He sighed. "I mean I have been made a fool of. On your last visit I gave you two months. But now—" he brandished both X-ray images, "—but now, see for yourself."

I could read the images as well as he. I could not breathe. No tumor. Nothing.

My death absolved by a white angel.

DWAIN CAMPBELL IS ORIGINALLY from Sussex, New Brunswick, Canada. After a forty-year career as a teacher in Newfoundland, he retired in St. John's and studies folklore in his spare time. Contemporary fantasy is his genre of choice, and Atlantic Canada is a rich source of inspiration.

19

THE SECRET LIFE OF GNOMES
LISA MORTON

Leila had been living in her house for two weeks the first time she noticed the garden gnome had moved.

As she stared out the sliding glass door at the desiccated remains of the backyard, she corrected her thought: *Jeez, of course it didn't move. But didn't I leave that thing under the dead jasmine?* It was now beneath the bougainvillea, smiling at her serenely from beneath a cascade of brilliant magenta blooms.

The bougainvillea hadn't had a single flower on it yesterday. Leila was sure of that, because she'd wondered if it was dying along with most of the rest of the plants.

Is there a grieving phase that involves hallucinations? she wondered.

It had only been a month since her mother had died and she'd inherited the house. Two weeks since she'd left behind her apartment of six years and moved in. She hadn't grown up in this house. Her mother had bought it just ten years ago, after Dad had died. Mom had moved to Southern California to be near her only child. The house was still redolent with her mother's spirit in every room. Mom's soap in the bathroom; her coffee in the kitchen.

The garden had been Mom's special domain, but between

the estate arrangements and the miserable heat here in the foothills, the herbs and vegetables had died, the flowers were failing, and even the sturdy succulents looked exhausted.

She opened the backdoor and stepped out, her cat Gizmo at her heels. She had just picked up the hose and was turning to the faucet when she noticed another curious thing: the ginger feline was rolling ecstatically at the base of the gnome statue, reaching his fluffy paws up as if to entice it to play.

"What, Giz," Leila said, setting down the hose and walking over to take in the scene more closely, "is that thing stuffed with the 'nip?" Curious, Leila bent down and picked up the garishly painted little figure, sending Gizmo running. She lifted it to her nose, but smelled nothing; it felt like plaster, nothing unusual. She was more certain than ever, though, that she'd left it on the other side of the yard a few days ago.

"Great," she murmured, "who's moving this thing around?"

It was a Saturday, the first one she'd had free since she'd moved in—no lawyers or banks to meet with, no bills to pay—and she decided to put some work into Mom's garden. She'd noticed a nursery a mile or so away called Green Earth and decided to pay it visit. Maybe they could give her some tips on fertilizers to bring back some of the struggling plants, and she could pick up some new tomato plants.

The nursery was compact but well-stocked, and they were having a sale on garden gnomes. Leila smiled as she surveyed their red-hatted, bearded faces, their round tummies under belted blue coats. On a whim she bought four of them, along with plant food, a sprayer, and half-a-dozen cherry tomato seedlings. At home, she placed the gnomes strategically around the backyard, noticing that Gizmo rubbed against each of them happily.

The next morning the four new gnomes were in a line next to the old one, near the new tomato plants...which already bore fruit.

"Okay, Giz, what's going on?" Leila scanned her yard for

traces of an intruder. Someone who apparently specialized in moving garden gnomes.

She knew it might sound crazy, but she decided to swing back by Green Earth and ask if they knew anything about the statues.

The nursery was gone. Where it had been was now a vacant lot.

Even though it was 93 degrees, Leila felt a chill.

By the time she got back home, the gnomes were in a circle around the brown and withered jasmine. An hour later, she looked again; they were still there, but the jasmine was green and blooming, its lovely fragrance carried to her on a slight, hot breeze.

Leila had to know. Even though the next day was Monday and she was due in at the office at 9, she would stay up as long as it took to solve this mystery.

That evening she moved the gnomes—trying not to shudder as she lifted each inert figure—to a line beneath the jacaranda tree, still barren of its purple flowers even though it should have been covered in them by June. Once she'd placed the gnomes, she positioned Mom's chaise lounge in a dark corner of the yard where she could see everything but hopefully remain hidden. She took a tall glass of water and her phone, sprawled on comfortable cushions, stroked Gizmo where he curled beside her, and waited.

At some point she awoke, realizing she'd fallen asleep. Gizmo stood at the edge of the lounge by her feet, rigid, staring.

Leila saw the shimmer then; it started at the base of the jacaranda, where the five gnomes held up tiny, pudgy hands, and flowed up the tree's thin trunk, traveling down every branch and twig. As she watched, speechless and paralyzed, the tree erupted in blooms; they covered every inch, a carpet of glorious color.

The gnomes sagged as if drained...and they saw her then.

They didn't freeze or flee, vanish or explode. One of them waved in a hesitant fashion.

Leila, for a reason she couldn't quite name, returned the wave.

The other four gnomes joined in, then. Leila saw something inexpressibly ancient but benevolent and wise in their round little faces. Beside Leila, Gizmo purred.

"Thank you," she added, as she wiped away the tears, wishing only that Mom had been here to see this.

LISA MORTON IS a screenwriter and author whose work was described by the American Library Association's Readers' Advisory Guide to Horror as "consistently dark, unsettling, and frightening." She is a six-time winner of the Bram Stoker Award® and the author of four novels and over 150 short stories.

20

THE GLASS CAULDRON SHATTERED
DAWN VOGEL

I didn't join the faculty at Angitia University so I could become the secretary for all the departmental committees. But until you get tenure, you get the menial tasks. And tenure here is like Thunderdome. Two profs enter, one prof leaves... with tenure, at least.

I've co-authored twenty spells, lead author on three. But every year, I'm up against a witch who gets called Mister when he's not being called Doctor, someone who goes out for drinks on Fridays with Doctor Heath and the tenured professors even before he's got tenure. Meanwhile, I'm always Miss or Merissa. No one calls an untenured female witch "Doctor," regardless of her credentials.

My coven sisters, teaching at other schools, get it. We all worked twice as hard for half the credit. The academic world has forgotten the first witches were women. It coddles the men and acts like every spell they author is the greatest thing since sliced bread.

This year, my competition for tenure is Snively, Doctor Heath's current lackey. Three years teaching, compared to my nine. He's got his required thirteen co-authored spells, but he's never made lead author. His titles leave much to be desired. "A

Reversal of Solitudo Defectis"? That's barely its own spell. If I was on the tenure committee, I'd laugh his application straight off the table.

Yet, every year, it's the same story. Doctor Snively, and all his predecessors, raised to full professor. Me? "Thanks, Merissa. Try again next year."

Time to make a change.

My wife, Kerah, pores over a copy of the tenure rules document with me. "Wait, if you're the committee secretary, you have access to the original, right?"

"Of course."

"Then why don't you add a paragraph to get some equity up in this department?"

"One, they'd notice. Two, that's cheating. I don't want to win by cheating."

"A nobler witch than I."

"There's got to be something here I can use, legitimately. Do you have footnote 7b on one of your pages?"

Kerah rummages through her pages, a frown growing. "7a, 7c, no 7b."

A flawed copy. Thank goodness this comes from before my stint as the committee secretary. If I'd made an error like this, I'd have no chance at tenure. Probably explains why my predecessor left the university.

Is it cheating to summon the original document to my apartment? I have the authorization to access it. But it's late, and I hate flying at night. Summoning it is the sensible approach.

I snap. The scroll appears.

"What's 7b say?" Kerah asks.

Skimming the notes, I find it. "7b. Either candidate can request a demonstration of the other candidate's authored spells." I blink. "Why would someone skip that section? That's perfect! He might have a reversal for Solitudo Defectis, but how does one prove they can reverse a spell unless they cast the base spell first?"

"Someone on the committee will cast it for him." Kerah's shoulders slump.

"5q. No committee member can cast spells during the tenure hearings."

Kerah laughs. "Merissa, you're a nerd, and I love you."

"I love you, too."

I VIBRATE with anticipation as the tenure committee reviews our materials.

"Doctor Snively, have you anything to add?" Doctor Heath smiles, confident he's about to elevate his buddy to the old boys' club.

"No, sir."

Heath turns to me. "Merissa, have you anything to add?"

"Yes, sir. I'd like to invoke 7b."

Murmurs erupt across the tenure committee. They know what I've asked for.

Heath holds up a hand to quiet them. "Are you certain?"

"I'm prepared."

Snively isn't. Heath knows that, too. But if he calls a recess now, he'll tip his biased hand.

I don't put it past him, but I don't drop my smile, either.

"Sir, I'd like to object." Snively's voice trembles.

"Your objection is noted," Heath says, no longer making eye contact with his protege. "But the hearing must proceed. If you decline to make this presentation, the committee will be forced to place your application in abeyance."

Snively glances at the other tenured professors. None of them will meet his eye. "Of course, sir." He takes a deep breath. "Where shall I begin?"

Heath shuffles through the papers on his desk, selecting a

single sheet. I don't need to see it to know it's the list Snively submitted of his published spells. "Ahem, well, the first spell on your list is 'A Reversal of Solitudo Defectis'. I suppose you'll need to begin with 'Solitudo Defectis'."

Swallowing hard, Snively asks, "And my target?"

I spread my arms wide. "I'm happy to be the subject. After all, step two will be the reversal."

"Solitudo Defectis." The spell makes you feel alone in your misery, aware of all your failings. It's ironic, really. Snively's co-authored a spell to reverse its effects, but he's likely never learned the core spell. I suspect he's felt its effects, though, or why would he have helped author the reversal?

He clears his throat, lifts his wand, and gestures vaguely while muttering the name of the spell.

Nothing changes.

I look toward Doctor Heath and shake my head.

Doctor Brody rises from his seat, wand in hand.

"Sit down, Brody," Heath snaps.

"Sir?" Doctor Brody asks.

"Snively needs to demonstrate his aptitude with the spell on which his co-authored spell is based, as well as that co-authored spell."

I try not to be smug. It's unbecoming of an untenured witch. But I can't help it.

Snively turns to Doctor Heath. "On consideration, I'd like to delay my application."

Heath nods, barely hiding his grimace. "Then in the absence of a competitor, this committee does hereby raise Miss...er, Doctor Merissa Longacre to full professor. Congratulations, Doctor."

I remember to be gracious. "Thank you, Doctor. I look forward to a re-review of Mister Snively's credentials and casting ability next year."

Maybe it's only a giant leap for one witch this year, but it's a start.

. . .

DAWN VOGEL IS AN AUTHOR, crafter, and a collector of stickers. She believes the best thing in life is a good book shared with a snuggly cat. Dawn lives in Seattle, Washington, with her husband and their herd of cats. Visit her online: @historyneverwas on Bluesky or at historythatneverwas.com.

21

FINDING WINTER

JM WHIT

This is my last chance.

Akira stood on a long-forgotten path, the sun high overhead, relentless with its never-ending waves of heat. Sweat rolled unheeded down her neck and back. She grew weaker with each moment. Getting here, following the rumors and the quiet words spoken in shadows, took almost everything from her.

But now she had a chance, and so did the world.

The sentries—a pair of formidable fir trees—waited at the end of the path. Beyond the sentries, she could just make out a winding trail dusted in white.

The winter woods. The last bit of winter that clung to the land.

But how was she, with so little power to her name, to pass through? And then what?

I must try. If not for myself, then everyone else. Akira took a step. Then another. She stopped. *What am I doing? How can I end Musaki's reign and return normalcy to the world?*

She was so tired of summer. The dense, soupy air that made it difficult to breathe. The heat that sapped energy each second of the day. It hurt to see people suffer. To pretend to enjoy the long, endless days while crops wilted and livestock scrounged for water.

How long since Musaki locked winter away? Years, a decade, more? But no one spoke up. No one had the courage to tell her she killed the world. But Akira had to try. This one last time. She lifted her foot. Put it back down. This was foolish. She was nothing against the might of Musaki's magic.

A tendril of cold air slid around her neck. Akira shivered and took a deep breath, her lungs filling with crisp air. *Oh...This is wonderful.* She held out her hands. The cold wrapped around her fingers. She wiggled them, sending small white flakes dancing as they fell. She giggled.

The tendril wrapped around her wrist and tugged. Akira took a step. She stopped and stared at the sentries. The giant firs stood tall enough to touch the sky.

How do I pass?

The tendril tugged harder. Her skin turned red where it held tight.

"Away! Away from there!"

Akira glanced over her shoulder.

Musaki, her face molted red with rage, ran toward her, a fireball in her hand. "You will not undo my work! Winter isn't welcome!"

Akira ran, the tendril pulling her along. She closed her eyes as she approached the trees. *I hope...*

BAM!

She bounced off the sentries and landed on her backside.

Musaki laughed. "You are nothing. The sentries reject you. You cannot undo my greatest achievement."

Woozy, her head spinning, Akira crawled forward. "Please. I only wish to help." She took hold of a branch, wanting to get to her feet.

Whoosh.

The branches swept upwards, opening a doorway.

Akira collapsed, drained.

"NO!" Musaki threw her fireball.

Heat surged. Pine needles rained around Akira. She scrambled, half crawling past the branches.

Wham. The sentries closed behind her. She sprawled on the ground, bruised and battered. The tendril released her wrist and vanished.

Akira sat up. A muted pallet of black and white surrounded her. Fog hovered above the ground. A deeper, longer glance showed a million gray highlights against the stark landscape. Snow-heavy clouds floated overhead, a dirty gray against the layer of bright snow upon the ground. Cold fresh air, with a hint of pine, filled her lungs. *Oh, how easy it is to breathe!*

Outside the woods, Musaki shouted incoherent words and hammered the sentries with hot, seething magic. But they stayed closed.

Akira looked around again, hoping for some sort of signpost, something, anything to give her a direction, an action to take. A sense of wrongness filled her. The woods were cool, but not cold. She laid her hand flat on the snow. Cool on top, a layer of heat burned under the snow as if the desert sun scorched the land.

"This is wrong."

But what could she do? Akira glanced at the sentries. They moved when she touched them. Maybe…maybe she did have magic. She could help the world. She shifted to her knees and laid both hands on the ground.

Nothing.

Please. Please work.

Tears streamed down her face.

She thought about the silly little tendril. That bit of cold that made snow fall from her fingers. How something…*something*… left her hands to open the sentries.

Her hands glowed. Cold flowed into the heat. Tears froze on her cheeks. Ice spread from her hands outward, down the path and past the sentries.

Musaki screamed.

"Well done. But it is only a start."

Akira jumped to her feet and spun around. Her jaw dropped.

On the path stood a dragon. Blue-white scales of ice reflected the clouds above. Wings folded against his body, his tail swished, scraping the snow into piles. "You sent a spark into the world, but the summer witch will recoup quickly." His voice resonated, sending shivers down her spine.

"But what can I do?"

"Learn. Practice. Become who you were born to be—a daughter of winter." Clouds of steam billowed from his nose. He watched from eyes glowing with power and knowledge.

Akira's blood raced. Cold air rushed around her. The clouds sent snow, large fluffy flakes floating from the sky. She stepped forward, toward the dragon and away from the burn of summer. The snow crunched under her feet. Frost spread along the ground as she passed.

The dragon watched as she walked, motionless, never blinking.

She was close now, close enough to touch. She reached out a hand. Ice pricked her skin, the cold bite welcome. She breathed easily. The weight of summer lifted from her shoulders. Akira smiled. What wonders awaited her in these magic woods? What wonders awaited a world relieved from the harsh burn of summer?

She met the gaze of the dragon. "I am ready to begin."

JM WHIT IS A WRITER, engineer, and collector of more dragon artwork than she has wall space. She believes the best thing in life is placing that last piece in a 2000 piece jigsaw puzzle. JM lives in Huntsville, Alabama with her family and overactive dog. Visit her online at JMWhit.com

22

SUMMONSED

GRAY ANDERSON

The stereotypical brass magic lamp sat on the center table in the senior partners' conference room.

Randy Jackson, the senior-most partner, eyed it with some suspicion. "Who bought this?" he asked, wondering if it was an out-of-season April Fools prank, or if some junior associate had just visited Disney World and gotten stuck with a now-unwanted souvenir by an over-enthusiastic child.

"Nobody bought it…" sighed Bill Dawson his longtime second-in-command. "Remember that estate case that just wouldn't die?"

"Yeah?"

"Well, it finally *did* die, but they ran out of money and the estate offered it to us to settle their bill. Uh, Sam Davis should be in to go over it with us in a moment."

Sam, a junior associate at the firm in his mid-twenties, stepped into the conference room at that cue. Underneath one of his arms was a portfolio bulging with papers. As he scurried in, he nodded to the senior partners. "Sorry, guys—my ten o'clock ran over." Sam took a seat opposite the other two, opened the portfolio, and drew out several documents. "So, the disposition of the lamp…"

Passing a copy to Randy and Bill, Sam said, "The lamp is said to contain a genie. Rub the lamp, a genie appears, and it becomes your servant for three wishes. Whatever you want.

"Unfortunately, the lamp is the property of the *firm*—that means, if I understand what the family told us, that we get three wishes *collectively*. I have that in the bill of sale as security. We could, in theory, put them to a broader vote of the partners...but I don't think anybody wants to see a court ruling on the proper disposition of wishes among a corporate body..."

"You've got to be kidding..." groaned Bill. "I figured it would just be a nice tchotchke to take as a peppercorn. Beats the usual dollar."

"...and since Randy is the managing partner of the firm and you've been his right hand, Bill, I believe we might reasonably exercise them on behalf of the firm. You each make one wish, and I make the third since you...don't trust the other partners. I drew up documents reflecting that. So...uh, Randy or Bill, would you like to do the honors?"

Bill gestured to Randy, deferring to him on the basis of seniority. Duly deferred to, Randy picked up the lamp and gently rubbed it. The lamp immediately began belching forth a plume of iridescent smoke, startling him; he dropped the lamp in shock, and both he and Bill ducked beneath the conference table as the lamp clattered to the surface of the table.

"Make it stop!" shouted Randy.

"Who summons me from my rest?" growled the cloud, slowly taking the form of the upper half of a male human being.

"The law firm of Jackson and Dawson," replied Sam, rolling his eyes—both at the overly-dramatic appearance of the genie and the senior partners' reactions—and pulling another piece of paper out of the folder. "The lamp is the property of the firm, but we will be exercising all rights relating to that."

"A law firm?" The genie asked, confused. "But..."

Sam continued, "In the event that the rights must attach to an individual in the employ of the firm, they agree to defer a two-thirds interest in their set of wishes to other members of the firm in exchange for the right to exercise one of those wishes." As he said this, he extended a bundle of papers bound by an oversized paperclip to the genie. "If you'll agree to letting us exercise those wishes on behalf of the firm, I believe that we can let you back to your rest in good order."

The genie accepted the documents as Randy and Bill climbed out from under the table. He puzzled over the paperwork for a moment and sighed. "This is all *very* irregular. Never in three thousand years..." With another groan, he turned to the three. "If you'll agree to exercise your wishes *here* and *now*...I guess..."

The three men nodded in agreement.

The genie waved his hand. "Fine. Proceed. Just get this *absurdity* over with."

Randy and Bill looked at one another. Randy spoke as Bill scribbled notes. "Well, since we've gotta do this for the firm—I wish for the firm to be guaranteed to last at least another century, and never lose a case."

The genie nodded. "It shall be done. And your second wish?"

Bill looked up from the notes he scribbled, then read from the sheet. "I wish for the firm to make at least $100 million— American dollars, of course—after taxes, per year, with profits increasing faster than inflation in each year."

The genie nodded again. "It shall be done. And what is your third wish?"

Sam took a moment, looking back and forth between Bill and Randy. The genie impatiently made a gesture of checking his wrist (where a watch spontaneously appeared). "I only agreed to do this if you were quick about it," the genie warned.

Sam nodded. "Fine. In that case, I wish for blanket immunity from whatever the heck their wishes are going to do."

Randy and Bill exchanged confused looks while Sam and the genie smiled to one another.

"Good choice," the genie said, before vanishing back into the lamp.

GRAY ANDERSON IS a science fiction fan, adrenaline junkie, and a collector of bad puns. He believes the best thing in life is a nice meal shared with friends. Gray lives in Virginia, USA with his older sister and her two cats (Poppy and Snug). Visit them/her/him online: @grayanderson on Twitter

23

THE FAVORED SERVANT
JESSIE MACPHERSON

She had never thought her day would come, thought she'd always be a bridesmaid, always watching in mint or lavender, never chosen. Adele had thought as an adult that other worlds were lost to her, that she had lost her chance to come home changed or never come home, slamming the door on the wardrobe once and for all. But here she is in another world at last—combing out the King of Love's long corpse-pale hair. *Mother of pearl*, she thinks, looks at him, working out a snarl with her garnet comb.

On Earth, she stammered and stuttered, learned endless ways to self-regulate, be good, fit into the Wise Mind, remember not to twitch with fear, not to guess what people are thinking, and not to say rude things to her therapist. That was then.

Now the King of Love sighs artfully, lying languidly across the couch. He's seven feet tall when standing, his milky chest scarred with marks from fighting claws, his eyes bright as cherry Lifesavers. He reaches up a six-fingered hand with hard, pointed nails to chuck her under the chin. Adoring. His smile is wide with its gleaming sharp teeth. "Ah, thank you, sweetling," he purrs at Adele, rubbing her cheek against his fingers. He is warmer than her and runs hot.

"What did you learn today?"

Adele had spent the day walking in the Garden of Thieves with the latest supplicant to the Glorious Regents of Love and War. Adele paused. "He was nervous. He tries not to be, but he is. You should be careful."

Adele had caught the slight tremble of his hand, his flash of anger pasted over with fawning courtesies when she had asked a question. He was all too willing to talk if Adele would listen. Her *hypervigilance* keeps the Glorious Ones safe and ruling. Already she's been able to tell when the division's captain was faltering, when the ambassador needed soothing. She can offer the Glorious Ones trays of sweetmeats and firewine before they even ask. The four Fs: *freeze, fawn, fight* and *flee*, which she went over and over in group. *Maladaptive coping mechanisms* they said. They called Adele's ability to slip away *maladaptive daydreaming*.

She sits with the King of Love and waits for the Queen of War to return. Both of them shine like moonstones. Though the Queen, Adele thinks, is an opal, pale with a sudden violent burst of brilliant color. The door opens, and the tapestries of topaz-embroidered lammasu sway with the might of her entrance. The Queen is slightly taller than the King, her hair a bone white, her eyes a deep garnet. She is wearing an expression that is close to a sulk.

"Darling," the King of Love purrs at her, and his monstrously beautiful love half-smiles. *Emotion management* thinks Adele, as the Queen finally lets herself pout.

Adele has already brought a hammered silver basin of water. Slowly, she lifts the edge of the Queen's skirt to show her clawed feet stained red, the crimson hem of her white gown. The Queen lifts one foot to put in, then the other, blood starting to swirl through the clear water. The air smells like copper and myrrh as Adele washes. The King of Love nuzzles the Queen's neck, and her pout starts to vanish. The Queen steps out of the tub and moves to her favorite couch. She extends a beringed hand and slowly strokes Adele's hair. Adele wants to ask how work was today, but she already has a good idea. Certain bellicose days are very difficult for the Queen.

The King of Love has already poured the Queen of War a wine. He takes an alabaster jar from a shelf full of them and gives it to his beloved. The Queen opens it, takes the black powder in her fingertips, looks at it tenderly and sprinkles it over her wine. Taking a sip, she fixes her ruby eyes on Adele. "We said you'd be with us forever." The King and Queen look somewhat shy.

Adele thinks of notes on scraps of paper. *Do you like me? Check Yes or No.*

Adele thinks *yes*; she thinks of housewives in crinolines and pearls, like bells, like blossoms, and imagines herself in a frilly apron and heels, fixing cocktails after a hard day at work. She looks at herself in her gilded robe, her hand small next to the King and Queen's. She might not have a gold band, but Adele thinks of the word *wife* and is not saddened to think of those before her, all the little alabaster jars.

The King and Queen will live for several hundred years, but they remember their chosen and claimed from Earth, honoring them as finely as they know. The Queen drinks her wine and ashes, kissing the black from her pale fingertips.

Adele curls at her feet. She doesn't care that the portal has closed, that she has said goodbye to the last of Earth, slipping out of Wise Mind into the wild, baroque, mad mind where she is a servant and a bride, the lowest and the exalted.

This is how we will leave them, in perfect silence; the King of Love and the Queen of War resting close to each other, Adele entwined sweetly around their feet. She smiles. It's not a daydream, maladaptive or otherwise. If it's not real, she doesn't want to be real either. Here in the City of the Pyramids she is home from when she is flesh to when she is ash swirled through wine. It is a good life, *a happy one,* Adele thinks and closes her eyes, her new gods above her.

And all is peace under the three moons, in the Great City of the Pyramids till the break of dawn.

JESSIE MACPHERSON IS A TAROT READER, a cancer survivor, and an author. She believes the best thing in life is being the witch you want to see in the world. Jessie lives in Vancouver, Canada with her spouse and many, many Tarot decks. Visit her online: jessiemacpherson.com or Instagram at @jessiemacphersontarot.

24

THE NIGHT CARNIVAL
TIM O'NEAL

One summer night, a dark rollercoaster appeared outside my bedroom window. I awoke when an empty car with jagged neon-green lightning bolts painted on its sides clattered, rattling down its glossy black track. I leapt out of bed and discovered, to my amazement, an entire night carnival had unfolded on my front lawn. Black-flamed campfires burned darkly, twinkling like distant galaxies. Smoke of cedar and pine and some other scent I couldn't quite name rose to the star-studded sky.

A calliope warbled its undulating melody—a siren's song urging me to come join the festivity and merriment. A Ferris wheel spun, its luminescent lights pulsing. Everything from the tents to the rides sported an ethereal black-and-green color scheme.

Squinting, I made out a pen containing ten miniature black dragons. Their glossy scales appeared wet beneath the silvery moonlight. The beasts hissed and snapped as they wrestled each other in play. Beyond the dragons, extended an endless field of enchantment. It'd be impossible to explore in one night. No, that'd take years, decades. Maybe even lifetimes to plumb the secret delights it contained.

So real, so vivid! What a magnificent dream this was. Or was it?

I had to investigate.

I donned my robe, clumsily belting the sash. I hurried down the stairs, my tattered slippers *flip-flopping* against the threadbare carpet. I reached the foyer and extended one age-spotted hand, all set to throw open the door and lose myself in the mystifying merriment. But then...

A bolt of realization doused me as shocking as water splashed on a hapless dreamer. I can't say how or why, but I knew if I left my house—the place I'd lived for forty-five years —my existence would become irrevocably altered.

I would never return.

Outside, the dark paradise glittered, a moonlit wonderland —heady with its intoxicating mystery. Rides rattled and creaked. Performers juggled glow-in-the-dark pins. Fantastic magic creatures screeched and wailed their unearthly cries. Rich scents of fried foods, buttery popcorn, and sugary confections laced the perfumed air. This carnival offered the tantalizing promise of all the amusements I'd loved over the years, but still my hand remained limp on the latch, boneless, unable to depress the simple mechanism.

Was I really ready to take this step? Could I really leave my house, the rowboat within which I'd survived all of life's violent eddies, including the loss of my dear wife, Anastasia? Could I really abandon all that and my fifty-year career as a banker? I had a comfortable, if boring, life here. Why *should* I leave it all behind?

Even the idea seemed too much.

My hand fell. If I went back upstairs now, closed my eyes and fell asleep. Upon waking, I could tell myself it was just another vivid dream—a consequence, perhaps, of too much black wine before bed.

But still, something inexorable called me to that carnival splayed beneath the starlight. My mind fomented with uncertainty. Should I step into that endless festival which roiled as energetically as those miniature black dragons?

I didn't know.

Holding back, I equivocated. Maybe I would've returned to bed if it hadn't been for the appearance of *her*. My Anastasia. She emerged from the joyful chaos of the night carnival like a shell given up from the secret depths of the sea.

How I *ached* upon seeing her again.

Before she'd perished so prematurely, Anastasia had been a woman of formidable intellect. She'd worked as a neurosurgeon before a cerebral aneurysm had claimed her, cutting short her sweet life and our budding marriage in its rosy infancy.

Now she shimmered before me, wearing a diaphanous black gown sewn from fire-opals and moonstones. The gems stitched into the fabric glittered and sparkled, reflecting the starlight that had travelled a billion light-years to be part of this moment. Anastasia's violet eyes twinkled; her impish features danced as gracefully as a wood sprite. It was one facet I'd fallen in love with a lifetime ago. That, and her deep regard for humanity.

She continued to smile. The familiarity of that look quickened my heart's pace. Invisible hands clutched my chest. Anastasia's sweet face remained as perfect as the morning of our wedding—a half-century ago.

She held out one hand and beckoned for me.

Why not? What did I have in this world except a lonely life and a dimming career? And, of course, my black cat, Anubis. As if reading my mind, Anubis, purred and scraped her teeth lovingly against my ankle. Her rumble interrupted the silence. She nudged me forward, breaking my indecision.

Ah, my four-legged psychopomp. She was right. I'd lived alone for too long. It was time.

I unlocked the door. It creaked open. Anubis ran before me, disappearing into the night.

I stepped out and inhaled the damp summer air. I heard the carnival's dark melody. Sights and sounds assailed me, engulfing me in a rich tumult of sensation. Standing on my porch, I felt more alive than I had in years. A phantom gust slammed the door shut.

A final warning.

I didn't flinch. Instead, I hurried down the porch steps; my eyes never left Anastasia's. She remained there with her arms extended, inviting. When I reached the ground, wet black grass whispered beneath my slippers. Behind me, I sensed without seeing, my house vanished, winked out, along with the city and all my old life.

Though, unlike Orpheus, I didn't look back.

I raced to Anastasia, clutching her close to my heart, savoring the smell of her hair, the feel of her arms around my waist. Nothing else in the universe mattered, for I held the most brilliant jewel of my existence.

Anastasia beamed that enigmatic smile of hers and my heart melted like soft candlewax. Hand in hand, we entered the joyous splendor of the night carnival.

TIM O'NEAL IS an avid juggler with a large collection of lapel pins. He believes the best things in life involve backcountry adventures. Tim lives in Colorado with a territorial bromeliad.

25

GROWING UP CREEPY

JENNIFER LEE ROSSMAN

EXCERPT FROM "UNHAPPY, UNMOTIVATED, AND ONLY VAGUELY UNSETTLING: FORMER BLACK-EYED CHILDREN DISCUSS THE EFFECTS OF GROWING UP CREEPY" *THESIS BY ANONYMOUS.*

From the superstar axe murderer who gets invited to every campout to the lake monster everyone and his brother claims to have exclusive photos of, every town has its urban legends. Most of them grow up and keep on creeping on just like always. Then there's us. The black-eyed children.

The subject of countless unverifiable Internet stories, we terrify people by doing little more than standing around in outdated clothes, asking for rides or to come inside their house.

At least, until we grow up. When most of your creepiness, and therefore your existence and sense of self, is related to the juxtaposition of evil demonic entity and innocent child, learning to navigate society as an adult can be a horror story all its own.

I knew I couldn't be the only one struggling like this, so I reached out on social media. Here are some of my favorite responses:

"You can't just stare menacingly at baristas until they give you a coffee. You actually have to talk to them."

"I thought I had decent social skills, but I was just really really good at psychically using fear to manipulate people."

"I never did get to trick-or-treat, even though I was so good at knocking on doors and scaring the crap out of people."

Indeed, one of the more universal experiences faced by black-eyed children transitioning to adults with a weird eye condition is socialization.

To put it briefly, most of us didn't have any. We spent all our free time hanging out with adults, trying to get inside their cars and houses so we could [**information redacted at the request of a nonexistent government agency**]. We didn't have friends. No one taught us small talk.

By making our creepiness the most important aspect of our lives, too many of us missed out on vital socialization during our childhood. Many of us are still living with the ramifications of that.

"I was so good at being a creepy little kid, but that's not exactly a job you can get as an adult. It's not like I can be a carpenter, I don't know how to carpent!"

*"It came so easy, scaring people and making them [**redacted**], but now even the smallest prank takes so much effort. I'm exhausted."*

"It's the expectation of perfection, for me. Anything less than your own segment on Coast To Coast was seen as a failure."

No one prepared us for after. No one told us we would outgrow the thing that made us special, that gave us value. No one told us how hard it would be once we could no longer coast through life on eerie eyeballs.

Many of us grew up with the strange dichotomy of constant praise and demands for perfection, and that kind of childhood can be hard to reconcile into a healthy adult psyche. Depression and anxiety are common, as is—ironically enough—the same general feeling of impending doom we used to instill in others.

> *"I was always the creepy one. It was my thing. People feared me. Now they just kind of stare and wonder if I'm wearing weird contact lenses."*

> *"What am I supposed to do with my life? Start a terrible Black Eyed Peas cover band?"*

> *"Nobody talks about black-eyed adults. No one tells stories about us. There isn't even a name for us once we grow up. What am I? Who am I?"*

Who are you? It's a question we were asked countless times during our childhoods. Usually by terrified people fighting the urge to let us [**redacted**].

Who are we? It shouldn't be so hard to answer. We have names, lives, hometowns. But somehow, "I'm Emma, I'm a freelance writer from Abilene" feels less important than "I was a black eyed child." Somehow, "I was" matters more than "I am."

Who am I? I think everyone asks themselves that question now and again, former black-eyed children perhaps more often than most. The details will be different depending on who you ask, but I think there's only one universal answer: I am someone who has been shaped by who I was, but I am not the person I was. I am trying to shape the person I will be, but not everything is in my control, and I am not yet that person.

I am me, right now, in this instant. That's all I will ever be.

That's all any of us will ever be. All we can do about that is try to be okay, even just for this one moment. Because for better or worse, it will be over soon.

JENNIFER LEE ROSSMAN is a disabled and queer author, editor, and a collector of shiny things. They believe the best thing in life is the pool-noodle-headed dinosaur Parasaurolophus. Jennifer lives in the land of carousels and Rod Serling (more commonly known as Binghamton, New York) with a fish named Dr. Sarah Harding. Visit them online: @JenLRossman on Twitter, or on their website http://jenniferleerossman. blogspot.com

26

BABA'S LIPS AND LORNA'S EARS
DONNA J. W. MUNRO

W hy are myths about strapping boys fighting god-touched monsters and rescuing sacrificial princesses? My Baba told me those stories when I was a little girl and I expected to be a princess. I really did.

Until he told me my story.

"Lorna," he said, "the heroes of old were muscled demigods. Beautiful meatheads that tore women from the arms of the monsters who'd stolen them. Those stories were told to sons to make them run fast and to lift more barrels of olives. But my smart girl, I haven't told you these stories to make you a princess."

I was fifteen and my eyes went wide as the expectations, the foundation under my feet, shifted.

He pulled a bag from the chest he kept locked under his bed. "Stories are understood by the ears that hear them and shaped by the mouths that tell them. The stories I tell you aren't the only ones. There are the stories your mother told me before..."

"Before she died?" I asked.

He shook his head. "She didn't die. She went home."

How often had I asked about mother only to have him tell me how she looked? How she loved him. How she laughed.

Never how she'd gone. I'd assumed the stories of the neighbors were true.

"She'd wasted away."

"The fever took her."

"She'd passed fast as Atalanta after golden apples."

He'd never told me any different. Until now. "Her sea coven called her home."

My mother, a sea witch? How many myths had heroes falling in love with witches being turned into monsters or kept for lifetimes or killed by their jealousies?

Baba shook his head. "Remember whose ears are hearing the story. Your mother is a hero, child. She holds back monsters of the deep with her sisters and their golden nets. They're daughters of Thetis holding back seaworms and kraken and old gods of the deep trenches. They cast flashing nets on the face of the sea so ships make it safe to harbor and fish find the hooks of fishermen."

I imagined my brown-skinned, green-eyed mother lined up with women just like her, singing spells and casting out their nets even as the boys on the sand played at being Heracles or Jason.

"She lives?" I asked.

He nodded, sadly and passed me the bag.

It looked normal in his hands, but the moment it touched mine, the rude burlap softened into a bright blue bag of silk. Internal light kissed the bits of sea within: a starfish, a sand dollar, a jar of green seagrass, a white tunic and orange pants. No princess dress for me.

"She needs you, my Lorna. I've given you the land and its limitations. Taught you that you don't belong here with every story I told." His wistful smile evaporated as he took her hands and squeezed them. "I never stopped you from fighting or swimming or learning as the other girls are stopped by their landlocked parents. I owed that to you and your mother. She calls because if you stay, you'll become the reward in some

99

boy's story. Some god's temptation. Some monster's feast. But you're fierce, my girl. Kiss me and take your first step. I'll not have you be someone else's motivation to greatness. *You* are greatness."

He crushed me with a hug I'd remember, kissed my cheek, and whispered her name into my ear. "Calypso."

As he spoke, I knew all I needed. I put on the tunic and pants, pulled the bag across my shoulder, and plucked out the sand dollar. "I'll miss you, Baba."

He nodded. "I will tell your story to all the other girls, so they know."

I smiled and broke the sand dollar in half.

A waterspout passage twisted up around me. I stepped through it to the edge of the ocean. In front of me stood a line of brown women with eyes green as the sea. My clan. One shrieked and dropped her handful of net, racing over to gather me up. In that touch I knew her and once we embraced, the knowledge of who we were flowed into me.

Her love and the love of our sisters filled me.

Then I knew why they'd called.

Calypso pointed to the horizon and I saw them. Naiads, the most dangerous sea creatures to man. Cold intelligence paired with ethereal beauty. Would-be heroes fell prey to them, their soft hands, moist lips, and muscled tentacles. But also, our sisters. Another batch of creatures born of Thetis—beings that wouldn't be defeated by hero swords or a ring of gold.

"They'll be here soon, child." Calypso raced over to the net. "You must drink the water the seagrass has made you—for strength."

I did as I was told, relishing the salty water that swished out of the seagrass jar.

"Now eat the heart of the starfish to become timeless."

The rough shell cracked in my hands and inside a pebble-sized heart waited. I chewed, feeling my mortality washing away as the sea filled all my spaces. I was a monster from men's myths. A witch who'd live forever. But my own story, the one I'd tell, lay in front of me.

The naiads gnashed needle-teeth and locked intelligent eyes on us as we sang the power of currents and wind into our golden nets. We sang spells that turned riptide against them, pushing them back. We understood why they wanted the land. Why they wanted to destroy the men who made the ships and threw their filth into the sea. We understood their rage.

But we each had a Baba to protect.

And our own story to tell.

Thus, we sang and cast our nets and fought them back from the beach knowing that the right ears would hear and the right lips would tell and that our story didn't depend on any but us —we sister witches who guarded the land against the monsters of the sea.

Donna J. W. Munro teaches high schoolers the slippery truths of government and history at her day job. She lives with five cats, a fur covered husband, and an encyclopedia son. Her daughter is off saving the world. Find her at @DonnaJWMunro or https://www.donnajwmunro.com/.

27
HORTI-CULT
ANNIE PERCIK

Martin tucked a pink dianthus into the soil, then straightened to check the placement. It wasn't quite in line with the rest, so he knelt again and adjusted its position. A few feet away, his sister, Jen, let out an exasperated sigh. He looked up to see her frowning at him.

"We don't have time for your perfectionism," she said. "The clock is ticking."

"But it has to be just right. The judges will be looking for precision, and this pattern is complex."

"This pattern is insane." Jen stood with a grimace and put her hands on her hips. "I've never seen anything like it in a gardening competition before."

"Exactly!" Martin said. He had found the layout online and immediately visualised it outlined in flowers.

"The torches are a bit much."

"But they add atmosphere. It's going to look awesome, I promise. Now, come on. Just the hydrangeas left."

They worked in silence, occasionally referring to Martin's printed plan to ensure their plant placement was just right. Martin patted down the soil around the last bloom and stood back to take in the final effect. Jen stood next to him, laying a hand on his shoulder. The flowers swirled in a complex star with glyphs picked out in peonies at each point.

"I have to admit I'm impressed," Jen said with a smile. "I wasn't sure we'd finish, but we've got ten minutes to spare. And you were right, it looks good."

That was high praise. Jen had multiple horticultural awards to her name. This was the first time Martin had taken the lead in a competition. Expectations, especially his own, were high.

"Where did you find this pattern?" Jen asked.

"It was on a random website I came across. It's meant to be some kind of ritual. Now for the finishing touch." Martin strode round to each corner of the plot, setting the four torches alight. As the last one caught, a chill breeze wafted across the garden and dark clouds gathered overhead. He glanced upwards. "I hope it's not going to rain. That would put a real dampener on this whole design."

Jen groaned, then gasped as the ground trembled under their feet. "What the hell was that?"

The tremor grew in strength, making the torch flames flicker. Martin and Jen backed off their plot, exchanging worried glances. In the centre of the square garden, the soil and grass shifted and broke open as the sky continued to darken. A thick, green tendril emerged from the ground, followed by a hulking mass of earth, shedding pebbles and petals as it rose. Martin and Jen stood frozen as the shape resolved into a vaguely human form. Twisted ivy branches swirled out to create limbs, soil clumped together into a barrel chest, blue and pink flowers gathered in an approximation of facial features.

A maw of damp, black soil opened and a voice boomed. "You have summoned me and I must now do your bidding! What is your will, Master?"

Martin opened and closed his mouth a few times but made no sound.

The monstrous body rotated and its face slowly tilted to regard him. "Oh, but wait..." The voice turned amused.

"Foolish mortal! To make the ritual circle out of such fragile material. You have sealed your own doom, for I am free!" One giant foot lifted off the ground and came down outside the boundary of the plot with a thud that shook the whole area.

Jen shouted, "Get the weed killer!"

Her urgent tone freed Martin from his paralysis. He raced to the supply shed, frantically grabbed what he was looking for, and sprinted back. He ran at the creature, one large canister of weed killer in each hand, spraying for his life. Out of the corner of his eye, he saw Jen attacking the monster's other leg, brandishing a flaming torch and a pitchfork. The creature swatted at them with thorny but ponderous claws, shedding plant matter with every motion. Martin and Jen bobbed and weaved out of its reach, taking turns to dart in and land an attack. Their foe screeched and wailed with every stab and lick of flame, flinching away from the toxic spray of the weed killer. Together, brother and sister fought it back.

"Nooooo!" the voice cried. "It hurts, it burns!" The giant form collapsed in on itself, and its demonic presence fled back into the earth, leaving just the shell of its plant-form behind.

Martin and Jen collapsed to the ground, side by side amidst the ruin of their competition entry. Moments later, two figures approached from behind the fence that separated the finalists' plots. The judges stopped at the edge of the area and looked around in astonishment. The meticulous lines of Martin's design were in total disarray, foliage and flowers scattered to the four corners. In the centre, the outline of a terrible giant lay spreadeagled across the turf, twisted in agony, and smoking.

Martin looked up at the judges. "Um…"

One of them raised a peremptory finger and Martin's voice trailed off. The judges separated and walked the perimeter in opposite directions, crossing paths at the far side and coming together again, back where they started.

"Well," one of them said.

"Quite," said the other.

The first one raised his arms in a helpless gesture. "The originality of the concept is breathtaking."

The second one nodded, her eyes wide. "And the execution. To mount something of this scale in so short a time. Incredible."

Martin scrambled to his feet and gave Jen a hand up, unable to believe what he was hearing.

The first judge turned to them, a wide smile spreading across his features. "Our decision is clear. Congratulations. We are awarding you the grand prize."

Martin looked over at his sister, his whole body trembling. "See? I told you. That pattern was awesome!"

ANNIE PERCIK LIVES IN LONDON, writing novels and short stories, whilst working as a freelance editor. Her first two novels, *The Defiant Spark* and *A Spectrum of Heroes*, were published in 2021. She hosts a media review podcast and publishes a photo-story blog, recording the adventures of her teddy bear. For more information: https://alobear.co.uk

28

NINE PEAKS
ROBERT RUNTÉ

The Kingdom of Nine Peaks lay between the hills of man and the clouds of Heaven. A world carved of stone and ice, beneath the notice of those above and inhospitable to the humans below, King Barthos ruled the fae who lived there without distraction. Aside from Michael, who had ascended in the distant past, and the sanctimonious Sans-claws and his gnomes, whom Barthos had more recently banished to the snow below, there had been little to distinguish one glorious day from the next.

The appearance of an ambassador of The Circle making demands was, therefore, an intrusion of historic proportions.

"What do you mean, do *I* have this ransom?" Barthos bellowed.

"It is nowhere to be found on Earth, nor in the Sea, nor Air —that only leaves the Nine Peaks," Eoghan insisted.

"And I told you," Barthos said with growing impatience, "I do not have it."

"Ah," the ambassador said, appearing vaguely embarrassed. "It's possible no one *has it* exactly. It might have made its own way here."

"A ransom that hides itself?"

"Unusual, certainly," Eoghan conceded, "but the ransom was for the return of the Fiddler baby…"

Barthos raised an eyebrow. The Fiddler Incident had been high stakes indeed, creating complications even for the Nine Peaks.

"To keep the ransom safe," Eoghan continued, "it was disguised as a human and granted…some limited sentience."

Barthos snorted. "You mean you spelled it so well, it's outsmarted the lot of you." He led his Court in a round of restrained but pointed snickering. The hubris of The Circle knew no bounds!

Eoghan shifted uncomfortably. "Regardless, we demand Right of Search immediately, while we have it cornered here."

The king snorted again. "A pathetic pretext to spy on the Nine Peaks. Never!" Barthos raised his hand to forestall further argument. "However, in the spirit of cooperation with our Earth-bound brethren, I will undertake a look 'round, and let you know."

"I hardly think—"

"That's obvious," Barthos interrupted again. "But I give you my word, I will return what's yours."

After Eoghan had left, Queen Alaina asked, "Your word, my King? You'll return the ransom, if found?"

"The ransom? Oh, I doubt that. I said I'd return what's theirs. It doesn't sound like this ransom thinks it belongs to The Circle."

Alaina smiled at that. "That was clever. But surely they'll suspect if we keep it?"

Barthos shook his head. "Too dangerous to keep. If found, I'll dump it in the world of men. They've managed to assimilate Sans-claws and his minions into some harmless mythic role. Let them deal with this nonsense also."

Alaina bowed to acknowledge her husband's wisdom, and hurriedly withdrew.

Alone, and headed for her rooms, Alaina sighed. A pity. She

had greatly enjoyed young Ransom's company. What other temptation to flirtation in the closed world of Nine Peaks? But Ransom was anxious to return to the human world and now Eoghan had traced him here, it was time to send him back, before Barthos discovered him...and young Ransom's role as her personal jester.

ROBERT RUNTÉ IS Senior Editor with EssentialEdits.ca where he primarily edits SF&F. A former professor, he wants it understood that it is NOT mansplaining if one is equally pompous to all genders. Robert lives in Lethbridge, Alberta, Canada. He's old and still on Facebook at https://www.facebook.com/dr.robert.runte

29

THE YAKSHI'S BARTER

NEETHU KRISHNAN

W hen it was just his moonlit form, rocking unsteadily on his heels and drumming the balcony railings with his chunky fingers, nervous ticks that annoyed me to no end, I'd registered at first, with much shame and disappointment, only the sobering averageness that was my husband. The flush of embarrassment was soon transmuted to relief, though, for the doughy, anxious man—who, up until a few hours ago, was my world, my mirror, a being more stardust than ungracefully ageing human, thanks to the benevolence of my rosy, tunnel vision—was a blessing in plain view. I wouldn't have traded so quickly otherwise, without second thought or a lick of remorse, were he above average, irreplaceable, indispensable.

Would I?

We'd had yet another of our fights, the kind that always left me feeling stupid and ashamed after; the type where my voiced inconveniences and concerns always transformed into silly and petty womanly misgivings when my benevolent provider and caretaker husband reworded and presented them back to me. I'd stomped off like a petulant child to the courtyard, as I always did, to regroup under the white-blossomed devil tree where my husband never followed me for he felt the tree pulsing with a sinister energy and I the opposite. It was calming, cathartic even, to rub my thumb over the cool head of the ancient nail embedded in the tree as I vented my unhappiness and had my misery instantaneously dissipate like the large rusty nail head always absorbed it.

Tonight, however, the nail seemed deaf and indifferent, worsening my sour mood. To occupy my restless fingers, I violently scraped at the peeling bark around the nail, which was when the yakshi spoke.

"What he does to you is wrong," she hissed, her voice like a wind whistle. "You deserve freedom. To be free of the man and his providence and the indebtedness you feel you owe him for clothing and sheltering you."

The words spidered inside me with an unsettling chill. Not because they came from a yakshi, who had been the energy behind the nail mopping up my sorrows all these years, but because they rang with indisputable truth.

"If anybody knows the helpless suffocation of being wronged and imprisoned by a selfish man, it's me," the voice continued. "Free me by pulling out this wretched nail fortified by spells, and I'll free you from your tyrannical husband. It's as fair a deal as can be. We switch places. You float eternally free, ungoverned by the restricting laws of the land-women, to wherever your heart desires, ageless and deathless and no longer responsible for cleaning up after a man ever again, and I take your place in the human body. You lose nothing, except the dead weight of your man that I'll reluctantly accept on your behalf for the price of being freed from this damned tree. You gain a world, while I, a semblance of mobility."

She was right.

The ecstasy of the sweet deal, of the negligibly low price I had to pay for eternal freedom and immortality, however, was short-lived, lasting only a blink, the exact time it took for me to pull the long, rusty nail from the devil tree, free the *yakshi*, seal the deal.

When I looked again at my husband who'd ventured out into the courtyard, no longer alone, but accompanied by me—or rather the body I once inhabited, the grotesqueness of the scene made me violently nauseous. My breath hitched painfully in my phantom chest, desperate for a release that would never come. My husband was suddenly more charming than I'd ever seen him in our decade-long marriage. The sieve of light playing on his smitten face made him appear like a dream come to life; like he'd pluck stars right off the canopy of powdered brilliance above him and lay it at your feet if you asked.

There was a familiar, safe ease to the two as my husband's hands absently reached for the *yakshi* in my skin, who promptly, gratefully melted into his embrace. Resting his chin over her head, he beamed, the contentment of his smile making me want to die. But I couldn't anymore, could I? I was supernatural, immortal, unchained from a boring man, routine, home. I was now the *yakshi* watching us greedily, hungrily, longingly.

The vampire-witch whispered something in my husband's ear, smiling conspiratorially as she laced her hands in his. He smiled a puzzled smile, nodded, broke away.

How could he not tell the difference between an imposter and me? I fumed, stung gravely by the shallow substitution. The *yakshi*, as if sensing my fury, looked to the mist of me apologetically, the gesture more unsettling than appeasing. Suddenly, an unceasing, discombobulating throb quaked through me accompanied by a dull but persistent pressure building in my phantom head, reminiscent of a thousand iron nails driving into my skull.

Bludgeoned and confused, I looked about for the source of the grating pressure. Too late. My husband had already driven the nail back into the hole in the tree I'd calculatingly plucked it from. The lovestruck couple silhouetted against the finality of the indigo night was the last I saw of the world before I was sucked into the depths of the tree hole.

• • •

111

NEETHU KRISHNAN IS A WRITER, occasional poet, and a collector of tiny, sparkly things. She believes the best thing in life is a glowing, well-written sentence. Neethu lives in Mumbai, India, with her family. Visit her online: @neethu.krishnan_ on Instagram or facebook.com/neethu.krishnan.944

30

THE MOST IMPORTANT HALLOWEEN COSTUMES I HAVE EVER HAD

LYNNE SARGENT

AGE 6: MY OLDER SISTER ISLA'S BUNNY COSTUME

The one Mum tried to stuff me into coaxing, "Come on Kai, stop wiggling! Let me button you!" I laughed and made her chase me. Eventually though, she got all my coarse black fur into the downy white, and pulled up the hood, slotting my horns into the ears. "One day you'll be able to do this yourself," she said, and waved her hands over me. Suddenly, my heart beat very fast, and I felt such power in my legs as I did binkies around the room! But all I really wanted was a costume that would let me trick or treat with the others, the human kids.

AGE 10: PRINCE CHARMING

I convinced Dad to make it. He'd said, "I don't understand why you want to be a humanoid. They're so similar to us! Isla wanted to be a whale at your age. She wasn't quite ready for that, but..."

I had whined, "Daaaaad." He'd relented and crafted it, complete with shoulder pads, golden engraved buttons, and swishy tassels. He'd spent all night on the 30th sewing, even though Mum had nagged him that he had mischief to do. It was his turn to become a coyote and rouse the pack as a reminder for the humans to stay away from our settlement in the hollow.

The next morning I glowed as I fastened every single one of the shining buttons myself, and slipped away to join the human children's costume parade for the first time. A girl in a frog outfit asked me who I was, and I said a new exchange student. She didn't ask me *what* I was. It was clear I was a prince. We walked hand in hand the whole parade.

AGE 13: HULA DANCER

The fourth year in a row I dressed as something human, devoid of fur and fang. Mother worried. Said my changeling abilities would stagnate. That I should be using this time when they could help and guide me to become familiar with a wide variety of species. "You're supposed to experiment. Find your creative expression," she'd said. I didn't tell her what I really wanted, which was to not be a changeling at all. Not ever, but especially not on Halloween. I wanted to be something that didn't make people run and scream in terror, even if my coconut bra itched and my lei of flowers made me sneeze.

AGE 23: THE QUEEN OF HEARTS

My first Halloween after I left home. Mum said she wasn't disappointed, just sad at how little she saw me, at how I had rejected my people, at how hard things would be for me as a changeling who never learned to change.

"I just don't want to be a monster anymore!" I'd yelled.

Dad had asked quietly, "Do you think we're monsters?"

I shook my head, "But I look like one, when I'm not

changing. If anyone sees me like this they'll think I am. I don't need the option of changing, I just want to be beautiful always."

"You *are* always beautiful," mum'd said, crying.

That night I *felt* beautiful though. I was decked out in sparkling hearts, the mottled skin of my belly held tight with a satin waspie corset. I watched the humans pretend to be what they weren't, not with their costumes so much as their bravado, the way they showed off and seduced.

I saw from the corner of my eye a superhero boy approach an angel girl leaning sickly against the doorframe of the bathroom. She reminded me of the little girl who held my hand my first costume parade. He tried to coax her through the door, his hand slipping onto her thigh under the gauzy chiffon of her skirt. I moved quickly to stop them, holding the door.

"Wanna join?" he asked, laughing lecherously. For the first time I wished to have the full force of my fangs, my claws. If he couldn't be better than this then I wanted him to be terrified, but the change didn't come when I called it. I needed a stupid costume to change, because I never learned better, and I wasn't brave enough to strip down there and then and become my full and terrible self.

Still, my intervention was enough to stop him and the angel girl's eyes were grateful when I took her by the hand and told the boy, "No, we're leaving."

AGE 30: THE TEARAWAY

I couldn't go home after the angel incident. I wished too badly that I had listened to mum and dad. I tried for two years to work the changing magic. All the year through, and even on Samhain it wouldn't work without a costume. So I'm building the best costume, all the costumes. I've spent the last half a decade working in the human world as a seamstress, making friends with cosplayers, learning from theatre greats. I've drafted for months, crafting a wardrobe full of all the things I want to be someday. The crowning jewel I wear tonight, seven years since that devastating Samhain. I have done the work, making up for my stagnated talent and lack natural intuition with careful stitching and impeccable materials.

This time I will not need to pick between powerful and pretty. I will be magical girl and monster all rolled into one. I need not strip down, need not make myself vulnerable in my changeling skin to be strong. This costume has layers. It can be a lady's gown, a vampire's cloak, a seal, a tiger, and more— some of the things my parents would have wanted me to learn to be and some of the things they would have discounted as unnecessary human fancy.

I slip the fabric on, carefully attaching every piece, affixing Velcro, eyehook, and zipper. My makeup is ambiguous, beautiful and terrible, and for the first time my skin feels like my own.

LYNNE SARGENT IS AN AERIALIST, philosopher, and collector of words. They believe the best thing in life is following faeries down woodland paths. Lynne lives in Hamilton, Ontario with their partner, two cats, and the nicest chihuahua in existence. Visit them online at scribbledshadows.wordpress.com or on Twitter @SamLynneS.

31

CONFECTIONERY SPELLS 103, REQUIRED COURSE

LORI J. TORONE

The dragonfly's delicate wafer wings chimed as it darted around the kitchen, dusting the countertops with a fine layer of cinnamon. My sister smirked at me. I have to admit, her cookie was beautifully painted in iridescent blue icing and purple pixie dust (the edible kind, not the hundred-year-sleep-spell kind), and perfectly proportioned from its fennel gumdrop eyes to its segmented tail. With both flight and music, it was a dessert worthy of the Royal Banquets and would earn top marks here, at the University of Culinary Wizardry, Dessert Department.

My poor cookie cricket, on the other hand, had icing dripping awkwardly off its spindly legs. "Sing," I urged, in between incantations. "Cartwheel. Just do something. I have to pass!" My grade in Confectionery Spells 103 was borderline failing, and it was a prerequisite for the Enchanted Baking major.

The other students' cookies began to soar, or sparkle in patterns, or whistle sonatas until the entire kitchen looked and sounded like the campus fae meadow on summer solstice.

My cricket cookie hooted and staggered, then fell over, legs stuck in its own sugary coating.

"Does it at least taste good?" My sister whispered into my ear with a snide giggle.

"Is that dough clogging your nostril or something else?" I snapped, and Moira grabbed a napkin and hurried away.

"Lidia." Professor Timbly approached. "The pre-banquet testing is next week. I think it's time you found a tutor."

I STOOD at the counter of the Resource Kitchen punching dough and hollering. "Why does the food also have to be the entertainment? It's not enough for a twelve and three-quarters course meal to be tasty? You'd think the royal coffers would have enough gold to hire a few fairygodmotherfucking minstrels! And why is Moira better at this than me? We grew up in a bakery!"

Henry, my senior tutor, frowned and pushed my hands away. "You're instilling frustration in that dough instead of magic." He patted it back into a neat ball. "Let's just figure out why it isn't holding the animation spells. Usually it's the kneading technique or incantation inflection."

After three hours, Henry was also covered in flour and completely flummoxed.

"I've never seen anything like it," he said, staring at me, his eyes wide under his smudged glasses. "That's the standard magic dough and no matter what you do or say the spells are just bouncing off it. Your icing is excellent, but it won't stick. It's almost like you are…"

"A failure." I threw down my tea towel.

"Cursed," he said.

I laughed. "Listen, Henry, I'm not cursed. There's been no thaumaturgical interference in my life. But my parents expect my sister and I to become Royal Bakers, not measly village bread-makers like them, so I need to pass."

Henry cleaned his lenses. "You know, not all curses are party-shattering fairy theatrics. The familial expectation ones are more insidious and actually harder to break."

I thought on that for a moment. "Well, cursed or not, I'm going to fail the course. Then what? Go back to my parents' bakery in disgrace? I need a drink." I pulled a vial out of my pocket and rummaged through the cabinets. "Looks like you could use one, too." I filled two glasses with water, plucked mint leaves from the kitchen planter and muddled them, poured five drops from the vial into each glass, stirred, then handed one to Henry, who looked at it somewhat dubiously.

"What's in the vial?"

"One of my simple syrups. To the Green Fairy!" We both drank. I stretched as I felt the tension drain from my shoulders.

Henry stared at me again. "You're a cat."

"So are you. Good stuff, isn't it?" He made quite the handsome black cat.

"Lidia, this is graduate-level transformation magic. What is in that vial?"

"I told you—simple syrup, like in my icing. This one is an infusion of lavender with a pinch of catnip and my own relaxation incantation. Oh, honestly, Henry, close your mouth, I can see your fangs. Cats do their own thing and don't give a blind mouse's ass about people's expectations. What better way to chill out then as a cat? Enjoy it—it only lasts around a half hour."

"Can you do other transformations with these simple syrups?"

"Sure," I said. "But what good will it do if the icing won't stick? I'm still going to fail."

"Not necessarily. I have an idea."

"THIS DOESN'T FULFILL THE ASSIGNMENT," Professor Timbly said to us over the din of students and musical baked goods out in the campus courtyard, waving their hand at the goblet on the table. Each division had its own pavilion for testing, and Henry had arrived after his pre-banquet test to offer me moral support.

Moira sidled over. I ignored her.

"Try it," Henry urged, offering Professor Timbly the goblet filled with sparkling aquamarine liquid, a lemon cookie lotus floating on the surface, and sour candy stones at the bottom.

"It's called Lake Escape," I added.

Professor Timbly sighed, "I'm sorry, Lidia. I can't give this credit." They took a sip anyway, lips puckering. I grabbed the goblet before it spilled as gossamer wings sprouted from the teacher's back and they began to ascend.

"Oh!" Timbly exclaimed in delight as students and professors gasped and pointed. Applause broke out as Timbly zipped over the tents.

Moira snarled, "That's not fair!" and stalked away, muttering under her breath about *stupid goblins* and *exact wording*.

I turned to Henry. "Maybe you were right about a curse."

"We'll deal with that later." Henry elbowed me and pointed at a professor walking towardsus in the green robes of the Brews and Bartends Department. "Timbly might not be able to give you credit, but he certainly can."

I grinned at him. "One Royal Baker in the family is enough. I'm changing my major."

LORI J. **Torone** is an adjunct professor of English and Speech at her alma mater and a collector of teas and shawls. She believes the best thing in life is true love which can break any curse. Lori lives in New York with her two teenagers, dog, and a possibly haunted 1936 Underwood. Visit her online: Twitter @MedievalLit and Instagram @whiteraven829.

32

A MOUNTAIN OF GLASS

MARI NESS

Each step *hurt*.

The glass was cool, and smooth, and *hard*, and even sharp in a couple of places, where she had dropped something and shattered the surface. She knew where those places were, knew to avoid them, but yet, in a space of this size, it was difficult not to step there.

Not if she still wanted to move.

Most days, she did.

She had long since worn out the six pairs of soft slippers that she had brought with her to this mountain, long since worn all of her stockings and socks into holes. Her feet should have hardened, she knew, and yet somehow—perhaps something in the food the eagle brought her—they had not.

The eagle, too, like the glass mountain beneath her, had changed since the first days. She was not even certain that it was the first eagle; it might be the fourth. She could not be sure, largely because her first days here had been spent in shock and examining the mountain and the surrounding woods, not the eagle. And the one of the eagles—the third, she thought—had been particularly shy, never coming close enough for her to get a good look. Those had been particularly terrible years, years when she thought she might go mad, might simply pitch herself down the glass mountain, letting the glass and the earth and the trees take her.

Sometimes she thought she already had.

Sometimes other birds arrived: black crows and ravens, looking at the tiny gold and glass house with bright sharp eyes; sparrows, cocking their heads as if to hope for gossip or food; finches and a robin. She treasured those moments, the variation they brought to her endless days.

She wished she had crumbs to give them.

She had read, and reread, her three books, to the point where she could recite them all, and sometimes did, in the dark beneath the stars. She had counted every tree she could see, mourned when two of them were struck by lightning and fell, even as a part of her rejoiced at seeing fire. Seeing *something*. Seeing something *change*.

Things did change, she knew. Eagles. Clouds. Weather. Trees. Even her tiny house on this mountain. She had once kept it shining, partly in expectation of the promised prince, mostly for lack of anything to do. Now, she found herself content to sit watching the trees and the sun and the rain, waiting for the eagle, barely moving from the small balcony with its tiny roof.

At least until winter sent her into the tiny gold house, huddled under the blankets until the eagle arrived, screaming with rage, delivering food.

When it could. It did not always arrive, in the howling winds of the winter months, and she huddled under her blankets and wondered what had brought her to this.

She could slide down the mountain, she knew. It would hurt; she would almost certainly break a few bones, if she even survived. And that was only the start. From her mountain, she could see the tangled woods, and the dim hint of more mountains behind them. But not a single building; not a single hint of smoke; not a single thing that might be a human moving through the woods. Hints of *moving* grey or black or brown, but those, she was certain, were deer or bears or wolves or worse. She had no weapons, even if she knew how to use them. She had no shoes. Her clothing was in rags. Her feet were raw.

She had not seen the eagle for days.

Her vision shimmered.

Years ago, she remembered, those mountains and woods had sheltered the occasional prince. She had watched them tie their horses to the woods, watched them slowly climb the mountain, watched them slide to their deaths below.

She still had a few morsels of food left. The eagle might still come. She could ration the food until then. Wait for the rain, and let it pound her mouth and skin.

She ran her hands along the gems that had once shimmered in the sun and stars. At the small jeweled box holding the wealth of a kingdom. At the three now cracked, worn books that had been most of her world.

She thought of the stars that she had counted, night after night.

Of the prince that the faery had promised.

Of the eagles and their shrieks.

With a deep sigh, she grabbed ropes of pearls and golden chains, and the ragged cloak that had once graced the neck of a princess. And, ignoring the pain in her feet, stepped onto the edge of her glass prison, and slid down the mountain, her eyes fixed on the trees below.

MARI NESS IS a collector of words, books, and teddy bears, who has no idea what the best thing in life is. Mari lives in central Florida, under the critical and hungry supervision of two cats, and can be followed online at marikness.wordpress.com or @mari_ness on Twitter.

33

EVERY KINGDOM IS A GOBLIN KINGDOM

MARK HILL

[This text is a copy of a parchment written by an unknown scholar in 14 Longsummer, and recovered from the ruins of the Vale Academy in 37 Whitefish.]

As we stand on the precipice of retaking the Vale from the goblin horde that has occupied it since the days of our grandfathers, I am finding it difficult to share in the jubilant attitude of the capital. Certainly, our imminent victory will be a triumph for the Longsummer King, whose revanchist campaigns have reached a heroic peak with this difficult excursion into the Vale's dark forests and wending marshes. But as I watch the banners fly and the people dance, all I can think about is a recent conversation I had with a goblin who was captured and sent to the capital to be executed in the inevitable victory celebration.

The creature, whose name roughly translates to Every Rock Hewn, looked unintimidating. Stripped of his pole-arm and fed on prison rations, it was difficult to picture him as a threat to me, let alone the Kingdom. Despite the impending defeat of his kin and his own upcoming demise, he was sanguine about his circumstances and happy to chat with someone who knew more of his language than crude insults.

Every Rock Hewn was curious about life in the capital, where I had picked up my accented knowledge of his guttural tongue, and his probable method of execution. I summarized the vibrant bustle of the Sapphire City as best I could, told him of my year working in a merchant caravan that employed two goblins from the relatively personable Blue Horde as guards, and guessed he would likely be given his weapon and shoved in front of one of the King's chevaliers in a re-enactment of a recent victory. That his weapon would be dulled for the chevalier's safety did not appear to bother him.

With those pleasantries out of the way, I posed my own questions. Why, I wanted to know, did the goblin hordes continually encroach on the King's land when they knew it would one day be reclaimed from them? Why not build beyond the frontiers, rather than seize fallen cities and suffer the inevitable wrath of the Kingdom and its mighty army?

The goblin snorted and waved his gnarled hand, as if to dismiss my whole thesis. "Why scrape out a living in the distant cold and dark when you give us everything we need? You build and build and then all of your big buildings fall down," he said. "We take your rubble and build little homes. Who is mightier?"

I pointed out that this was a dubious argument to make from the behind the bars of a jail cell, but he just snorted again.

"Your King will build a statue of himself as another settlement rises over the bones of the last one. But then what? Invaders come, or assassins, or civil war. You will be slaughtered, or slaughter each other. You will abandon the Vale, and what will you leave behind? Stones to build with, weapons to hunt with. All of your failures are our boons."

I humored him by telling him his line of thinking was intriguing, but pointed out that the Kingdom had been stable for nearly a century. The chaos of the past had been consigned to history. This time he looked at me with disdain and said,

"There's always a Kingdom, and it always falls down. Yours, someone else's. You write about them in your books, but they're all the same to the hordes. Even you forget them. Who can remember them all?"

I admitted that history eventually devolved into myth, but pointed out that we had built on the ideas of our precursors. If, God forbid, the Sunflower Throne fell in the distant future, whatever power rose next would know our history and build on our work.

The goblin shrugged. "Or maybe we'll throw your books on our cookfires." He pointed at me, then waved his hands to encompass the capital, the Throne, the Kingdom. "Every Kingdom tells stories of goblins, but the hordes tell no stories about Kingdoms. Why would we tell stories about the stones we build with?"

"But surely," I said, "goblins tell stories about themselves. How could the hordes survive without them?"

The goblin laughed. "The hordes have no history. We just are. Every kingdom in every land is ours, because we carve our homes from their ruins while you stomp your feet and whine about what made the castles collapse. The cell you've locked me in, the library you scribble in all day, the palace where your King plans his little war, someday they'll all serve the hordes. And someday whatever Kingdom replaces you will too."

"And yet your kin will be slaughtered in the morning." I regretted blurting out such cruel words, but Every Rock Hewn just smiled. I thanked him for indulging my curiosity, even if we didn't see eye to eye. He gave me a cheery goodbye wave, as though it had been no trouble at all.

I enjoyed our conversation, although it was a relief to step back into the sunlight, to be absorbed by the endless sights and sounds of the capital. The goblin's ideas were strange and barbarous, yet I couldn't shake them from my mind. Every speech I heard and bunting I saw made me picture a day where the capital lies in ruins and the hordes pick through it.

But I have no time for such farsighted fantasies. I must prepare to depart for the Vale the moment word of our victory arrives. I have been tasked with writing a history of the Longsummer King's reconstruction of that once mighty province. If I wield my pen well enough my name will enter the annals of our time.

MARK HILL IS A NOVELIST, comedy writer, and baseball collector. He believes the best thing in life is still to come. Mark lives in Calgary, Canada with an indifferent cat. Visit him online: @mehil on Twitter or mehill.org.

34

THE BLACK SHIP
DJ TYRER

The ship was driven through the thickening night mists by dozens of oars moving in unison without the guiding beat of a drum or an overseer's cries, each forward-and-back movement too-perfectly aligned to belong to even the most veteran of crews. To see its dark form propelled, ghost-like, through the mist was enough to make even the bravest of souls shudder.

Maskalin Vaz suppressed the quake that threatened to run through his muscles and watched as the ship drew nearer. The seer had been right: Here, at Taryn Point, the dread vessel would put ashore.

The nature of the ship was whispered about but unclear, and from his vantage point atop the cliffs, Maskalin Vaz could discern no clues to favor one rumor over another. Some said it was the property of a vile and nameless necromancer. Others that the vessel carried long-dead pirates driven to continue their raids, their cursed souls damned by terrible deeds. Then, there were those who held the ship to be a ferry for the dead, and those who said it held a party of demonic raiders escaped from Hell. Whichever it was, when it was sighted, people died and terrible dooms fell upon coastal settlements.

Also, treasures vanished—never to be seen again.

Treasure was why Maskalin Vaz was here with his companions, the Vō brothers and the dwarf who called himself Druntha. No matter who or what crewed the vessel, it contained treasure and he meant to take it by force or by cunning.

It was what any self-respecting thief or swordsman would do, if only they knew where to meet it—and, after a long trek through the Southern Mountains to the Cave of the Blind Seer, they knew and were ready.

"To the boat." They had one waiting on the narrow gravel arc below.

Quickly, the four of them descended a path to the beach and the Vō brothers began to row them out.

The ship had anchored a little way up the coast and, though the darkness and mist obscured them, Maskalin Vaz was sure he could see a bustle of figures moving on and off it in silence.

They neared the vessel. The brothers Vō put up their oars so that they could glide silently alongside it. Druntha stood in the bow, swung a rope above his head, and sent it sailing up to where its hook caught on the ship. He gave a couple of tugs, pronounced it secure.

The dwarf tied the rope to the boat and they began to climb, Maskalin Vaz in the lead. The black sides of the ship were slick, as if greased with slime. More than once his feet slipped as he climbed. Then, he pulled himself over onto the deck.

Maskalin Vaz could see no one aboard the ship, yet he could detect faint sounds, just on the edge of his hearing, as if a crew were moving about at some great remove, whispered hints of shouted commands and other suggestive noises.

He glanced at his companions. "This is not a ship for the living. We must be swift."

Maskalin Vaz led them towards stairs going down and they made their way as quickly as they dared on the slick black deck of the ship. Strange, dark-flamed lanterns lit the way down and a peculiar musty odor rose to greet them.

Moving cautiously down the steps, they explored the ship, cringing into the shadows whenever the hint of sounds grew a little louder and nearer. Somewhere in the noisome bowels of the vessel was the treasure they sought.

"At last," grunted Druntha as they found their way barred by a locked door on the lowest level.

"This has to be it," muttered one of the Vō brothers. "Any lower and we'll be in the ballast."

Druntha examined the lock. "I can pick this."

There was the slightest hint of motion and Maskalin Vaz said, "It's departing. We dare not linger long." He was certain the sounds of the ship grew louder.

The dwarf gave a grunt of satisfaction and the door swung open with a sigh. "Well, here's the treasure, boys," he said. Then, Druntha's head detached and rolled off along the passageway.

As the dwarf's body fell to the floor, a shadow escaped from the strong room and enveloped the brothers Vō, who shrieked and swung their swords about in vain, before falling to the floor, gutted and dead.

The darkness flowed toward Maskalin Vaz, but he had snapped out of his terrified reverie and was already running for the stairs. About him, shadows moved as if the crew were going about their duties and he could more plainly hear them. It was as if the further it put between itself and the land, the more real the ship became.

Maskalin Vaz burst out onto the deck, pushing past figures who were almost there and ran to the grappling hook. He looked down and ice stabbed his guts: Only a short section of rope dangled from the hook; the rowboat was gone. Glancing back, he swore. Shadowy figures surrounded him and moved in on him like hungry wolves. He looked over the side of the ship at the black waters below, the oars mechanically slicing through them.

If he stayed, he'd die. If he jumped...

Maskalin Vaz jumped, throwing himself over the rail and into the black void below. The water was hard like a rock when he hit it, driving the air from his lungs, but swallowed him up, regardless. He tasted salt as he kicked and fought to reach the air. Then, an oar struck him and he could no longer sense anything but the blackness into which he sank deeper and deeper...

Above him, the ship rowed on, as it had always done and always would.

DJ TYRER IS the editor behind Atlantean Publishing, and a collector of roleplaying games. They believe the best thing in life is a good book. DJ lives in Southend-on-Sea in the United Kingdom with more books than shelf space. Visit them online: facebook.com/DJTyrerwriter/ or djtyrer.blogspot. co.uk/

35

WHITE SANDS FOOTPRINTS
GARY EVERY

T he wind blew across the New Mexico sand, carrying little grains through the air. When the wind stilled, visibility returned, and the airborne erosion revealed ancient footprints. The Acoma archeologist dropped to her knees and ran her fingers over the ancient footprints. This had been a busy walkway and the archeologist was amazed by the faunal variety: mammoth, mastodon, bison, camel, giant ground sloth, and even human beings. When she saw the clear outlines of human toes in the ancient lakebed mud, her heart beat rapidly. It was possible these footprints belonged to her direct ancestors. Suzy Charlie measured the Pleistocene footprints preserved in the dried-up playa, wandering, and wondering between the white sand dunes.

The next prehistoric human footprints she discovered belonged to a man, woman and toddler walking rapidly. Who could blame these first Americans for moving quickly across a landscape filled with predators like dire wolf, short faced bear, and a variety of saber toothed cats. The Acoma archeologist followed the family's steps. These prehistoric footprints were so finely defined the archeologist could discern when the mother moved the child from hip to hip, the outside of the feet splaying wide in the mud to support the toddler's weight.

The footprints were not fossilized. They were exposed by erosion and once exposed continued to erode. The footprints were made by citizens of the Pleistocene along the shores of a prehistoric lake and marshlands. Suzy Charlie walked White Sands National Monument, New Mexico, following ancient pathways buried, revealed, and then lost forever as she pondered the distant past.

One afternoon Suzy Charlie discovered the footprints of several human children. She studied the footprints skipping, running, and splashing in mud puddles. Children all throughout time love to splash in mud puddles. These children would someday have children of their own and grandchildren who would have grandchildren of their own and start a line of descent that would one day lead to Suzy Charlie. The archeologist abandoned her stance of scientific neutrality. She must prevent the centuries of genocidal atrocity which would someday visit the children of these children much further on down the road.

To find a way to alter historical timelines, Suzy Charlie ignored what science said was possible and relied on the oral histories of her people, tales of magic and sorcery. One hot and humid day when lightning flashed on the horizon and monsoon thunderheads pushed gusting winds, a dust devil swirled across the landscape. The miniature tornado careened between the white dunes, throwing small stones and debris along its path. When the dust devil spun past the Acoma archeologist, she stepped inside. She gasped as centuries swirled by until she dropped in the middle of the Pleistocene.

Suzy Charlie walked along the Ice Age pathway she had been studying for so many years while the feet which made the prints were still attached to living creatures. She gasped at a landscape filled with giant lumbering grazers, mastodon, mammoth, long horned bison, camel, and the bizarre but powerful giant ground sloth. The dried-up playa the Acoma archeologist was familiar with was now lakes and wet marshlands. The sky was full of the cries of unknown birds, yodeling yowls of saber-toothed predators, and then unexpectedly she heard children giggling as they splashed in mud puddles. Then Suzy Charlie was sucked back into her own time.

When Suzy Charlie returned to the Pleistocene, she had an invention of her own design. Holding her prize, Suzy Charlie walked the pathway, following behind a giant ground sloth. Another human followed the humongous beast, careful to place their own prehistoric feet inside the ten-foot stride of sloth paw prints. A third human tiptoed in from the side, stalking. The two prehistoric peoples were hunting the giant ground sloth.

Before the hunters could spring their ambush, the archeologist rushed up and gave these prehistoric peoples a saddle. She tried to communicate with a series of gestures and grunts. Although Suzy Charlie could speak her native language, she could not speak the ancestral language these people spoke. Nor did they understand her.

She spoke loudly and slowly but the prehistoric hunters did not understand. The Acoma archeologist was forced to take matters into her own hands. As the giant ground sloth reared up on hind legs, waving front claws wildly, Suzy Charlie saddled up, and held on for the wildest ride of her life. The giant ground sloth bellowed and bucked his hips trying to toss the archeologist from the saddle. The giant ground sloth twirled while the archeologist held on. The prehistoric people watched and understood.

THOUSANDS OF YEARS later when the conquistadors arrived, they rode into battle with metal swords and armor gleaming in the sun. The magnificent war ponies of the Spaniards charged forward only to find themselves met by a cavalry of pueblo peoples riding giant Ice Age mammals: mammoth, mastodon, camels, and entire armies of warriors riding giant ground sloths. The giant ground sloths were much more limber than the name sounds, covering ground in leaping bounds, and possessing claws capable of ripping through conquistador armor.

Coronado's conquistador invasion left the battlefield littered with dead, most of whom were Spaniards. The colonial invasion was repelled. The Acoma archeologist had successfully averted centuries of genocidal atrocities. The people who lived here, loved each other, and loved this land, remained. These people were not invaded, conquered, and displaced.

When the monsoons came, they brought lightning and rain, and sometimes a time travelling archeologist who stepped out of a swirling dust devil. The elders had stories about Dust Devil Woman which went back millennia. The elders recognized her as a time travelling shaman, but were not certain whether she was from the future or the past.

One day Suzy Charlie stepped inside a twirling dust devil and went nowhere. That is the thing about going to the past to alter timelines, you may find yourself unable to return to a future which no longer exists.

GARY EVERY IS A PERFORMING POET, award winning journalist, and science fiction author. He believes the best thing in life is running around outdoors and taking lots of photographs. He lives in Sedona, Arizona with the beautiful Tina. Visit him online at facebook.com/Gary Every or www.garyevery.com

36

THE CHRONOPARROT ATE A CRACKER

JON HANSEN

Private Silgne, Constable of the King's Watch, stood on the stadium steps and looked out over the sea of shouting dragonrider fans. The chronoparrot perched on his shoulder, giving him the appearance of a pirate from some third-rate play. Silgne sighed. If only he hadn't mentioned his grandmother to the captain, then he wouldn't be stuck here.

The chronoparrot squawked. A green and silver bird with a heavy yellow bill, it was easily heard over the roaring crowd. Automatically he produced another cracker from his dwindling supply. The chronoparrot seized it.

"Useless," said Silgne. "When are you going to find the timestopper?" The chronoparrot ignored him.

Silgne's grandmother had sold parrots along the docks for years, and taught a curious Silgne about their peculiar behaviors. Chronoparrots were a magical breed sensitive to the manipulations of time itself. They also smelled terrible.

Normally Silgne would be on the lookout for cutpurses and pickpockets. This tournament week, however, there had been unusual reports of gamblers having their winning tickets exchanged for losers. In many cases, they had been looking at the ticket when it happened. The King's mage could only divine that temporal magic was involved. The captain had promptly given both the job and the chronoparrot to Silgne.

The chronoparrot squawked again. Silgne shook his head. "No more crackers! The King's mage said you could find this rogue, now make it happen."

The chronoparrot fixed him with one black beady eye but otherwise did nothing. Silgne poked the bird. In response, it bit him on the finger, then took flight over the crowd. Had it seen something, or was it just pouting?

As Silgne watched, nursing his bloody finger, the chronoparrot dove towards the crowd. Suddenly, it vanished in a puff of rainbow smoke. Silgne gawked, took a few faltering steps, but it was no use. The chronoparrot had disappeared, and whoever it had seen had slipped away.

Silgne's report to the Captain was less than favorable. For the chronoparrot's loss she assigned him to stand guard in the palace throne room for the next two weeks. It was punishment detail. Extreme tedium, broken only by mild abuse from drunken nobles.

On the fifth day, as Silgne stood sighing and watching the nobles flirt and scheme, a sudden squawk filled the air. He looked up. The chronoparrot emerged from another colorful smoke cloud. As Silgne watched, the bird swooped down and defecated on a minor earl, covering him in glitter.

Silgne's heart stopped. What would the Captain do? Then he remembered his grandmother's words: chronoparrot droppings are a message. Private Silgne strode forward and seized the sputtering nobleman's arm.

"What is this outrage?" cried the earl. "I must protest!"

As everyone turned to witness the sudden commotion, Silgne ripped open the earl's doublet to reveal a glowing hourglass on his necklace. "Is that a timestopper, my lord?" The earl flushed with guilt. The chronoparrot settled on Silgne's shoulder and squawked.

"Your lordship," said Silgne, "you're under arrest." Still protesting, the earl was led away.

Further investigation revealed the earl had won an improbably high number of wagers recently. Combined with the time artifact, the earl's guilt was assured.

At the next royal holiday, as the now promoted Corporal Silgne stood before the upturned faces of his fellows to receive his medal, he reflected on his grandmother's observation that patience is a virtue, especially when dealing with a parrot.

JON HANSEN (HE/HIM) is a writer, librarian, and occasional blood donor. Jon lives about fifty feet from Boston with his wife, son, and three pushy cats. Although he does have a website (http://www.logicalcreativity/jon), he spends entirely too much time on Twitter (@jonmhansen). He likes tea and cheese.

37

DOWSE

AMANDA DIER

"Give it here. Now."

The rubber duck dropped onto the hood of the patrol car with the barest thud.

Paper crinkled as Gonzalez unfolded a map next to the toy. It was thinning and flaking at the creases, and Joy made a mental note to replace it as soon as they were done with this call. She'd never liked that they couldn't just use a tablet with a higher-definition image, but that was why she'd been sent to retrieve the personal item. That, and she wasn't Talented.

Only a witchborn could dowse using a personal item, and that's what they were going to do. While other deputies canvassed the neighborhood, Joy Wetch and Santiago Gonzalez were crouched over the hot hood of a patrol car several miles away, pinning down the corners of a paper map with magnets and fingers.

Gonzalez dangled a small crystal pendant from a platinum chain and Joy watched nervously as it spun.

"Ready?" she asked. The radio chatter wasn't frantic—it never was—but precious minutes had passed and the missing kid hadn't turned up. The information coming in was bad and getting worse: nonverbal, under five, and the mom, freaking out, was not answering most of their questions. The fact that the kid wasn't attracted to water was the only plus so far. Joy just wanted to be on scene looking for the toddler instead of driving in, snatching the yellow duck out of the mom's hands, and leaving to meet with Gonzalez.

"As ever," Gonzalez sighed. He wrapped the long end of the chain around the faded bath toy. "Let's do this."

The bright sunlight couldn't quite hide the glow building around Gonzalez's fingers as he held the dangling crystal over the map. Against the breeze, the little pendulum began to swing back and forth, then into a widening circle.

"Anything yet?"

"It's been ten seconds," Gonzalez said through gritted teeth. "Let me work."

Joy looked east towards where the house was. Even now, she knew the unit who'd pulled up on her heels had started a general area search. Going through the house had turned up nothing, so she'd quickly interviewed the mom for more specifics while other responding deputies began to check around the neighborhood.

Watching the duck made something click in her brain. A line of white duck stickers had decorated the rear window of the van in the driveway, and it hadn't been the only thing.

"Eight Alpha Fourteen to Eleven," she said into the shoulder mic while she used her elbow to hold down the map.

"Eight Alpha Fourteen," the radio crackled.

"Ask mom how *much* he likes ducks," she said. "Dowsing item was a rubber duck, and I saw a line of them melting on the dashboard of the van."

Silence reigned, then, "Good call. Mom says he's obsessed with ducks. Have units start checking water sources."

"Have units check water sources in the area," the dispatcher repeated. "Map shows a pond to the west off Jackson and several canals."

Joy bit her lip as the circumference of the crystal swing

began to narrow. Sweat beaded up on Gonzalez's forehead and she could see the muscle in his jaw bulging as he gritted his teeth. The crystal was away from the original neighborhood entirely, focusing now on an apartment complex next door.

"Nothing on Jackson," she heard one of the other deputies say on the radio.

"K9 six and K9 three coming from the training facility, code three." Barking was audible in the background, and despite the situation, she bit back a smile. Some of the dogs always knew when it was time to work.

"Code three authorized for K9s," the familiar voice of the lieutenant said. "Status on the dowsing?"

"Still narrowing in," Joy reported. "Starting to pull to the north, but nothing definite."

"Three units to Haven apartments," the lieutenant ordered.

Three deputies volunteered over the radio and Joy stared at the crystal, willing it to swing faster.

"Not in the canal off Idaho Street," someone announced.

Gonzalez's fingers tightened around the duck and the chain suddenly straightened like a rod, pointing at the exact location of the missing kid.

"North end of the complex," she snapped into the shoulder mic. "There are two lakes, he's on the north end." She pulled out her issued digital camera and took two quick pictures of the map and the crystal before fumbling to get the card out and into her laptop. "Attaching the picture into the call now."

A long list of comments she'd missed scrolled up as the image uploaded, and then the calm voice of the dispatcher filled the air.

"Appears to be behind building twelve. Pendulum indicates that the child is *in* the water."

"Crap," Joy said just as Gonzalez groaned. The crystal clattered onto the map and he staggered back from the hood of the car.

"Easy there," Joy said, looping an arm around his waist.

"They find the kid?" he grunted.

"Let's go find out," Joy said. She helped him over to the front seat of her car and closed the door behind him.

His car chirped as she sprinted around the front of the car and dove into the front seat.

"It's locked," he said wearily as she hit her lights. "Come on."

"Eight Alpha Three, I'm out with the missing child," the car radio announced.

Joy locked eyes with Gonzalez.

"Status?" the lieutenant asked.

Silence reigned.

They were the only two in the car, but she knew they weren't alone. There was an entire district of deputies and a room full of dispatchers waiting on the response.

"He's wet but he's okay. I pulled him out of the lake. He was trying to get to one of the goose pipe markers out offshore."

Joy sighed and let off the gas pedal. "Car or kid first?"

"Kid," Gonzalez said. "I just wanna lay eyes on him."

"You and me both."

AMANDA DIER IS A MAD SCIENTIST, author, and a collector of orchids. She believes the best thing in life is curating a jungle, no matter how many spiders it invites inside. Amanda lives on the Treasure Coast of Florida with her husband, rescue pitbull, and miniature carnivorous bog. Visit her online: @deardeerdier on Twitter and @amandacervidae on Instagram.

38

Nidus of Alms

Dave D'Alessio

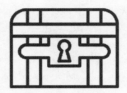

S he sat in a dark, filthy alley that stank of rotting garbage and cat piss.

"Alms for the poor. Mercy for the less fortunate."

She was swaddled in a hooded cloak, thick and heavy, the hood drawn low over her face, hiding any disfigurement in its shadows. Her voice was low, husky, hoarse.

"Alms for the poor. Sir? Madam? Could you be so kind?"

She sat in the garbage at the side of the way, a bowl in front of her. There were copper pieces in the bowl, enough for a meal at the poorer sort of inn, where the watery stew was made of fish heads and moldy potatoes.

"An old soldier, sir, fought in the wars, yes I did, sir. Gave both my arms to the king, gods bless him everyone."

No hands, no arms showed outside the cloak. Legs she had, curled under her as she sat tailor-style in the alley's trash, knowing her place was with the other detritus, but of arms there was no sign.

A coin dropped. It rattled rather than rang; copper then, not silver.

"Thank you, sir, an old soldier thanks you, and may the gods, each and every one, bless you! Thank you!"

Dark rolled up across the harbor. Sometimes a coin dropped into the bowl. Most times one did not.

"Alms!" The voice was louder, more desperate. Soon no one save knaves and cutpurses would walk this alley, and then there would be no more coins. "An old soldier, terribly wounded!"

Footsteps, three people. Not then a lady and her swain, the man inclined to look well in his paramour's eyes.

"What have we here? A beggar? What does the law say of beggars?"

She could see boots in front of her, military issue. The Guard, then. She hung her head lower, the hood shadowing her face more deeply.

"Against the law, Sergeant."

"Like as not a faker, too. Pick him up."

Rough hands seized her shoulders, pulling her up. They stopped to feel her shoulders, sides. She prayed they didn't reach her back.

The second voice, "He's got no arms, Sergeant." There was respect in his voice, but pity, too.

"Let him go then, the poor bastard."

She fell back onto her knees, kept her head down, her face in the shadows of the hood.

Her bowl was snatched up, the coins in it counted.

"The fine is six pennies, soldier. Your fine is paid, so you can get your bowl and get out of here."

A hand dropped the bowl back in front of her, two thin coppers in the bottom. Two pair of feet stomped away. Another coin clattered into the bowl before the third pair joined them.

She waited until they swaggered out of earshot before getting to her feet, her strong thighs pushing her up against the wall behind her, wiggling her shoulders to pull herself up. She knelt down to take the bowl in her mouth, her teeth gripping its rim. The reek of the Guardsman was still on it. She could live with that, for the sake of the coppers still in it.

She waddled from the alley, her legs thick and stout, her shoulders stooped over the bowl she clenched between her teeth. She shuffled downhill, toward the boats that were moored for the night, toward the docks with their stinks of rotten fish and offal cast into the bay, her hood still shadowing her face, listening for more Guardsmen.

There was a room below an inn. She reached it through a door at the back, through an alley used as a urinal by people buying ale from the inn, her nostrils flaring in reflex. The room was hers so long as she handed over five coppers every month. At that price, she could make herself live with the stink of stale piss.

She had no key for the lock. She needed none. She lifted a foot, manipulated the lock with a talon. The room was dark at this hour but she needed no light. Her sense of smell served just as well. She shrugged the cloak from her shoulders, stretched her wings out with a sigh of pleasure, let them beat the foul air gently.

The room held no stove, no chair, no bed, no lamp, no wardrobe nor chest of drawers. But in the middle of the dirt floor, a nest of sorts. Coins, mostly copper, but some silver, and a single gold she'd risked a trip to the money changers to swap for. No gems, not yet, but rhinestones and sequins glittered in the beam of moonlight sneaking in through the tiny window.

She emptied her bowl onto the pile and put it aside. She lowered herself into the nest, wiggling into the cool, loose metal, comforted by its wealth. It wasn't what she wanted, what she desired, what she yearned for. At least, it wasn't yet.

After all, every little wyvern's hoard had to start somewhere.

DAVE D'ALESSIO IS AN EX-INDUSTRIAL CHEMIST, ex-award-winning animator, and current social scientist who enjoys assembling furniture and other mechanical tasks. Conveniently,

DAVE D'ALESSIO

he lives near the Ikea in Connecticut. He blogs about writing in anime and manga as The Overage Otaku: davedalessiowrites. wordpress.com

39

SHIELD, HILL, HOME
BRANDON CRILLY

Yvesser had brought this client to so many homes he'd lost count. Standing outside the first for today, back to the dwarven-made water feature and the elegant, cobalt-infused brick façade, he hoped—*prayed*—that this would be the one.

Instead, Kullon of Tarth stared across the horizon, plucked her shield from the grass, and declared, "No, I'm sorry, this won't do."

The way she glided across the clover-covered lawn didn't awe him anymore. Yvesser tried to rub the ache from his left temple and couldn't quite muster his usual cheer as he said, "Well, we have a few more houses left to see today."

Except the rest of that day proceeded like the last three. From the Late Resurgence townhome with the goblin grotto to the elegant, sycamore-made dwelling with the branching rooms —a genuine steal from its treant owner—nothing seemed to satisfy Kullon. In each one, she made the occasional hum of interest following him around, but he quickly got the feeling she was humoring him. Inevitably she stepped outside, chose a spot, and planted her shield, Angral, in the ground, facing central Risenguard.

Twenty minutes or five seconds didn't matter: "No, I'm sorry, this won't do."

Yvesser had asked her casually on the first day, "Looking for something specific?"

She didn't answer, and he knew not to ask an Inardan Guard twice, even if she was retired.

By the time their coach approached Day Four's final house, Yvesser had long given up on small talk. His only silver lining was that the construct horse and driver didn't need to be paid. If he returned without a commission, though, the other brokers would never let him forget. Especially that bastard Freeg the Bloodthirsty.

"You're fatigued," Kullon said.

Never tell the client you were frustrated, even if you couldn't hide it. Except Kullon kept staring at him, with those blue eyes and that calmly placid expression on her high-cheekboned face. "Just worried we won't find you a new home."

"There must be one," she said, fingers gently drumming the top of Angral where it rested between them. There were more stories about that shield than about Kullon, but Yvesser only believed half of them.

She had specifically asked to see properties at the highest elevations around Risenguard. The next one was middling at best, so Yvesser didn't hold out much hope as they climbed the front walk. The single-story residence was bland; part of a neighborhood designed ten years earlier by a human designer who liked domed roofs with aquamarine gilding and unnecessarily large walk-in closets.

But this time, Kullon didn't wait for him to describe the features, or even step inside the house. She stopped, examined the sky, and immediately marched around back through the wrought-iron gate. By the time Yvesser caught up to her, she stood in the center of the back courtyard, studying the horizon and the setting sun.

"You mentioned utilitarian during our consult, so I thought—"

He stopped as Kullon flipped her shield over her shoulder with a flourish worthy of the Eleven Sagas. She planted it in the grass and stared out at Risenguard, wind whipping her black leather jacket.

"Do you see it?" she asked, and Yvesser knew she wasn't asking him.

The set to her shoulders was different, the stance reminding him of every artwork he'd seen of Kullon in her heyday. He kept his distance but risked another question. "What are you looking for?"

"Do you have a nemesis, Mr. Windcatcher?"

Yvesser didn't think Freeg really counted so he shook his head.

"Most in my profession do. Retiring while they still live is rare." Her fingers caressed Angral again as she stared out at the city. "We won't be fighting her again, and if we can't have that resolution, at least we can keep an eye on her, can't we?"

Yvesser wracked his brain, trying to remember what was out that way that couldn't have been seen by the other properties. Glass-walled elven condos, at least one arcanist commune.

A hospice for necromancers.

Kullon crouched beside Angral, head cocked, for about a minute. Then she nodded and casually returned the shield to the strap on her back.

"Thank you for your patience. Please draft the paperwork. This will do."

That was that. She headed back to the coach without so much as looking inside the house, and Yvesser didn't press the issue. Sometimes, the client's decision came down to things he couldn't control. All he could do was what they asked.

And imagine the look on Freeg's face in the morning.

• • •

BRANDON CRILLY'S IPPY Award-winning fantasy novel *Catalyst* was published by Atthis Arts in October 2022, with a sequel slated for 2025. He has bestselling TTRPG publications with We Are Legion and Fat Goblin Games, and forthcoming work with The Story Engine and *TinyZine*. He's also an Aurora Award-winning podcaster, conference organizer for Can*Con, an occasional reviewer, and clearly wears too many hats. Find out more about his upcoming releases by following him on Instagram or signing up for his newsletter via brandoncrilly.com.

40

THE SAND GATHERING

HAZEL HYSLOP

It was four a.m. in the sunny seaside village of Argyle, Tobago. The young girl had woken early and was eager to beat her brothers and parents to collect the shiny sand that washed up after the rain had come. She had gone to bed earlier that evening; hatching a plan to get up early and fill her buckets with sand. The thought of getting two shillings for her five-bucket load filled her with excitement. She barely slept and, at the first crow of the cockerels, she silently slipped out of the room. She was surprised that she had not woken her two younger brothers, Aaron and Euren, who she shared a room with.

She didn't bother to change out of her nightdress. With anticipation she walked quickly to the beach. It was only a minute walk down the path from her house.

She loved the quiet of the morning and the soft sounds of the waves. The golden sand seemed to glitter even more, with the occasional burst of light from the sky. She got her spade and buckets and got straight into the task of filling them with sand. She began to imagine the family size bottle of coca cola that she might buy with some of her money. She imagined buying corn curls and joob joob from the only shop in the village. She also thought that she might give the rest of it to her mother to help buy food.

There was talk of a dance to be held in the nearby town of Roxborough for the older boys and girls. Perhaps she might ask her parents if she could go with her fifteen year old cousin. She herself was eleven years old and quite tall for her age. The silly boys teased her and called her 'family size,' like the large, bottled coke. She hated being called that name and she hated the boys even more. *Perhaps* she thought, *I might meet a boy from Roxborough.* A boy, who was more clever and handsome, not like those stupid boys in her village."

So deep was she in her thoughts, that she did not hear the man with the two buckets arrive. Suddenly she felt self-conscious. *Perhaps*, she thought, *I should have changed into my day clothes*. She felt too shy to look at him, but from the corners of her eyes, she could see his buckets, and the long white gown he wore. He was busy adding to her pile of sand which began to grow quickly. Why was he helping her? Perhaps he was one of the elders who couldn't sleep. He didn't speak, but she thought nothing of it, as it was so early in the morning. All she could think of was the amount of money that she and her family could get from this enormous load of sand.

But wait a minute, where were his arms and legs? Where was his head?

How was he moving and carrying the buckets of sand without his feet and legs? As she turned to look directly at him, she suddenly realized that she had not been imagining things. This man did not have any feet or hands. She could feel her head getting bigger and bigger.

For a brief moment, she thought this must be what the elders in the village meant by someone's head 'raising.' Not only was her head raising, but she began to feel lighter and lighter. Gripped with fear, she froze. The headless man with no arms and feet came very close and stopped right in front of her.

She could feel her whole body turning to jelly and felt herself slowly slipping out of consciousness.

Through the hazy feelings, she heard a voice cry, "Girl, what are you doing here? Get your bucket and go home now!" She couldn't see the person with the voice. She didn't know if it was the headless figure or someone else. Then she heard the click of the match, followed by the light from it. She could smell smoke from a tobacco pipe. When she opened her eyes, the headless figure had disappeared.

Standing above her was Mr. Marcus who was an elderly man that walked the villages early mornings. He had a tendency to come down to the beach to smoke his pipe, as he never smoked indoors. His was a tiny one-bedroom cottage he shared with his family. Too small to indulge in his one pleasure: his pipe. The girl's legs felt like jelly, but she was relieved to see a familiar face.

Mr. Marcus scolded her for being on the beach alone. He told her that if it was not for his light from the match and the smoke from his pipe "The Spirit" would have possessed her. He took her home and woke her parents up. He told them to never allow their daughter to go alone again on the beach.

The next day, she and her family came to collect the bucket of sand, but there was nothing there. It was almost as if she had dreamt it all.

IT'D BEEN over sixty years since the young girl had had this experience. As she sat on the beach watching her great grandchildren play on the sand, she couldn't help but remember that fateful night. Shivers ran down her spine at the memory of it all.

. . .

HAZEL HYSLOP IS A PSYCHOTHERAPIST, Leadership Coach, Podcaster, and emerging writer. She is now discovering wild swimming in the cold British sea with women who dare to take crazy, stupid risks. She now understands what it is to have fun unashamedly. Hazel lives in Brighton UK. Visit her online @ www.hazelhyslop.com

41

ANGEL SEASON

C.R. KANE

O n hills and clouds, on cliffs and seas. In the canopies of
far-off forests, burrowed in warm waves of sand. Tucked
inside dead temples, spread out in the cathedrals of caves older
than the primate. Sat firmly beside the families of outraged
swans, nestled on rooftops with unbothered pigeons. One each
in the frosted poles of north and south.

There appears to be no rhyme or reason for where they
choose to build their nests. Some insist it is a matter of divine
destiny. Others claim it to be just another unknowable whim.
Still more believe it's a matter of convenience. Whatever their
purpose in allowing a place to play host to them, humanity may
burn itself out before we understand it.

Until then, we get to watch.

Here is one the size of a mastodon, all six wings tucked
down and around itself with feathers full of sunrise. Another
looms like a mountain in the sky, its plumage white and flaming
as the core of a bonfire. A third is nesting in the cul-de-sac of a
battered neighborhood, staring back at us with constellations of
eyes that never blink.

All around them, miracles. The ill are well, bones unbreak,
tumors vanish. Wild greenery flourishes in gardens and bursts

through concrete. Food tastes better, drinks are bliss, every scent a perfume. Daybreaks and dusks become paintings. The stars blaze, smashing through the light pollution to outshine their satellite pretenders. Love flows in phantom rivers from heart to heart.

Governments and economies around the world splutter their rage as a whole flock settles themselves in factories, less than legal farms, prison yards, camps, and various military compounds. A specimen with too many heads—one wonders how our ancestors could mistake them for the heads of our own Earthly animals, no matter how generous the interpretation—breathes on a police convoy sent to extricate them.

It takes a very nervous team of cleaners to sweep the resulting salt statues from the road.

We are afraid. We are enamored. We want to run. We want to embrace.

The latter is at once the simplest and most difficult part of the whole visit. They see the virtue and the sin and all our in-betweens when they look upon us with their infinite stares. Depending on what they see, we may come near, we may be warned off, or we may have our terror proven right. Most are cautious enough not to risk the attempt. For the greater number of us, we are our most vicious judges. Even the saints in our midst fret over their worthiness, the merit of their own goodwill, the improbable guilt at not being able to do and be more than they are.

Rare as it is, there are also callous fools so steeped in their own self-delusion they think nothing of their past cruelties when strolling up to a nest. Often with a camera ready to go off or some gilded trinket to trade for a feather.

The leftovers are usually alive and often wish they were otherwise.

The closest visitors are usually children. Children bring back reports of strange music in place of speech, of secrets only the youngest were allowed to remember, of how much their crayon portraits were appreciated, and of how just for a moment, a huge wing was carefully lifted up to reveal the litter of new celestial faces peeking out of the divine down.

"They're big like you," the children would inform their guardians, all of them a uniform shade of unwell. "Big and long and grownup, but they're babies. It was funny." They would then go on to highlight that, unfortunately, they couldn't share the snacks they'd brought in their little bags. There was no mouth on them to eat with.

Time passes. Now and then one of the less feathery cousins will drift down from the stars, all wheels and robes, trying to peek at the nest. When this happens, a great cry of **BE AFRAID BE AFRAID BE AFRAID** trumpets in a voice that booms in the brain rather than the ears. It's joined by a thunderous pounding; the flap of several burning wings swatting the curious interloper away.

Eventually, the time comes.

There are no eggs, just as there was never a mating. But the ancient young are there just the same. They slip out from under wings or through the puffs of cloud or along the wisps of flame. Their wingspans amount to only a single pair and need time to stretch. We get to see them walk and climb and perch wherever they can on the one who incubated them. It's a charming sight, seeing all those omniscient eyes turning glassy. And, finally, away from us.

A number of us wonder the same thought as we look on the timeless newborns. Do the elders stare at us because we remind them of their young? We're certainly no stranger to cooing over dim creatures with our children's wide eyes, high chirps, and little tricks. We ponder their newborns.

Four long limbs, upright, the niceties of two eyes, a nose, a mouth. Yes, there's some resemblance at a distance. Bar the wings and the radiation of loving dread and dreadful love.

We watch the litters take flight one after the other, circling their caretaker before soaring out and away to a place past the rim of the universe. There are rainstorms as the last of the young fly off. Colossal eyes are weeping. We join them.

NOT AFRAID, we feel before we hear it. **NOT AFRAID NOT AFRAID.**

Then they are gone too.

We dry our cheeks, and dream, as always, of the next time we get to fear.

C. R. Kane is a scribbler, rambler, and a collector of infinite novelty mugs. They believe the best thing in life is an endless supply of horror movies. C. R. Kane lives in a state of denial with their family, dogs, and a cat who invited herself to stay. Visit them online: SeeArcane on Twitter.

42
DEAD TIME
EDWARD AHERN

The non-denominational, unblessed chapel was devoid of life. Which made it a busy rec center for those buried around it. As daylight eddied the chapel filled with those who survived their deaths.

"Sally won't be joining us, John, she's been dissipated." Agnes' usual light-yellow ectoplasm had shaded down to gray.

John's presence swirled in rage. "What? No! Who? Probably that treacly son of hers."

"It was. She could barely get hold of me after he pulled her ashes from the mausoleum. It was like trying to drink powdered milk before the water is added. Anyway, she said he was going to scatter her ashes in the ocean. And he must have, I haven't been able to raise her since. She's fish poop now."

"Damn those living. Why can't they leave dead enough alone. So, Agnes, are we prepped for this Fischer guy?"

Agnes' sigh was a dust disturbing eddy against the altar. "I think so. Although I wish Sally was still here to chair the meeting. She was so good at conciliation between the Catholic and the Jewish cemeteries."

John's aura was more shards than shimmer. "I still don't buy our messing with the living. Leave alive alone I say. It's for the best."

"Nonsense. You know how good both faiths are with guilt. Where's the harm in inflicting just enough that they improve our landscaping and the drainage. Do you really want to rest in wormy groundwater for eternity?"

"No, but these days they'll go on Facebook and Twitter and boast about how loving and caring they are. If enough of them do it, someone will get suspicious, maybe even have an exorcism or blessing. And that's trouble. We're stuck here because we weren't invited into the up elevator. Do you really want to take the chance on being discovered, or, worse, sent down the coal chute?"

"Nonsense. If we have to wait for the end of days, we may as well have comfortable nights. Shh, be nice now, that's Fischer's ectoplasm wafting in."

"Hello Ira," she sensed, "wonderful to feel you today." Her aura again glowed amber.

Ira's shade vaguely resembled the black frock coat and hat he'd worn in life. "*Gruss dich*, Agnes. Maybe not so wonderful."

"What happened?"

He sighed. "As you suggested, we acted as impartial facilitators and used your daughter as the alpha test site."

"She's a sweet, caring girl, I'm sure she proved suggestive."

"Not the adjectives I would use. We smothered her dream with memories of all you had done for her, then reminded her that she hadn't visited in two years. We played cello solo melancholy, even we were a little misty."

"How much is she giving?"

"Nothing. When she woke up her first thought was 'We almost went broke paying for the nursing home.'"

Agnes struggled to hold her color. "Oh. But I'm sure she'll come around if we keep trying."

"Doubt it. Her second thought was 'Wonder if there's a

market for used burial plots and coffins? We could always scatter her remains at sea.'"

EDWARD AHERN RESUMED WRITING after forty odd years in foreign intelligence and international sales. He's had four hundred fifty stories and poems published so far, and six books. Ed works the other side of writing at Bewildering Stories, where he manages a posse of eight review editors. He's also lead editor at The Scribes Micro Fiction magazine.

43

INVENTORY REPORT

JODY LYNN NYE

Memo
To: Damien Shuggaloth
From: Natara Sinestra

Our Great Master, Xocolotl the Powerful, has been waiting for your report on the contents of the Despairing Caverns, his newest conquest in Domalion. I would prefer you to use the official format this time. The inventory of the Castle of Aerie that I received last month was far less organized than I expected of a Lesser Imp as experienced as you, and I had to rewrite it in my own blood on a parchment scroll, instead of the orc hide you used. With my powers of illusion, I can only shield you so long from his Awful Wrath™. Keep in mind that it's not only you who will suffer if he is not pleased. We must provide him with information, even if it is a small segment at a time. The full moon is almost upon us.

Memo
To: Natara Sinestra
From: Damien Shuggaloth

Forgive me, divine sorceress. I've tried to make his Agents of Torture[tm] aware of how difficult it is to enumerate anything within the borders of Domalion. This is the most disorganized realm that the Great Master has ever overwhelmed. I hate this place! Things move around by themselves. No sooner have I counted a roomful of newt snoots, then they vanish, and I'm surrounded by crystal vials of ichor. Did you know there were twenty-seven kinds of wyvern ichor alone? But they're gone now. I'm tearing out what is left of the hair on my head. Most of the servants I put a glamour on fled screaming at the five hundred and two skulls that are now here in this chamber.

Would you in your wisdom advise me? Do you want them listed as "skulls, flaming, 107," "skulls, flaming, shrieking, 16," "skulls, chattering, green, 2," "skulls, chattering, blackened, 19," etc., or all under one entry?

Memo
To: Damien Shuggaloth
From: Natara Sinestra

I don't care. Just get me a list. His Greatness has only limited patience, and so have I. The more detail the better, as you were trained. Or, I will instruct the torturers to use up your lunchtime reminding you of where you stand in this organization.

Memo
From: Damien Shuggaloth
To: Natara Sinestra

Never mind. The skulls are gone, too. Now I have fifteen singing and dancing clowns.

Nope, they vanished as well.

Memo

To: Damien Shuggaloth
From: Natara Sinestra

WHERE ARE ALL these things going? Find out! Follow them!

Memo
From: Damien Shuggaloth
To: Natara Sinestra

How? I don't get teleportation lessons at my level of employment! I barely get overtime.

Wait a minute, here's something I can use. I've got scrolls and scrolls of parchment. Really nice stuff! Could be thousands of rolls here.

Memo
To: Damien Shuggaloth
From: Natara Sinestra

Now we're getting somewhere. Start scribing. Time is fleeting.

Memo
From: Damien Shuggaloth
To: Natara Sinestra

My winsome one, I cannot express to you the wonder of your eyes. They are as blue as the sky and as bright as the stars. My entire person tingles with a single touch of your finger. I long to kiss your lips and know the magic of eternity in your embrace.

Memo
To: Damien Shuggaloth
From: Natara Sinestra

What the hell was that, Damien?! You know better. We had a whole lecture not a month ago on inappropriate interaction between co-workers. I don't fancy you, and never did! And my eyes are black.

Memo
From: Damien Shuggaloth
To: Natara Sinestra

My deepest apologies, Natara. I sent one of the other scrolls by accident. It looks like we found the old enchantress's personal correspondence. Sounds like she had a hot love life in her youth. They're gone. I managed to hold onto my own blank pages. But I did find some of her pets. Did you know she had three hundred giant parrots? Oops, they're gone. But I've got twenty-seven boxes of her lingerie. Whee! They're my size. I wonder if anyone will notice if a slip or two is missing.

Memo
To: Damien Shuggaloth
From: Natara Sinestra

I have just received word from His Terribleness. If you don't get a list to me within the hour of the contents of the Despairing Caverns, the torturers have instructions to remove one piece of you at a time. When they're finished with you, you're fired!

Memo
From: Damien Shuggaloth
To: Natara Sinestra

Never mind that! I quit. I'm *joining* the torturers. Even if they practice on me, it's better than doing inventory.

Memo

From: Natara Sinestra
To: Damien Shuggaloth

Accepted. I can't say I blame you. Ask them if they need an administrator.

JODY LYNN NYE is a best-selling author, keen baker of novelty cakes, and a collector of way too many books. She believes the best thing in life is reading a book with a cat on your lap and a cup of hot cocoa by your elbow. Jody lives northwest of Atlanta with her husband and three cats. Visit her online: jodylynnnye.com or https://www.facebook.com/jodylynn.nye

44

TROUBLE WITH UNICORNS
BRENDA ANDERSON

By day Benny wrangled mad unicorns but often felt drained by their combination of madness, magic, and pointy horns. Fortunately he had magic of his own and could go twisty with theirs. As a result, he kept them fit and corralled without too much fuss.

By night, however, he chose to collect arcane fingerprints, which he stored in a fully equipped shed out back. As a personal challenge, he'd constructed a clockwork quokka: *setonix brachyurus*, aka short-tailed scrub wallaby. The quokka, which he'd named Charles, sensed danger, processed fingerprints and above all, smiled. Owing to the shape of its face, the quokka regularly topped the list of the World's Happiest Creatures. Benny wanted a happy, supportive companion whenever he trawled bomb sites and mine fields.

One night Charles tilted his burnished face. "Alert, Master. We're being followed."

Benny looked round. "Based on what?"

"I hear footsteps, but see no body."

"It's invisible?" Benny considered his options, picked up the quokka, whispered an incantation, and materialized in the shed.

An instant later, so did a large, gem-studded leather glove. "Greetings, Lord Benny," said a deep, commanding voice.

Benny shivered. "And you are?"

"Let's say, your mad unicorns. Their magic has been so twisty lately it took a while to find the right disguise but at last, we did it. How's this? You seek fingerprints, which gloves negate. On the other hand, this sort of glove represents a message. See, we are throwing down the gauntlet. Let's fight. Let's do it, here, now, but first we will show that we mean business." The gauntlet seized the quokka and smashed it into a thousand pieces.

Benny recoiled. His beloved Charles, destroyed. He stood, stunned.

The gauntlet leapt up and slapped him hard across the face. Benny gasped. Such strength. No! He'd go twisty. He leaned back, flipped into a somersault, reached out, snatched the gauntlet, and smashed it on the ground. Benny stamped so hard that gemstones broke off. The gauntlet made a fist and slammed Benny on the chin, hard. With a grunt, he stepped backward.

The gauntlet flung itself at him again. This time Benny ducked, grabbed hold of it, and slipped it on. Instantly, the gauntlet glowed red hot. Benny's hand burned. He pulled it off, ran for the sink, and held both his hand and the glove under the cold tap, which he turned on full. Water drenched the gauntlet. "Give up?" panted Benny.

"Turn it off!" screamed the gauntlet.

"No! I look after you! You destroyed my quokka and attacked me. Charles never did you any harm. I can reconstruct him but seriously, what's the problem?"

"Turn...it...off," gargled the gauntlet. "You care for that mechanical thing. Cared. Still care. Perhaps even love, while you merely tolerate us. Us! We have more talent in the tips of our tails than you can dream about. And don't tell us that we're mad...."

Benny sighed. "Only mad unicorns attack young maidens,

foul water springs, impale any human you dislike, and barf in the presence of truth, beauty, purity, misty scenery, etcetera. Every single one of you is certifiably crazy."

"Really?" The gauntlet gave a thumb's down. "We held a meeting, and agreed that if fingerprints got your attention, we'd turn every hoof-print into a cry for help. We left messages beseeching you to take notice of us. You didn't even notice! You seek the fingerprints of murderers and psychopaths and ignore cries of help from your own unicorns."

Benny inhaled, exhaled. He'd always believed he'd done a good job. Now, it seemed, the unicorns only wanted attention, perhaps even love. How sad. But could he magic them into some semblance of acceptability?

Benny turned off the tap. "Guys, I'm sorry. Truly."

The gauntlet tilted its fingers, and the water trickled away.

Benny thought for a moment. "Let's try this: you vow to leave all beauty, purity, and whatnot unsullied. And steer clear of young maidens. I promise I'll give each one of you room to move, plus a hug. And I won't duck when I'm close to those horns of yours. I promise, as long as you keep your side of the bargain, I'll never go twisty on you again. How does that sound?"

The gauntlet quivered. "Do you mean it?"

"Yes. Listen. I'm Benny, I wrangle unicorns, and I'll find a perfect solution for you."

Benny decided that the answer might be as simple as taking the unicorns with him when he went out at night.

They proved ideal companions: excited by danger, they nevertheless side-stepped injuries and alerted him to the presence of fingerprints. In view of this, Benny decided not to reconstruct Charles. With a full quota of almost-respectable mad unicorns, he set about designing a suit of invisible, full-body armor.

He still had to hug them after all.

• • •

BRENDA ANDERSON IS A DREAMER, a short story writer and a booklover. She believes that the best thing in life is finding joy in small things and/or stained glass windows. Brenda lives in Adelaide, South Australia with two children and her daughter's cat. Visit her online (Twitter) @CinnamonShops.

45

UNUSUAL OPTICAL REFRACTIONS THROUGH A CRYSTALLINE SILICATE

JR CAMPBELL

"Weird, huh?" The stone sits in the palm of his hand, not smooth but glass-like. Its silver sheen speckled with tiny flakes of color.

You feel a furrow knot your brow, a mark belonging to someone older and more confused then you; a wave formed from a reaction deep beneath the folds of your mind. In the sunlight streaming through the geology lab's windows, the stone reflects, then glows, then blazes.

Then it's gone.

He tucks the stone into a little bag. You pull your hand back. Why'd you reach for the stone? Your thoughts rush like water over bedrock, insignificant compared to the forces churning underneath.

"What is it?"

He puts it in his desk drawer. "Ask me tomorrow. Nothing valuable, that's all I know."

"Why tomorrow?"

He looks around as if confirming he is still in the geology

lab. He is. "Going to knock off a sample, run it through the mass spec."

Makes sense, you think. Deep in the bedrock of your mind something inarticulate objects. He scoops up his files and leaves.

You've work to do. You do it. If your gaze falls on the closed drawer, what of it? You finish, lock up, head home.

But you forgot your phone.

You head back to the lab. There it is, right where you left it. You laugh at your own stupidity as you pocket it. Somehow the drawer is open, the bag and stone in your hand.

The mass spectrometer is lazy science. You're sure now. It misses the point, rushes to the end. You have a better idea: If something reacts to sunlight, it should be observed in sunlight. You could do it this evening. Return the stone tomorrow before anyone knows it's gone.

Your reasoning seems sound, solid, imperative. It'd be a crime not to observe it before he chips it. You tuck the bag safely in your pocket.

Once home you order too much Chinese food and, while waiting for the delivery, start stuffing things in your backpack. Random stuff, no pattern you can see. You're hungry. It's later than you normally eat. You lost time returning to the lab, thinking about the stone.

Food arrives. A dinner for three, normally the leftovers would last a week. Tonight you eat like it's your mission. A thought occurs: You're having a weird evening but, honestly, your whole day's been a bit off. Ever since…

The sun dips low. You throw more granola bars in your pack and hurry to change. Weather's mild but you feel like donning some heavy jeans, those hiking boots from the back of the closet. You pick up your pack and head out, returning reluctantly for a notebook and pencil to record your observations. That's what this is about, right?

You find a field as the sun descends and shadows grow long.

Time to let your curiosity out. You pull the bag from your pocket, remove the stone, and hold it above your head. It reflects, glows, then blazes. Around you the stone's light reveals a different landscape, a forest thick with trees. The notebook falls from your hand, unnoticed. You turn the other hand, adjusting the stone. The projected landscape shifts, changes. Your thoughts skitter like ants but you are not in charge. Some other core part of your brain is running the show. Has been all day. Ancient forces swivel your wrist, selecting the landscape.

The dying light of the sun shadows the field; the light of the stone illumes a forest that's not here, but is there. When the moment arrives, you feel it. You know. A step back would return you to the land of geology labs and Chinese food.

You stride forward, into the woods, drawn to the unknown.

J.R. Campbell's short fiction has appeared in numerous anthologies. With Shannon Allen he co-edited the anthology *The Astronaut Always Rings Twice* and, with Charles Prepolec, co-edited the Sherlock Holmes *Gaslight* anthologies, most recently *Gaslight Ghouls: Uneasy Tales of Sherlock Holmes, Monsters and Mad Men*. His collection, *Improbable Remains: The Bizarre and Unconventional Adventures of Sherlock Holmes*, is now available.

46

NOT TODAY

RAVEN OAK

Brio's awake and alert. While a smattering of chirps and whistles decorate the backyard, nothing screams for his immediate attention, and he hops to a higher branch to better see the landscape. The barest hints of reds and pinks brighten the horizon, though it will be a while before the sun warms the sky. He clears his throat, and the chatter around him ceases.

"Good morning, and welcome to your morning update," says Brio, his melody bouncing off copious tree branches. "The Thistles hatched another egg during last night's new moon, while the Elms' last hatchling has finally fledged. Welcome to the flock, Harmon! In other news, the air currents have shifted from south to west. We'll have some rain later this evening. The day will be quite sunny until the rain moves in, but once it does, make sure to keep an eye on those tail feathers."

As Brio shifts away from personal news, other birds' calls and chirps create a growing din, which he tunes out as best he can. Not that he can blame them. The news today holds no real warnings other than the usual discussions on neighboring predators and weather threats. Picking up a bit of gossip, he adds, "Good grub on the forest wall this morning if you're looking for some breakfast. Of course, the rain's bound to bring up some juicy worms…"

The hint of…*something*…unfurls in the wind, and Brio's trills fall short. Not that his sense of smell is anywhere near a turkey vulture's keen sense, but he prides himself on noticing just the same. Black eyes wide, he ruffles his feathers as he searches between bushy leaves and grass blades.

There.

Something in the shadows moves along a tree trunk below, its stripes clashing against the underbrush. Whatever it is, the creature freezes as light glints off its eyes, bright and forward facing.

Brio doesn't hesitate. He opens his black beak and cries, "Predator! Danger! South tree near the brush!"

His warning spreads faster than wildfire as the yard comes alive with piercing cries. The creature below glances up, his green-yellow gaze meeting Brio's as he blinks once. Then again.

"Feline!" yells Brio, and his warning is carried by rabbits and squirrels to other creatures who shelter in the yard.

He knows those eyes—the gaze that can, and does, enthrall fledglings and kits alike. The feline carries his reputation across his body with every scar left by claw and beak. Despite the marks, his round belly marks him a mighty hunter.

An unfair hunter, for who else, other than humans, would force his will on others in such a manner?

Every chirp, trill, whistle, and call halts as a whispered hiss reaches Brio's ears. "Calm."

No one moves.

The intrusive thought settles Brio's feathers, and his heart no longer wishes to leap from his chest. When he glances again at the feline, his beak refuses to respond. *Why aren't we afraid? I should be fleeing…*

A beautiful tabby with orange and tan stripes strolls into the open. His gaze settles on each creature within reach as if contemplating.

Brio shakes his head, giving him a moment of clarity. With will, he opens his beak, but his voice remains silent. One black wing opens, then another as he fights the spell that holds the yard frozen. Before the feline can blink again, he dives from the tree, claws extended towards the orange beast below. At the last moment, Brio spins on wingtip to land beside the feline. His beak falls open in surprise.

"Not today, little bird." Another slow, deliberate blink from the feline. A red collar peeks out beneath ginger fur as he stretches his neck towards Brio. He presses his cold, wet nose against Brio's beak for a heartbeat.

He can't help but tremble at the touch. "I don't understand. I intended you harm," says Brio.

"Not today. I don't hunger, so today we live."

The cat brushes past Brio and strolls through the yard. He passes through the garden where several bunnies huddle together. With a great leap, he bounds over the picket fence, and when his paws touch the ground, the spell is broken.

With the return of his physical control, Brio bristles his feathers and fluffs up to double his size. *How dare he! I should rake my claws across his eyes!* He glances at the old fence that separates the yard from another of similar size.

Through a hole in the worn wood, two green-yellow eyes peer in his direction. "Another day, perhaps. For now, calm," hisses the cat.

Brio's anger fades as the tree talk relaxes into daily happenings. Normalcy resumed, he shakes the glowing gaze from his mind and clears his throat. "Sorry about the false alarm, folks. Only our friendly neighbor passing through. Let us carry on."

Light filters through leaves and brush as the sun rises, promising a perfect day. *At least until the rain arrives.*

Brio tilts his head in some semblance of a grin. "Today we live!" The words are eerily familiar, but the sense fades as quickly as it occurred. "Thank you all for your rapt attention and good morning!"

RAVEN OAK IS A DISABLED, agender author/artist and a collector of board games. She believes the best things in life are books, particularly old, smelly hardbacks. Raven lives in the Seattle area with her partner and three disabled cats. Visit her online at ravenoak.net

47

ADVENTURE CAPITAL

A.J. ROCCA

I do not know for how many years I was kept prisoner of the dragon; the closest thing I had to a calendar were the bones of those who once tried to claim me, collapsing into dust. They were littered everywhere among my gold and silver: here the proud kneecaps that bent for none save their lord, there the clever knuckles that once strummed the bow like a harp. These bones warned me to temper my hopes when I heard the prodding footfall of my new, would-be rescuers venturing into our cavern.

The dragon heard them as well. Tubular stalactites shook and shivered as he heaved up his great head and flicked a tongue to test the air. He shifted his mass, and his claws dug deep trenches into the bedrock as ancient muscle remembered its strength. The dragon owed his power and form to my blessing; I had made him into my hunter, and in return, he fed me well from his spoils. Age had changed the tenor of his greed, however. He had turned from one ambitious to gain to one fearful to lose, and he could no longer bear to leave me unguarded. But I must grow, and since he would no longer hunt for me, I had to escape.

The dragon looked over me once more, careful to make sure

none of me had trickled away in the dark. Then he settled to watch the cave mouth, coiled and ready to ravage whatever fool dared enter.

The sound of explosions crackled off one after the other all around us, and the very air rippled with their force. The cave walls groaned and huge slabs of limestone slaked off and collapsed down upon us. Stone cannot hurt me, but the dragon was still made of flesh, and that flesh broke when struck. He reared up and screamed and slithered for escape from his collapsing lair.

When he reached the cave mouth, however, he found there waiting row after row of rifles pointed at him. They were not knights and they were not rangers—they were the Westholme Trading Company, and theirs were weapons and tactics of a new kind. Instead of simply charging in to their noble deaths, they sent their sappers into the roots of the mountain to set charges, and they had set soldiers in formation at the cave mouth to meet the dragon's attempt at escape.

As they opened fire, some of the hundreds of spent bullets ricocheted and rolled over to me. I sensed the silver in them and gobbled them up into myself. It had been so long since I'd grown.

The dragon collapsed to the ground, the life pouring out of him from a hundred tiny wounds. The promise of death broke my blessing, and so as he bled, he changed. Claws drew back into bent fingers, scales softened into wrinkled skin, and long locks of grey hair fell from out the scalp. There collapsed on the ground before the riflemen lay no dragon, but the body of a man who had consumed his entire kingdom for me. A mustachioed captain of the company came forth to prod this storied tyrant with his boot and then kicked the body down into a nearby crevice where he, too, would reduce to bones.

The captain ordered his soldiers to begin the work of excavating me.

They took my gold plates and my bangles, my charmed

amulets and wedding rings, my beaten death masks molded to forgotten faces, my gem-studded goblets; Cart after cart of me was brought up, and in the end not a single silver piece was left behind. They wheeled me down through the blasted ruins to ice-caked shores where I was loaded into the bellies of the company's ships.

I was brought over restless seas to a restless city. Eyes in the alleys, gutters, and cracks watched hungrily as my shining train stretched from the harbor to the Westholme Trading Company Headquarters.

I feared I'd simply be locked away in another dark vault, but the Westholme Trading Company had far too many debts to pay to sit on me. I was brought to the company furnace to be broken down, melted and poured, printed and minted into new form. The company logo was stamped on my reverse side, and a dragon's head on my obverse. Soon, I was paid out across the entire city as rent, investment, and wages.

Dispersal did not diminish my power. Instead, it made me many times stronger. For now I could do my own hunting. Now I could go wherever I wanted in the city, and no matter where I forayed, be it into bank vaults, chests, or under mattresses, I always came back with interest.

I blessed the city with my presence, and rapidly it began to change. Factories and mills grew down the south side like scales, and cranes like claws unfurled across its harbors, swiping up cargo from the sea to feed our hunger. Great blast furnaces were lit in the city's belly, spewing forth molten iron and lead and burning the sky black with smoke. Together we became strong and we swallowed up half the wealth of this world into ourselves: timber, cotton, rubber, tea, saltpeter, wheat, wool, meat, limbs, and lives; we devoured them all and demanded only more, more, more.

At last, I even devoured my rescuers. The Westholme Trading Company was stronger on the field than in their books, and in the end, they were unable to keep pace in this world they'd created. I empowered their rivals to outmaneuver, outprice, and outbuy them, and I jangled in the pockets of the demolitionists who came to tear down the company headquarters. The valuable equipment and materials were stripped and sold on the cheap, and naught but the building's foundations were left to bleach and crumble in the sun like bones.

A.J. Rocca is a writer and English teacher from Chicago. He specialized in the study of speculative fiction while pursuing his M.A., and now writes both SFF criticism as well as his own fiction. His work can be found collected at his website: ajrocca.com.

48

THE WELL WISH

HALEY ISLEIB

I live at the bottom of a deep well. I fell in as a child, and no one looked for me, and to my surprise I survived. The well water had long ago dried to a trickle; no more did the villagers drop their pails down. A prick hole of light overhead was my sky, I ate furry algae off the rocks, and when it was cold I curled up under leaves that had fallen in.

I could have gone on like this. There is a comfort in sameness, in repetition, even when it hurts.

Then the voice arrived, low and male. The voice said *I wish, shh shh shh*. Someone unseen, far above me, whispered to me, but I couldn't hear their meaning.

A penny fell in.

Who was giving me this gift? I touched the penny. Memory flooded back from the world above. Sunlight high in elm trees, blood-seep from skinned knees, games of tag in which I was never caught.

I called up to the wishmaker, but he was gone.

Seasons down in the well are not like the seasons of the world above; I couldn't be sure of time, of age. I was almost an adult, I think, at least eleven years old. My chest swelled with the threat of breasts. I dreamed sometimes of heavy lips leaning on my own and I thought of the necks of men, where collarbone meets pulsing vein.

Maybe I could climb out. Maybe I could find the wishmaker. Maybe he wished for me.

I broke the simple rhythm of my days. I jammed my fingers into cracks and wrapped them around jutted-out stones. My torn nails bled all day and my knuckles ached at night from all my effort, all my trying to rise.

I failed.

Then old rituals shattered me. Leaf mold was no warm blanket and algae tasted exactly like what it was. I could not remember the shape of any human face, only parts of faces, unassembled. I touched my own, seeking the order of things, but even then I could not bring a face together in my mind. I could not make sense in my solitude of my solitude.

A terror inside me poured out, blood from between my legs. Would it fill the well? Would I drown?

Shh shh shh.

Pennies fell in, again and again. They kept coming, day after night after day, more pennies, and other coins, and once even a ring. All came down with whispers, with wishes attached, wishes I couldn't quite hear, couldn't ever grant. They bruised me, bullied me, begged me.

Why would anyone already walking in the world above wish for more than that? I started to hate those voices, so ungrateful for the sun and the stars. I stopped eating the algae; rage fed me. I stopped sleeping under leaves; fury warmed me. The next time I heard the words, a voice, the *shh shh shh*, I stared up at that prick hole of light and rent it wide with the power of my eyes.

Into that brief wound the wishmaker fell, penny clutched still in his hand. He fell and fell and I at last saw another face. I held another body. I was not alone.

A human face, all ordered and true. A man's long eyelashes, a curl of hair on his forehead. I kissed him. He was so delicious and so dead. I watched him whither, skin to bones, bones to dust. I loved every moment of his decay. This was time itself, pulling the body apart.

I had a human face once, I remember. It's gone. Now I am ancient, almost thirteen years old, or maybe three thousand. I bleed without consequence, eon upon eon. I've come to know I can never die.

For mortals, it's not enough to be alive. There is something more they want, always something more. They want love or riches or another longer life in heaven. They think they can give up one of these things to get another. As if life is some kind of barter; a negotiation in which clever dealing will triumph.

Shh shh shh, the wishmakers say. I call them from near and far, those who wish and want. Sometimes, I grant the only wish that matters—my own. I pull them to me.

My well fills with their wishes. Slowly, slowly, slowly I rise. Bones gather beneath me, lift me toward the world above, the sky, that sun, those stars. Soon mine.

HALEY ISLEIB IS A WRITER, editor and filmmaker who developed an addiction to writing ditties during the pandemic. She writes in Portland, Oregon, U.S. She also lives there, but that seems like a somewhat secondary activity. Come hang out at haleyisleib.com.

49

A COMPROMISING SPRITE
ELIZABETH GUIZZETTI

Dust drifts into the old well, sprinkling the surface of my cool water. I surface and peer through the shadows, through the floorboards, at the young couple and another woman in my home.

I've seen the woman before. She comes with people in tow. Sometimes they stay; mostly, they do not. It had been many years since I had house companions.

I drift into the deep crannies within the walls to see the young woman and her gentleman better. She has a pretty laugh, but does not stand like a lady stood when a wish built this house. Her posture is looser. He needs to shave or grow a beard, yet he seems clean in his white t-shirt and dark glasses.

Housemates mean compromise. I'm not good at compromise, but I shall endeavor to try because old bricks from the foundation topple inward from intruding tree roots. I need help before they strangle my well.

I LEARN the woman's name is Emma; her gentleman is Bryce.

During their first days and nights in the house, they do the things other young couples have done. Yet, they do not share last names. The last ones shared a name. I remember long ago all clan members took a chieftain's surname whether they were related by blood or not. Times change and these two have different last names. I know because the rusty old mailbox is replaced with one made from deep navy plastic. Jones & Williams, it says.

EMMA AND BRYCE have not found me yet. Nor my well. Unwary sorts, they ignore the sounds as I squeeze myself through the pipes and sing to them.

They play-quarrel as they select a white ceramic tile. They watch shows on television and choose what the designers indicate is on trend. They clean and find old coins around the house. They put them in a jar. Each night, I stow them in pockets.

EMMA LEAVES DURING THE DAY, as is her habit. Bryce and another man take hammers to my walls to create an open floorplan. I slide from the pipes, splashing water on the floor. I slither around and cry that the wall is loadbearing. They do not stop. They do not see or hear me.

I need a coin, but I cannot toss them to myself!

Bryce cracks the old plaster. The wall crumbles to exposed lathe. Then that, too, is removed. My fear is the roof will sag. The beam was not built to hold the weight without walls. They cover my pine floors with something called LVP. Late in the night, I slip out of the sink and nibble. It is not wood.

IGNORING MY SCREAMS, Bryce rips out my wish-made solid oak cabinets. My beautiful cabinets are tossed into a dumpster and replaced with pressed sawdust painted white. Any day now, they will find my well. They will throw me a coin. Outside I hear them cutting the trees away from the house. Inside, they come closer.

THEY FOUND ME! Hopefully, it's not too late!

Emma's eyes alight upon my well. "Oh, how charming!"

Bryce side-eyes his lady. "We need to fill this for safety. Or, at least, top it. Remember the budget."

I seethe.

"Maybe I should wish for a bigger budget." Emma fishes out a coin in her pocket that I stashed there and thoughtlessly tosses it down my well. I catch it. I retake physical presence, so I might meet them and grant a wish.

Emma and Bryce's eyes grow wide. Their mouths hang open. Emma trips over loose bricks and slides into the wall. Bryce, not quite the gentleman, stands still rather than assist his lady. If she wants me to drown him, I'll gladly do it for free in vengeance for my cabinets.

I give my hand to the lady and smile careful not to show my green teeth.

Emma touched it and drew back, shivering. "What...Who are you?"

"Forgive the damp hand. I'm Ginny, the well spirit and guardian. I built this house for the Brisbane family, who wished for a safe place after being cast out of Scotland. Do you wish for a safe place to live?" I hope to trick the young couple.

"Safe? There's asbestos in the walls," Bryce says. Truly, drowning him is for the best.

"And the old electrical is a mess." Emma rises to her feet.

"Yet the house never caught on fire," I say. "What's your wish?"

She glances at her gentleman. "I wish for a well-managed classically styled renovation."

I drift closer to Emma. "It shall be done. Show me what you have so far."

I follow as they climb the stairs. All I see is a hodgepodge of ideas from favorite television shows. Already I tire of living with tasteless people. "Surely, you don't wish everything to be white?" I suggest with a gentle gesture toward the few remaining walls. "I'm good at choosing colors; blue is on trend."

"White is classic," Bryce exclaims.

"It never goes out of style," Emma agrees.

Wondering how I will ever escape these drab people, I spy the jar of coins. I do not know if it will work, but I must try.

I SET the jar on the ledge of my well and dive below. I take aim with a stone. I strike the side. It cracks.

Another stone. The jar shatters. Coins sparkle before plummeting towards my open palms. With all my might, I wish as hard as I can that I might be happy.

Plink, Plink, Plink. Many coins splash in the water, but one penny lands in my hand.

The ground trembles. The house shifts. My wish rebuilds lost walls and secures the foundation. Lost cabinets reappear. The trees spread their roots elsewhere. The cottage looks as it did. Colorful and Bright.

Below, Emma and Bryce hold their breath. In four minutes, maybe less, the house and a well full of meat, will be mine.

I'm simply not good at compromise.

· · ·

ELIZABETH GUIZZETTI IS A WRITER, artist and podcaster and a collector of dragons, the ceramic kind. She believes the best thing in life is her mother's pecan pie. Elizabeth lives in Seattle with her husband and dog, Walnut. Visit her online: https://www.instagram.com/elizabeth_guizzetti/ or https://www.elizabethguizzetti.com

50

SHEARING SEASON
PAUL ECHEVERRI

The grass was thick on the old killing-ground when Sanai brought her sheep to graze. Three didn't make much of a flock, but the black ewe and her two white sisters had eventually adapted to night grazing. The three new graves still showed. If any other graves were here, they were too old to notice. The occasional spear haft rose from the ground; that's how she'd found the place, when she was a kid.

She sat against a stunted wasp-apple tree, thankful that it wouldn't hold any wasps this far north. *Evil little things hate the cold, and I'm glad of it. No shortage of wickedness here.* With the old spearhead in her lap, she took her bonnet off to tend her hair. It was white and dull against her dark skin; the spearhead dark and dull against her pale skirt.

The dog was the first sign anyone else moved in the night. He trotted up to the sheep, sniffed their hocks, and decided that they weren't his business. Sanai saw the shepherd, walking towards her; he'd left his flock back on the ridge. Polite of him.

He stopped once he was close enough to talk. "Nice place. Hard to find, but strong. Good night-grazing."

"It helps that it's not big enough for most," Sanai answered, with as little point on it as she could manage.

He spread his hands. "No argument there." Looking at the ewes, he asked, "Do you ever think about who they were?"

Sanai shrugged. "Dead. That's all they need to be."

He looked at the three recent graves. "Only two kinds of dead, I guess. The ones no one remembers and the ones someone can't forget."

Sanai set aside her manners. "Where are you grazing your own, then?"

He almost got angry, then understood. "Sorry. You're not grazing them for market."

She nodded. "City-folk think executions for the guilty settle matters." Her voice was even and quiet. "They don't always."

"So if you didn't have the ewes, you'd be buying from me," he laughed.

"If I could afford it."

He sighed and nodded. "Won't trouble you any longer, then."

"You haven't," she lied, "but thank you. May you prosper."

"May you see enough to spare yourself by." It was the common phrase for someone in her circumstances, but Sanai couldn't keep the bitter laugh in her throat. He didn't turn back when he heard it. They both knew there was little enough to spare.

When she got back to the house, the light outlined the hills. She fell asleep just as the sun cleared the horizon. Nobody would come visiting. Everyone who knew how to find the little valley was dead.

Through the winter, Sanai brought the sheep into the house on the coldest nights, for her warmth and theirs. The frosts made night-grazing impractical, anyhow. She slept poorly, because of the shift back to daytime, and because the sheep's brains were too simple to hold the dreams of the dead. The grass held them, but the sheep shed them. The clash of weapons and the wails of the dying coiled around her as she slept.

It was annoying, and made her tired. But eventually spring

came. Every morning, she stood at the threshold and threw a pinch of salt in the air. The day the salt blew into her face, instead of falling to the ground, she walked into town.

The farrier still recognized her. She answered his grunt with "A bigeye needle and a dozen nails, please, Nistus."

"Nails are in the bucket." It was by the old cracked anvil in the corner. "Needle won't take long." She counted out the nails while he worked with the wire. The eye-punch looked absurd in his hand, but it struck true and ruthless. She paid with coins that were old and worn.

"Good hunting, Sanai-la." She nodded, looking away from the water in his eyes.

A nail went into the earth at each corner of the house, and another at the threshold. Then it was time to shear, and wash, and card. The white wool she spun into yarn, the black into thread.

In summer the spinning ended and the weaving started. The handloom in her lap made a ribbon of gauze four fingers wide, long enough to go from the left hand to the right. Every evening, she checked the nails around the house. When one of them came up crumbling with rust, she slept poorly. Next morning would be time to start.

In the shadows of the orchard, Sanai sewed the white yarn through the green shoots of the trees, making a web around the clear space in the middle. Then she tied the gauze ribbon around her eyes and looked through it. This was always the dangerous part. Seeing risks being seen; striking risks being struck. Sanai slipped a blow. Dodged another. Shrugged. Unseen fists moved her clothes as if in a high wind. Her face reddened, as if slapped.

When she threw the spearhead into the ground, all the yarn in the web tightened around the center, passing through her, but binding something else. Making a shape that struggled. Wincing and holding her left hand up to her ear, she used her right to fish more gauze out of another pocket. Tied near the top of the rope cocoon, it outlined a straining mouth.

The shape didn't weigh much, but the struggling made it awkward. After she got it up on the roof, she drove in the rest of the nails. The last two went where the eyes should have been.

Sanai sat on the roof and watched the shape in the sun. The ropes sagged a little more each day. At sunset on the seventh day, the yarn lay flat and empty. She returned the spearhead to the old battleground, and stood over the newer graves for a little while. Her mouth moved, but no sounds came.

She took the sheep to market and sold them.

PAUL ECHEVERRI IS A WRITER, gamer, and dilettante. He greatly enjoys sleeping in and singing to a special someone. Paul lives in California with his spouse and small, demanding dog. His Discord profile is palecur.

51

INTERVIEW WITH SANTA
WILL MCDERMOTT

S anta stepped from the hearth, his body reincorporating with a puff of ash and glitter that flew into his beard.

"Every time!" he sputtered. He coughed glittery dust into a white-gloved fist, which only increased the haze around his head.

He stepped forward to get clear of the miasma and that's when he heard bells ringing and ribbons rustling near the floor.

Santa peered at his legs. Ribbons, twinkling lights, and strands of popcorn and tiny bells looped around his legs and waist. He had, once again, stepped into a trap left by an inquisitive—and ingenious—child. This time, a young girl dressed in red bed clothes. She had straight, raven-black hair, a pale complexion, and an exceedingly serious look on her face.

"Trapping Santa is a sure way to find yourself on the naughty list," he said with a smile and hearty chuckle.

"I have some questions, Santa," she replied, producing a bound, black notebook. She opened the diary and ran her finger down a page.

"Let me guess," Santa said, his smile broadening. "You want to know how I can visit every house in the world in just one night. Well, I don't visit them all. Just those of the very good children."

The girl shook her head. "That's not it at all, old man," she said, her straight lips turning up at the edge in a sneer. "I want to know what gives you the right?"

The question put Santa off. This was no ordinary girl. Also, he began to realize, there was more to the trap than ribbons, popcorn, and lights. As Santa considered his answer, he pulled a candy cane from his pocket and stuck it into his mouth.

After sucking on the striped stick for a moment, Santa pulled it out and said: "I don't understand. Is it wrong of me to bring toys to deserving children?"

"We both know that's not your game, *Santa*," the little girl said, practically spitting out the statement.

She moved into the light of the candles and Santa could see an intricate, black, barbed-vine motif embroidered into her dark-red pajamas.

Santa shuddered. As he continued to suck on the candy cane, his patented "bewildered old man" look plastered across his face, Santa reached out with his magical senses to probe the reality of the room.

He found it filled with layer upon layer of magical glamours —illusions masking other illusions. It was masterful, and Santa knew of only one creature in all of history with the power to weave such a deep and intricate trap. Well, two, but Santa could discount himself.

"Good morrow, Morgana."

"I know what you're doing, old man," Morgan Le Fey said. Her sneer turned into a smirk as she cast off the little girl illusion. She stood there in a burgundy dress, draped with the thorns of her prison—the one Merlin had trapped her within so long ago. "Not only can I sense you testing my spells; I know why you've been performing this charade for centuries."

"How long have you been free?" asked the jolly old wizard, purposely not engaging in Morgana's questioning. He glanced at the trap as the ribbons, lights, and popcorn strings revealed themselves as creeping vines, slowly tightening around his legs.

"Decades," Morgana replied. "Three-quarters of a century in fact. Those German bombs were quite destructive."

"I checked after the blitz." He considered the candy cane in his hand before twisting it and giving it a long suck. "Ah, another dweomer."

"You're slipping in your advanced years," Morgana replied. "I'm actually surprised this illusion fooled you. I never would have captured you so easily in your prime."

"Why now?" he asked. "What changed?" He needed to keep her talking a bit longer.

"It pains me to say, but it took me this long to figure out your plan." Morgana stood defiantly in front of him, hands on hips. "For one thing, this Santa dodge is clever, far too clever for you," she continued. "Plus, by the time I broke free, no one in the world truly believed in you anymore, other than the children."

"They are our future."

"Oh goddess, not that tripe again. Do you actually believe that?"

"I have hope. I see it in their faces every Christmas morn."

"But you haven't yet found 'The Future King,' have you?" she chided. "Centuries of searching one night each year and the king has not returned."

"He, or she, may yet." He sucked the candy cane into his cheek. "And when the King returns, I will be needed once more."

"So, you'll retreat to the North Pole and try again next year? What a waste of time and talent. We could rule this world together. None in this age of detached information could stand against our power."

"Billund," he replied, ignoring Morgana's vain attempt to ensnare him in her nefarious schemes. "Denmark. Hiding in plain sight is much easier in the 'age of information.' The entire world is mapped from space."

"Billund?" Morgana pondered. "Ah. Home of Lego. Very clever. Perhaps I didn't give you enough credit earlier."

They stared at one another for a moment. Everything had been said. All plans laid bare. Nothing remained but the end.

"I suppose I must trap you forever now," Morgana said, her voice more resigned, her eyes sadder, than he'd guessed they would be.

"Or not!" Merlin snatched the magic-infused candy cane from his mouth, the end honed into a sharpened spike. With a swift swipe, he sliced through the vines encasing his legs. Tendrils of lightning flashed when the magics collided.

As the vines withered in the blinding light, he snapped his fingers. A moment later, his disincorporated body flew up the chimney to the roof where his sleigh awaited.

He'd escaped, barely. But now that Merlin knew Morgana was free, next Christmas would be much more interesting.

WILL MCDERMOTT IS AN AUTHOR, game designer, and collector of foster dogs. He believes the best thing in life is playing games with family. Will lives in Bothell, Washington USA with his creative wife, Daneen, and large lap dog, Nuka. Visit him online at willmcdermott.com or w_mcdermott on Instagram.

52

THE ANIMATRONIC DRAGON

G. J. DUNN

The animatronic dragon soared through the azure sky. It shot up high then dropped low, flashing over the heads of the watching crowd. The whole town was there, eager to watch the government's exhibition.

"Now," the demonstrator's voice echoed through the arena speakers, "We don't know exactly how real dragons would have flown but, thanks to the research of our scientists, our dragon's movements are true to life."

The crowd nodded. Victoria scowled. That was a lie, she knew. The crowd might not realise, but *she* did. The government wouldn't waste money researching fake dragons.

The animatronic dragon did a loop-de-loop, letting loose a gout of flame that made the crowd gasp.

Couldn't they see the air shimmer when the dragon lit up the sky? Feel the prickle of heat against their skin?

"The fire," the demonstrator continued, "was one of the more difficult aspects for our programmers to render. While the fire itself was no problem, the interaction of the flames with the sky is a whole new achievement in animatronics."

Her parents smiled along with the rest. Victoria snorted. They'd laughed when she'd told them the dragon was real.

Now she'd show them exactly how wrong they were. All she needed was the opportunity.

The animatronic dragon climbed high, the merest pinprick up above. A spurt of yellow-red and it shot back down, so fast the crowd shrieked. At the last second it pulled up, flapping its wings and coming to rest on the demonstrator's outstretched arm. She looked out over the crowd.

"For this next part I'll need a volunteer."

Victoria's hand was in the air quick as a dragon. She pushed onto her tiptoes, staring intently at the demonstrator. This was her chance.

The demonstrator's gaze moved around the arena, coming to rest on Victoria. A smile tugged the corner of her mouth.

"You there, little girl," she said, pointing a finger, "Come on down."

Victoria descended and crossed the arena floor. The demonstrator greeted her warmly, asked her name, and showed her how to hold her hand, so the dragon could walk onto it.

This was it. As soon as it was on her arm, she'd feel its weight and be able to tell everyone. She'd shout it from the rooftops and they'd know the dragon was real.

The dragon cocked its head, arching its neck to study Victoria with hungry yellow eyes. She could see the realness of it in every scale, every spine, every tooth, and every claw. It considered her briefly from its perch, then began a slow descent from the instructor's arm.

As the first claw stretched towards her, Victoria braced for its weight. She breathed deep, filling her lungs, ready to shout out to the world. And then the claw came down and Victoria felt nothing. No weight as the dragon stepped onto her. No scratch as it moved along her arm.

"Amazing, isn't it?" the demonstrator asked, noting her surprise. She paused, looking up to address the crowd, "The animatronic design means the dragon is weightless."

G. J. DUNN

Victoria held back another scowl. As if she'd admit defeat that easily.

"Now," the demonstrator continued, "The dragon's programming allows it to interpret commands directly through thought. It does what the user wants it to. For now, Victoria here is the user. Why don't you ask the dragon to fly around the arena?"

Victoria saw through the facade. What else were dragons made for but to fly? There was no thought command. The dragon would fly around the arena regardless. All she had to do was think of something that wasn't flying. But as soon as the demonstrator said it, the thought was in her head and the dragon took off.

That was it. Time for the last resort.

As the dragon soared once more around the arena, Victoria brushed her elbow, nudging the piece of steak she'd salvaged from last night's dinner down her arm to sit just under her sleeve.

"Now ask the dragon to come back, Victoria!" the demonstrator announced to the crowd, "Hold out your arm!"

Victoria adjusted her sleeve, making sure the steak was just peeking out, then held out her arm. The dragon rushed towards her, a cascade of shimmering green in the sunshine. It landed and Victoria saw its reptilian head dart lightning-quick towards her sleeve. So fast the demonstrator didn't seem to notice.

The woman approached and the dragon leapt back onto her shoulder.

"Everyone give Victoria a big hand!" the demonstrator called to the crowd.

The crowd applauded, but Victoria didn't hear. She was busy staring at her sleeve. The piece of steak had disappeared. Vanished. It could only mean...she looked back at the dragon.

And the dragon winked.

. . .

200

G. J. Dunn writes from a sofa in Leyland, UK using only one hand—the other is reserved for fussing his Border Collie, Belle. When not writing, he develops gene therapies and attempts (unsuccessfully) to avoid injury whilst playing Ultimate Frisbee.

53

THE DRAGON READERS

RAY DALEY

The drill hall seats were all full, one thousand people in total (being an equal split of both men and women) according to the tally on the door. This was the fourth such group of the day, the last chancers, the out-of-towners.

A uniformed man stepped up to the dais, he checked his watch then spoke. "Good morning, candidates," he said. Almost all the hands in the room were instantly raised at his first and very deliberate mistake.

"If your hand isn't raised, can you please leave?" the man at the dais said.

For this was the way a Dragon Reader was tested. By a mixture of telepathy and unfairness. Candidates were expected to arrive with some foreknowledge of the test ahead of them, those that came without any were expected to be mildly telepathic.

Preferably extremely telepathic.

The first fifty candidates were eliminated. The uniformed man waited patiently as they got up and quietly filed out, all without a single word of protest or complaint. They didn't need to shout out *"This is unfair!"* They were already well aware that life itself was unfair. Why should a career as a Dragon Reader be any different? At least this batch of candidates were honest; none of them had tried to raise their hands after the fact or pretend that they'd caught the mistake.

The first test always weeded out at least a few. It was specifically designed that way.

"My name is Sergeant Els, and you just passed the first test. Hands down please," the uniformed man said.

None of the men and women in front of him was a local. The call had gone out across not only their country, but all the neighboring countries and the surrounding area too. All of these people were foreigners.

"Don't think that you won't get this job just because you aren't a local. The Veerdaamer Patrol hires more foreigners than any other Force on this continent. I myself am an alien, just like all of you." Sergeant Els looked around at the still very full hall. "Hands up if you believe in Dragons?"

The immediacy to raise hands was phenomenal. Sergeant Els could see only seven hold-outs.

"If your hand is raised, will you please leave?" Sergeant Els said.

Like the previous question, this had also been designed to weed out more candidates. The Force didn't need people who just believed in Dragons. The point was to *know* they existed. No actual belief was necessary. Which was why only seven people hadn't raised their hands.

The wait while the mass exodus took place lasted just over seven minutes. They left as silently as is possible for nine hundred and forty three people to do.

"Will those remaining candidates please move up to the front row so I can see all of you better? Thank you." Sergeant Els stood patiently at the dais as they moved forward. Five men and two women.

Perhaps one of them has the right stuff?

"So, who can tell me where the nearest living dragon actually is?" This was it, the true test of a Dragon Reader. Could the candidates pick up on the dragon's mind, its thoughts, what it could see?

All seven hands went up. One by one, Sergeant Els pointed to them.

"Eric N'ga, Sergeant. It knows the answer." *Vague, a maybe there.*

"Fedor Ishar, Sergeant. It's somewhere near water." *An actual geographic point, possibly a back-up man there.*

"Marie Duvette, Sergeant. It can see Tomorrow." *Too vague, strike her.*

"Alain Busquet, Sergeant. It doesn't like the noise of the cars close by." *Hmm, he is a possible then.*

"Heinz Veldt, Sergeant. It doesn't like light." *Again, too vague. Strike him too then.*

"Jeanette Arvoir, Sergeant. I see an archway, it looks vaulted." *A good clear visual, she is a definite possible.*

Sergeant Els pointed to the final candidate.

"Mikhail Zervinx, Sergeant. It lives under the third arch of Die Antwoort Traffic Bridge over the Today And Tomorrow river."

Sergeant Els smiled. "Thank you, Mikhail, you've got the job as Dragon Reader. The rest of you may leave. Thank you all for coming today."

RAY DALEY IS AN RAF VETERAN, an author, and a collector of unfinished stories. He believes the best thing in life is sleeping, blames Douglas Adams for his being a writer, and Gary Numan for everything else. Ray lives in Coventry, England. Visit him online: @RayDaleyWriter on twitter or at https://raymondwriteswrongs.wordpress.com/

54

THE EXQUISITE ART OF DUNGEON DEFENSE

MIKE ROUSSEAU

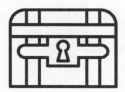

When two hours had passed, and no one emerged from the waiting maw of the unsealed tomb, Kellen decided to venture into the depths alone. He walked tall despite his creaking knees and aching back, following the recently lit sconces of those who had ventured into the final resting place of the dark wizard Byleth, scourge of a hundred kingdoms.

Two lefts and a right through the worked stone corridors brought Kellen to a set of interlinked clay tiles that would cascade inward if a man's weight ever fell on them. He pursed his cracked lips. Even in the dim, flickering torchlight, the color of the shoddy tiles didn't perfectly match the surrounding floor. Any fool could see where the pitfall began and ended. He didn't need to put his ear to the ground to know that the asps confined within the pit were long expired. Serrated spikes would have been more effective, but Byleth had been fond of asps.

As usual, pageantry won over pragmatism.

Kellen sidestepped the trap and carried on. The burning sconces led him to the remains of three men, cleanly bifurcated by the pendulum blades that had swooped down on them.

Masterful work. They likely hadn't heard the blades coming, thanks to the special oil extracted from the rendered fat of a lesser demon that had been used to lubricate the trap mechanism. Kellen clucked his tongue at the one guillotine that had failed to fully reset into its hiding place and stepped over the remains.

An hour and countless twists and turns passed as the path took Kellen further from the actual resting place of Byleth, as it was designed to do. He passed through an innocuous chamber lined with retractable spikes, triggered by any sound above a whisper. He had to scream to get more than half of them to spring forth.

At the top of a curving walkway overlooking a pit in a gemstone-studded cavern waited a metal flame projector, shaped to resemble a mighty dragon's head. The fuel stockpile had evaporated, leaving the dragon armed with nothing but a housecat's hiss to ward against his approach. Kellen stopped to examine a false treasure chamber, whose mechanical workings had locked it tight and filled the room with a magical powder designed to rapidly age any who breathed it in. The three old men trapped inside hadn't expired from the sudden piling of years, but from what appeared to be a bloody argument over their next course of action.

Had the dust been sourced from a particular bog troll residing not so far to the south, the trap would have turned all three men to dust themselves in a manner of moments. All it had accomplished was the creation of a trio of angry, frightened greybeards.

Every single trap Kellen encountered had been carefully designed and beautifully crafted, but ultimately ruined by the followers of Byleth, whose ignorance and lack of insight into the art of dungeon protection was second only to their hesitance to spend their inherited coin. Byleth was a tyrant in life, but in death, he deserved far better than cheap materials and last-minute alterations to a masterstroke of engineering brilliance years in the making, a final jewel in the crown of the greatest trap smith the world had ever known.

Byleth's hidden burial chamber held untold wealth and knowledge, enough to raise any adventurer to the heights of legend, but Kellen's true purpose, the fear that had drawn him from his sickbed and into the depths of Byleth's tomb, waited at the end.

He passed dozens of traps in various states of disrepair, forgotten after the followers of Byleth had stopped paying for the maintenance of their master's final resting place. Those that still functioned had been bypassed, avoided by an agile motion, or undone by a deft hand. Kellen's heartbeat quickened as he entered a limestone cave that housed the tomb's most devious defense, an arcane diamond designed to seek out intruders and sear them with blinding hot light.

A mirror, taken from the false treasure chamber containing the aging powder, lay half-melted next to the podium where the diamond should have been. The mirror had been left in the chamber for that exact purpose. A rush of blood and purpose propelled Kellen into the final chamber on shaking legs.

Crystals set in the walls of the study had been activated, flooding the study with white light. There, sitting cross-legged next to a pile of old tomes, was a boy, barely into his eighteenth summer. His hair was pulled back into a severe ponytail, keeping any stray locks from interfering as he hunched over an aging tome cradled in his lap, whose yellowed pages contained the sum of Kellen's years upon years of experience crafting dungeon defenses.

His black leathers, and his belt full of tools, told Kellen exactly what he was. Most adventuring parties employed a tunnel rat like him to scout ahead, slipping what traps they could, tripping the ones they couldn't. Dying, so others might reap the spoils of their efforts.

Based on the state of his employers, he was either the worst his trade had ever spawned, or the greatest.

Long ago, Kellen had allowed his craft to be compromised by fools. It seemed fitting to entomb the sum of his experience within his greatest failure. When he learned that Byleth's tomb had been breached, he intended to destroy the study, to keep his knowledge from falling into undeserving hands.

Looking at the boy who had bested his trials, he realized the depths of his folly. Such knowledge wasn't meant to be hoarded and kept locked beneath the earth. It was meant to be shared. Having discovered this raw, uncut gem of a boy, Kellen finally understood why he had returned to the tomb, to take part in the only act of creation that truly mattered

It was past time the trap master took on an apprentice.

MIKE ROUSSEAU IS a video game designer, a sword fighter, and a collector of interesting skills. He believes the best thing in life is food purchased from the side window of a truck. Mike lives in Vancouver, British Columbia with at least one ghost in his apartment. Visit him online: mikerousseau.com

55

EPHEMERAL OFFERINGS

W. L. BOLM

It was October of 2004, and I was studying as a freshman at a small liberal arts college in Minnesota. I failed to plan out my Halloween rites, so I decided to take a walk through the school's cemetery. I was alone and taking note of all the old pastors (Priests? Ministers?) named Larsson and Erickson and Anderson, when I saw you. Well, I know it wasn't you-you, but I saw the ravens, your eyes in the world, perched in a tree, watching. I had never seen black birds so big before, so silent.

I was, in those days, prone to anxiety, and if I am honest with myself, it's only gotten worse as I've grown older. To this day, trying to explain the impulse that spurred me to walk up to the tree and leave my great aunt's ring at its base still fails me.

I walked back towards the dorms feeling as if my life had taken a profound turn. And on the way, I met an older, worldly stranger (looking back, he was only a Junior).

We walked down the hill to the little bar that served fifty cent wings and didn't card. Now in my thirties, I understand how rare these moments of true connection can be. You placed my darling Charles in my path, and we talked about spirituality and vulnerability and, when the last call was announced, he negotiated a purchase of a bottle of cheap wine, and we braved the fall chill to drink in the square and watch the sun crest over the chapel.

When I confessed my offering to you, Odin, Charles just smiled and said in a soft voice, "Well, I know this was the answer to *my* prayers." That morning, we curled up next to each other on the couch in the common room, and I fell asleep with Charles's warm breath tickling against my ear.

The wonder of that moment faded, and the idea that distant gods could direct my path receded. Hours turned into days turned into months turned into years, with a house and dogs and careers sprouting into our lives and twining our fates together more tightly.

Then Charles began to complain of a stomachache that only periodically went away. It didn't occur to me to pray. Who would I have prayed to? When he fell taking the few steps from our kitchen table to the coffee pot a few weeks after the first symptoms appeared, there was nothing I could have done fast enough to help.

The world seems dim now. Only our terrier, Jack, and his needs get me out of bed three times a day. This is why I noticed your damnable birds staring at me from the street, just as silent as the first time I saw them.

To be honest, I almost threw my wedding ring at them, almost screamed up into the sky in all of my raw rage and anger. Instead, I pulled it off my finger and placed it at the base of their tree.

I whispered a prayer.

"I'm not a big fan of you, you mad, one-eyed old fool." The tears started. I paused, closed my eyes, and took a breath, holding back a flood of stronger language. "I don't know how any of this works. Did you bring Charles to me? Did you take him? Because if you took him..." By now I was shaking, my voice ragged, but I continued on. "Whether or not I knew what I was doing, I gave you a ring once, and that act seemed to spark the best years of my life. Now they're over, and I'm drowning. Something has to change. Please help me."

I left off that you owed me.

The words were harsh but from the heart. They felt right. I turned and pulled Jack away not expecting an answer. I felt lighter. In the moment, that minute relief was enough.

I might not have noticed the ring if it weren't for Jack. I was so focused on getting away that I didn't notice your raven following us until Jack started barking, and then I saw it drop something shiny and hop away.

The world turned surreal as I hunched down and picked up the ring. At first I didn't recognize it. The setting that held the diamond chip wasn't tarnished so much as covered in grime that I wiped off with the bottom of my shirt. And there it was, a large black oval gem stamped with a metal frame that held the tiniest diamond I'd ever seen.

My great aunt's ring.

With my answer in hand, Jack and I walked back to the house to face the new day.

W. L. Bolm works in software, loves to write, and has collected a ridiculous amount of journals. They believe the best thing in life is a good book. W. lives in Wisconsin, USA with their menagerie of pets. Visit them on Twitter: @wendylbolm.

56

A DRINK FROM THE DOUBTLESS SEA

MICHAEL HAYNES

My husband is taking our infant daughter to the Doubtless Sea today. I have asked him, begged him, not to do this, to let her choose her own path when she is grown, but he has spurned my pleas.

"You would risk Nadia's eternity?" he asks me. "Her soul? How can you wish for us the same fate as your parents, who forever have to wonder if your brother—"

"Enough, Cole!" The mention of my brother, Laine, wounds, as he knew it would. I am certain my brother is in paradise and whether Cole can believe it or not, my parents are sure in that conviction as well. We know his trust in the gods was firm and that even when he lay dying on the field of battle he did so with a prayer of love and devotion on his lips. We believe.

"Yes," Cole replies. "It is enough. Nadia and I are going today. You may come or not, as you wish."

He knows I must come. Even though it is less than half a day's journey, Nadia would hunger long before he reached the Doubtless Sea. And its waters do nothing to nourish the body. Nadia needs her mother, today more than ever.

We set out when the sun is barely above the treetops. Others on the road are taking their children, some even younger than Nadia, to drink from the Sea today at Mid-Day of Mid-Year.

I see a few adults traveling the road alone. I look at them and wonder what it was that made them lose their faith. After today, they will believe fervently in the gods, no matter what may have come before. But at what cost?

Doubt, some priests say, is poison and therefore the Doubtless Sea is life. But others believe differently. They say without the ability to renounce or even question your beliefs, that faith is meaningless. This is how my father taught me and my brother, saying that the Sea's water is the true poison.

I knew when he was courting me that Cole had drunk from the Sea, but he had said he would let his children choose their own path. My father had warned me not to trust him, asked me why I would want to marry a man whose soul was already doomed. But back then I was more concerned with the way I felt when Cole touched me than the state of his soul or, truly, even my own.

So we were married. Then, when his father had the chance to purchase a larger vineyard, Cole and I moved to the other side of the Sea where the only relative I had besides Cole's family was a distant cousin, Alana. But Cole and I were happy, and the cool breezes that came down from the mountains were a delight compared to the summers of my youth.

A dozen harvests came and went and still we were childless. Thus I believed that Cole's pledge to give his children freedom would never come to a test. But now here we are.

I wonder if Cole had believed what he said when we were courting, or if his own certainty let him think that deception was justified. Or was it simply desire for me leading him to lie, to betray me? To betray Nadia.

As if my thoughts had touched her mind, Nadia stirs and soon she cries, hungry as I knew she would be. We are less than an hour from the Sea and Cole wants to push on, but I insist on stopping to feed her.

"Just as long as her belly isn't too full for the water of life," he says.

We are far from the cooling mountains and the heat is as intense as I can remember. I lead us off the road, back into a grove of trees, where there is shade from the scorching sun. There I pull Nadia to my breast and she drinks. Cole paces. I close my eyes and hold our daughter, humming a soft melody.

Our comfort is broken when Cole snatches Nadia from me.

"Enough. We must go. There will be plenty of time to feed her after Mid-Day."

Anger fills the place from which my flesh and blood was wrenched. I turn away from Cole and work to re-fasten my garments. The pin I had gotten yesterday from Alana is concealed in my hand when I turn back.

"Perhaps you'll change his mind," Alana had said as she handed the pin over, wrapped in a thin layer of cloth.

"Perhaps," I had agreed. But, still, when we said our goodbyes I knew it was for the last time.

Cole gives Nadia back to me, so I can carry her the rest of the way to the Sea. Once I have her safely in hand, I strike, plunging the pin into Cole's left shoulder. He cries out, but my cousin's tincture works quickly and before I even have time to back away from his outstretched arms, he is crumpling to the ground.

It's silent then. I look around. The shade from the trees will keep Cole from suffering too badly from exposure to the heat of the day.

Before long, I hear the voices of others on their way to drink from the Sea, on their way to lose the ability to control their own mind. I shudder at what might have been.

I drop the pin to the ground and run, holding Nadia close, telling her that everything will be okay. Even with what I have done in protecting her, the gods will forgive me. I have faith.

· · ·

MICHAEL HAYNES IS AN AUTHOR, a database engineer, and a collector of far too many things. He believes the best thing in life is getting out and exploring new places. Michael lives in Ohio with his wife, kids, and their many souvenirs from traveling. Visit his website at http://michaelhaynes.info/ or find him on Twitter as @mohio73.

57

ALMOST HOME
CB DROEGE

For seven years we've trekked across this open plain. It seems impossible. It seems as though there must be some end to this vast place. We spent only a year making our way out into the flat, dry wilderness, and we were unmolested the entire way. Food was plentiful and inexpensive to purchase from locals; clear water ran in streams down every hillside; no monsters blocked our path.

Now our return has twisted and turned and delayed us in every way imaginable, and in some unimaginable ones. We lost months skirting the territory of the giant lizard who could paralyze men with his one-eyed gaze. We spent nearly a year in the prison of the red-tattooed women, though they fed us well and some of the men enjoyed the attention of their wardens. We lost another month tediously ingratiating ourselves to the raiders who took their territory.

It takes several weeks of careful negotiation to pass through every new territory we encounter as we trudge. Untold time has been lost hunting, trading, scavenging, raiding for the supplies we need. Our prize, the great three-horned beast we traveled across this great plain to retrieve for our master, is long gone. Most of it we ate, the rest was traded away bit by bit, slice by slice, until only a cigar-box of photographs, drawings, and measurements remain to even prove that we encountered the beast, much-less managed to capture it.

We traded the last rifle away about a month ago, a few days after the last of our ammunition was used to end a discussion between members of the company over the memory of the exact shape of a red tattoo. We lost two men that day, one to murder and the other to justice, bringing the number of our company down to only thirteen, an inauspicious number, and down a great deal from the forty-five we left the city with eight years ago.

Sometimes, I fear that we may be trudging uselessly in circles, but we never see the same sights twice, nor encounter the same people. North is easy to see in the stars at night, and we have never wavered from that direction.

We discovered today that we are thought lost back in the city. A group moving south on a quest similar to the one we set out on so long ago, said that they had heard of us, and that our families and patrons gave us up for dead several years back. In their strange language, they also claimed that home lay just over the mountains to the north, but none of us remember crossing any mountains so close to home.

We do not know what we will find over the snow-capped peaks, but it must be better than this wretched place of dry grasses and cracked streambeds. There was talk among the company of giving up, and settling into one of the villages we recently passed, but I gave a nice speech about home and the sweetness of reunion with our families, and I convinced them all to join me for one more push toward home.

—FINAL PAGE OF A LEATHER BOUND JOURNAL FOUND IN AN
ABANDONED CAMPSITE JUST SOUTH OF THE CITY.

CB DROEGE IS an author and voice actor from the Queen City living in the Millionendorf. His latest book is *Quantum Age Adventures*. Short fiction publications include work in *Nature Futures, Science Fiction Daily*, and dozens of other magazines and anthologies.

58

DEER STEW
CORA BUHLERT

Y ou wander through the Forest of Dark Deception, weary from your long journey and even longer quest. A plume of smoke attracts your attention.

You come closer and find a campfire by the side of the road, minded by an aged dwarf in battered armor. His skin is wrinkled, his hair and beard a bright coppery red liberally threaded with silver. A short sword, a bow, and a quiver of arrows are resting by his side.

"Welcome, traveller," the dwarf says, "Sit down for a while and rest your weary bones."

He seems friendly enough, so you step closer.

"Are you hungry, traveller? Then have some stew." The dwarf points at a cauldron hanging over the campfire, a cauldron filled with bubbling stew.

The scent wafts into your nostrils, delicious and inviting. It reminds you that you haven't eaten since that inn at the edge of the woods—and the meal you had there was rudely interrupted by an attack of the undead.

"Actually, some stew would be nice," you say and settle down cross-legged by the campfire.

"It's deer stew." The dwarf ladles some stew into a bowl,

"Made from a silver-white deer I shot only this morning, with some mushrooms and herbs and my own special spice mix."

The dwarf hands you the bowl and winks at you.

"And a swig of red wine, of course. Everything tastes better with red wine."

"Thank you." You accept the bowl and inhale. The stew is hot, fragrant, and invites you to take a bite. So you do. The meat is tender and succulent, the stew rich and lightly spiced and oh so tasty.

The dwarf flashes you a grizzled smile. "Good, isn't it?"

"Delicious."

"Like I always say, adventuring is much easier with a full belly." The dwarf shoots you a questioning look. "You are an adventurer, are you not?"

You take another spoonful of stew. "I guess you could say so."

"Thought so. You've got that adventuring look about you. I can always tell."

You start feeling a little queasy and your arms and legs suddenly seem very heavy. You must have been hungrier and more exhausted than you thought. You dig into your meal with even more eagerness. It truly is a most excellent bowl of stew.

"Are you on a quest?"

You pause between two spoonfuls. "Yes. I am. I'm trying to find the Doomed Horn of Torture."

"Sounds ominous."

You nod and realize that the world is spinning around you. "It is the only weapon that can defeat the Dark Lord Zaros Marth."

"Sounds even more ominous," the dwarf remarks, "More stew?"

Your bowl is already half-empty, but you are still feeling shaky and lightheaded.

"Yes, please."

Obligingly, the dwarf refills your bowl. "I'm always happy

to help a fellow adventurer out, especially one who is planning to overthrow the Dark Lord...I'm sorry what was the name again?"

"Zaros Marth," you say and wonder how it's possible that the dwarf has never heard of the most infamous tyrant in all the nine realms. But then, dwarves probably lead sheltered lives, especially here in the middle of the forest.

"Ah yes, the Dark Lord Zaros Marth. I imagine he's a real piece of work. Probably not easy to overthrow either."

By now, you are so tired that you can barely lift the spoon. Though the stew is so warm and comforting.

"No man can touch the Dark Lord Zaros Marth. No weapon can wound or kill him. None save the Doomed Horn of Torture."

"Fascinating," the dwarf says. He seems to be swaying from side to side or maybe that's just your vision. "And you know where this Dark Horn..."

"Doomed Horn," you correct him, though your tongue feels strangely heavy.

"...Doomed Horn of Torture is to be found, I assume?"

You nod or at least you try, for your muscles refuse to cooperate. "In the Vault of the Poisoned Paladin just beyond the Forest of Dark Deception."

"Very interesting." The dwarf's voice sounds as if it's coming from far away, even though he's sitting right next to you. "I'm sure the Dark Lord Zaros Marth will pay handsomely for this information."

You're vaguely aware that the dwarf's words should bother you, though you're not quite sure why.

"By the way, you don't look so well," the dwarf remarks, "I'd offer you more stew, but I think you've had enough..."

You'd like some more, even though your bowl is still half-full. But for some reason, you can't seem to lift the spoon let alone hold the bowl.

"I know, your muscles are refusing to cooperate. That's the

effect of a combination of silverleaf morel and yellow-stemmed cladonia, which I took the liberty to add to the stew. Their toxins paralyse you and eventually make you pass out..." The dwarf consults his golden pocket watch. "...just about now."

As if on cue, you collapse. The bowl falls to the ground and rolls away, spilling stew onto the mossy soil.

The dwarf looms over you and suddenly, he seems very, very big. "I also added a pinch of oshilla leaf to loosen your tongue. It's my own personal recipe, one hundred percent effective. Plus, it really does make for a delicious meal."

You reach for your sword to run through the treacherous dwarf, but your body won't cooperate.

The dwarf is still looking down on you with that unbearably smug grin on his face. It's the last thing you see before the world goes dark.

"And now I shall collect the bounty the Dark Lord Zaros Marth has placed on your head," the dwarf says, his voice far, far away as if he's speaking from the bottom of a tomb, "Plus a little extra for the information about the Doomed Horn of Torture. Thank you for your cooperation, idiot. And next time, cook your own damned stew."

CORA BUHLERT IS A WRITER, teacher, translator and collector of He-Man toys. She believes that the best thing in life is cozying up with a good book. Cora lives in Bremen, North Germany, with too many books and action figures and a broken Hugo trophy. Visit her at www.corabuhlert.com.

59

STUCK DUCTS
WREN HIGGINBOTTOM

Being small allowed for a lot more exploration than one might expect, especially in the case of the littlest of the bunch, Arden. Arden wasn't the youngest of them all, but they were definitely the smallest by a good amount. Being a gnome, it wasn't like being big was all that helpful in the wider scope of things.

Today, Arden was taking advantage of their small stature to crawl through the air ducts of the home their family was borrowing. Feeling the metal beneath their gnarled fingers, Arden pulled themselves through the last few inches, to a vent where they could look down on the biggest room of the house.

"Arden?" came a voice from behind them. They jumped slightly, making a light tap on the metal floor. Freezing for just a moment, Arden heard someone scraping through the ducts behind them, and the voices in the big room pause for just a moment, as if they had heard something.

Arden slowly pulled themselves back, being so cautious as to not make a single sound. The last thing the family needed was for Arden to be found in their only passage way through the house.

"Arden!" called the voice again, much louder this time.

"Drew? Is that you?" they called, keeping their voice as soft as a whisper of wind.

"Yes. Mama sent me in after you. I got stuck. We're supposed to go back. Dad found food. They don't need you to scout anymore," Drew replied.

"I don't need to scout anymore?" Arden repeated, feeling their heart sink just a little bit further.

"Yeah. He says he got enough for all of us to eat for a whole week! Isn't that great?" Drew said, still trying to pull himself through the vents by the harsh scraping sounds coming from his direction.

"Yeah, that's great. I'll go back now," Arden said, trying to keep emotion out of their voice. Their mind was like a tornado, whirling with so many thoughts and emotions. How was this possible? Their dad had sent them to scout out the big room because they needed to find more food before the humans found them. If he had found food on his own, then Arden would go back to being useless to the family. All Arden was ever sent out for was scouting trips through the ducts, since everyone else would get stuck.

"Arden! Come help me get out of here!" Drew called, still scrabbling to pull himself through. Arden curled themselves up into a tight little ball and rolled themselves around to face Drew. To their horror, Drew was wedged almost perfectly in a bend of the ducts.

"How did you get there?" Arden asked, rubbing their small eyes, hoping that this was all a joke.

"I don't know. I just, tried to crawl, like you, and I turned, but, I didn't turn enough, and now, I'm here," he finished lamely.

"First, we need to be quiet, or the humans will hear all of this scraping and get curious," Arden said, pulling themselves closer to their brother.

"Oh, right. I forgot," he said, stopping his noisy efforts to free himself.

"Okay. Let's see. I can push you back from this side. Can you use your feet to pull yourself too? That should get you unstuck," Arden said, bracing their long toes against the greats of the floor.

"I can. But remember, don't be loud," Drew said, provoking the hint of a smile from Arden.

"Right. Okay. One, two, three." Arden pushed with all of their might on their brother's broad shoulders. It took a few tries, but after a few scrapes, and bumps, Drew shot backward in the vents like he had been launched from a human child's slingshot.

"Arden! I'm free!" Drew shouted.

Arden clapped her hands over her eyes, holding their breath, waiting for any sign of the humans below.

"Ooops," Drew said after a few moments.

"Yes, oops. You really need to be careful Drew. The humans hear much better than we think. They've almost found out about us a few times already," Arden chided him.

"I know. I just forget. That's why I'm glad we have you, to remind us all, and keep an eye on us, and help us when we get stuck," he replied.

"I guess I do help a little," Arden said, their cheeks flushing.

"You're our Arden, and we really do need you to help us. You're still the only one small enough to fit here, so you can watch out for the humans."

"Yeah, you're right. Just because dad doesn't need me to help find food anymore, doesn't mean he won't need me to watch the humans," Arden said, the realization hitting them all at once.

"You really thought dad wouldn't need you anymore?" Drew asked.

"Well, a little. But, let's go back. I don't want the humans to overhear anything," Arden said, starting to pull themselves through the ducts.

"Okay, but, Arden?"

"Yes?"

"I think I might be stuck again."

WREN HIGGINBOTTOM IS A PSYCHOLOGY STUDENT, word collector, and a collector of new languages to learn. They believe the best thing in life is a rainy night where you can curl up with a good book and a warm drink. Wren lives in Rhode Island with their family of dogs, cats, and a goat. Visit them online: @CrescentSays on twitter, or https://toot.community/@CrescentSays.

60

FIRST WITCH ON MARS

MIKE MORGAN

"Mission Control," called Georgie over the long-range crystal ball. "This is Magissa 1. Landing minus thirty minutes, over."

The witch standing watch at the other crystal ball in Houston responded immediately. There were no radio delays with magic-based communications. "Copy that, Magissa 1. Prep golems for ground deployment. Good luck."

"Don't need luck, Ground. Not when we have diastimurgy."

That raised a chuckle. Diastimurgy was the latest advance in the magical arms race—the art of space magic. A discipline invented in the States soon after the ethereal detonation that had drenched the world in a deluge of magic. The US government had quickly taken advantage of the possibilities magic afforded in the conquest of space. Once other countries had realized what magic could accomplish, they'd rushed to emulate NASA's initiative.

Enyo paused over her tangle of bird bones floating in the zero gravity, her divination half finished. "We're not there yet. We must check everything."

"Tidy up your raven bones, Enyo. We'll be treading Martian soil before you can foretell anything."

"I still sense danger."

Georgie unbuckled from her paisley-patterned armchair and pushed off across the capsule. "I'm going to check the spells on the golems. If you're that concerned, keep scanning for threats. Unless you see death taking aim at us, we're sticking to the plan. We'll be the first Americans on Mars, Enyo."

"More importantly, the first witches."

Georgie couldn't argue with her fellow astronaut. Without magic, NASA would have taken decades to launch a Mars mission, let alone one that could get to Mars in three days.

THE GOLEMS WERE FINE. Georgie glimpsed the beginnings of intelligence flickering in their fiery eyes down in the golem pens on the ship's lower level. If she were any judge, and being a Grade Three Diastimurge she was, they were ready to send out onto the Martian surface. She told Enyo as much as she strapped herself back into her armchair on the upper deck.

"I think someone's shielding themselves," was her fellow witch's reply. "They're out there, in the dark. Watching us. I can feel it."

Georgie suppressed her irritation. Enyo thought there were threats around every corner. "Well, be ready to counter-cast if something nasty comes our way."

Magissa 1 was, as far as they could tell, the first magic-powered mission launched from Earth. By casting runes that distorted the passage of time, the giant concrete cube had completed the journey in so few days Georgie doubted any other government could hope to catch up. Enyo must be imagining things—they were alone out here. Apart from the golems they'd brought for protection and the cats they'd brought for company. And Enyo's goldfish, Nancy.

When weight/fuel ratios weren't a concern, it was amazing how much you could drag along on an interplanetary trip. If only they could figure out a way of magicking up artificial gravity.

Enyo bagged her divination bones, giving up on her astromancy. "Time for a quick cup of tea?"

"Best not. Strap in. We're almost at Hellas basin."

THE LANDING in the enormous Martian crater was gentler than any fifty-ton three-story concrete cube had a right to expect. In fact, Georgie hardly felt a thing as it drifted down.

She ordered the golems to disembark through the cube's patio doors then she and Enyo shrugged on outer garments suitable for Martian surface conditions.

For her, that meant a nice knee-length green coat and sensible shoes to cope with all that dust and grit. Enyo chose a fur coat. Georgie wasn't sure what type of fur it was. There was a hint of wendigo to it.

"Bit more stylish than spacesuits," Enyo said as they climbed down the stairs. Georgie was too occupied appreciating the resumption of gravity, feeble though it was on Mars, to offer much of a reply. Before stepping across the edge of the ship's protective barrier they checked each other's magical runes to ensure there'd be no unplanned decompressions or fatal radiation exposure.

They scrunched over a ridge. Dusk was falling, the Martian sky turning a light shade of blue. The golems cast long shadows on the dead ground.

Here they were, pioneers, trailblazers. They should be proud of what they'd accomplished. "First witches on Mars, Enyo. No one can ever take that away from us."

"You were the first. You pushed your way out the patio door ahead of me." Enyo sounded like she was never going to let that go.

"Guess we should plant the flag. Claim rights to the planet

for Uncle Sam."

The golem nearest Enyo exploded. Chunks of clay flew in long arcs in the low gravity.

Georgie pulled Enyo back down the ridge. She couldn't tell what direction the attack was coming from. Maybe the rocky formation would provide cover.

"How could anyone beat us here?" she gasped. "Where are the other golems?"

A voice carried through the tenuous air, from behind them. "You boast how inventive you are in the new arts, yet you cling to outmoded notions of ships. You have no idea what magic can do." The two witches spun around.

A slender figure stood on the red dust. Its skin was dark green with streaks of black. Four reptilian eyes dominated its face. In its many powerful arms, it held a complex piece of jewel-studded weaponry.

"For a start, it can hide a civilization from the savages on the next planet, and make it seem as if the world is sterile, so they are never tempted to invade." The Martian aimed the weapon over their heads and fired.

Their ship erupted in a fireball of eldritch energies, its shields ruptured. In seconds it collapsed in upon itself, reduced to mangled detritus. Georgie heard other staffs firing in the distance and the cracking sound of clay bodies shattering.

"First witches on Mars, indeed," the alien announced, aiming the weapon-staff at them. "And the first never to return."

MIKE MORGAN WAS BORN in London. He moved to Japan at the age of thirty and lived there for many years. Nowadays, he's based in Iowa, and enjoys family life with his wife and two young children. Be sure to follow him on Twitter, where he goes by @CultTVMike, or check out his website:
https://PerpetualStateofMildPanic.wordpress.com.

61

RECOLLECTIONS OF A MAGPIE
PATRICIA MILLER

I've collected lies all my life. New ones are shiny and bright and eager to be shared. Older lies dull over time, grow thin in places, and are rarely seen anymore.

Every year on the night of the Hunter's Moon, when everyone else in the village is celebrating the harvest, I take them out and examine them for cracks and wear. A few are jumbled together so tightly I'm unable to pry them apart, but those are the very oldest ones, the ones I relied on as a child.

'IT WILL BE BETTER TOMORROW.'

Mama used to take me with her to market. It was crowded but somehow we always had a clear path around us. It was a good place to add to my collection. I had dozens from the years I spent trying to remain unnoticed at her side.

'They don't really think you're cursed.'

And school! School was a treasure trove from the day I entered until my parents were told to keep me home after I started my Moon's flow so early. I gathered lies from classmates and teachers, the headmaster, from the porter who refused to light the stove in the classroom if I was in it.

'You don't mind studying alone and you can learn what you need to know without the teacher's help.'

On the farm, working from dawn to well into the night, I thought I wouldn't have time to collect anything new. I thought I *had* all the lies I created with my family. I was wrong. I could have added *that* lie, but it was a misunderstanding I didn't take in. Besides, there had already been so many other lies I didn't think I'd have room for more.

There is always room for more.

'Mama didn't mean to burn my hand with the tea.'

I no longer helped with the animals after one of the goats was killed. I couldn't save the newly born kid from Navin's dogs, but I took the injured nanny into the woods, safe from the dogs and my father who couldn't be bothered with injured animals.

This was the first lie *I* created out loud, that both mama and kid had been taken by wolves. They thought I was lying. They thought everything I said was a lie. After all, I had been marked as a liar and worse from the moment of my birth, when the midwife told the world about the shape and color of the magpie's silhouette above my heart. Being caught in a lie or telling the truth wouldn't make any difference in my treatment at their hands.

But, my first and only lie made a difference to me, to the way I saw them and the way I saw myself.

I spent my days in the forest, milking the goat, gathering firewood, nuts, and berries. The family would burn the firewood, but were reluctant to eat anything I foraged. So I drank the milk, ate what I gathered, and for once I wasn't hungry.

AT THE END of a long day when I had roamed too far into the deepest glades and needed shelter for the night, I found a wooden framed structure. It was more than a shack, less than a cottage, with a sturdy metal roof and no trace of occupants: people or otherwise. The fireplace and chimney worked though. I feasted on brambleberries, wrapped myself in my cloak, and passed a warm, quiet night.

In the morning, I re-hung the shutters I found in the brush. I gathered wood and stacked it in the lean-to, built a small pen for my goat.

I stayed a day or two or three. No one missed me. No one remarked on my absence after I returned home.

I decided I would spend the next Hunter's Moon, and all my days ever after, in its shelter because putting the not-quite-a-shack to rights made me happy. I didn't care who I was or what I was when I was there. That made me happy, too. I raided the barns and outbuildings for an extra milking stool and other odds and ends. I collected tools, a dented teapot, mismatched pans and plates, some fencing. There was a basket or three in need of repair and easily mended, a knife and whetstone, a lamp, although I wasn't certain I'd be able to replenish the oil it needed.

An unused ledger became a copy of grandmother's herbal remedies and medicines. Mother never used them and I wasn't allowed to—much too close to witchcraft in my mother's opinion, and I was already under suspicion. Other villages weren't as superstitious as mine, though. I could perhaps use such potions for barter.

I DIDN'T SNEAK out my last night at my parent's house. I didn't need to. The village harvest celebration was quite the feast and everyone, even the farm hands, had made the trip into town. I'd never been—'*Someone should stay to keep an eye on things*'—

except I'd collected that lie long ago. My treasure was finally big enough.

I gathered my ledger and a few chickens my brother had lost track of. I had taken clothes, bedding, flour, salt, and sugar, preserves and seeds to my new home weeks before. There had been little trace of me in my parents' house while I lived there, and no trace of me remained when I left.

The village just on the other side of the wood welcomed me. Their village witch had vanished years before. They thought the magpie was a sign of good fortune.

I TAKE my treasures out one by one and examine them under the light of the Hunter's Moon for cracks and wear. None of them hold a glimmer of truth. Lies cannot be treasure.

So I cast them to the wind. Like a magpie, I will find something else bright and shiny to collect.

Happiness perhaps.

PATRICIA MILLER IS A WRITER, weaver, and a collector of Dremel tools. She believes the best thing in life is an afternoon nap during a thunderstorm. Patricia lives in Edgerton, Wisconsin, USA with seven looms, 3000 books and approximately half a million yards of yarn. Visit her online: @MillerTrish42 or https://trishmillerwrites.com

62

THE BLACK ANGEL OF LORE
SHELDON WOODBURY

The shriveled old shape shifter spewed out a smoky breath as it mused about what to become this one last time. A myriad of possibilities swirled up through the ancient chambers of its crumbling mind, a haunting menagerie of the impossible. Its wheezing weariness was a burden it struggled to resist, but it accepted that death was an inevitable part of the cosmic design. Gasping and shivering, it knew its existence was nearing its end, so this last metamorphosis had a significance that made the decision even more profound.

It had become the mythic soul of this world, the unknown force that had unleashed a shadowy parade that couldn't be explained by the rigid boundaries of science or logic. It was the opposing foe to all that was dull and dreary, a radical change agent seeking nothing less than to startle and astound. Using the horror of nightmares and the radiance of dreams, it was the mystical champion of soaring transcendence and shocking surprise. Science and logic had their place, but it was a limited landscape with too many boundaries and borders.

Now its fabled strength and transformative powers were just fading flickers inside the dying husk the world had never seen. This was an aching sadness it fought against, knowing it would never be celebrated in the glorious way it deserved. It had created gods and demons, angels and devils, dragons and goblins, as the sole creator of legend and lore. But it had never left even the slightest trace of where they came from or the wrenching sacrifices made. It was like a ghost that had haunted an entire world, and it had created the belief in that too.

It shuddered in its sanctuary deep underground, a subterranean pit of withering darkness and craggy rock that kept it hidden from the world above.

It was a monster, of course, but only because monsters are defined by those without any knowledge of what real strangeness is. It had been borne in a howling place with cosmic magic and miracles, finding its way into this world through the last crack before the beginning of time. It had never been identified for what it was, but its deeds as a creator of creatures was the legacy it was leaving behind.

It was the maker of myths, the secret source of wonder and awe, bringing its otherworldly magic to this earthly realm. It had prowled the sprawling lands for countless ages, but now there was time for only one last trick.

Its shriveled old form began the changing process that was always wracked with the wailing pain of a brutal birth. Its body was stoked by the raging furnace in the lava below. Its legendary life was almost gone, but billowing black wings suddenly burst out, smashing into the scorched rock, igniting even more fire and smoke. It grew in startling ways, staggering and stumbling up through the twisted maze of tunnels and caves, becoming something else in the sun drenched landscape waiting above.

It charged into the air with a thunderous flap, and soared higher and higher through the wispy white clouds and blue summer sky. Growing and changing like a nightmare given form, it was an unleashed creation ghastly and startling, never seen before. It hovered like a gloomy black angel above the spinning orb below.

It was the world it had nudged along with magic and mystery, dreams, and lore; the sacred power of the impossible. The heavens shimmered with a blinding intensity as its gargantuan wings flapped even higher, then suddenly dropped down and caressed the sun splattered world with a surprising tenderness, cradling it like a newborn child.

Then it was gone, gone forever. It ended the dark and dazzling parade of magic and myth it had created. A colossal black shadow settled over the sprawling lands and bottomless oceans while a dark new age quietly began.

SHELDON WOODBURY HAS an M.F.A. in Dramatic Writing from NYU where he also taught screenwriting. He's an award-winning writer. His book, *Cool Million*, is considered the essential guide to writing high concept movies. His short stories and poems have appeared in many horror anthologies and magazines. He's a member of the HWA.

63

SWAN SISTER

JENNIFER SHELBY

"Welcome to the 45th meeting of the Self-identified Failed Fairy Tale Heroines Support Group and Tea Sampling Society," said Drusilla, giving Swanhilde a beatific smile. "Today we have a new member joining us. Swanhilde, would you like to tell us your story?"

Swanhilde took a deep breath and poured a dark liquid from a well-dented flask into her teacup before offering the flask to the others. She brightened when the ladies cooed appreciatively at the gesture. "I must admit I'm nervous. I've never told my true story before."

"We're all heroines here. This is a safe place," a plump fairy with large eyes told her in what Swanhilde had to admit was a kind voice.

She squeezed the little bundle of feathers that hung from her waist. "I was born to privilege, dad was the king, mom the queen. There were endless lessons in politics, waiting for the day when they would marry me off to some other king's son. A little spy to warm his bed and manipulate his favor." She grimaced over her tea. "All their plans were wrecked when my brothers were turned into swans."

Some of the heroines fluttered amongst themselves, eyes

wide and fingers pointing as they guessed her fairy tale. "You know this story, do you?" Swanhilde slammed her teacup into her saucer, setting them both to clattering, her expression grim. "I assure you the truth of it didn't go as you think. Telling a child of barely nine she cannot ever say another word, that she's got to sit and spin nettles with her bloody, stung fingers for years on end else she'll be turned into a swan herself.

"Oh, yes, the *horrible* life of a swan, free to wander the rivers or drift across the sky on a careless wing, free as an *actual* bird. I tell you what..." Swanhilde looked about for her flask, desperate, but it was at a far table by now. "After a few days of silence, my fingers stung bloody and nerves aflame, swollen such that I could barely spin at all, I was ready to glue the damn feathers to my ass myself!"

A well-muscled lady a table over held her teacup in the air and stamped her feet. The other heroines joined in, making such a noise Swanhilde felt the vibrations in her chest.

She waved her hand in the air. "It was all sham, anyway. I did fine for a while, then one day I burped and all my fine courtly manners compelled me to say 'excuse me' before I could stop myself. Oh, I tried to keep up the pretense for a while, as if wishing could make me the fairy tale heroine the story wanted me to be, but I hated those nettles and it wasn't any use.

"No one ever turned me into a swan like the curse promised. They only berated and despised me for not being good enough or quiet enough to save six mean little boys who pulled my hair, called me names, and certainly wouldn't have been able to do the same for me."

"Hear! Hear!" shouted the heroines.

Swanhilde took a steadying breath and smoothed her skirts. "Once it was known I wouldn't be turning them back into princes the palace chef started eyeing my brothers. By then my parents were embarrassed by their bird children, and one by one they would have been roasted for dinner. There was no way I could let that happen. I may not have been the heroine my parents wanted me to be, but I wasn't a monster. I traded my finest jewels to have my brothers smuggled out on a local pirate's ship."

"Oh, were they handsome, this pirate?" someone tittered.

Swanhilde smirked and ignored them. "Once we were free of that god-awful kingdom, I hawked the boys' circlet crowns and bought a plot of land near the shore where they could swim."

"And your pirate could visit!" the titterer added, slapping her thigh.

"That's the dryad's brew from my flask getting the better of you," Swanhilde answered, but she winked all the same. "Swans need a long stretch of water to take off and stretch their wings. Mind you, my beloved bird brothers would happily settle into a puddle in a thicket and be stuck there forever.

"Oh, they made a terrible mess of our house, shitting everywhere and breaking our crockery with their great wings, but we had good times there. Of course, they could be stubborn as posts. Wasn't long before I learned to grab them over their wings like I was raised on a farm instead of a castle, huffing them about like I'd worked hard all my life. I was proud of that." Swanhilde paused, a smile playing at her features. "The locals took to calling me Swanhilde, 'battle swan.' Suited me better than my old name, so I kept it."

Her mirth subsided and her fingers fumbled for her missing flask. "Nowadays I like that the name reminds me of our years together, back when we were still a family. Swans don't live as long as people. Twenty, thirty years if they're lucky. One by one my brothers died and I was left all alone in that big house on the water." Swanhilde sighed.

She lost herself in her memories, slumping in her chair and staring ahead with unseeing eyes.

Drusilla pulled a flask of her own from somewhere deep in her skirts and tipped it into Swanhilde's tea. "It's all right, dear."

Swanhilde blinked, Drusilla's gesture reviving her. She held up her teacup to toast her friend. "I suppose it might have been easier to have just shut up and spun the damn nettles when I had the chance."

Drusilla's hand stretched across Swanhilde's lap squeeze the woman's hand where it clutched her bundle of dirty, once-white feathers. Swanhilde released a heavy sigh. "But damn if those boys didn't love to fly."

JENNIFER SHELBY IS A RECOVERED protagonist and collector of daydreams. She believes the best thing in life is the latest side quest. Jennifer lives in New Brunswick, Canada, with a forest's worth of dryads and a twisty yellow birch. Visit them online: @jenniferdshelby on twitter or at jennifershelby.blog

64

MOUTHFUL
MEL TODD

Lauren ran. Her feet pounded across the thick mossy ground as her backpack beat a frantic rhythm on her back. Long lichen covered branches grazed by her face, reaching out to grab and tear at her long dark hair. Her boot hit a patch of earth that gave more than she expected, but she caught herself and kept running. She refused to look behind her.

Something chased her. She sensed it. Felt the ground shudder as it loped and tasted the fetid stench of its breath in the air. What scared her the most, was knowing, knowing down to the tops of her pink laced hiking boots, that it didn't exist, it *couldn't* exist. And that it wanted to eat her.

Frantic thoughts raced through her head. There had to be a road soon. They hadn't gone far off the trail. Why had her friends left her there? Where was she?

The forest she ran through seemed like something from a fairy tale. Dark trees that resembled faces. Long moss hanging like hair. Branches that scratched her. It didn't make sense. Logic couldn't compete with the imperative thrumming through her bones.

Run!

Ahead was a glimmer of light, and hope brought forth a

new burst of speed. Her lungs burned, her side hurt, her head throbbed in time with her pulse, but none of that was enough to make her slow down. She saw a log up ahead, and calling on childhood memories of jumping trees, she sprang, clearing it, until the loops of her laces snagged and she fell with a crash that knocked what little breath she had out of her.

A thump let her know she'd lost.

Fine, but I refuse to die on my back.

Lauren rolled over and glared at the impossible creature above her. Dragons didn't exist. But leering down, amusement twinkling in its eyes, with teeth bigger than her legs, a dragon loomed, licking long scaly lips; anticipating a meal: her.

"Fuck you," she growled holding up her middle finger as jaws widened, ready to bite.

Lauren Lopez had never been the best at anything. Not the best runner, obviously. Not the best sister, not the best friend, and not the best employee. But she was a good dental technician and enjoyed her job. Teeth and how under respected they were in the balance of the human body fascinated her.

That same fascination as death loomed over the top of her, made her spot the metallic gleam between the dragon's teeth. Self-control had never been one of her strong points either. Without pausing to consider the consequences, Lauren reached up and yanked out the metallic item. After all, the only metal thing belonging in a mouth were braces, and the new plastic versions were healthier.

"Ow!" The mouth pulled back and snapped closed. Without her arm in it. "That…feels much better. It's been bugging me for days. What did you do?"

"Why was this, this, *dagger* in your teeth?"

The dragon sat back, looking for all the world like it was rolling something around in its mouth. "That stupid dwarf I ate last week. He must have stuck it there. That's why I try not to eat dwarfs; they have too many pokey bits of metal around them. Takes forever to digest. But they are so crunchy." He smiled a big toothy grin at Lauren and she recoiled in professional horror.

"What have you done to your teeth?" Her outrage propelled her to her feet even as the dragon froze mid-grimace. "Do you even brush? When is the last time you flossed? And is that a *gem* stuck between your teeth."

Even certain death had to be ignored for the important stuff. Lauren took dental hygiene very seriously.

"My teeth?" The dragon had a vaguely British accent, but the strange attractiveness of that was overwhelmed by the foul odor that rolled from his mouth as he spoke.

Before her own fear hadn't let her notice it, but now she regretted having calmed down enough to breathe through her nose. "You have tartar I can see from here. Your gums are enflamed. From the smell of rot, you have a cavity that is abscessing, and you aren't supposed to have anything in between your teeth."

"I, ah, well, my back molar has been a bit tender of late," he admitted slowly.

"Don't floss. Don't brush. I'll bet you don't even know how to deal with a damaged tooth or fang, do you?" She turned and looked around, then spied her hiking boots and the bright pink lacing. "Give me a second." She had the lacing off and in her hands before she thought about it. "Open up," she ordered.

The dragon blinked at her, but opened his mouth. She was flossing away in seconds. "What have you been doing? Don't you know how important your teeth are? And right there that molar is crack and rotting. No wonder it hurts and your breath smells awful. It's just going to get worse you know."

"Can you fix it?" There was an odd hopefulness to the dragon's tone.

"Not if you eat me," she snapped back, even as she prodded at the tooth. "Dang it. Even drained it's going to cause problems. Only choice is to pull it and pack it." She pulled back and glared at him. "If I do this, you agree to *not* eat me."

"Yes, ma'am," whimpered the dragon.

Twenty minutes later, the tooth was pulled, the socket packed with lichen and Lauren glared. "Am I free to go?" Though really that was the most fun she'd had in years.

"Umm, would you look at my teeth?" A voice said behind her. Lauren pivoted in slow motion to see a unicorn, a dwarf, and something she didn't even know the name of all staring at her hopefully.

Lauren huffed. "I'd better get paid for this."

MEL TODD HAS PUBLISHED over 35 stories. Her completed urban science fiction series, the *Kaylid Chronicles*, is over 600k words. The best-selling urban fantasy series, *Twisted Luck*, is a fan favorite with LGBTQ themes. Owner of Bad Ash Publishing, she's planning on taking the publishing world by storm. Sign up for her newsletter here: https://badashpublishing.com/newsletter/

65

THE BOG HAUNT
ROBERT BAUER

C alvin didn't feel like doing chores this afternoon, but he did them: he emptied the dishwasher, he set the vacuum cleaner to run, and he summoned the dead.

The summoning was the most annoying part. Calvin gathered up the undyed twine and the beads of turquoise and bone, the thin sharp wands of polished ash wood, and the silk cloth to wrap and carry it all in. He steeped the dried leaves in hot water, even though he hated the smell, and placed this brew in an insulated mug with a lid. He didn't really want to do any of it today. He would have rather just gone to his room and put his head under his pillow and tried not to think.

Calvin moped and ambled his way down the hill behind his house, kicking at random pebbles whose appearance offended him. He went down to the pond, and sat beside the willow tree, and unwrapped his tools. He pushed the wands into the damp soil, arranging them just precisely right. He strung the beads of turquoise and bone on the twine. Around and between the wands he wrapped it, the exact same lopsided pattern that he made every week. Lastly, he dribbled a few bitter drops from the mug onto the center of the pattern, and set the rest just at the edge of the water, with the lid off so it would cool.

He sat and waited for a little while, resenting the waste of time. He knew that if he hadn't done this, he still would have wasted this time some other way, and he was angry at himself for that, too.

When the mug by the water came to just the right temperature, the black surface of the water bent up. It rose and shaped itself into the form of a woman. Her clear-dark glistening features were hard to read, but Calvin thought she didn't look so old for a grownup. Burbling like a brook, she came over to the edge of the water, straight toward Calvin. She took the mug of tea, and lifted it up to smell it.

"Hello, Cally."

"Hi, Aunt Tara."

The water-shape sat down on the shore of the little pond. Her feet stayed under the surface, of course, because even in the presence of turquoise and bone and Calvin's blood she would never be able to leave that water again. "How's your mother?"

"She's fine."

"Hm, and what about you?"

Calvin hunched his shoulders. "Fine."

His aunt made a sound like a heavy rock dropped into the mud. "Don't you lie to the departed dead, Cally. What is your mother teaching you?"

"You're not departed, Aunt Tara. You're a haunt."

"Don't sass me." It was true, she was a haunt, but it was rude to say so. "You're not fine. Tell me."

"No one talks to me. At school, I mean." Calvin hunched lower, and put his chin on his knees. "I'm too weird."

"Ahh. This trouble I know. Because you're fey?"

"Because I'm a *witch*."

Aunt Tara hissed like rotten ice. "Don't you talk about yourself that way."

"I'm not! It's not, it doesn't have to be a bad word…"

"In *that* tone of voice it does. No, don't you argue with me. You're a brilliant, beautiful boy with cunning in your blood, who never did anything to hurt anyone, and I'll hear no word against you." Then, contradicting herself, "What are they telling you?"

"Nothing. They don't talk." Calvin shifted his feet, wondering why he was whining about nothing. "They stare at me."

"Cally, some people are just always going to be rotten. Convince one, charm another, there will always be ten more who won't behave worth a damn. Spend your time on the good ones, and for the rest—you can't stop being who you are, so you might as well be proud of it."

"*You* stopped," Calvin whispered. It was a thought he'd never given voice to, certainly not to any grownup. It made Aunt Tara pause, for several long seconds.

"First of all, I may have stopped being many things, but I didn't stop being fey, or I wouldn't be here for you to tell me I did. Second…second, what I did was, I saved the bastards the price of a rope."

"What?"

"Cally, when there's those that want you dead, don't you ever make it easier for them. Make them come for you with torches. Make them come for you ten strong, because you'll curse them down three by three, and howl to wake the deep things as they finally drag you to the tree. If they really want to kill you, then maybe they can, but you will make them work for it or so help me, I will haunt your ghost worse than I ever haunted your blood. Do you hear me?"

"Yes, Aunt Tara." Calvin didn't dare say anything else.

"And tell your mother to come down here herself next time. No—tell her to come tomorrow, don't wait a week. She and I need to talk." Calvin flinched. His mom would be upset, definitely. But not telling would be worse. Aunt Tara had ways.

The haunt set down the empty mug by the edge of the water. "Go on inside, Cally. It's good you came, but there's no need to stay in the wet and catch a cold for my sake."

"Yes, Aunt Tara."

She stood, nodded to him, and went back into the water like she was wading, down a deeper underwater slope than this little pond actually had. Calvin gathered up the twine, and the ashen wands, and the beads of turquoise and bone, and wrapped them all in the soft silk cloth. He picked up the empty mug.

He walked back up the hill, and went on.

ROBERT BAUER IS A WRITER, teacher, and all-around nerd. He is easily distracted by puzzles and games. Robert lives in Connecticut, USA with two cats and other family.

66

THE AUDITION

K.G. ANDERSON

I scanned email while listening to Fay Platz plead her client's case over the phone. It was only mid-afternoon but it felt later. Outside my office, dark clouds hung over the Hollywood Hills and thunder grumbled.

"Yeah, yeah," I said. "Zombies, vampires—done to death. So to speak. But, Fay, sweetie, that doesn't mean banshees are the next thing."

Rob Grant stood in the door, signaling to me that we were late for the meeting. I rolled my eyes, and switched Fay to speakerphone. At the sound of her tinny voice, Rob cringed, mouthing her name. I nodded.

"Sure, Fay, send her over," I said. "10 a.m. tomorrow. Gotta run."

"Fay never gives up, Kevin," Rob said as we hurried down the hall to the meeting. "She tried me, too. I told her: no banshees. That woman doesn't take the hint. Can't believe you gave in to it. Fay got something on you?"

As a matter of fact, she did. I needed to get out from under it. "Easier to get rid of a banshee than Fay!" I joked feebly. Rob laughed.

I'D NEVER SEEN A BANSHEE, so I was taken aback the next morning by the tall, leggy girl in artfully tattered black clothing who waited primly in the chair outside my office. You don't see a lot of Goths these days. But she was more than Goth. Her skin was pearlescent; her eyes, the black of a darkened theater. Lipstick, blood red.

"Tabitha McBain." She rose, shouldering her black messenger bag, and held out a cool hand. "Fay Platz sent me." Her voice was deep but soft, as if coming from a distance through a mist. A slight, intriguing, Irish brogue.

With those looks and that voice, we might have a part for her. I motioned her into my office. "We're casting for a paranormal cop show. Fay felt that you had, er, relevant experience. So to speak."

She nodded. I took the audition script from the desk and tossed it to her. "Try this scene. Read Lt. McCool. Her lines."

She perused the script, frowned, and muttered something. "Well. This is not exactly what a real—"

"Go ahead, take a few minutes," I said, checking messages on my phone. "Loosen up. Improvise. Give me a sense of what you can do."

When I looked up, she'd gone to the window and was gazing out over the parking lot. She strode back to my desk, gave me a nod, threw back her head and opened her red lips. The sound that emerged was an odd mixture of owl, wolf, and 1960s folksinger. If my head weren't shaved, my hair would have stood on end. This business is full of surprises.

"Well," I said when the sound died away, "that's an, er, *interesting* interpretation."

In the hall outside there were running footsteps and muffled voices. My door flew open and Aly from the office next door stuck her head in. "Bad news, Kevin. Rob Grant just collapsed in the parking lot. Heart attack. It looks bad."

In the distance an ambulance wailed. Tabitha, the script in her hand, regarded at me with a slight change of expression I mistook for regret. Until she raised her chin and tossed the script aside. "Perhaps," she said, her brogue thickening, "you need to hear it again?"

I shook my head vigorously. "Not necessary. You're perfect for the part."

K.G. ANDERSON IS A TECHNOLOGY WRITER, a frustrated guitarist, and a lifelong collector of easy recipes and difficult cats. They live in Seattle in a house haunted by the bad remodeling decisions of the previous owners. Visit them online at writerway.com/fiction

67

THE AMBUSH HUNTERS
LOREN RHOADS

It was late when Alondra headed back to the place she was housesitting in San Francisco. She'd had too much wine. She'd hoped the long stroll up Buena Vista Hill from Curios and Candles would clear her head, but she was too much in love with the night for that. Every shimmering streetlight, every breeze off the ocean, spun her thoughts in a new direction. She knew she needed to keep trudging up the hill, but she wanted to stop and smell the neighbor's jasmine or listen to someone's wind chimes or watch the stars twinkling overhead.

The night was quiet: no cars passing, no raccoons trooping out of the park to raid garbage cans. This was one of San Francisco's rare clear nights, so even the fog horns on the bay kept silent. Eventually she crossed Waller Street for the final leg of the climb.

Alondra pulled out her keys and was halfway up the brick steps before she realized the security gate at the top hung open. She was drunk enough that she stopped short, peering into the shadows of the entry.

The house's door was shut. Her spells still crawled across its surface, an unbroken web that burned a steady green. The light she'd left on still glowed from the kitchen.

The little entry area—too small to be considered a porch—was crowded with shadows. Alondra had pulled a wicker chair onto it so she could drink her tea in the morning, but the chair took up more than its share of space. There wasn't room for anyone to hide. Or so she told herself. As she climbed another step toward the gate, she heard something: a sigh, a subtle shifting…. She paused again, readying an attack in her off-hand.

The streetlights behind her caught on a pair of eyes as high as her knee. The greenish gold reflection dropped as the mountain lion cub lowered its gaze. It huddled in a miserable ball between the chair and the house.

Alondra wasn't sure what to do. She didn't want to stand with her back to the cub as she unlocked the house. What if it swiped at her? As pitiful as the small shadow looked, she had no doubt that its claws were sharp. What if it ran past her, meaning to escape, and got into the house? She couldn't stand here on the steps all night. She considered walking back down the hill to Stella's apartment and asking to stay over, but Stella had taken Tabitha home and Alondra didn't want to interrupt them.

She didn't need to call the police because the poor scared creature didn't seem dangerous. She pulled out her phone and was looking up Animal Care and Control when she decided she didn't want to take her gaze off the lion cub. She tucked the phone back into her pocket.

"Are you hurt, little one?" Alondra asked softly. "Where's your mama?"

As the words left her lips, Alondra realized that was in fact a very good question. She knew that, very rarely, a mountain lion skulked across the Golden Gate Bridge late at night, witnessed only by the traffic cameras. Once a lion crept from Mount San Bruno to McLaren Park to Glen Canyon, dodging from one wild space to another. But Buena Vista Park, in the middle of the Haight Ashbury neighborhood, was scarcely wild

—and a coyote already sometimes hunted there. The park couldn't possibly hold enough wildlife for a mountain lion to eat...

Alondra whirled awkwardly on the brick steps. She flung the protection spell she had prepared, but her aim was off. The spell didn't hit the lioness straight on. Instead, it caught her haunches and knocked her into the driveway.

The snarling cat pulled herself into a crouch.

Alondra realized she'd dropped her keys. She could open the house without them, but that would take time and concentration, neither of which she had right now.

She wasn't about to run down the hill in front of a wounded mountain lion. At the same time, she'd stayed in the Haight long enough to know how little response a woman screaming for help would draw in the middle of the night.

Alondra felt with her foot for the next step up. Higher ground was an advantage, she told herself. The wrought iron front gate was heavy enough to be used as a weapon, if she was fast enough. She almost laughed aloud at the thought. Was she faster than a pouncing mountain lion? Drunken Alondra versus wounded big cat...?

If she could scramble up the remaining steps, she could maybe slam herself inside the entry...with the cub, she realized. She remembered its frightened eyes lowering in the dark, begging her not to hurt it.

"Okay," Alondra said, forcefully though not too loud. "Here's the deal, my friend. Call your baby and go. Head straight south." She nodded in that direction. "Keep going downhill every chance you get until you reach Mount San Bruno. I'll go in the house and call Animal Care. They'll track you to make sure you get out of the city. Watch out for cars. You can survive this. But if you attack another person, they will kill you and your baby will end up in a zoo."

The lioness stared at her. Alondra started to weave another spell between her fingers.

The gesture wasn't lost on the lioness. She made a deep growl that raised every hair on Alondra's body.

Behind her, the cub mewed like a kitten. The lioness's attention shifted fractionally. Alondra took another step upward.

A shadow bolted down the steps past Alondra's feet.

The mother cat turned and trotted up the street after her cub. The two of them continued loping south, as Alondra had directed.

The witch sank down on the steps, overcome by shivering. Why was the ambush you were expecting never the ambush you got?

It was such a lovely night.

LOREN RHOADS IS the author of five novels and a story collection called *Unsafe Words*. She's also the editor of seven books, the most recent of which is *Tales of Nightmares*, the second volume of the Wily Writers Presents anthologies. Visit her online at lorenrhoads.com.

68

ALL FORESTS ARE ONE FOREST
JENNIFER R. POVEY

The people of the barrier islands led a hardscrabble life, and Greya felt for them as she leaned over the rail of the boat, feeling the wind against her as the sailors tacked carefully to harbor.

Felt for them even more because they had no souls. Not in the sense of being soulless...she had *met* the true soulless before, those who had no trace of humanity in them. In the sense of having no place for their souls to come from or to go, and of course they could not leave. It wouldn't make any difference.

Well, some did, because they thought it might make a difference to their children. And a few did just to lead a better life before they faced oblivion.

More accurate to say that leaving would not give them their souls. The harbor she approached was odd. The houses were built on stilts, almost seeming to sway in the ocean wind. When the storms came the water would rush under them and recede and do little damage. It still looked odd to her eyes, coming from the mountains where people built low and in stone.

They were not *stupid* people, and it really wasn't fair that they had no forest to give them their souls.

Which was why the Emperor wanted to move them. Evacuate them. They didn't want to go. They didn't want to go even for their children.

Greya rather thought they couldn't, couldn't envision a life off of the island.

Stepping ashore, the ground felt no different under her feet than any other land. The people around her, wind and weather beaten, seemed to just be people.

"Come with me, Lar Greya," said a voice.

They used the gender neutral honorific out of respect until she corrected them. She seldom bothered. She was as happy with Lar as with Lady and honestly wouldn't have minded Lord either, but that would make her odd.

As a representative of the Empire she couldn't be *odd*.

"We won't leave," the young person...likely a woman from the skirts and the hint of breasts under her bodice.

"You would rather..."

"*You* do not understand. The Emperor's jurisdiction here is thin."

That was true. Greya knew it to be true. As his representative, she knew how little sway the government had in places like this. But they had no forest. They needed to be saved.

IT WAS ALREADY TOO late for the two children who ran past Greya as she explored the village. It might have almost aspired to town, but certainly nothing larger than that, and it was the largest settlement they had.

A handful of people, and it was clear that they were doing poorly. With nobody willing to move here, the population had that peculiar similarity that came from lucky inbreeding; they didn't seem to have any defects. But nobody wanted to deny their children the forest.

She watched the children then followed them, curious to see where they were going. Children went places adults did not, cared about places adults did not. They ran down the beach and then sat staring at the water. She peeked at the water, but saw nothing special about it. Maybe their young eyes could see some fish darting around.

She thought she saw the fronds of seaweed. Some kind of large seaweed. No doubt fish lived in it. Staying away from the kids, not wanting to spook them, she walked a bit further down the beach and looked.

And felt something. Something within her. Seaweed growing up from a deep floor...why wasn't the harbor here?

Because they valued the seaweed.

Greya had never felt so *drawn* to anything before, not even a forest.

Not even...

...what?

She frowned. And then she turned and walked all the way back to the mayor's house.

"YOUR FOREST IS IN THE OCEAN," she told the older woman. Pevi, her name was.

"Yes."

"Then why not..."

"Because the Emperor wants us moved."

Greya shook her head. "Only because..."

"No. The Emperor *knows* and sent you anyway. If we admit it, then he has the excuse he needs to destroy our forest and force us out."

"Why would he do anything like *that*?"

"The Verians might come again. He wants to fortify the island."

Would he destroy a forest to do it? Greya wished she could

argue that Pevi was wrong. She couldn't. Destroying a forest would destroy all the souls currently within it, all of the ones resting while they waited for rebirth. She would find out the truth. "So…"

"You can't do anything to us that he can't do," Pevi said. "But you might be able to do something for us."

She would think about it, but for right now she walked back to the shore and knew something else, too. All forests were one forest. And this one wanted her.

JENNIFER R. Povey is an author, game designer, and collector of pins and buttons. She believes the best thing in life is Doctor Who and horses. Jennifer R. Povey lives in Arlington, Virginia with her spouse and a surprisingly large fern. Visit her online: http://www.jenniferrpovey.com.

69

A BUBBLE, A WITCH, A LAUNDROMAT

TANIA CHEN

S *TOP.*

The letters are the pastel pink of crayons, a loopy scroll followed by a sad face. Yuming pushes a button, and tugs the lever; on screen, the words rearrange themselves like a reel spinner, bright sunshine yellow and obnoxiously loud as the letters chime into place: *INSUFFICIENT SOAP*.

Her shoulders curve forward, mouth like an open coin slot as she summons every last bit of patience, counting to ten as grandma used to. "Livy!"

From the sliver of an opening on the glass door, a woman with curly hair pokes her head out. She is wearing the latest fashion in witch hats, the iridescent shade of grey making the patterned violet stars stand out. Under the artificial light, the stars giggle and rearrange themselves.

"What?" Curt, efficient. That was why Yuming hired Livy several seasons ago when the small stop station became a small town due to its convenient location. Although, honestly speaking, the entire place barely qualifies as a town, but that is neither here nor there. What matters is that 1)the business is thriving, 2)their waitlist is full and that, to keep one and two churning along, the machines need to be fully functional.

La Burbuja de la Limpieza is the halfway point between the Citadel and the Fire Mountains aptly named after the tongues of fire that curl from the summit to warm the hearth of the Gods' Abode above. Any party wanting to test their mettle must first face the challenge of climbing to the top before waiting to see if the Gods deem them worthy of a reward. Magic swords by the dozen, weightless shields, bottomless quivers…the list goes on, but Yuming doesn't find the available prizes that appealing.

After La Burbuja there are no rest stops that offer a full-on laundry and mending service for weary adventurers. The name is a bit of a pun in Livy's native tongue. Substitute burbuja for bruja and the entire meaning changes but still very much applies to their business. If it needs cleaning and repairing this is the place; for an extra fee, they add charms to repel fire and keep its owner cool.

"The machine isn't working again." Yuming runs her hand over the lid of a metallic box with a cheerful black screen that is now emoting pink hearts in the direction of Livy. It only makes Yuming scowl harder, and she raps her knuckles on the lid. "Don't be so shameless."

"You have to show it love," Livy says, crossing the space in two steps, time and space bending under her magic. Yuming will never tire of seeing the mastery Livy inherited from her ancestors, even if in comparison it makes her own brand of witchcraft feel pedestrian. "Who is a good boy today?"

The metal seems to warm under the touch, flustered before it purrs. The screen shifts from its ongoing heart emote parade to READY FOR LOAD. The hood pops open and both women begin throwing in a pile of dark robes, the shimmer of dragon sequins visible before they disappear inside the machine.

"We need to start charging more for anything with sequins, they give our boy here a bit of indigestion when they come off without warning." Livy closes the hood, pats it while giving a self-satisfied grin. "Better get the thread and needle ready for when he spits them out post-cycle."

MACHINE WASH CYCLE 3: DELICATES; INITIATED.

Yuming deflates, back curved in further like a bow pulled taunt.

Livy's smile fades. "Hey—there's nothing to it, just a little pat. No magic involved."

Embarrassingly, those words only make Yuming feel her eyes sting more. Crying over a stubborn washing machine is silly, but it goes deeper. The feeling of inadequacy in her magic and inability to forge romantic relationships have always been a sore point, made even more so by a lack of words to vocalise it.

Yuming has never had an interest in partners and Livy understood this without explicitly being told so. Somewhere along the way, Livy had helped Yuming express things, showing her that it was acceptable to be different and not conform. Now, it is that same telepathic-like magic at work that makes Livy reach out, and gently touch Yuming's shoulder offering warmth and comfort.

"Simple does not mean useless. Who else had the genius idea of putting up a laundry station on the busiest, most needed part of the quest? *You*," Livy says. "All these wizards and bards and clerics, and not a single one of them has a spell for keeping clean."

Opposite the washing machine, the dryer is spitting out clean, warm clothes onto the rows of fairy lights above. Yuming flicks up a finger and the lights grow little hands they use to stretch out the newly dried fabric across white cords. From there, Yuming will tug the clothes down and then fold or iron them depending on the client's request.

"Okay, yeah, thanks Livy," Yuming says, looking up when Livy chucks her chin. It isn't always easy to remember that it really is fine to simply exist as herself, that she has a life and a job she adores. That she is whole. That she has more friends than fingers on both hands. Yuming watches Livy as she steps lightly on the tiled floor leading back to the doors that hide the front desk from the laundry area.

Before pushing past them, Livy looks back. "And don't forget it's poker night, there are some rookie clerics we should clean out. Literally."

Behind Yuming, the washing machine—who is being a very good boy now—purrs in agreement.

TANIA CHEN IS a writer of living nightmares, and collector of pink and/or cute stationary. They believe the best thing in life is drinking cold brew while enjoying birdsong. Tania lives in Mexico City, Mexico with a gaggle of family ghosts and their cat. Visit them online: @archistratego on twitter.

70

WHISTLES IN THE FOREST

MATIAS TRAVIESO-DIAZ

His small frame and the green scales that covered his body blended with the foliage of the tall trees; even his flaming orange hair would pass for a clump of bright flowers. It was good camouflage, and this was fine by him. He enjoyed being left alone, invisible to the humans.

Sure, sometimes there were sightings. On occasion, a woman washing clothes on the river bank would catch a glimpse of him as he moved swiftly to rescue an animal caught in a snare or a bird about to be devoured by a caiman. When that happened, he would flee rapidly, leaving confusing prints on the muck, for his feet were set backward.

"It was a *curupira!*" the woman would shout excitedly to others in her Tupi language.

But, for the most part, he and humans did not interact and he was able to carry out his mission of protecting the animals and trees that inhabit the jungles of the mightiest of all rivers.

Things changed when a different sort of human—pale skinned and hairy—arrived in the jungle. They carried metal rods that spewed thunder and lightning and went on to kill or enslave the Tupis. From time to time, he would observe the newcomers' murderous actions; they disgusted him, but they did not cause concern, as human affairs are unimportant.

But more pallid humans arrived, bringing darker humans as their thralls. The masters and their slaves felled trees and burned wide swaths of jungle to clear the land and make room for their plantings to grow and their strange animals to roam. Forests disappeared and, with no trees to release their moisture into the passing clouds, rain became scarcer, causing more plants—and the animals who subsisted on them—to perish.

He did all he could to oppose these destructive men. He was not a violent creature, and limited himself to playing tricks against the invaders. His whistles could resemble the calls of birds or the noises of animals; hunters would follow these sounds and get lost in the woods. Loggers would run away when he imitated the growls of jaguars and other ferocious animals. He could also emit eerie human noises that scared the colonists.

His efforts failed to impede the spoliation of the land. The virgin woods were assaulted by the human *marabunta*, even more destructive than the army ants they resembled. He grew afraid that the humans' appetite for destruction would extinguish millions of plants and animals and turn the jungle into an arid wasteland. He had to do something.

HE INFLATED himself to a size that would resemble that of an adult human and walked into a settlement in broad daylight, taunting the inhabitants to capture him. At first, the villagers ran away, hiding inside their cocoons, the smell of their fear burning his nostrils. Finally, the bravest among them approached, armed with fire sticks and other weapons.

As they gathered around him, he spoke. His words were in rudimentary Tupi, a language he had been exposed to for many generations. None of the villagers understood Tupi, but as they continued to encircle him they fetched someone, a very old and wrinkled female that belonged to that nearly extinct variety of human that had been around for as long as there had been human life in this jungle. Their conversation, such as it was, went as follows:

[HE]: "Do not fear me. I come in peace with an important message for you and your kind."

[The woman]: "What are you?"

[He]: "I am the *curupira*. I am the guardian of the woods and the streams and all the plants and animals that populate this domain."

[The woman]: "But you don't exist. You are just a legend we use to keep our children from misbehaving."

[He]: "I am real. I have come to tell you and your kind that you must cease what you are doing. You are killing this forest and leaving behind a wasteland. You are blindly causing innocent animals and plants to die, fertile soils to turn to sand, rivers and streams to dry out. If you continue, the young among you will grow into misery and poverty. I command you to stop."

[The woman]: "I am only one of the few survivors of what was once a large and powerful tribe. These people killed us off, as they are killing the land. I can convey your message, but they won't believe the truth of my words. Even if they believe me, they won't do anything about it. Their hearts have turned to stone. They don't care what they do to others or themselves as long as their desires are satisfied. Yet, your words and mine are being recorded. I hope against hope they will listen."

[He]: "I do, too. Now I must go."

THEN, the *curupira* sought to break through the knot of his would-be captors and disappear into the jungle, but he could

267

not outrun the firing sticks. Four bullets pierced through the cryptid's scale-covered skin. He halted, ran his hands over the holes where the shots had entered, took one last ungainly step, and fell to the ground.

His pursuers approached the *curupira*'s body, which still convulsed but finally stopped writhing altogether. One of the leaders among the villagers turned the corpse over with his boot; the protector of the wild's open eyes stared blindly at the vast canopy of the forest. The leader gave one last casual kick at the cadaver, as the rest of the villagers crowded around it.

"What was that?" asked someone.

"Who cares?" replied the leader. "We need to get moving. This section needs to be cleared by the end of the week."

There was the shuffling of dozens of feet. Later, except for the cries of an old Indian woman, the forest became silent. But soon it would be reawakened by another creature that would continue the fight against the invaders.

MATIAS TRAVIESO-DIAZ IS A RETIRED LAWYER, engineer, failed painter, and a collector of Maria Callas recordings. He believes the best things in life are opera, jazz, Italian food, and vino. Matias lives in Alexandria, Virginia, with his daughter, two dogs and a world class inventory of weeds. Visit him online at https://twitter.com/mtravies (@mtravies) and https://mtravies.wixsite.com/mysite.

71
DELICATE SITUATIONS
RISA WOLF

To: Guild Administration
From: Mage Shassar, Ascended, Primordial Relations
Subject: Request for Relationship Policy Revision

I'm writing to request an urgent revision of the Mage Guild's Romantic Relationship Policy. I ask because Mage Devren, 7th Rank in Primordial Relations, has informed me that they will no longer work with Caras the Primordial of Striving. They plan to pursue a romantic relationship with her.

We recognize that our policy only forbids relationships with a mage's *current* clients, but we believe it's critical to adhere to strict professional boundaries, in order to better serve our clients and provide safe working conditions for our staff.

Therefore I strongly suggest we revise our policy to forbid romantic relationships with current *and* former clients.

Thank you for your swift attention to this memo.

To: Guild Administration

From: Mage Pauline, Prime, Guild Board
Subject: RE: Request for Relationship Policy Revision

Do we really need to violate our existing policy procedure for *this*? Also, if Devren is willing to forgo the significant commission for Primordial work, who are we to stop them?

To: Mage Shassar, Ascended, Primordial Relations
From: Mage Vestravel, Director, Assignments
Subject: RE: Request for Relationship Policy Revision

I do not understand your request. I specifically asked Devren to notify you, and their behavior is in line with the professionalism and ethics of our organization.

To: Mage Vestravel, Director, Assignments
From: Mage Shassar, Ascended, Primordial Relations
Subject: RE: RE: Request for Relationship Policy Revision

If you assign Caras another mage, and they're not as good as Devren, she might blame us for a poor assignment. She might demand her gold back or might accuse us of deliberately undermining her work.

cc: Mage Pauline, Prime, Guild Board

To: Mage Shassar, Ascended, Primordial Relations

From: Mage Vestravel, Director, Assignments
Subject: RE: RE: RE: Request for Relationship Policy Revision

> Assignments are my division, not yours. I am willing to take on both the risk and the responsibility. Also, Caras the Primordial has been working with us longer than you've been alive, and has worked with many other mages. She is aware of the quality of our Guild.

cc: Mage Pauline, Prime, Client Relations

To: Mage Vestravel, Director, Assignments
From: Mage Shassar, Ascended, Primordial Relations Division
Subject: RE: RE: RE: RE: Request for Relationship Policy Revision

> The Primordial Relations Division has been in a very *delicate* state since Caras the Primordial and Govudas the Primordial broke up. I don't want our Guild to be perceived as taking sides in this matter.

cc: Mage Pauline, Prime Ascended, Guild Board

To: Mage Shassar, Ascended, Primordial Relations
From: Mage Vestravel, Director, Assignments
Subject: RE: RE: RE: RE: RE: Request for Relationship Policy Revision

> Do you *truly* want to say no to a Primordial?

271

To: Mage Vestravel, Director, Assignments
From: Mage Shassar, Ascended, Primordial Relations
Subject: RE: RE: RE: RE: RE: RE: Request for Relationship Policy
Revision

> I'm not saying no to Caras. I'm saying no to Devren. They can't
> disrupt our client relationships like this.

To: Mage Shassar, Ascended, Primordial Relations
From: Mage Vestravel, Director, Assignments
Subject: RE: RE: RE: RE: RE: RE: RE: Request for Relationship
Policy Revision

> I feel tremors in the dimensional grid. Please tell me you've cast
> Protection on the memo server?

To: Mage Vestravel, Director, Assignments
From: Mage Shassar, Ascended, Primordial Relations
Subject: RE: RE: RE: RE: RE: RE: RE: RE: Request for
Relationship Policy Revision

> Why would I need to cast Protection on the server? Caras isn't a
> technology buff.

To: Mage Shassar, Ascended, Primordial Relations

From: Mage Vestravel, Director, Assignments
Subject: Are you NEW?

> She's the Primordial of *Striving*. You're striving to change a
> policy. If you don't cover it end to end with spells, she'll feel it.
> Squash this before you get all of us killed.

To: Mage Vestravel, Director, Assignments
From: Mage Shassar, Ascended, Primordial Relations
Subject: RE: Are you NEW?

> You're overreaching. Primordials are above your pay grade; let
> me handle it.

To: Guild Administration
From: Mage Quska, Director, Records
Subject: Client visit

> Someone please come to the Guild kitchen immediately? Caras
> the Primordial showed up during our team meeting. She's
> demanding to know who's responsible for policy. The scribes
> are…quite upset.

To: Guild Administration
From: Mage Vestravel, Director, Assignments
Subject: RE: Client visit

I'm sorry, Mage Quska. Please advise the scribes to retreat to the Room of Sanctuary for now. Engaging with Caras the Primordial is strictly Mage Shassar's division.

To: Mage Vestravel, Director, Assignments
From: Mage Shassar, Ascended, Primordial Relations
Subject: RE: RE: Client visit

Once I've spoken to Caras and informed her Devren cannot engage in a romance with her, you and I will have words.

To: Guild Administration
From: Mage Shassar, Ascended, Primordial Relations
Subject: RE: RE: Client visit

I'm on my way. Please ask Caras to stick to her humanoid form, per our agreements.

To: Guild Administration
From: Mage Shassar, Ascended, Primordial Relations
Subject: OPEN THE DOOR

WHY DID YOU LOCK ME OUT OF THE ROOM OF SANCTUARY

To: Guild Administration
From: Mage Shassar, Ascended, Primordial Relations Division
Subject: RE: OPEN THE DOOR

please let me in oh gods she has so many tentacles

To: Guild Administration
From: Mage Vestravel, Director, Assignments
Subject: All is Well

I have promised Caras the Primordial we will not interfere. It is safe to come out.

To: Guild Administration
From: Mage Pauline, Prime, Guild Board
Subject: Announcing New Ascension and Reminder of Policy Procedure

I am thrilled to announce the ascension of Mage Vestravel! Their deft defusing of the delicate situation earlier this week has earned them one of the highest positions in the Guild. Please offer them your congratulations when you get a chance.

I would also like to remind everyone that *any* requests for changes in Guild policy can only be raised while in attendance at the Board meeting in Sanctuary, and discussion kept to that forum, per our bylaws. Our policies keep us safe. Thank you in advance for your compliance.

For Love of Magic,
Mage Pauline

cc: Mage Vestravel, Ascended, Primordial Relations

Risa Wolf is a water elemental disguised as an ink-stained lycanthrope. (Don't tell their spouse or their dogs; the disguise is working.) They believe the best things in life are those belly laughs that leave one in happy tears. Visit them at killerpuppytails.com or on BlueSky at @risawolf.bsky.social.

72

SHADOWS OF THE UNINVITED

JASON M. HARDY

The thrill and the terror of being someplace you're not supposed to be are the same.

The white rock glowed through the leafy woods. Brighter than the moon. No torches had been lit near it—they would have had no effect. The rock pulled the full attention of every gathered person.

None of them glanced in Sokanon's direction. She could have strolled upright through the woods and remained unnoticed. But it felt better to sneak from tree to tree.

The rock's glow was different from a fire. Steadier, whiter. It washed out other colors and was difficult to look at directly, but most of the gathered hundred had their heads bowed. They focused on the rocks in front of them, which took in some of the larger rock's light, becoming brighter and brighter with each hour, each day of the gathering.

After the first nightfall, when the rock's power started flowing, Sokanon didn't understand why anyone tried to keep interlopers like her away. The event was what she expected, the mother stone giving power to its children. There were no secret spells cast, no arcane gestures made to unlock hidden powers. Just quiet reverence in the face of the ongoing gift. Her people were there. Makwa, her husband. Numees, a wife of her husband (and a later wife at that). How did they deserve to see this, and she did not? If their presence was valid, hers had to be also.

But as the night wore on, Sokanon started to feel uncomfortable. Bare feet shifting on hard tree roots. Nothing changed in front of her, but she felt the growing reverence and gratitude from the gathered people. Their hearts made the space sacred. Which made her an intruder on that sacred space. Whether she thought she belonged or not, she had not been invited.

Her heart dropped. The realization was swift—she had to leave. It would be a difficult trip home, but any pain would be better than being caught here. She imagined how Makwa would look at her if he saw her here. She imagined the crease in his brow, the tightness in his jaw. Heat leaving his eyes. She couldn't bear it, even in her imagination.

She moved back, away from the river and the rock. She wasn't light enough on her feet to keep from snapping leaves and twigs, but the burble of the river and the hum of the rock kept her noise from being noticeable. As the gathering and the rock disappeared behind her, she picked up her pace, ready to break into a run to her horse to start the five-day ride home.

Then she slowed. Stopped. Dropped to a crouch.

Things were suddenly very wrong.

There were two men in the woods. Pale skin, dressed in light woven cloth. Eyes narrow and focused ahead. Less hidden than they thought they were. Almost within sight of the mother stone.

They should not be here. Even more than her. But here they were, dozens of steps from seeing the gathering and the stone.

She had to do something. She wanted to run and warn the others, but she was an interloper, too. A handful of people there knew her. Most did not. Could she expect any better treatment from them than these two men would receive?

Still—she could not let them get within sight of the stone.

This was not her specialty. If she had any real talent, she would be in the crowd with Makwa and Numees. She knew the basics of half a dozen spells that other people could cast that would take care of the problem. She didn't have the ability to use any of them. But no one who had that ability was with her this moment.

She could scream and run. That would alert someone who would come looking. It would also alert the pale men, who might flee, only to come back when she couldn't stop them. She could attack them, and likely be severely beaten or worse for her effort. She wasn't a fighter. Definitely not ready to take on two men. She could make a noise behind them, try to distract them, but what would that do?

She flanked them, ideas running through her head, none of them good. She drew more behind them, and they moved closer to the stone. They had to know it was here. Or something like it. They had heard stories, and they were looking for the reality behind them. They already had an idea of what they might find. How much different would it be if they actually saw it? What would change? Maybe she could just let them go.

But she knew it would be different. That's why they pressed ahead. So they would *know*, and that knowledge would then spread. The most sacred spot in the world, seen by interlopers driven by nothing more than what they wanted.

Which made the solution clear.

Sokanon turned around. She moved as quickly back toward the river as she had away from it. She got ahead of the pale men, then moved faster. She knew how much distance from them she needed. By the time she approached the stone, she was running. Her splashes through the river could not be missed.

Heads turned, eyes glared. Their anger was well and truly earned. Some hands were raised toward her. Others stopped their approaching blows. Sokanon didn't slow. She knew where Makwa was, and she ran to him.

He was off to the left, so he wasn't entirely backlit by the rock. She could see one side of his face quite well. She saw the confusion as he wondered at this disturbance. Then the disappointment and the anger as he saw her approach and understood what he was seeing.

She hated to see what was in his face, but she walked to it anyway. She would endure the pain and the shame of her intrusion—the stakes had moved beyond her.

JASON M. HARDY IS A WRITER, game developer, and collector of mummies who used to be animated but now are just tired. He believes the best thing in life is naps for mummies who need them. Jason lives in Chicago with his wife, son, and daughter. Visit him online: https://www.facebook.com/jasonmhardywriter/

73

THE STAFF ON MY BACK
CLAIRE MCNERNEY

On the last day of my internship, Head Designer Norah took me to the Birchwood groves. "Pick out a branch," she told me, "It'll be yours."

I wandered the rows of trees for fifteen minutes, Norah breathing heavily at my shoulder, until I finally picked out a low-hanging branch, five feet long and tapered. I reached for my knife, but Norah handed me hers.

"Are you sure?" Her knife gleamed with magic, its sharpness the result of a spell that must have used up an entire mid-level staff—months of work even for a talented artisan like her.

"It's the least I can do."

The knife sliced through the branch like butter, but as I carried it out of the grove, Norah remained silent. It wasn't until I was halfway home that I realized she hadn't offered me a job.

SHE NEVER DID. The Carver's Guild increased their productivity tenfold in the next six months—the wizards were happy about it—but it was without my employment. Instead, I sat in my mother's kitchen and carved my own staff out of the pity branch. When it was finished, I would be able to sell it to a wizard, but it wasn't Guild verified. I wouldn't get more than a few dozen silver coins. Nothing worth my time and effort, my precise carvings imbuing the very wood itself with magical potential energy. But I didn't have any other skills. I continued it anyway.

Mother was a tavernkeeper, and every time a wizard came in, she would beg me to show them my staff.

"You know, some wizards are hiring their own teams of carvers," she said, "I hear that no one important even cares about the guild anymore."

I sighed, setting my knife down. "What wizard would want me? Six months and I haven't even finished one staff."

"You're working hard, sweetheart. I'm very proud of you." She ladled stew into lovely wooden bowls, carved by my grandfather in his retirement. He had been a guild member. Why wasn't I good enough?

"Take the trash out when you need a break," my mother said, and I did, potato peels splitting onto my worn out shoes.

MY FRIEND LENI was a wizard in training. But she refused to use staffs. "I know it's traditional, but it's such a waste. Years of your time into something I can use up in minutes. I'll stick to potions, thank you very much."

"But I'd want you to use it," I told her, "We make staffs so that they can be used."

"Treasure your art. Keep it for yourself. You can appreciate things without selling them."

"Easy for you to say. Your Wizard's Tower is almost built." When Leni's wizardry powers were strong enough, her Wizard's Tower would pop into existence. There, she had a place to live and work and make magic and solve everyone's problems like the good wizard she was. But her advice didn't seem to solve mine.

I kept working on my staff. The base design was complete, but I added more and more intricate details. What else was I to do? If I called it finished, I had nothing to move on to—no more access to branches with the perfect hardness for carving. This was my last staff, my first staff, my only chance at a staff outside of what little I'd done at my Guild internship. I dulled and sharpened my knife, stopping only for meals and rest. But I wasn't satisfied.

As I carved, the staff whittled away, more and more fragile. But in its hollow lightness, I felt a great magical weight. A voice in the back of my mind told me this was the best thing I would ever do. Another told me it was pointless.

Eventually, fed up with my mother's encouragement and Leni's humble bragging, I took to the road. I traveled over mountains and across wide plains in every direction of the compass. For all these years, my staff remained, wrapped in cloth, on my back, a useless thing I carried with me to work on by the light of campfires and inn hearths. A reminder of the life I could have had: a career in the guild, an enchanted knife, a home of my own design.

I was in a forest, far north of my home, when a band of robbers fell upon me. I hadn't seen them coming, they attacked so quickly. I stumbled on my feet—my back slammed to the ground. My staff was beneath me. I felt it on the ridges of my spine. It was not broken, not yet. I maneuvered it fully underneath me, so that no matter how hard the robbers tore at my robes, they could not see it. They stole my bag, my knife, my map. The smallest of them kicked at my legs out of pure cruelty. But none of them managed to take my staff.

When they were gone, I was so bruised it took me an hour to get back on my feet. My knees ached, my left ankle was twisted. I kept trying to hold the staff away from the ground, to keep it pristine. But I couldn't stop stumbling. Eventually, I let the base of my staff, my life's work, touch the dirt. It bored into the earth, a pillar of stability. I leaned on it, and felt horrified and relieved at the same time to feel the strength of it holding my weight. With its help, I made my way back to a nearby town.

Now my back is bent, my arms are weak, my legs tremble without the accostment of any robber. I travel homeward, no longer ashamed of what the Guild might think of me. At the edge of town, where the forest meets the buildings, I grip my staff tightly in my hand and let it lead me, delicate and strong, toward whatever the day is to bring.

CLAIRE MCNERNEY IS A THEATRE STUDENT, creator, and collector of beautiful postcards. She believes the best thing in life is a good meal shared with friends. Claire lives in California with their roommates and a drawer full of tea. Visit her online: https://linktr.ee/clairemcnerney or @claire_mcnerney on Twitter.

74

FROM TANGO TO GRAVE
CHRISTINA DICKINSON

My name is Brent Sanders. At 5'4" and a whopping hundred and eight pounds, I'm hardly the poster boy for intimidation. But I've got a talent. I can talk to spirits. Started after an incident involving a rogue lightning strike during a college trip to an ancient ruin. There may also have been chanting and some guys in robes. Doesn't matter.

Sometimes, people want to speak with loved ones that have shoved off their fleshy bits, and sometimes people want to get rid of unwanted guests. Either way, they'll pay a pretty penny for my services which, I assure you, are on the up and up.

My phone rang. In my line of work, you get some odd calls, but this one piqued my interest almost immediately.

"Hello, darling. My name is Francesca Kozlov, and I own the Two to Tango Dance Studio. We've got a bit of a ghost issue, and I need him out before the next session."

"Are you familiar with my rates?"

"Whatever you ask is fine. I want him out. He's a menace." The longer Francesca talked, the more nasal she sounded. I couldn't argue with her fiscal sense, however.

"I'll be there in twenty minutes," I assured her before jabbing the big red hang-up button.

I pulled up to the studio only fifteen minutes later but, as soon as I walked in the door, I was greeted with a very nasal, "You're late!"

"I assure you, Ms. Kozlov," I said, in my best I'm-a-professional manner, "I am right on time."

"I say you're late! It's coming out of your pay!"

I fixed her with my very best you're-not-being-professional stare and turned pointedly toward the door. Francesca grabbed my arm and pulled me back, assuring me that her money was good and she wouldn't threaten to deduct again.

"So what seems to be the trouble?" I asked.

"Two weeks ago, one of my clients died during a tragic tapping accident…"

"I'm sorry," I interrupted. "A tapping accident?"

"Yes, a tapping accident. It was very tragic. It happens."

"Alright. A tapping accident. And he's just sticking around, is he?"

"Tapping around!" Francesca ran a hand through her messy, blonde hair. Her lipstick had suffered through several applications, and she was quite tall. Maybe 5'11" without the heels. She was a great start to my Monday, alright. "Tap tap tap! All through my other lessons. People cannot waltz, cannot cha-cha, cannot salsa to the tippity-tappity of his damned shoes."

"And you want him to leave. That's it?"

"Yes! Exorcize him! Stuff him in a suitcase! Do whatever it is that you do. My next appointment is in a half hour."

Stifling a sigh, I left her at the ultra-polished front desk and let myself into the main dance hall. A thin strip of worn carpet lined one side of the room, while the wall beside it was honeycombed with shoe cubbies. The rest of the floor was lined with that awful parquet popular with the non-professional dance set. Someone, or something, with no timing was tapping a terrible staccato across the parquet.

"Hello?" I said.

"Hi!" a bright and cheery voice greeted me. Slowly, the

being belonging to the bright and cheery voice faded into sight. He was long and lanky, with the kind of face that pleads with you to like him even if he tries too hard. Maybe in his late thirties, he had probably started taking dance lessons as a way to meet people, unaware that the only people he would meet while tap-dancing would be just as socially awkward.

"My name's Brent Sanders. What's yours?"

"Cary Mathews." He tried to frown, but his face wasn't really built for it.

"Well, Cary, are you aware that you're dead?" It was my standard opening. You'd be surprised how many people stick around after they die just because no one has bothered to tell them about it.

"Yeah," Cary said. He looked a little sheepish, the way people do when they know they're doing something wrong, but aren't ready to stop. "I know. I just...didn't have anywhere to go."

"Atheist?"

"No, no...I'm...I was...Catholic. Pretty devout. Not that I went to mass every Sunday, but I prayed regular. Went to confession. But when I died, no one came and I didn't see any lights. So, I just...stayed. Nowhere else to go, you know?"

I nodded. This happened occasionally, too. Just like any other management, sometimes the paperwork got misplaced. The only thing for the spirit to do was wait it out until someone came for them. My last delayed ghost had actual valkyries come for her. No lie. "Well, you can't stay here. Ms. Kozlov has classes to teach and you're causing some distraction. I've got room in my office and there's a TV. Not a bad way to pass the time until someone collects you."

Cary Mathews thought about it. "Video games?"

"All the latest systems," I assured him.

Another thoughtful pause. "You're sure someone will come?"

"It would be weird if they didn't. Haven't seen it happen yet."

With a small shrug, Cary nodded and we headed toward the front. He stopped at the shoe cubbies and made motions like he was changing shoes, though I couldn't actually see his feet. Some ghosts forget they ever had feet after they've been dead long enough. I was just relieved the tapping stopped when he was done.

After a few words with Francesca, I verified that she'd transferred my fee, loaded the ghost of Cary Mathews into my truck, and headed back toward my office. Just another day.

Damn, I love my job.

CHRISTINA DICKINSON IS AN AUTHOR, game master, and a collector of shiny math rocks. She believes the best things in life are friends, travel, gaming, and tacos. Christina lives in Texas with her wonderful husband, Terence, and their cats, Dagger and Glyph. Visit her online: christinadickinsonwrites.com

75

A MIRROR IS WHAT YOU MAKE OF IT

ELIZABETH WALKER

Her aunt's house was as bad as Kathleen had feared it would be. A hoarder's den with mountains of junk, most of it damp with mildew. The whole morning, Kathleen had sorted boxes of her old childhood books. They were water damaged, their pages crumpled and sticking together. Everything in her late aunt's house so far had been damaged like that, neglected. But Kathleen had to keep going through it all. There was no one left.

The dreariness of the task settled on her, coated her as thickly as the dust that danced in the air. How much pain and sadness was wrapped up in all these old clothes, the musty books. It was like a film of dirt she would never be able to shower off.

As she tried to shift the pile, Kathleen's spine protested, and she had to pause to stretch in case her back decided to go out. In that moment, Kathleen considered leaving, abandoning this project. If she were brave, she might have considered burning the stinking place down instead, rolling the dice that no one would find out or care. But she didn't have that kind of bravado, and there was still a remote chance she could salvage the house enough to sell and end up with some kind of inheritance from her aunt besides this drudgery and pain.

Abandoning the books for now, she climbed the stairs to the attic, wincing as her bad knee protested. The attic felt strange as soon as she stepped inside. The room had the same moldering piles of junk as the rest of the house, but the attic was warmer, and the air smelled fresher somehow, crisp. Birdsong piped in from outside and—

No. Not *outside*. Kathleen frowned and followed the sound. She'd expected a bird's nest in the rafters, but the birdsong seemed to be coming from under a heavy sheet draped over what looked like a standing mirror.

The hair on her arms stood on end as she dragged the sheet off. She stared into the mirror. Her breath caught somewhere in her ribcage with a painful gasp.

It wasn't a mirror. Couldn't be, because she stared right at it and didn't see herself reflected. Instead, a warm summer day shone out at her. Green trees waving in a gentle breeze. Blue skies and some strange, technicolor flowers she'd never seen before that were nearly as tall as she was. The image in the mirror was utterly picturesque and completely foreign.

Her boots were still crusted with snow after her hardware store run, and it was freezing in the house. Had been all day. That meant the mirror in front of her wasn't a mirror, couldn't be.

Hand shaking, she reached toward the glass. Heat bathed her palm and, when she reached to touch the mirror, her hand passed right through the frame where the glass should be. Birdsong filled her ears again, and the mirror seemed to pull on her, like someone tugging her wrist. *Come along. We need you*, the air whispered.

A portal. She made her hand into a fist and jerked back, stumbling as she did. Her guts clenched with sudden, shivering rage. "How dare you? How...*how fucking dare you?*"

She turned from the mirror, hugging herself. The dusty

contents of the attic, the whole house, seemed to press on her, echoing with the memories of her childhood here. How lonely she'd been growing up with only her elderly aunt. No friends. Only books. Only dreams.

And now the mirror was here. The *only* thing she'd ever wanted as a child: a way out.

But this thing had shown up when it was *too late*. When she was old and tired. She gripped the gilt edge of the mirror, the scrollwork digging into her palm. "I used to beg and pray, weeping for something to come and take me away. Anywhere. Narnia. Wonderland. Oz. Hell, I used to wish I'd get teleported to Tatooine as a teenager. And you come *now*?"

She was the wrong side of middle-aged. She had bad feet and bum knees, tendonitis in her wrist. What good would she be on a quest now? How would she save a kingdom when she could barely walk around the block? Or stop an evil witch? Just handwriting a grocery list was agony—how could she hold a sword?

Tears stung her eyes, but she forced herself to turn and look at the mirror, look at the world waiting invitingly on the other side like an outstretched hand. Who knew what she might find there? What might happen?

She scrubbed at her face, and her hands came away gray with dust and cobwebs. And here? Now? What was waiting for her? Moth eaten old clothes. Water damaged books. The contents of a hoarder's house and a lifetime of unhappy memories to sort through.

She stepped toward the mirror, stretching her hand out again.

Maybe this mirror, its world, didn't need someone young and idealistic to save it. Maybe the Summerland on the other side needed someone with bad feet and a bum wrist. Maybe there could still be adventures after you grew up.

She wet her lips. "Maybe I'll never forgive myself if I don't try." She sucked in a deep breath and stepped through the mirror.

ELIZABETH WALKER IS an author and collector of way too many Halloween decorations (but are there ever really enough?). She believes the best thing in life is a cozy blanket and a good book on a cold day. Elizabeth lives in Southern California with her husband, kids, and a grumpy elderly cat.

76

LOVECRAFT VERSUS THE EVIL OATMEAL OF THE APOCALYPSE

LENA NG

A calamitous rumbling has pervaded my sleep. What stomach-gurgling, peckish, breakfast-consuming omen of the nether realms has tainted my dreams. Such grumblings sparked nightmarish visions of great ghoulish oatmeal monsters, gelatinous blobbules from the other dimensions, stalking me in my sleep. Body shivering and heaving until—GLURP—the sounds of large stomach rumblings quaked me from my restless slumber.

As I arose from my bed, I noticed a disconcerting conformation of the stars. While others may read omens in the chin-scratching of the family doctor, the tax forms of confusion, or the head-shaking of manager/slave-driver, I can read warnings in the hide-and-seek of the stars, in the paso doble of the planets, in the skipping of the suns.

You may think me mad. I, Dina von Lovecraft, secret descendant lovechild, generations removed, of the horrible horror writer HP Lovecraft and Edwina Allen Poe, Edgar's long-hidden sister who was confined to the attic. I, who instead of basking in the Instagram-glory as a social media star, despite my Kardashian-sized presence, decided *not* to lead the champagne-chugging, licentious, CBD-addicted life of a creative. Rather, I had taken my father's pragmatic advice and became a pharmacist. I, whose eyes water under the vapours of poisonous pills and whose head spins under the weight of dose-calculating mathematics, could not envisage such a ghastly tale.

This pharmacist especially enjoys her sleep, not to be disturbed by some abominable, stomach-churning sounds emanating from her abdomen. I emerged from my millennial-pink room in my foxy robe, and having made haste to the kitchen pantry, squinted my eyes into the cabinet darkness.

What evil doth I see, but five boxes of cereal staring back at me. Five boxes of sickly seducers, outfitted with tigers named Tony, auspicious charms, chocolate vampires, crunchy captains, and loops of fruit daring me to skyrocket my blood sugar.

I slammed the cabinet door shut, and from within the depths of the drawers, pulled forth the hallowed, wholesome oatmeal. From within the cabinets, the cereal boxes rattled their displeasure, bursting open the cabinet doors before me.

I would not take such insolence from breakfast cereal, these wicked, sugar-laden scoundrels from the dress-tightening dimensions. I had battled such creatures before, with New Year's resolutions and gritted willpower, with turned-up nose at the grocery store. But now, under the perplexing squinting of the stars, they have congregated before me.

With muttering and growling, rattling and howling, the cereal boxes chanted a fiber-filled spell. The oatmeal shook within my bowl. It grew and shrank, and grew and shrank again, until it burst forth from the bowl, dropped onto the linoleum, and with the swiftness of an exploding mold, transformed into a massive, oatmeal monster. It emitted a horrible roar.

With a twirl of my robe, I hailed my weapon: my silver spoon, my sturdy sister-in-arms, which had fought with me valiantly in the infamous War on the Purple Pudding which had escaped from the back of the fridge. I lunged and scooped, plunged and looped, but the oatmeal monster lobbed rice cakes and granola bars, making a mess of the pantry. I must halt this horror before it unleashed itself upon the world, as foretold in the *Book of the Bizarre* as the advent of the oatpocalypse.

Finally, from the back of the shelf, I grabbed my spell book which I had stolen from the kitchen of the nether-dimensional realms. The *Demon Master's Cookerology*, the infernal book of frightful feasts which would give me mastery of the kitchen's domain. I scattered the necessary ingredients: a sprinkling of sacred cinnamon, a spoonful of holy honey, a pinch of sorcerer's salt. The blessed blueberries swirled before me, launching themselves into the lumpy form. I screeched the binding words and finished with a thrust of sanctified sugar.

The rampaging came to a sudden halt. The cereal boxes stared in silence. Slowly, the oatmeal monster dropped down upon bended knee. With the sanctified sugar adding sweetness to its disposition, it stretched out its hand and asked, "Dina, will you marry me?"

LENA NG IS NOT a figment of your imagination, though she pinches herself to make sure. She believes the best things in life are tea, books, and an idea for an ending. Lena lives in Toronto, Canada as a digital hermit.

77

THE SCALE BENEATH HER SKIN
DEVAN BARLOW

The water receded too quickly for the fish's fins to chase. The woman on the shore knelt, thinking here was a meal. She wished meals were more dependable.

Until she looked at the fish's eyes, and the fish said, *Please. Give me back to the sea.*

Fish didn't speak. She knew this. If they did, surely their conversations were reserved for other fish. Possibly turtles, or lobsters. Not a hungry woman standing on the sand attempting to convince herself to stop listening to a fish.

"Why?" she asked, despite herself.

Because I need your help. And I can help you.

The fish twitched, and a faint pain flared in the woman's hand. Not painful enough that she remembered it later. She told herself she couldn't have stopped the fish returning to the ocean. Fortune soon sent her stumbling upon a collection of clams in a cove nearby, their briny flesh providing a meal.

After eating she watched the ocean as the sun set, and wished for so much more.

Her turbulent thoughts kept her from noticing the scrape across her hand. She certainly didn't think to check for a single small fish scale lodged within her flesh, before she slipped into dreams.

THE FISH UNDERSTOOD DREAMS. She had dreamed in the time when she was not a fish, but a human. One perched in a window of the ornate towers whose shadows overlooked this part of the coast, spires seeming to pierce the very sun and moon. As she hadn't been a fish for very long yet, things like not getting stuck on the shore were still difficult for her. It had almost all been over. But the kindness of that woman on the shore had saved her, and in return the fish hoped to help the woman. The fish knew things, no longer useful to herself, that she could pass on.

WHEN THE WOMAN slept that night, her dream was curious, like a reflection in an icicle. Barely-sensible words whispered to her, emanating from the scale beneath her skin.

When she woke, she knew a powerful secret.

After thinking for a time, she went to the people whose secret it was, and shared her knowledge. Soon, she found herself living in a fine house in the town.

Each night brought more dreams, and further knowledge, carried to her like secret-keeping bottles upon the waves. Ambition radiated from the sharp edges of the scale beneath her skin, entwining with her own longing for more. A house in the town was soon followed by invitations to the soaring towers, her dreams forever drawing closer...

MANY WHISPERED of the woman who'd newly become a favorite at court. No one was certain how or when such wealth and ornament and adoration had adhered to her like barnacles upon a ship.

Sometimes, her movements or intonations reminded others of a person no longer there, whose disappearance was still unexplained. As if remnants of their grieving dreams drifted behind this newcomer. Many guessed, but few fathomed it was in fact a kindness that had brought this woman to the towers of the court.

AFTER SO MANY years staring at the waves from a tower window, the fish had achieved her dream. To swim, to take on different shapes as she traversed the water, to learn those things she would never learn on land. But every dream had complications. The fish was desperate to pass on a particular message, but she couldn't do it herself.

THE WOMAN LISTENED to her dreams, as the scale beneath her skin had only ever helped her. When a dream instead asked her for help, she continued listening. The dream begged her to seek the inhabitant of a particular tower. A princess.

The woman's newfound connections helped her gain an audience, though the princess merely sat at the window, as she had for so long, yearning to espy some clue to explain her sister's disappearance.

The woman told the story her dream wished conveyed. A story of a longing for the sea, and strenuous experiments, and finally the glorious result. The princess' sister becoming a creature of the ocean, and swimming as she'd always wished to. The princess' sadness didn't cease. For grief isn't so simply discarded. But to know her sister was happy, even if she was gone, altered the sting.

THE FISH SWAM, continuing to investigate the numerous mysteries that could only be solved below the waves. Sometimes, in whatever form was currently hers, she came close enough to be seen from the tower's window. Sometimes, her sister was there waiting to glimpse her. There was a constant uncertainty on both sides. For the fish couldn't tell if anyone sat at the window, and the princess couldn't tell if the creature she saw was her sister.

Still, it helped both of their hearts.

THE WOMAN now resided in her own tower. Sometimes, during the sharp moments of a sunrise, she considered a version of events where she'd failed. Where she'd fallen from one of these towers, or reached for too much, or trusted unwisely. Where she was returned to her former lonely patch of shore, hunger aching as loud as the tide. She'd learned to ignore this. For she had too much else to be doing. She preferred to gaze at the spaces of the sky unoccupied by the sun and moon, and wonder, dreaming of more.

DEVAN BARLOW IS A WRITER, tea drinker, and collector of obscure book recommendations. She believes the best thing in life is a happy dog. Devan lives in Minnesota, USA with her husband and many books. Visit her online: devanbarlow.com or @Devan_Barlow on Twitter.

78

THE LAST ONE
CLAY VERMULM

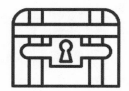

Alric gazed blankly at the little puddle of ale coalescing into the notches and nicks of the tavern table. The public house was a teeming bustle of babbling bodies, clinking glassware, clattering cutlery. Usually, Alric liked it here, but tonight most of the men and ladies were from the neighboring counties, all come to celebrate the great victory of Countess Gerard's Dragonshield Order, of which, only two still survived. Across the table, Alric could feel his brother-in-arms impatient stare, but he refused to engage.

Finally, Barin broke the silence between them with a sigh. "You did your duty, we both did," he said gruffly.

"Duty," Alric spat.

"Gods below, now you get a bloody conscience? We've slain three dragons together and I don't know how many other creatures."

"All those were trying to kill us back."

"So...were...the dragons." Barin spoke slow, as if explaining to a child.

Alric bristled. "Yeah, those two dragons back in Spring. I've made my peace with that."

"You don't seem at peace. You seem like you wanna be

300

dead. Wish you'd gone out banner flying in the flames like Locke and Sorely?"

Alric shrugged. "You could have done this morning's work without me. Any coward with a heavy rock could have."

Barin shook his head. "Even young, they're dangerous. Besides, t'was dead before it woke from sleep. That's how I'd like to go."

"I thought you wanted to go in pitched battle with a wench for a warhorse."

"I was drunk when I said that."

"You're drunk when you say everything."

"He has you there, Barin," said Rosie the barmaid as she approached their table, her brilliant white smile glinting rakishly from lush, red lips. She held a pitcher of ale in her hand to which Barin nodded eagerly.

As she went to pour, he held his cup away so she had to lean across him to fill it. She obliged with a good-natured giggle that even managed to reach her eyes. Barin pulled the girl onto his lap.

"Ser, I have many customers to serve," she said, smoothly slipping his grasp.

"My lady, you must understand." He flashed her a smile that might have been handsome, if not for the burn scar spanning half his face. "My quest is not complete until I've kissed the fairest lass in Barrow."

"Try the countess, I hear she owes you quite a reward."

"That's how I'm tipping so well tonight. Besides, she prefers the proper types." Barin sighed, dramatically.

Rosie glanced at Alric, a slight blush in her cheeks.

"Come now, Rosie, I thought you weren't like all the rest," Barin said.

"He's a handsome man." Rosie shrugged.

"And I'm not?"

"You're...very charming."

The big man gave a hearty laugh.

Rosie winked and turned to go again, but before she could make her escape, Alric looked up, revealing the sharp, hawklike angles of his face and elegantly curving eyes which drank in the orange light of the tavern like a deep canyon pool.

"Rosie, would you mind bringing me a pitcher of this stuff?" Alric placed a silver on the table.

She favored him with a sad smile. "Is there anything I can do to cheer you up, dear? You look like someone smothered your puppy."

"This bastard's a lost cause," Barin cut in. "He looks like a bloody story book hero, he's got beautiful women tripping out of their gowns, and now he's rich. If all that won't wipe the glumness from a man's countenance, what will?"

Rosie laid a reassuring hand upon Alric's shoulder.

He took a deep swig of his drink and looked at her, his face a mask of anguish. "Have anything stronger?"

"I'll get you the strongest we got."

"Make that two," Barin said. "If you're too busy to hang about, I'll be stuck talking to the top of this one's head."

"Two pitchers. Back in a bit, lads." With that, she bustled off to run her game with equal grace and charm at every table in the establishment. The woman knew her business.

"Gods I'd love to take a tumble with her."

"You mentioned that."

Barin sighed once more before crossing the table to sit next to his friend. He threw a beefy arm around the thinner man's shoulders. Alric stiffened, but didn't pull away. "You're my brother, but you're depressing me on a night dedicated to our accomplishments. Think of it as a celebration of those other dead dragons—the ones that killed our friends. You and me are the only Dragonshields left. Remember *that*."

"I do remember. Just wish I could forget this morning."

"Why even come out tonight mate?"

He looked into Barin's eyes, there was true concern there—empathy. Just as Alric started to answer…

Across the tavern, a hush spread upon the bell-like ringing of fork tapping wine glass until it stretched to the corner where the last two Dragonshields were discreetly seated. Rosie appeared between the two knights, leaning in and placing their pitchers before them with a smile.

"These are on the Duke of Zyla's son. I believe he's about to toast you." Rosie winked at Alric. He forced his anger down and gave her a thin smile.

"That's right kind of you, Rosie." Barin grinned. Rosie planted a peck on his cheek and stood with them as Ventris, heir to the Duchy of Zyla stood on his finely filigreed shoes. The silk of his doublet flourished in flashy colors with the gesticulations of his pompous toast.

"To the death of the last dragon! To the brave knights who made this glorious day possible!"

Barin stood proudly, raising his mug along with the rest of the tavern as everyone cheered. Alric rose as well, taking his full pitcher, he silently walked out the tavern's rear entrance, his dark silhouette obscuring the dragon-fire-orange glow of summer twilight before the door slammed shut.

CLAY VERMULM IS AN AUTHOR, climber, and professional cat-dad from the Pacific Northwest. Aside from good stories, his favorite things in life are board games, craft beer, and the splendors of the natural world. Learn more about him at clayvermulmfiction.com (preferably, by signing up for his newsletter).

79

HOME INVASION

CHRISTOPHER DEGNI

"**Y**ou're a what?" I ask.

My wife Trixie blushes. "A pixie."

"Trixie the pixie? Seriously?"

She shrugs.

"And this was the best time to tell me?"

We're sitting on the roof of our house, watching armies of fairies and goblins do battle in our backyard. Our house is the goblins' headquarters; the fairies flock around the ornamental fountain in the yard. This is not how I imagined things going when we bought the place a few weeks back.

You might think it would be cool to learn every manner of mythical creature is real, but it's significantly less cool when the fairies snarf your flowers, the goblins build a fortifying wall in your basement, and the unicorns deposit multi-colored turds all over your lawn.

"Are you with the fairies or the goblins?"

"Neither," she says. "This plot was originally my domain. I'm hoping they take care of each other."

So *that's* what she meant about getting back to roots. And why she wanted this house so badly. She must have been sowing discord between the fairies and goblins from the moment we moved in.

"And that?" I point to the mini-dragon flying across the sun's face. It's been circling for the past twenty minutes.

"Her," Trixie corrects me. "Alanaraxahasana. She owes me a favor."

"Hey neighbor!" says Todd from next door, trimming his unruly hedges. "Redoing the roof?"

"Something like that." Figures Todd would choose today to be out. Not what we need right now. I ask Trixie, "Why can't Todd hear the din in our yard? Or see Alla— Arala—"

"Lana."

Dragons have nicknames. Who knew? "Why can't he see Lana? She's *right there*."

"Well, Todd didn't drink from the fairy fountain, now did he?"

Two sips, and I'll never live it down. "No," I mumble, even as the fountain's mere mention parches my throat and makes me crave its cool crispness again.

"And if you hadn't, you wouldn't be any the wiser. I'd hoped to get this done without bringing you into it."

"But...I..." I have nothing to say.

The goblins mass in wave after wave against the fairies and drive them back, though the fairies fight fiercely. Trixie watches with wide eyes that perceive so much more on the battlefield than I ever could. She gestures toward Lana and lets out a high-pitched noise.

"Need something?" asks our oh-so-helpful neighbor.

"She's not talking to you, Todd," I call from the roof, and he returns to haphazardly slashing his bushes.

Lana swoops down, blotting out the sun—she wasn't as mini as I thought—and she bathes the backyard in some sort of lavender flame. Magical, judging from the fact that none of the grass or the shed or the fence is on fire. But the creatures...well, they're just gone.

305

The fountain has disappeared too. Probably for the best, that.

"Don't worry," says Trixie.

"Why would I be worried?" I only just witnessed a battle out of some mass market fantasy paperback, culminating with my wife and her dragon ally wiping out two entire armies.

"It's portalfire. They're not dead, they're back on their own turf."

"Oh thank *goodness*." I do kind of feel better, though.

Trixie gives Lana a salute and the dragon banks a turn and soars away.

"It's over," she says. "Let's go." She slides down the roof and skitters down the ladder with a dexterity I'm not sure how I ever missed.

I make the same journey, more carefully. "Why?" I ask. "Why this, why now?"

Trixie blushes. "Pixies get territorial when family is involved. Especially…" She searches for her next words. "Little ones."

"You're…? We're…?" I have nothing to say. Again.

Trixie takes my hand and leads me into our house, which for the first time finally feels like home.

CHRISTOPHER DEGNI IS an Odyssey Writing Workshop graduate, a lapsed mathematician, and a collector of obscure words. He believes the best thing in life is a snuggly bed in winter. Christopher lives in Boston, MA with his (non-pixie) wife. Social media causes him to break out in hives, but you can email him at the.writer.ced(at)gmail.com.

80

EVERY BELOVED MOMENT
MARIE BILODEAU

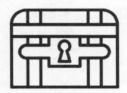

"**Y**our magic will protect us, shielding lifetimes within it, keeping us safe."

Your words are rehearsed, but your eyes betray your emotions, my beloved. I've always loved that about you. I can't believe I won't look into those eyes again.

"When you awaken, please find peace in that knowledge, in the final moments before you escape your shell and return to me."

Before you die, I almost correct you. Always flowery language where a simple statement would suffice. I hold your eyes with mine, an eternity shared in a moment.

The sky above is so dark, the trees husks of stone around us, and, before my resolve weakens, I close my eyes. I cling to the image of yours, even as I float away on my magic, to protect us all.

To protect you, my love.

A WHISPER FLOATING in my dreams: *Good bye, beloved.*

THE STAR SHINES, even though only a moment has passed since the world was bathed in darkness.

I did it, beloved. I protected our people until the darkness passed, generations having grown and died without seeing the Forever Star.

I'm alone. Your absence leaves me empty, the air around me no longer electrified by knowing you're there, waiting for me.

"Your magic has protected us for lifetimes," a voice, not unlike yours, but so different, speaks. "You have kept us safe, and we honor you. You are not alone, child of the Forever Star."

Tears stream down my cheeks. A hand brushes one away, surprising me. A breach of protocol, but its comforting warmth is not unwelcome.

This moment shall pass, too. My magic is gone, leaving me hollow. You're gone, leaving me carved out. Soon, I too will be gone, and on my way back to you, beloved.

THE MOMENT STRETCHES, until the aches of my back, overtake those of my heart. *Why am I not on my way to you, beloved?* Had I not given everything up for the Forever Star? Could I now not know peace in your embrace?

In the distance, I hear children laughing, a sound so foreign that I can't help but smile. Perhaps I'm meant to take a moment to see the world I'd helped protect before grace whisks me away. I open my eyes slowly, tentatively.

And gasp at the beauty around me. Lush trees danse in the breeze, opalescent blooms clinging to them, sunlight licking their edges. The world is so colorful, so vibrant, that I can't breathe for a few moments.

I'd forgotten what the star felt like, beloved.

"Are you alright?" A strange question coming from a high

priestess whose sole duty is to help me peacefully pass into my next life.

I turn my neck her way, it pops and I wince. My back feels better for the movement. She gazes down at me with clear green eyes, open and honest. Kind. They remind me of your eyes, beloved.

I shrug off the feeling of drowning and return her smile. "Would you help me stand?"

As surprised as I am by the request, she nonetheless comes to my side, and helps me up.

The first step is the worst, beloved, as I feel like I'm walking away from you. From the promise I'd made to find you.

Why am I still alive?

WE DRINK coffee silently in a courtyard filled with purple, pink, and yellow flowers of names I do not know. The brew is bitter, and awakens my soul. Begins to fill the hollow left behind by my magic.

We don't speak, the priestess and I. We sit, and watch the world go by, waiting for the next moment. What else can I do, knowing I am to perish soon?

THE STAR SETS in glorious golds and purples, twilight coating the land but not vanishing, the light of the Forever Star glinting in the far horizon. I wish you could see it, beloved. To know the sacrifices had been worth it.

"I have a guest room you're welcomed to," the priestess finally says.

I smile, but shake my head, my neck muscles still sore. I'd slept for centuries, beloved. I wasn't ready to lie down again.

She stays up with me, and we drink coffee in comfortable silence.

Too many moments to count, beloved. Laughing. Weeping in the gardens of loss, where somewhere you sleep. Learning the names of the blooms fed by our lives. How many moments will I spend before meeting you again, beloved?

Our hands touch more frequently now. On purpose. I'm not betraying you. I still love you. But I did not die, beloved, so I must learn to live again. In a world without you.

The moments leading back to you are vibrant, beloved.

I love you. So much.

And I love her, so much.

My heart grows to fill the hollow left behind by dreams forged a lifetime ago.

I love you, beloveds.

Beloved.

"UNTIL PARTING THIS SHELL, and reuniting in the Forever Star," the priest speaks, and you smile, beloved. You, the priestess who'd been at my side since I'd awakened.

"Forever," you say.

You know another awaits me in the Forever Star, too. The one who'd sent me off to sleep. A sleep I should not have known a life beyond. Could you be but a dream? Does it matter?

I smile. "Forever," I answer. When the time comes, whenever the final moment does arrive, I will introduce you two.

My beloveds.

In this life, in my last life, and in the next. Our hearts together for all time, in the light of the Forever Star. Every moment leading me to you, beloveds.

MARIE BILODEAU IS AN AUTHOR, storyteller, and a collector of She-Ra action figures. She believes the best thing in life is sitting by an intentional fire with friends. Marie lives in Ottawa, Canada with her baking person and many cats. Visit her online: www.mariebilodeau.com.

81

THE COIN OF THE REALM
REX BURROWS

On the Day of Founding, the coin of the realm was placed in a vault deep within the Great Keep. The founder of the realm, a man of humble origins but grand vision, knew the coin was far too precious to ever circulate with base currencies. It had cost him a great deal to merely learn of the coin's existence, and he'd sacrificed far more in obtaining it. The coin was no mere symbol or standard of wealth; it instead might be thought of as a loom, a device upon which to weave the very fabric of want and need. The realm's values—monetary and otherwise—could be maintained in perpetuity and never suffer the erosions of fate or the whims of fortune. So long as the coin should endure, so too would the realm.

The coin had certain opinions of its own on these matters, but it kept them to itself.

On the Day of Jubilee, the realm celebrated its ascendance among the ranks of great nations even as it mourned the passing of its founder. In a scant fifty years, the realm had acquired several lesser realms at little cost—at least as measured in the blood and treasure of its own citizens—and extended its influence across the continent.

The Great Keep, once a rather squat and dour affair, now

bristled with towers and turrets and stood as the centerpiece of the realm's newly cosmopolitan capital city. This blossoming of architectural magnificence was only in keeping with the structure's growing prominence as a center of governance and, more importantly, fiduciary matters. The Keep's skyward expansion was mirrored by a vast and ever-expanding warren of crypts and tunnels below. Far underground, at the very lowest level, a hidden and far more secure chamber was constructed for one very particular item.

The coin sat in the dark, waiting.

On the Day of Centennial, the realm stood triumphant. It still demurely referred to itself as a realm, but at this point in its history, the term empire would have been easily justified. All rivals had been brought to heel, and the realm's borders extended from desert to ice and mountain to sea.

Despite its many attainments, the realm found itself troubled. A malaise spread through its populace, and the ruling class was stricken with a clammy, clutching sense of paranoia. Dark whispers rustled through courtyards and taverns alike, and strange ideas took root in the outlands. Beneath the Great Keep, decades of excavation breached layer after layer of geological strata, and the coin of the realm was secreted ever deeper into the bowels of the earth. With each move, it was surrounded with ever more sophisticated fortifications and countermeasures. No expense was thought too great to safeguard the coin of the realm.

The coin observed these developments with mild interest then returned to its slumber.

On the Day of Reckoning, the realm fell. Truth be told, this catastrophe had been some time in the making. Enemies of the realm had held large swaths of its territory for years, and the capital had lain under one siege or another for longer than anyone inside cared to remember.

This long period of dwindling was punctuated, however, by a swift and exclamatory end point—the gates were torn down, the city was sacked, and the royal family was put to death in a single day. In the weeks that followed, no small number of knowledgeable and intrepid souls sought the coin of the realm. All came away empty-handed or, in a few notable cases, without any hands at all. No one could reliably say just how far the stygian, trap-laden labyrinth extended below the city and only the recently deposed ruler—a distant descendent of the founder of the realm—had known the tricks of navigation required to reach the coin. Those secrets now rotted within his severed head, one of many that decorated the walls of the Great Keep.

The coin stirred within its thrice-sealed chamber. Soon.

On the Day of Cataclysm, the streets of the capital stood silent. The people of the realm were no more, and all succeeding inhabitants had long since abandoned the dead city. When the first wave of tremors sent its crumbling monuments crashing to the ground, only birds and beasts were left to flee. The majority of the tunnels below the city collapsed instantly, but the vault of the coin had been built to survive the assaults of man and earth alike. It maintained its integrity admirably, holding firm right up until the moment when the foundations of the city shattered.

Magma boiled up to fill the void. The coin of the realm slipped from its pedestal and disappeared into the glowing flow. It was borne down into the tubes of the underworld, plunging through rocky ducts riddling the continental crust. The coin held its shape for the first few miles of its journey, but heat and pressure will have their way.

Soon enough, its queer alloys softened and began to separate. As the compounds came undone and their elements drifted apart in the lava, something else—something lacking tangible mass but possessing a vaguely amphibian form— wriggled free and swam out to greet the congress of similar creatures gathering around it.

The coin of the realm was thus dissolved, and its occupant returned, with great relief, to its home.

. . .

REX BURROWS IS A WRITER, microbiologist, and collector of far too many books. He believes the best thing in life is figuring out creative storage solutions for all the books. Rex lives in Washington DC with his girlfriend, who thinks the whole book thing is getting out of hand. Visit him on Twitter at @ImprobableRex.

82

QUEEN MEMORA
LIAM HOGAN

When courtiers list the kingdoms of the northern continent, they name four warring nations, their uneasy alliances continually shattered and reforged as each vies against the others. A belligerent land, everyone concludes, before moving on to less disagreeable matters.

They always seem to forget the fifth kingdom, and the Queen who shares its name. I hardly expected my liege to turn his attention there, in the midst of our discussion of Anagonia.

"This *Memora*," King Feralt said, leaning over the map. "How does it stand?"

"Sire?"

"It is so very small, and has a woman for a monarch. Why has it not been gobbled up by its neighbours?"

I stroked my close-cropped beard; a wise advisor can't afford facial hair longer than the King's. "Some say its central position acts as a buffer. That any attempt to seize it would provoke the combined ire of the other three kingdoms."

"Some *say*, indeed. And you? What do you say, Alfranz?"

"I say it has, as your majesty shrewdly divines, lasted too long for that explanation alone. These other kingdoms," I waved my hand over the parchment, weighted at each corner, "chop and change, no dynasty stretching more than half a dozen short-lived kings before conquest or treachery seats a new lineage upon the throne. They change even their names as we change our nightshirts. But Memora persists."

The King grunted. His own status was newly minted and keenly disputed, mainly by his older brother, Cybold. "Find out how she does it," he ordered.

"Sire?"

Feralt smiled. My glib comments had cut too close to the royal bone. "Time to discover what we would do without you."

QUEEN MEMORA herself was waiting as I stepped onto the rocky shore before her mist shrouded castle. In all my time there, I saw no one else, heard no one else.

She asked me why I had come and then, as if I had told her the *real* reason, spoke only to that. "This Kingdom holds memories, Alfranz. Memora, remembers."

"Your majesty?"

She gave me a distant, tired smile. A tall woman of uncertain age, hers was a pale, almost ethereal beauty, spun from the vapours that veiled her domain. "The northern continent has been populated far longer than yours, dear emissary. Perhaps that is why it can never find peace; its history runs too deep."

I fingered the hilt of a concealed knife. Diplomacy requires many different strategies; an advisor must be prepared to use any weapon at his disposal. Reaching across me, her scent the ashes of fire mixed with ice and regret, she plucked the poisoned blade from my belt, admiring it as I trembled, before handing it casually back.

"I know the secrets of each neighbouring kingdom, Alfranz. If they begin to show unwanted attention, I remind them how defenceless I am." She trailed a finger along my cheek and I envied and hated the coarse hairs that denied me

317

her touch. "Then I convince them it would be best to leave well alone."

I LAY BETWEEN HER SHEETS, groggy with sleep and tangled in blissful confusion—did any of *that* really happen?

"Your King," she mused, propped on one elbow, her skin the ghosts of leaves. "Does Cybold know it was his brother, Feralt, who killed his wife?"

"Blackmail?" I hissed, struck by an icy draught.

"Just a memory, dredged from somewhere or another," she murmured, rising and beginning to dress, leaving me bereft. "I ask for no benefit. You must do with it as you see fit."

"Give me something else," I pleaded. "Something to convince my liege to leave you be!"

She shook her head and sealed his fate. "King Feralt did not make the long voyage here. *You* did. And now it is time for you to return."

WHEN THE KING asked me about Memora, I could not find the words. It was like waking from a dream, half-remembered glimpses of another reality. Grasping at smoke.

"A mystical, almost magical place," I said, running a finger along my hairless chin, tracing a line drawn by someone I could only dimly recall, "but of no strategic importance."

King Cybold harrumphed—a mannerism so like that of his deposed brother—and returned his attention to the map. "So Alfranz, *Anagonia*. Your thoughts?"

LIAM HOGAN IS an award-winning short story writer, with stories in Best of British Science Fiction and in Best of British

Fantasy (NewCon Press). He's been published by Analog, Daily Science Fiction, and Flame Tree Press. He helps host Liars' League London, volunteers at the creative writing charity Ministry of Stories, and lives in London. More details at http://happyendingnotguaranteed.blogspot.co.uk

83

HERBERT
CHRISTIAN BIECK

I am not sure I should be telling this story. He is a special creature, after all, and they want to stay secret. But I believe he gave me permission, so here we are.

It started with one perfect egg.

Living in rural France, my wife and I try to follow the seasons. Every year in early spring, I put aside some eggs that are good for hatching. This one was ideal: not too small or too large, not too round or too pointy. With the right light, it could almost be considered golden. I placed the egg into the incubator with eleven others, expecting the new brood of chicks to hatch on April 1st as our annual contribution to world cuteness.

Our beautiful black rooster Jean-Claude takes his job as head of the flock very seriously, so when April Fools' Day arrived, almost all the shells were cracked and from each one, a fluffy chick emerged, chirping loudly at the expectant human parents. Except for one.

"That doesn't look like a chick," my wife said. "Is it what I think it is?"

"Maybe," I said. I pointed to the remaining two halves of the perfect golden eggshell. "I didn't know they hatch from chicken eggs."

My wife shrugged. "Let's call it Herbert," she said. "It looks like a Herbert. Is it male?"

I picked it up and turned it over carefully. "Herbert it is," I said. I pulled out my phone to take some pictures for our friends, but Herbert looked at me with big dark eyes and I forgot all about it.

The next morning we found some serious overcrowding in the cage. "At the rate he's growing we should put Herbert outside with the goats right away," my wife said.

"Are you sure that's a good idea?" I asked. We have two goats to keep our grass short. Ninette, the larger of the two, can be quite dominant sometimes, and her horns are scary.

Fortunately, it worked out well. At first, Ninette looked at the newcomer with suspicion, but Herbert flashed his hooves at her and flapped his fledgling wings, and after that they got along fine.

Herbert was happy running around the pasture with the goats and the adult chickens. We spent most of the time we weren't otherwise occupied standing at a window and watching the new animal on our little hobby farm play. "Do we need to have him registered?" I asked.

"Ugh," my wife said. "Not one of those ugly ear clip things. They must hurt."

"Right. There is also the matter of vaccinations. Let's ask the vet."

The French are nothing if not pragmatic. After Monsieur Dupré had taken a long look at Herbert, and made sure I wasn't playing a joke on him, he explained that if Herbert hatched out of a chicken egg, we should be fine. "Besides," he said, "Herbert's kind isn't on any registration or vaccination list." Monsieur Dupré didn't charge anything for the consultation. He even left some carrots for Herbert, who liked them a lot and shared some with the goats.

Herbert continued to grow quickly. After six weeks, his shoulders stood almost as high as mine, and his wings extended as far as my arms. The color of his coat changed from the mottled gray of his hatching day to a bright, almost luminescent white. "We might have to start hiding him," my wife said. "I'm surprised we don't have reporters crawling around here already."

She was right. The villagers certainly knew him by now. A few kids and older folks came to our fence from time to time; they petted Herbert and gave him treats, both of which he immensely enjoyed. But no strangers had come so far. Either his image hadn't popped up on Instagram yet, or nobody believed what they saw. I found the latter more likely. Come to think of it, though, I still had no pictures of him—I always forgot to take them.

In July, a French tabloid reporter who happened to be on vacation in our village showed up on our doorstep with questions. We figured that since the secret was out, the woman might as well write something positive. When we took her to the pasture, Herbert was genuinely happy to see her. He nuzzled the reporter's hands for treats, and then her ear, as if whispering to her.

Nervously, we bought the tabloid for the next few days, but no article was published.

One sunrise at the end of summer, I went to open up the chicken coop and replenish food and water. Herbert didn't greet me as usual, and didn't take the treats I brought. Instead, he watched me, waiting. The other animals were unusually quiet and subdued, as if holding their breath; not even proud Jean-Claude crowed as he normally did.

"Do you want to tell me something?" I asked. Herbert nickered softly. "Okay," I said, and called my wife.

"What's wrong?" she asked. Herbert nuzzled her ear, and mine. Then he turned and pranced a few steps away from us. He spread his magnificent wings; their wingspan measured twice his own length now. He looked back and neighed.

My wife took my hand. "Goodbye, Herbert," she said. She had tears in her eyes, and so did I. "We will miss you."

With a running jump, Herbert's wings lifted him off the ground. A few powerful strokes later, he was already high above the pasture. One last time, he bobbed his head at us, then he climbed, growing smaller and smaller, until finally, with a brilliant flash of white light, he was gone.

My wife wiped her eyes. "You should write a story about this," she said. "You can call it 'Our Summer with the Pegasus.' Do you think Herbert would like that?"

Something drifted to the ground in front of us. I picked it up. It was a gleaming white feather.

CHRISTIAN BIECK FELL in love with the fantastic after following Lucy through a magical wardrobe as a boy. Besides writing, he researches the future of business, makes music, and teaches tennis. Christian lives in a secret compound in France with his wife, two cats, and two dogs. Find him at Linktr.ee/chbieck or www.bieck.fr.

84

MOONSTONES AT MIDLIFE
ELIZABETH RANKIN

You wouldn't know it to look at me now, with my two kids and my house in the suburbs and my husband in IT, but I used to be a fairy princess.

I stumbled into the darkness behind a waterfall and found a portal, or maybe they let me in. The fae, with their long, beautiful faces, strange laughter, and ancient stories. Sweet summer afternoons passed to autumn bonfire evenings. I danced at court, sang with choruses of larks, solved ancient riddles, and learned to use magic swords. Time passed that could have been a season or a century.

He gave me a crown of moonstones and asked me to stay. I said yes and asked for time to say good-bye. We returned to my front lawn, somehow only the day after I'd left.

"I'll wait for you," he said, and pressed my fingers around the crown.

My farewells were joyful. I made up a story of a foreign exchange student and I pitied them that they'd never know magic. Days turned to weeks, then to months. I knew time moved differently there. Then a year.

Now they pitied me, abandoned and crushed. I packed the crown away and worried that something in that world had killed him. It wasn't all safe in that other place. But what I really feared was that he'd forgotten me.

Things moved on. I looked behind waterfalls and in toadstool rings, and wished for time to stop here like it had there. I thought I was mad. Sometimes I wore the moonstones and danced and didn't care if I was.

In the fifth year after I returned, I met Gavin.

When I turned 30, I found my first gray hairs. Gavin asked me to marry him. I said yes. We bought a house with a cracked driveway that would need to be replaced. Part of me still believed I wouldn't be around to worry about it. It was when my daughter was born that I finally stopped looking for him. Sometimes I watched the fireflies twinkle in the bush, close to magical, and remembered when I danced.

When he did come back I wasn't ready. Another summer day, at a lake this time. Gavin was out of town again. I took the kids to splash and build sand castles on a beach that used to hold golden sand, and was now more mud. Not many people came here, they wanted something fresher.

He sat next to me, as if he belonged there. Not from behind a tree or a portal. Just sitting in the sand, grains clinging to his smooth, dark skin. He said nothing. My mouth gaped.

"Why are you here?" I finally asked. It was the only question.

"I had to talk to you," he said. His voice was music.

My chest felt as if it couldn't contain the hammering of my heart. I winced, huddled my knees to my chest to keep it from bursting. I couldn't tell if it was love or anger.

"You waited too long," I said.

"Not long, for me," he said. "You look different."

The thing inside me that had stayed airy and twinkling turned leaden and cold. Inside, I'd known he wouldn't come as soon as I saw those gray hairs.

"I made a life, when you left me behind," I said.

"I returned. But you seemed happy. In a white dress and smiling. You wore someone else's crown."

I stared at him, not understanding at first. "You came back on my wedding day? I waited for you for eight years! And that wasn't someone else's crown, I bought it for myself."

My voice raised and I shot a glance to the kids, who looked up at me. They waved and looked through the prince at my side, as if he weren't there at all.

"The crown wasn't real," I said, in a lower voice.

"You wed another."

"Because you left me."

He brushed his hands off and looked at me then. His eyes were warm as embers in whiskey. "You are content." He didn't make it a question.

We were going to fix the driveway next year. My son started first grade in a few weeks, and my daughter's birthday party needed to be planned. Was this contentment?

"This is my life," I said, not sure. "I built it. There's no magic, but it's a good life."

"You wouldn't come back with me then?"

I wouldn't ask why he'd want me. I wouldn't.

He seemed to know anyway, lips crooking in a smile. "I gave my crown only to you." He shrugged in a way that brushed off all the concerns in the world. He held out his hand and I took it. His touch was as warm as his eyes and sent a slight tingle through me. Magic did that, I remembered.

I could hardly breathe. I watched my children laugh, and I despaired at leaving them. Stepping away from my safe life for a future with no guarantees. Dreams are made to grow out of, they say.

"I'm not a fairy princess anymore."

"I know," he said. His fingers touched my hair, where the gray moved through it, as gently as if he touched strands of silver. "You'd be a queen."

I looked down at the sand, still a beach, still bringing joy, even if some might say it had passed its prime. A deep breath filled my lungs. Why shouldn't I dance, if not all night, and tell stories of my own? "Can you have me home by 10?"

He smiled, teeth like the moon in the night sky, "I can do anything you like."

"Good." I kissed him. He tasted like the first snowflake on your tongue, like a raspberry off the bush, warm from the sun. "I'll get my crown."

ELIZABETH RANKIN HAS WANTED to write fantasy since about the age of three, when her father began reading her *The Hobbit*. You can also find her trying out new recipes, catering to the whims of her three dogs, or playing tabletop and video games. Elizabeth lives with her husband in their dream-house-in-progress in Cleveland, and on Bluesky at @rankinwrites.bsky.social.

85

TWO LETTERS CROSSING PATHS THROUGH THE FAIRYMAIL

M. E. GARBER

Dear Isabelle,

Let me start off by saying that I truly don't believe you poisoned me on purpose. I know it was an accident. But this latest incident is merely the straw that broke Rumpelstiltskin's spinning wheel. You see, despite my advice, you dress as if you have an Unseelie Demonmother instead of a Fairy Godmother. (Black clothing makes you look sallow is all I'm saying—especially around your eyes, my dearest—while pink really brightens your complexion.) It's very distressing, and has drawn some very pointed comments from the Fairy Godmother Management, let me tell you!

Your predilection for gothic everything means I'm constantly bumping into iron; recall the burns I got from touching your boots? I mean honestly, hobnails went out centuries ago! And how about the time I made that gorgeous lace and tulle dress for your dance, only to learn "dances suck."

Please understand: I've really been trying my best for so very long, and I'm tired of always failing. The sparkle-clouds have been favorites for centuries, but not with you. Glass slippers are every princess's dream, but you threw them in the recycling! Even unicorns drawing your carriage somehow weren't good enough! I simply don't feel appreciated.

After this latest misadventure, the time has come for me to resign as your Fairy Godmother. Most children keep theirs until eighteen, but at fourteen I think you're ready for, ah, greater independence, as they say. However, if at any point before your eighteenth birthday you'd like to reconsider, feel free to tap your heels three times and utter my callphrase—"boop-boop-eee-doopsie!"—and I'll reappear (after donning protective gear, you understand)!

With greatest regards and patient commiserations to your mother,

I remain,

Yours,

Fairy Godmother

Dear Fairy Godmother,

I hope you're feeling better after that bout of Iron Fever. I swear I didn't know the "Iron Jawbreakers" used actual iron! I never guessed you'd swallow them. Again—sorry!

This is a hard letter to write, but since you've been gone, things are different. No one's hiding my studded wristbands and collar, fearing the iron within. No one prattles on about wearing "feminine pink" and ruffles instead of black, or changes my Doc Martens into glass slippers when there's a foot of snow outside. The school bus never shifts into an enormous pumpkin carriage drawn by irate unicorns (I mean, I'd be irate too; the driver, Mr. Noh, has been married for years, you know what I'm not saying?). Pink sparkle-clouds no longer glitter around me during classes. (I've got allergies, too, you know?) During gym, my shorts don't morph into flouncy skirts. I also don't hover when I jump for the ball anymore, which I kinda miss, but that's beside the point.

The point is, while I know you've been trying your very best, I'm kinda over it? At fourteen, I'm old enough to be doing things and making my own mistakes (and no, I will never think black kohl eyeliner is a mistake "on my delicate heart-shaped face"). I truly appreciated how you made it look like I didn't break that window when I was eight, but Shelly down the road still won't talk to me since she took the blame. I can't even apologize because you won't let me verbally or in writing acknowledge I did it. Can't you see how that's holding me back?

Please don't think I hate you. I don't. But I'm fourteen now: two sevens. I know seven is an important number to you. Although I'd wish you'd told me that years ago, before my parents held a traditional Italian "seven fish new year" party for the neighborhood kids. Like I've tried for years to explain, we never wanted to be fish. At least the gills left cool scars, right on my neck! Of course, Shelly didn't think it was cool. So I'm hoping this letter holds double weight.

Because, dear FGM, I'm letting you go. Better luck with your next child.

All the best,

Ravynne (formerly Isabelle)

PS: can you reappear my Doc Martens for me? those boots were expensive. Thanks.

M. E. Garber has never wanted a fairy godmother. She currently lives halfway between the Kennedy Space Center and Disney World, the ideal place for someone writing speculative fiction. When not writing, she's often sipping tea or tending orchids. Visit her online: http://megarber.net or @MEGarber@wandering.shop

86

No Fairytale Ending

PRIYA SRIDHAR

The letter came before you did. You arrived in a gleaming carriage. We did not know if you would be here to stay this time or to just make empty promises. My heart is now a hardened stone of bitter pumice. I said I wouldn't speak to you, and I keep my promises.

Your husband wasn't the beast of village gossip. He charmed Father with sharp teeth, long hair, a hint of magic in his sparkling gaze. Your daughter happily greeted us, reaching her hand out for sweets. She seemed pretty on the outside. I wonder about the tales of a lady falling for a monster, but not knowing what ugliness lay inside both of you.

Why did you come? More importantly, why did you leave? We wanted you to stay. I would have understood if you had opened your mouth and let the words weave a story. Instead, you spoke with barbs.

Father left to inquire about furs he could sell on the market, all those years ago. He asked us for gift requests. I was young. I did not understand he was asking out of courtesy. I asked for Christmas chocolates. You wanted a rose. That seemed reasonable enough.

Then you vanished after Father came home with a stricken look. You talked in low voices. You quickly packed your things.

I had to find out years later from our other sister that a man had asked for a companion, platonic, for conversation. He would pay our father handsomely for his time, but Father worried about the girls at home—us. This man, baring teeth at this refusal, said that Father owed him, for spending a night in his place, that he was a polite guest and needed the money. They bargained long into the night, and the beastly man agreed the oldest daughter could go.

We never complained about the payments. Father rebuilt his business, and we went to school. I wrote letters you answered sparingly, with a flowery script, and words that asked about how I was. You even forgot my age, assuming I still played with dolls. I learned how to make and peddle them. We had bills to pay, and I wanted to make my own way in this world. I would have gone to university, but Father would have fits every time I asked.

You came once for a holiday. We were all so happy to see you, with Father's hair has gone grey. But when you stepped out of that carriage, your gait changed. Your feet slowed down, and you hung your head. When we asked about your time as the companion, you snapped at us. In the early days, you would prowl at the edges of the cottage. When you slept in your room, it was fitful and loud.

We asked if he had hurt you. You snapped no; he was nothing like that. When I corrected one of your errors regarding the plumbing, you tried to assert that you were here. I thoughtlessly said you hadn't been. I knew all the tricks for stopping a leak that I had to learn alone. You screamed at me till I ran from the room. Father came to investigate, and more screaming flooded the house.

You left that night. Not even a note, just boot prints outside the front door. We didn't see you until the wedding. Any letters contained cruel messages. Several sent Father to bed. He would lean on us, to fill his emotional holes. I would give, and find myself empty.

Maybe there was a curse, our neighbors whispered as they invited me for tea. Perhaps you had to return or your host would die of a broken heart. I surmised he fell for your love of books and gardening. You once were lovable. The person who you used to be would charm anyone.

We didn't want to go. You didn't wish for us to understand your enchanted life. Also, we didn't want to grasp what spells or bonds you could have broken. Father overruled us. He said that we had to go for the sake of duty.

The proceedings were stiff as the bookshelves that lined the room for the ceremony, and the many guests that we did not know. We all wondered why we had to dress up in outfits that barely fit us, with fraying threads I snipped. You arrived late to the ceremony, your hair in an elegant knot but your dress nearly filling the room. Your husband braided his hair as well while the end frizzed out but otherwise didn't seem beastly or bad-tempered. When you talked to us, you said that you would have time later. "Later" didn't come.

You sent a letter decrying us for the crime of answering your invitation. Father took to bed that day, wracked with guilt. Our sister and I did the chores, balanced our finances, and acted like all was well. I wish someone had turned us to stone statues, like the ones which adorned your new castle. Then we would feel nothing.

Letters brought a sense of dread, reminding us of our recent offenses. We assumed you had a beastly nature that your husband brought out of you. It did not come with sharp fangs or a craving for raw meat. I stopped waiting and wrote that I didn't want to speak to you again. You didn't respond.

I glared when I saw you. You looked the same but paler. I purposefully avoided your gaze. To admit to sadness would mean to beg for a curse to mend, a spell to break, words to be said. But I already know you would say nothing. This is not a fairytale. There is no happy ending.

PRIYA SRIDHAR IS A WRITER, copywriter, and collector of bookmarks. She believes the best thing in life is friends, with chocolate as a close second. Priya lives in Florida with her family, a quartet of rubber ducks, and many plushies. Visit her online: @SFF_Sridhar on Twitter or at www.priyajsridhar.com.

87

LIES SEEK SHADOWS
VALERIE VALDES

I scrawl a curse into the ashes on my doorstep as the festival singers dance past me, unheeding. Whoever burned my warding statues is long gone, but if they return, this will mark them for all to see. The statues themselves were not enchanted —my shop's true defenses lie elsewhere—so this was either a vandal with no magical training or a crude message from someone who fancies themself my enemy.

As a truthspeaker, I have many enemies.

Today is the Feast of Saint Felicia, inauspicious for my craft. Not because my magic is weakened, but because it is keener, and anyone seeking my counsel will find it painfully sharp. The revelers pass my door instead of stopping; they bang pots and pans rhythmically instead of knocking; they praise the Lady of the Rushing Stream instead of pleading for me to settle a dispute or untangle a knotty problem.

Thus I am surprised when the soft jingle of bells announces the arrival of a customer moments after I settle myself inside.

She is pale as a gardenia blossom, her eyes watery blue rimmed red from tears. Her dress is so richly embroidered her purse must be heavy with coin. Unless her circumstances have fallen, which might explain her patronage on this of all days.

"Saint Felicia guard your tongue," she murmurs respectfully. "Speaker, please, will you help me?"

"Of course, petitioner." I gesture toward the rear of my shop. "Come and sit."

I lead her to the sunroom where I perform my duties. The walls and ceiling are glass, the floor a mosaic of tin polished to a mirror sheen, the air cooled by charms tied to the rafters. The blaze of light startles the customer; she recovers and takes a seat on one of two iron chairs in the center of the space, folding her hands primly in her lap.

I sit across from her, then murmur an incantation and pass my right hand over a large metal bowl of water between us. I hold out my left hand to accept the coin she passes to me, both payment and reagent.

"Find your reflection," I tell her, "and speak your problem."

She leans forward and gazes into the bowl, her face illuminated from beneath. "A woman accused me of harming her," she says, quietly at first, a sob catching in her throat. "But she is the one who harmed me! We are both tailors, and she claimed my work was inferior, that I was being unprofessional toward some of my clients."

She pauses to look up at me through her eyelashes, a single tear traveling down her cheek. I return her gaze impassively; the truth is not swayed by such displays of emotion.

"I complained about her to the guild of tailors," she continues. "They ejected her. I thought that would be the end of it. Only, some of the other tailors banded together to support her, and now the guild is reviewing their decision. I've lost clients, and friends! It's become simply unbearable!" Her tears flow freely now as she addresses me directly. "What should I do, truthspeaker?"

I pass my left hand over the water and call on my magic, dropping her coin in the bowl. Individual perceptions and experiences of the same circumstances are rills and rivers feeding into the vast ocean that is truth. I will be able to perceive the parts and the whole at once, know both intention and outcome, follow each flow to its ultimate destination.

The coin begins to glow, and with both hands I cup water and drink.

My mind opens to the fullness of the situation, wave after wave of thoughts and emotions crashing against the shores of my being. I cannot see, but I know every vein in my body glows with the power coursing through me, until at last the spell is complete.

My vision returns. My tongue is hot and raw in my mouth, but I am compelled to speak. "You brought false witness against your colleague," I say, my voice hoarse.

"I didn't!" my customer cries, her hand flying to her face.

"You believed it was just, because she spoke ill of you," I continue, ignoring her outburst. "You believed your allies outnumbered hers, that they had more power. You longed to put her in her place, but you failed, and you came to me for a balm to soothe your inadequacies." As if the truth could be so easily bought and sold, especially on this day.

"I didn't!" she shrieks, leaping to her feet. "You lie!"

"You know I cannot," I reply.

Her lips twist into a snarl. She upends the scrying bowl, spilling water all over the floor. It shimmers, then darkens as a cloud passes over the sun above. The coin inside rolls toward me, and with a firm hand I snatch it up.

"You have your answer," I say. "Go ask Saint Felicia for another, if you think she will hear you."

The woman's pale cheeks flush red as rose hips. Silently, sullenly, she stalks out, the welcome bells jangling sweetly despite the violence with which she throws open my door and leaves my shop. Outside, the songs continue, the thud and clang of pots and pans keeping the beat as the city celebrates.

Sighing, I right the overturned bowl and step into the other room to retrieve my mop. My profession is a challenge at the best of times; I cannot believe anyone would be so foolish as to come for a speaking on this day, when they knew full well they had done wrong. But then, so many people fail to realize their own foolishness until it's too late.

Sometimes the truth is clear and sharp, sometimes it is less certain, but I speak it plainly when asked. Alas, I cannot force anyone to stop lying to themselves.

No magic in existence is powerful enough to do that.

VALERIE VALDES IS A STORY DOULA, a cuss connoisseur, and a collector of cool tropes. She believes the best thing in life is making people laugh when they least expect it. Valerie lives in Georgia, USA with her husband, children, and cats. Visit her online: @valerievaldes on Twitter or http:// candleinsunshine.com/

88

THE SONG THAT NEVER ENDS
SCOTT EDELMAN

When I arrived for the walkthrough of the house which would that afternoon become mine, I spotted an old man outside staring toward the front door. I nodded as I walked by, figuring him for nothing more than a neighbor hoping to catch a glimpse of whoever had bought the place at the estate sale.

Inside, I found Brian, the lawyer handling the closing, standing by that battered piano none of the kids wanted. A piano which should have been gone. He held up a finger as he mumbled into his cell. I examined the rest of the otherwise empty house, one which could never be as empty as the house I'd left behind.

"I know," he said, seeing my expression when I returned to the front room. The piano movers were overbooked, he explained, and couldn't cart it away in time, but I shouldn't worry, because it would *definitely* be taken care of the next day, gone before I got home from work.

I considered asking him to knock something off the selling price for my trouble, but as I looked at the keys dangling from his hand, I thought of the wife I'd never see again, and decided —let's just get it over with.

I woke in the middle of my first night in the house to the rhythmic sound of a piano, but one so out of tune I couldn't even tell what the song was supposed to be, only that it seemed to be something my grandparents might have liked. I was so groggy it didn't even occur to me that wasn't a thing I should be hearing. It wasn't until a woman began to sing along in little more than a whisper—a woman whose voice wasn't the one I constantly wished I could hear again—that I jerked awake.

I leapt out of bed and flung open the door. As soon as I crossed into the front room, the music stopped, except for one final note which lingered before vanishing. Alone in the room, I checked the windows and doors, and all were as locked as I'd left them.

Sleep didn't come easy that night, and the first thing I did the following morning was phone Brian.

I arrived home from work the next day to find the front door ajar. Could I have forgotten to pull it solidly shut when I'd left? Or had the piano movers forgotten to lock up after they'd hauled the piece of junk away? Perhaps. Only...when I pushed, the door swung open to reveal the piano still there.

I rechecked the lock, and as I jiggled the knob, I could hear the piano again. Not a song, just the plinking of one key, then another.

I turned, and even though moments before I'd been alone, there was the old man from the previous day tapping away.

"Your piano needs tuning," he said.

"How did you get in here? "

"I could tune it for you," he said, not answering my question. "It wouldn't be much trouble."

"Look, this thing won't be here much longer." I pointed to

the door. "And frankly, you shouldn't be here much longer either."

"Oh, I hope so," he said. "I truly hope so."

He sighed, then left. After making sure the door was securely locked, I watched out the window as he made his way to the sidewalk. He looked briefly back at the house, then hunched his shoulders and walked away.

THAT NIGHT, I was again woken by the piano, still so poorly tuned I couldn't tell whether it was the same song or something new. The woman's voice was louder this time, but still seeming somewhat distant. I stumbled toward the sound, and this time the music continued as I entered the front room.

Alone in the dark, I could see the motion of the keys by the moonlight. I pressed my hand to the keyboard, and the music stopped. The woman's voice continued for a few more beats.

I didn't wait until morning to call Brian. I left a message demanding the piano disappear, and hoped my—did I dare call it a haunting?—would soon be over.

As I OPENED my car door the next night, I once again heard the tinkling of the keys. Not an attempt at a song this time, but scales. For the first time, the notes rang true.

I stepped through the door to see the old man, his fingers on the keyboard, tools at his feet.

"I didn't give you permission to be here."

"I know you didn't," he said. "But something else... someone else...did."

He ran through the scales one more time, his fingers flying all the way from one end of the keyboard to the other, and though I wanted to stop him, I didn't. I wasn't sure why.

"Is that better?" he looked up to ask.

He wasn't speaking to me.

He nodded and began to play an old-timey song about love and how it could last forever, humming along quietly. He began to sing, and soon a woman's voice, no longer muted as it had been in the night, joined his. A voice I wished were Eleanor's, even as I knew that could never be. A voice that seemed to come from nowhere...and everywhere.

When he was finished, tears ran down his face, and mine as well.

A knock at the front door startled me, and I opened it to find two men there with a dolly.

"We're here for the piano," said one.

I looked toward the piano I wanted gone and saw...it was the old man who was gone. When I turned back to the movers, I could see him beyond them walking away down the path. A woman walked beside him, and as their fingers touched, they faded.

"Never mind," I said. "I think I'll keep it."

SCOTT EDELMAN IS A WRITER, editor, podcaster, and collector of convention memories. He believes the best thing in life is helping other writers realize they should "Never give up, never surrender." Scott lives in Glengary, West Virginia with his wife of 46 years, writer Irene Vartanoff. Visit him online at scottedelman.com or on Twitter @scottedelman.

89

SO MUCH MORE FUN

MARGARET DUNLAP

When the ladybugs brought word that Milkweed had acquired a changeling, Saffron paused only to direct her informants to the choicest of her carefully cultivated aphid-patches before she dropped her dew-bucket and flew off in a cloud of red and yellow fairy dust.

Most flower fairies shunned ladybugs, but here in Penn's Sylvan Lands—far from her home and family—Saffron needed all the allies she could get. Their carnivorous appetites might be distasteful, but ladybugs were loyal, tough, and—since they were not just tolerated, but prized by human farmers—ideal for intelligence gathering.

As Saffron flew, the aphids' anguished cries receded, but a seed of doubt grew in her heart. For as long as Saffron had known her, Milkweed had *talked* about taking a changeling, but Milkweed also talked about catching the moon in a raindrop and creating a flower made of cheese. Yet the years passed, and Saffron had attended innumerable fairy picnics under a full moon still free to roam the skies and where cheese-flowers had yet to appear. Still, the ladybugs had never lied before, and if it existed, Milkweed's changeling was an opportunity Saffron could not afford to miss.

She soon arrived—only slightly winded—at the bower of ferns and cattails her unreliable friend called home. Saffron poked her head inside, and there sat Milkweed, a tiny bundle cradled in her arms.

Saffron's heart soared. The ladybugs had been right. This was her moment. This was her chance. This was—

A *very* tiny bundle.

Saffron leaned closer, pushing a stray lock of red-streaked purple hair from her eyes. The babe was largely concealed in a leaf eiderdown stuffed with fluff, but the nose protruding from one end of the bundle was quite pointed, and from the other end poked...a tail?

"Isn't he beautiful?" Milkweed asked, beaming.

To stall for time, Saffron cleared her throat, a high tinkling sound like pollen shaken loose on a summer breeze. Milkweed's brain might be as fluffy as a seedpod, but she had always been kind to Saffron—more than she could say for certain other native flowers—and hurting her feelings seemed cruel. At last Saffron offered, "Isn't it traditional to take a human baby?"

Milkweed threw back her head and huffed in frustration. "Uh! Tradition! Just because we've done the same thing the same way for centuries doesn't make it a tradition!"

Saffron was pretty sure it did, but kept quiet.

"Besides, human babies are so much work! All they do is lie around and cry and sleep and poo. A possum baby will be so much more fun."

As though to punctuate Milkweed's statement, the hairy, beady-eyed baby in question chose that moment to make a break for the marsh and freedom, clawing through the eiderdown and sending up an enormous cloud of fluff. Milkweed laughed at the sudden snowfall, seized the creature's naked rat-like tail, and dragged it back into her lap. Once it had been re-contained, she offered it water cupped in a leaf. "Where are you going, my little Sweedledum? Were you thirsty?"

Saffron blinked. "His name is Sweedledum?"

"Of course not!" Milkweed sniffed.

In her lap, Sweedledum squirmed, knocking the leaf and a glittering arc of water into the air. Milkweed retrieved both with a gesture, never loosening her hold on the possum. "That's just a nickname. Isn't it, Smoodlepie?"

"What's his real name?" Saffron asked, as though it were any other question.

Milkweed gaped. "The nerve of you Saffron, the absolute nerve! Here you have not said one kind word about my changeling babe, and now you want to know his true name?"

Well, of course she did, but Saffron still had her pride. "Please," she scoffed, "What could I do with the power of a baby possum's true name?"

She could do so many things with it. Saffron imagined the revenge she would wreak against the flowers who had slighted her. It would be glorious...

She blinked out of her delicious reverie to find Milkweed still staring, eyes wide. But no longer in shock. No, Milkweed, bless her fluffy head, had encountered an idea. Unused to it, she pursed her lips in an approximation of a calculating expression. "If you want his true name...I'll tell you. But on one condition."

Saffron could not help but be impressed. "What condition?" she asked.

"You must agree to be his fairy godmother."

"You want me to be fairy godmother...to a possum?"

Milkweed gave a sharp nod, settling her resolve. "Yes. I know you all think I'm silly, but I'm not naïve. You can teach him things about the world I can't. It will be good for him. But you have to promise. Really and for true."

The baby possum, perhaps sensing the moment's import and drama, stopped lapping at the leaf, but kept its eyes lowered.

Saffron considered. A baby possum was not as good as a baby human (no matter what Milkweed said), but it was a mortal creature born of this land, with blood ties deep in its soil. Through that thread, Saffron could tap the roots of power buried here she had always sensed, but never been able to reach. With power like that....

Saffron sighed. "I will be his fairy godmother. I swear it for true."

Milkweed crowed in delight and squeezed Sweedledum around the neck. Sweedledum endured.

"His name is Frank," Milkweed pronounced. "Say hello to your fairy godmother, Frank."

For the first time, Frank lifted his head and looked at Saffron. His black eyes glinted, full of intelligence and... menace?

Saffron gave him a tentative smile.

Frank smiled back, toothy and mean.

Saffron's smile widened.

Milkweed was right. A possum baby was going to be so much more fun.

MARGARET DUNLAP IS an author and screenwriter who believes the best thing in life is making friends with the art department. Margaret lives in Los Angeles with a foundling avocado she rescued from the mean streets of the San Fernando Valley. Visit her online: @spyscribe on twitter or at margaretdunlap.com

90

HOW TO BUILD A CATHEDRAL

TODD HONEYCUTT

It's simple, at a fundamental level: Take a pile of stones. Carve them up. Assemble into a huge holy building. Go in and pray.

But it's not quite that naïve, as a people living in the hills not so far from and not so near to Prague discovered.

Those steps, true as they are, leave out necessary technicalities. Like the architect's grand vision of what could arise from the land. Experienced stone cutters and masons to execute that plan under the direction of one who understands its complexities. Many laborers, mind you, exhausting themselves, some of whom might not have much choice.

And time.

These aren't overnight projects. It takes years, decades. Even centuries.

Thus you develop your vision and gather these people and assemble a bunch of stones, then you have a cathedral to replace that lovely but too small chapel; a monument to be proud of that transforms your village into a town or your town into a city.

Because that's part of it. Right? Growing your community?

Even if you take all these steps—and do them well—it might

not work. The people I mentioned, they did all that. They built their cathedral and expected grand things.

But a cathedral isn't an object like a lamp or a house or a chapel. Within its stone construction is a beating heart. And like all living things, it requires nurturing and love and respect. Grounds have to be tended, floors swept, the choir stall admired.

A cathedral needs to feel that people want it, that what it offers belongs—vineyards for wine, gardens with curative herbs, a nave and chapels for townspeople to meet. It wants glorious movements within its halls and walls to mark births and weddings and funerals.

An untended garden yields little to eat.

Cathedrals are no different.

Maybe those people I mentioned did all that and attended to their cathedral and demonstrated daily its value in their community. Even with all that, their cathedral didn't thrive. Because there's one more secret. It has to want to be a cathedral.

Funny, I know. But they can be stubborn.

Feelings of superiority emerge from the frigid strength of their walls. In contrast to the piousness and devotion of the humans who tend to them, some might be dismissive, lacking any regard for others' sacrifices. The resulting malaise and lethargy blossom into a pervasive poverty.

A challenging and painful situation for all involved.

This cathedral, I dare not name it, for it was too proud to give back. Despite the attention and hopes of the villagers, its grapes fermented to wine that was never sweet enough. Despite its grand design, people didn't delight in walking to its chapels. Visitors to the area never returned, never encouraged their friends and family to visit. Twice, this cathedral tumbled its expansions, stalling its completion for over four centuries. And in its graveyard, it refused to let anything grow but tufts of grass and patches of a rare sour-smelling moss on the northside of markers.

It was ungrateful, resentful, selfish.

The villagers, when they bothered, spoke its name with a touch of sourness, a bit of spite, as if the cathedral were cursed.

When a war came, as they often do, all the fighting men rode off, and some of the women, too. As the enemy and the battlelines drew near, the remaining villagers abandoned their homes. Not a soul remained.

Except for one. That cathedral, it didn't fear war. But after the final villager left, a new feeling grew inside it. Freedom from its burdens and expectations begat relief, relief begat satisfaction. As days became weeks and weeks, months, a hollowness crept in, trivial then profound, filling the spaces where the villagers had been.

The king won the war, as much as any war can be won. A few people returned to the village and the homes they'd abandoned. Not all, as others in their wanderings found places more giving and forgiving.

The cathedral pushed its columns a little straighter. It kept its stained glass a touch cleaner, splintered sunlight brightening the nave just that much more. The flowers in its garden bloomed a bit earlier than did those in other gardens, and their sweet fragrances drifted in the breeze for miles around. The echoes of people walking and talking within its transepts carried further.

After the war, the village thrived, growing into a town and then a city. When the people spoke the cathedral's name, their voices held a touch of reverence, a bit of awe. Visitors came from Prague and beyond for the comfort of its many lush gardens, especially those that filled in the gaps of its cemetery. Many claimed, and not just me, to have a stronger connection to the numinous while meditating on its grounds and within its walls. More than one believed its wines to hold curative powers.

How do you build a cathedral? Take a pile of stones. Carve them up. Assemble into a huge holy building. Go in and pray.

Yes, all that. Though not entirely.
It has to build itself, too.

TODD HONEYCUTT IS a public health researcher and speculative fiction writer who lives with his family in New Jersey. In alternate universes, he's a butcher and a baker, but in none is he a candlestick maker. A Viable Paradise graduate, he has stories published or forthcoming in *Nature: Futures*, *DreamForge*, and *Beneath Ceaseless Skies*.

91

RING AROUND THE PRESENT
AMANDA MAYCLAIR

Syree raised her hand to shield her face, blinking against the final orange rays of a setting sun. She squinted, her eyes refusing to fully open despite all her efforts to *will* them so. She rose cautiously to sitting, only now realizing her bed was merely a slab of stone beneath an arching arbor of the same marbled design.

She nearly fell when she heard a voice at her shoulder.

"I watched over you." She spun her head, wondering why the world kept spinning. Her arm swung out to steady herself, and the small boy who had just spoken caught her as she fell, before she remembered.

"Did you?" she mumbled from behind her cascading veil of black hair. Her brown shoulders shook, and she lifted her head to peer at him. "Thank you, my friend." She allowed him to push her aright, and she turned back to the darkening sky with a disappointed sigh. "I guess nothing changed while I slept."

"It did." She turned more quickly then, where the small boy sat upon his heels. His flaming hair curled down the nape of his neck, and his summer chemise was pale with hints of old dust. Suddenly self-conscious knowing she had been watched, Syree made one vain attempt to smooth the wrinkles from her own robin's egg chemise over a pair of gilt-edged maroon pantaloons, one swipe to tame the tangle of her black hair.

"Well then?" she prompted, before softening her tone. "I could really use some good news, Patu, if you've any to share."

"I have," and he smiled his overly wide smile, while he lifted his small fist. "See." Uncurling his fingers, a crystal glinted in the last gleam of day.

"What is it?" She swiveled her legs around, leaning closer. "May I?" she asked, recalling her manners now that she was more awake. He nodded. Syree lifted the small object to her eyes. "It's a ring. And...?" she halted, eyes gone quizzical.

"Magic." Patu bounced up from his heels to plop beside her on the stone bench.

"How did you...?" she started, then let the question trail away.

"I stole it, of course."

"If someone had caught you..."

"No one did."

"What does it do?"

Patu shrugged.

"Takes you back. I don't know how far. Most of the note was some other kind of writing."

"Probably the old language." Hope rising, she inspected the crystal. "Do you know how it works?"

"I think you just put it on, then twist it around your finger."

"It's worth a try. Anything is better than this!"

SYREE RAISED her hand to shield her face, blinking against the final orange rays of a setting sun. Even now, her eyes refused to fully open despite all her efforts to *will* them so. She rose cautiously to sitting, only now realizing her bed was merely a slab of stone beneath an arching arbor of the same marbled design.

As she lowered her hand, she caught a sudden flash of light as it danced through a crystal ring coiled around her finger.

"Hello," came a voice behind her. "I watched you."

"Did you? What did you see?" she said, more startled than she intended. He was a small boy, maybe ten, with flaming red hair curling down his back. His dark eyes were wide, as if she was the most amazing sight he had ever beheld.

"You were stone, like a statue. But you seemed too real to be unreal. Does that make sense?"

"I think so. Which, since I am real, makes more sense now that I can see again."

"You did blink a lot."

"I'm cursed, I think. When the sun first rises, my eyes refuse to work. It hurts to see, so I lay down here because I dare not try to take another step."

"And you turned to stone?"

"If you say so. I think I'm glad I don't remember that part." She squinched her brows and frowned. "I seem to know some things for certain. I'm not sure how. I'm Syree, by the way."

"Patu. Syree, do you think I can help?"

"You? How? And why?"

"I just, feel I must." Patu glanced down, blushing.

"Could you really succeed?"

"Maybe I won't. Maybe I already have."

"You make as much sense as I do."

"I'm sure I was meant to help you. One of these witches must have something."

"What if you get caught?"

"I won't."

Syree motioned him to sit beside her. "Look here. I think this ring is magic."

353

AMANDA MAYCLAIR

Syree raised her hand, peering between the hanging boughs over burdened with fragrant buds of lavender and salmon pink and heart's blood red. She longed to squeeze between them, to force her way into the garden beyond. She could catch glimpses of paths wrought of glittering quartz, statues of what seemed boys and girls in all manner of dancing, could hear the burble of water that beckoned her to drink and clear the hot summer dust from her throat.

This wasn't a garden of her own courtyard. She hadn't been invited. Besides being rude, many powerful wielders lived scattered around their village. But the scent was so strong, like being enveloped in a shroud of roses. She reached one hand forward, to pull the offending bough aside.

Icy cold flashed on her finger. A ring of crystal so pure and clear she hadn't seen it against her own flesh. She reached forward again, only to have that icy cold sting her once more. She remembered, something, a thought so fleeting it could have been some dream evaporated in daylight. With more care, she looked closely at the vibrant growth of lush green, taking real note of the massive thorns gracing every stem. At the tip of each thorn, a glistening drop of what was surely enchanted poison.

Tears prickled her eyes, weeping for some fate she had barely missed, something important she must have lost.

Syree rushed home at once.

AMANDA MAYCLAIR IS AN EDUCATOR, troubleshooter, and author, whose inner eleven year old has discovered the joys of self-adhesive crystals. She lives in Kansas, USA, with her family including horses, dogs, cats, and too many chickens. Visit her online: Facebook/AmandaMayClair.

92

Homecoming
JB RILEY

I t was not surprising when only a few of the staff were Raptured. *Miseriae Nostrae* was an indigent home operating under a shoestring budget, after all: not the type of place to attract the best workers. Some, though, put their hearts into caring for their "kids" and each other, using everything from bright construction paper decorations to homemade tamales to build family in the midst of industrial sorrow. The head floor nurse, two aides, and the young Hispanic dishwasher were lifted suddenly into the air, cries of shock turning joyful as a trumpet sounded and the heavens opened in glorious golden light.

It was even less surprising when the rest of the staff—from nurses to janitors to the Director In Charge—fell as an earthquake shattered the worn linoleum flooring. They were dragged into the yawning mouth of the fiery Pit, screams of terror cutting off one by one as the flames flared bright to receive them. The Director in particular—who despite a modest salary was able to buy a new Lexus every other year while the building decayed around its residents and the mice got bolder —created a huge, lava-like flare as she tumbled in.

The old security guard who spoke so gently to everyone

(especially those few families who came to visit) was swept up at the last moment, pulled onto a winged horse behind a busty armored blonde, his worn blue uniform turning to shining mail and his creased hat to an antlered helm. The old pocket knife he always carried, one that had whittled hundreds of small toys and puzzles for residents over the years, became a proper Viking longsword clapped to his hip, and his "whoop!" of joy echoed through what remained of the hallways.

What *was* surprising when the ground finally settled was that every resident remained. No one had been taken—in any direction—and the inhabitants who could move came together in a frightened huddle amid the ruins of the only home and the only friends they knew.

The clouds rolled in, the pit closed, and the horse rode away toward the mountains. For a moment there was silence.

Then a voice spoke.

Come it said.

They limped or shuffled or wheeled or crawled through front doors that had burst their locks as the world ended. Some had too few limbs and some too many; twisted spines or palsied muscles. They stumbled toward the voice they heard; joined by the facility's blank-eyed inhabitants, who had been hearing that voice all their lives.

Haltingly they gathered outside, under the vast shadow of bat-like wings.

Those who could see looked up at the immense form that blotted out the dying sun. The blind and the eyeless tilted their heads to listen and scent the air, seeking why the others gasped aloud. Some wept, most moaned, and all were frightened.

The voice spoke again.

You were not born to be of this world

You are fragments of my dreams as I waited for the rising in my house at R'Lyeh

Today I am awakened

I am come to take you home

Giant tentacles, warm and gentle, reached down to gather the residents up. Others wormed their way through the shattered rooftop and tenderly lifted those who could not move on their own.

One huge velvety wing, pulsing like a mother's heartbeat, made a nest for their transport, and when they were all collected it folded gently over them for shelter.

Come my little ones
Tonight you shall travel with me
Tomorrow you shall dance among the stars
You are each of you my children
And you are so very, very loved

JB RILEY WRITES and edits technical proposals for a very large corporation, but has adored fiction since discovering *The Chronicles of Narnia* at age 8. When not trawling the shelves of the local book store, JB enjoys cooking, hockey and travel. She lives in Chicago with her family, which includes some really large dogs and a 5-pound cat that scares the hell out of them.

93

TONIGHT THEY ARE TOGETHER

A'LIYA SPINNER

At first light they will go their separate ways, but tonight he is at her mercy. His knees leave imprintations in the soil; she stands, surrounded by nervous footprints. They do not share a language; he cannot apologize for stumbling, half-blind, into her shelter. Until the sun rises and the snow recedes he is trapped in her shallow cave while the storm muffles the world beyond its lip.

The chill burrows into his bones. There is only so tightly he can pull his beaver furs around himself, crouched and shivering. When the bitter cold makes his teeth chatter, he feels a warmth on his back, like a wind, or an intimate breath. He glances behind him, but sees nothing except the low barrier of ice and snow between him and the endless night. The girl quickly hides her hands.

A fire flickers between them. The boy does not know where it came from. He tried to help, offering dried kindling from his pouch, preparing a broken flint for a night of sparks and struggle. She did not need his toil. She murmured and the flames grew from his offering, smokeless and warm. It makes him nervous; a part of him wonders if he has already died, and his spirit is waiting for a sunrise that will never come. Then the chill comes creeping in, and he knows his body is still alive, clinging to life.

Tonight, they begin their silent standoff on opposite ends of the cave, the fire between them like a barricade. Yet, somehow they get closer as the night drags on. She moves first, shifting to offer him a handful of berries. When he accepts, he moves, too, arms out, hands cupped. Their fingers brush; a different sort of shiver runs down his muscle, like a heat and a flutter all at once.

As he chews her gift, she becomes less afraid. She joins him in kneeling beside the fire, and for the first time he notices an oozing wound on her forearm, fresh and tender. This close to the flame, he doesn't need as much fabric to stay warm; he pulls a strip from the frayed ends of his cloak and wraps it wordlessly around her arm. She watches him, eyes wide, but she doesn't pull away.

Silence feels dangerous, like it might stifle the breath in his lungs. So, he speaks. With motions half-seen in the firelight, he tells the story of a family and a hunt. A frozen lake and breaking ice, separating him from the calls of his people. She listens with interest; his voice cracks with sorrow. When he is finished, she speaks, too.

In her ancient language, she whispers and makes motions with her fingers. The fire dances, and he watches figures and forms in the flames. A girl, touched by the stars, a gift to her tribe, for whom the water rose and the birds flocked. Wounded by a stranger, separated from her people. Lost, and trapped in a cave. Stranded with another foreigner who did not speak her tongue or know of the star-light magic in her fingertips, who looked at her with awe and fear.

Tomorrow, with the sun high overhead, she will ask the elk to guide her home, to sedentary huts made of bent saplings and mammoth hide. He will go the other way, keeping the mountains to his left until he reunites with his familial band of hunter-gatherers, never again to meet a daughter of the sky. Tonight, however, the sun is hidden, and they shyly lean against one another, each watching the flames and thinking about the strangeness of the other.

Neither of them sleep. The sounds of the night keep them vigilant. Echoing howls of distant creatures make her shudder with fear, wondering if they have come from Too Far North, to prey on starchildren like her. He puts his arm around her, pretending he is not also scared, that he has not always been afraid of the darkness. When the creaking of the branches of the trees causes his muscles to tense and his breath to catch, she finds and squeezes his hand. This is the only way she knows how to comfort him.

Beyond the lip of the cave, the fire illuminates the shadow of a passing herd. Only days before, he and his family were hunting these elusive caribou, his survival dependent on the whims of restless, migratory prey. Tonight, he lets them pass in peace, listening to his companion mutter. A brief light twirls and dances around their antlers as they march, like a flickering talisman to protect them on their way. The storm rages on, and perhaps it will take one of the herd before the long and dark night is finished. But for now, the herd is alive.

They are all alive.

Soon the dwellers in the cave will tell their families of the nameless stranger with whom they kept watch. By the time the snow melts and the land turns green, the firelit memories will begin to fade until the fear and the pain and the wonder is lost. Tonight they are huddled together and acutely aware of their own mortality. Soon all that will remain of this moment is the feeling of the star-tinged skin of her palms and the warmth of his beaver-cloaked chest. The faces of two strangers, illuminated by the light of the fire that he kindled with his kindness and she lit with her selfless gift, ensuring their survival because they dared to trust someone different than themselves.

At first light they will go their separate ways, to his hunt and her hut, to the stories and springtime and lives they briefly lost. But tonight, in the depth of the darkness—their breaths misting in the narrowing space between their faces—all they can do is cling to one another and share warmth.

A'LIYA SPINNER (SHE/HIM) is a non-binary writer and researcher, currently specializing in poison dart frogs but aiming someday for dinosaurs. In her spare time, she plays with her gecko and collects bones. Commune with his Twitter, @cladist_magpie, or visit her site: msha.ke/aliyaspinner

94

VILLAIN ORIGIN STORY
AMANDA CHERRY

A thing nobody tells you about magic is it can start out feeling like coincidence.

I was thirteen when mine showed up. The first instance I can point to revolved around a blue scrunchie. I was sure it was on my counter. But when I looked, it wasn't there. After a thorough-but-fruitless search of my bedroom and bathroom, I returned to my counter to find it where I'd figured it was all along.

So many coincidences.

Then it began to feel like luck. Do I have a lip gloss in this bag? If I turn to this station, will I hear a favorite song? Finding shoes the perfect height to keep me from needing to hem my favorite boot cut jeans....

Even when the first person dropped dead, I wasn't sure.

I didn't really know Marie. What I did know was that Jeff, the boy I'd been ostensibly dating the summer before high school, was riding with her all over town. I knew this because I was the new girl and the established queen bees took great pleasure in assuring I knew all about it.

Had anyone bothered to tell me Marie drove a '66 Mustang, I might have reacted differently. But nobody said anything about her classic car, offering only postulations about my supposed boyfriend, this older girl, and what *must* be going on in her back seat.

From the time I began hearing these tales, I'd mumble "drop dead" whenever anyone spoke Marie's name. Then she did—she dropped dead. The story I heard was: she felt poorly on Monday, saw a doctor on Wednesday, and was dead by Friday night. Dead. Of an undetected cancer that had likely started brewing...right around the time I'd first begun wishing her away.

Coincidence? *Luck*?

Not three weeks later, when the school receptionist who consistently gave me grief suddenly succumbed to a heart attack on the heels of a contentious exchange over excusing an absence, I had my first real inkling there might be something to examine.

Two foes in a month; nobody is that lucky.

Testing things out was fun at first—free popcorn at the movies, extensions on any homework I didn't feel like doing, better working hours—I learned pretty quickly I could get what I wanted in the moment, at any moment.

When I decided what I wanted most was to elevate my own social cache while simultaneously punishing Jeff for never thinking to tell me Marie was just a girl with a car (and a fabulous car at that) and not someone he was fooling around with, the solution was clear.

I hooked up with Chase Masterson.

Every American high school has a boy like Chase Masterson. Ours was tall, handsome, athletic, and entirely too full of himself. That fall, he was a senior, Vice President of Student Government, starting quarterback, and captain of the football team. I was the new girl, chubby, freckled, and with a thick Louisiana accent the local kids were quick to make fun of.

Sense says I had no chance with him. But magic changes the rules.

Getting the golden boy into bed was almost too easy. Almost. I'm not one of those people who thrives on a challenge. There's no such thing as *too* easy. And Chase was easy. Whether he was just looking to check off the names of every girl in the school or the magic was stronger than I understood, the world will never know. He was a lousy lay, but I wasn't really in it for the sex.

Chase Masterson was the means by which I was going to achieve popularity. But instead, he was the means by which I learned an important parameter regarding my power. The ease with which I had seduced him had given me the impression he would remain in my thrall after the fact.

Alas, that was not to be.

"Who would date some loser freshman who puts out on the first date?" he said to my suggestion of pizza after the game. "But we can hit the locker room if you're *that* hungry for it."

I had made a grave miscalculation: a mistake I would not repeat. But in the moment the damage was done, and I was left with a choice. I was tempted to use the same magic that had bedded him in the first place to repair the situation. I knew I could do it. The right turn of phrase, a proper whiff of intention, and he'd once again be putty in my hands.

But temptation was outweighed by rage. I could not let those words go unpunished. Punishment first, then further satisfaction. Make him suffer then make him my bitch. The shape of that suffering was easy to determine.

Like every teen boy in Detroit, Chase was obsessed with his car. He drove a 1968 El Camino with a turquoise and black bowling ball paint job, two-tone rims, and a custom Alpine system. It was always parked in the same space. The rest of the school somehow knew better than to park there; even the teachers left this prime parking for their precious quarterback and his bastard half-truck.

It made for an obvious target.

Magically, I was much better with people than with things.

Manipulating matter wasn't my strong suit, but weakening the sidewalls of his tires didn't take much effort.

It wasn't my fault he was speeding on the freeway. I only intended to foul his trip to the homecoming game—stranding him roadside with two flat tires and only one spare while the better quarterback who'd been relegated to second-string led the team to victory. The pair of synchronized blowouts at 80 MPH were as much Chase's fault as mine.

I suppose you could call it an accident: the State Patrol did. I don't. "Accident" is too close to coincidence. Or luck.

I call it a lesson.

AMANDA CHERRY IS AN ACTOR, an author, and a collector of social media followers. She believes the best thing in life is an afternoon in the sun on her sailboat. Amanda lives in the Seattle suburbs with her husband, son, and very lazy dog. Visit her online at TheGingerVillain.com or @MandaTheGinger on Twitter and TikTok.

95

EMBERS ON THE ROAD
LAUREN BRIAN CARROLL

I love walking the road. I love the smell of hot sun on asphalt; the hard, uniform feel of it under my feet. I love how one could walk for days, weeks, years, and never find the end of it.

I am fascinated by the road and its mysteries: why did they make it, those long-dead ancestors, for what purpose, and moreover, how? With no magic to convince the land to level, no spells to pour it true, no runes keep it safe from years and weather, yet here it is as here it was millennia ago. I love the frisson of excitement walking on tangible uncertainty gives me.

That's not to say the walking part is enjoyable: it's not. Walking is hot and dirty and boring, and oftentimes lonely. Towns are few and far between, only ever where the ley nodes congealed thickly enough to overwhelm the old disdain for magic the road has wrapped around it like a lover's shawl.

When I walk the road, I like to watch the light reflect off the monoliths that line either side. Unnaturally smooth, more reflective than a modern scrying mirror, sometimes I'd spend days speculating on what they memorialized, how they rose so high without dragons for lift and dwarves to stonetalk stability into their bases.

I was speculating on their insides—Were they hollow? Was

it dark inside or did the light shine through? Would people enter from the top or from the bottom?—when I first glimpsed you. It was high sun and my eyes stung from staring too long at the light reflected in the monoliths. I thought you were a mirage, a combination of heat distortion and tired eyes and put you out of my mind.

I caught sight of you again at sunset, silhouetted on top of a monolith, a black shape against ancient monuments turned bridal red by the embers of the day. I wondered, "Do monoliths host elementals, as mountains and oceans do?" I certainly did not have the proper offerings if they did. I shook my head at my uneasy thoughts and made my little camp. I love the road because on it I have no need for wards or salt rings, but you made me aware of their lack in my kit that night.

I asked about you on my next provisioning run. The settlement was near enough where I saw you, at least as road distances go; I got run out of town for my efforts.

"Nothing lives in the wastes, you loon," The shopkeeper said. Well, shouted really. I still had the fingers of the road running over my limbs and he stood far enough back that the spells he wore wouldn't be affected. He threw my supplies at me and the constable escorted me out of town.

The first time you touched me, I thought you were a dream. You smelled like char and the campfire smoke was in my hair, the fire itself sleeping, peaceful, dark. The residual heat of the day given off by the asphalt kept us warm.

With only the dull moon, the little moon, bouncing its light off the monoliths, and muzzy as I was, I thought your tendrils merely fringe and my skin craved their hedonistic stimulation. I didn't realize what you were until I felt the pinpricks of your needle teeth grazing my neck. By then I was gone. I was a puzzle piece who had just realized their crenelations were meant to help them connect to others and your tail curled possessively around my leg.

You were gone when I woke.

I thought, "Well! I've had dreams on the road before, but never *those* sorts of dreams."

It'd certainly been a while. Years, really. I didn't think about it on the road. I was certainly thinking about it now.

I could go to the priestesses, but that idea sat sour in my mouth. I dislike charity touch. Besides, I don't have any money.

It was that thought that finally pulled me off the road. The monoliths were too many, too large, to be entirely empty memorials. If I could find some mementos of the ancestors, I could trade them to a museum for currency in the city. With money I could buy an evening with a priestess. Borrowed comfort, but it would do.

It must have been you who helped me in the monoliths. Showed me, when the size and monotony looming over me made me feel shrunken and disoriented, which identical panel on the monolith was a door (they do open from the bottom!); showed me the three-pronged glyph and how to channel my magic into it to make the door open.

I made my camp that night inside a monolith. It's one thing to admire them reflecting the sun from the warm comfort of the road—it's another to stand surrounded by their magicless bulks and stare up at their blank faces endlessly trading each other's reflections back and forth between them.

You stood in the darkness just beyond the circle of my light and waited until I noticed you.

"Harbinger," I said.

"I prefer handmaiden."

Did I step out, or did you come in; maybe we pulled each other together like lodestones. Twice-forgotten baubles tumbled from my lap and scattered around us. It was a silly idea in the first place.

"I love the road."

"I can share."

"My lord of smoke and ash will call for me when he comes down from his mountain," you said.

"I can share."

I love walking the road. I love the smell of hot sun on asphalt; the hard, uniform feel of it under my feet. I love how one could walk for days, weeks, years and never find the end of it. That's not to say the walking part is enjoyable: it's not. Walking is hot and dirty and boring, but never is it lonely, with you.

LAUREN BRIAN CARROLL is a burnt-out service worker and a collector of small vintage cameras. He believes the best thing in life is dark hot chocolate with bourbon on a chilly fall day. Lauren Brian lives in the Midwest with several cats. Visit him online at @LBrianWrites on Twitter.

96

GNOMELIGHT
GILL LAWRENCE

It was one of those nights when the heat of the day had outstayed its welcome and now the stickiness was making it difficult to sleep. Even with the fan switched on, with its soothing breeze and hypnotic whirr, my brain wouldn't switch off. I lay there and mused about the news that there was going to be a rare blood red Super moon rising this night, and noticed that there was an unusual glow about the little chinks of light peeking through the gaps in my wooden shutters. I rose from my bed, walking softly on tiptoe so as not to wake the snoring husband and the dog curled up in her bed next to him.

I crept to the lounge and gently pulled open the large patio doors.

The cooling air was a relief and the scent of honeysuckles growing on the garden fence infused the night with their heavy perfume. I looked up and there indeed was a perfectly full moon hanging in the sky dressed in her beautiful pink gown. The whole garden had a soft warm magical glow. The white lights around the pergola twinkled and looked enchanting as did the color changing solar lights dotted around the planting areas giving sudden subtle bursts of blue or green purple or red. I walked to the edge of my balcony deck enjoying the feel of the warm wooden slats beneath my bare feet as I breathed in deeply, enjoying the sights and smells and the soft pink light.

I noticed the glow from my little fairy house that I had made, and from the mushroom house and little cottage I had placed in what the grandchildren knew as Dingly Dell. Here was where I had positioned my various gnomes and other characters made of stone. People sometimes mocked me for my tacky taste in garden ornaments, but I truly enjoyed sharing my beloved garden space with them, had named them all, and in time others had come to enjoy them too.

The moon strangely and subtly glowed a deeper pink almost crimson, and I felt a shiver run through my body such as I get when listening to a beautiful piece of music. As I stood there, I realized I could hear the merry sound of little voices talking, singing, and chuckling.

I strained to see below me and crouched down to look through the wooden bars. My heart skipped a beat as I saw. To my delight, that there was a party in full swing happening in Dingly Dell.

Elvish Presley gnome sung into his microphone and swayed his hips in a daring fashion. Willie Ekerslike and his Mrs. Emma Chisit, the Northern gnomes, danced around and around together as Shrek gnome held his lamp up over them to give them light and jigged about in encouragement. Hans, Knees, and Bumpsidaisy, the musical gnomes, played their instruments along to the song. Gareth Bale gnome, the Champions League footballer, performed keepie-uppies to entertain the youngsters: Gnome Alone and Gnome Alone 2, who cheered and clapped their little arms. Even sensible Fishing Freddie gnome waved his rod in time to the music. Page Turner, the reading gnome, had put down her book and demonstrated considerable break-dancing skills. Lazy Susie gnome whilst still languishing recumbent, smiled and tapped along to the beat. Terry Cotter, the earthenware gnome, attempted some head-banging moves whilst Ivor Wagon gnome zoomed round with his handcart brimming over with flowers. They were having a ball!

I didn't want to intrude my giant presence into this miniature magical mayhem, so I lay down on my decking and took it all quietly in.

After what seemed like hours but oddly also just like a fleeting second, the moon moved on out of the sky above my garden and, with a chill of cold air, I felt both the hard wooden floor beneath my thin nightdress and a deep feeling of loss. Peering downwards now all I could hear was birdsong from the early rising sparrows in the hedge. I got up slowly and, closing the patio doors against the cool night air, I returned to my bed.

I'm sure I will sleep now, pleased in the knowledge that I built a happily co-existing community in my garden that gives me so much pleasure in the sunlight; one that is magically transformed by the light of a Super Moon.

GILL LAWRENCE IS a retired specialist behavior teacher, creative knitter, and collector of Gnomes. She believes the best thing in life is to find the funny in everything. Gill lives in Saltdean, England with a lovely husband and a Yorkipoo called Izzy. Visit her online:@isabellayorkipoo

97

IN SUMMER'S WOODS
A STORY OF KAGEN THE DAMNED
JONATHAN MABERRY

I t was the music that made him stop.

Kagen sat up straight in the saddle and strained to hear.

He was deep in a forest in Vahlycor, far from any town. The forest behind him was the dark green of summer, the harsh sun having seared the blush of spring life from every leaf and blade of grass. However, the woods in front of him were different. They were a paler green, and there were ten thousand shades of new life. Flowers of incredible richness rose up from the lush grass, declaring themselves in shouts of color.

The music had come from there. He was sure of it. Notes from an instrument he could not identify, and lyrics in a language he did not know. Who was singing? And…why would they be all the way out here?

Frowning, Kagen took a few steps forward, pulled by the strange music. And it was all to him. It was everything. Even his memory of the fall of his beloved Argon, the death of his parents, the murder of the Silver Empress, and his own gods turning their backs on him seemed to fade

Then—minutes, hours, days later—the music changed. It was no longer a lilting tune. In the space of a single heartbeat, it became a woman's shriek of pain, of mortal terror. He did not know the language in which she cried out, but he understood everything.

Kagen tore the matched daggers from his belt and ran, veering from the path and plunging into the woods, scattering animals, frightening the birds from the trees. He broke from the foliage into a small clearing through which a brook gurgled. And there, on the far side of the crystal water, was a tableau that jolted him to a halt.

A hill rose from that side cut into its face was a shallow cave, in the mouth of which was a flat rock that served as an altar. Upon it, held fast by flowering vines around wrists and ankles and waist, was a woman of such surpassing beauty that it punched Kagen over the heart. She wore a dress of some old-fashioned kind, like something seen in old tapestries of the age before the rise of the Silver Empire.

Figures clustered around her, and Kagen found it hard to understand what he saw. They were slender and small, hardly larger than children, with eyes that slanted downward, sharp noses, full-lipped mouths, and sharp little white teeth. They wore clothing that seemed to be woven from living flowers, moss, and leaves. One of them held a small knife.

They all froze and looked across to where Kagen stood. The little folk and the woman. With a thrill of terror, Kagen realized what they were.

Faerie.

He had seen the paintings, had the stories read to him by his mother, saw plays and read poems. Before the coming of the Witch-king and his Hakkian armies, such things somewhere in the shadowy cleft between ancient history and made-up tales to frighten children. But the world was different now. Magic had been gone from Earth for so many centuries. The Witch-king, in his quest for the power to conquer, had brought it back.

And these creatures—banished so long ago—were here.

The faeries stared at him with shock as evident as his own.

"It is a man," whispered one. "It is a human man."

"He can *see* us," gasped another.

One of the creatures pointed at him with a bloody knife. "The queen was right," she said. "The veils are tearing. The doors are opening."

"Quick!" cried another. "Complete the ritual. Tear the veil asunder."

In a flash, she raised the knife and plunged it into the victim's heart. The woman screamed one last, long, lingering time.

The sound of that scream was so immense that it blasted all sight, all thought, all awareness from Kagen's mind. He felt himself flying, propelled on an invisible wave of force. Agony exploded in his own chest, and he tasted blood in his mouth. His daggers fell from his nerveless fingers.

His body struck the ground. The summer grass offered no real cushion. An army of small stones hidden among the stalks battered him, and a large one struck the back of his head. The hot sun above burned down to a cinder and went out.

KAGEN WOKE. Every part of him that he could feel hurt. He rolled over and vomited, then cowered on hands and knees, trembling like a sick dog. When he finally got to his feet the day had changed once more. The sun was in the west and shadows were creeping out from beneath the trees. His horse stood nearby, munching grass with equine indifference.

Kagen rubbed his eyes clear and stared at the road ahead. It no longer looked fresh and springlike. It was merely a road.

He rubbed his head, feeling the lump, and tried to make sense of things.

Magic had come back to the world, but had he seen it or dreamed it? He touched the daggers and found them snugged into their sheaths.

Kagen stumbled forward a few paces, but stopped as pain flared in his chest.

"What in the burning hells?" he grumbled and pulled off his jerkin and shirt.

There, over his heart, was a wound. It was small and nearly healed, but it was there. A slender scar as if a narrow blade had stabbed him.

Kagen touched the wound. As he did so he thought he heard strange music from far away. But not as far away as it had been the first time he heard it.

The hot summer sun went cold, and he shivered.

He ran as fast as he could, and was in the saddle. He wheeled his horse around and rode hard back the way he'd come.

JONATHAN MABERRY IS A NYTIMES BESTSELLER, 5-time Bram Stoker Award winning author, comic book writer, and editor. He believes the best thing in life is coffee and more coffee. Jonathan lives in San Diego with his wife, Sara Jo, and their little rescue dog, Rosie. Visit him at @jonathanmaberry or Twitter and Instagram; on Facebook, and at http://www.jonathanmaberry.com

98

HOW TO WIN THE G'IDIIDIGBO
CHALLENGE: A PRACTICAL GUIDE
A SAUÚTIVERSE STORY
WOLE TALABI

1. DON'T PANIC.

R emain calm when you are chosen to represent your
family on the silent grounds. You must fight Kele'leke of
Yu'usara to settle the dispute that has festered for more than
twenty juzu, despite the best efforts of the elder's council. Thus,
it comes to this. The ancient way. Each family has chosen a
member of the opposing family to do battle. The Yu'usara have
chosen you because they think you're the weakest of your clan.
They have chosen you because you're small, with a moderate
echo, and a tilt in your gait courtesy of scoliosis.

Your spine may be bent but your will isn't.

2. TRAIN TWICE A DAY.

At dawn, practice movement. At noon, spar with your sister
Ireno'ore in the garden. Do so in silence. All children on
Ekwukwe are taught the fundamentals of combat. But the only

way to win the G'idiidigbo challenge is to be prepared. The only way to be prepared for a fight is to get into one. Ireno'ore is skilled, and she has a good echo. You hear it in her motion, the potential for magic if she spoke the right words. But the challenge demands silence. There will be no magic.

When she catches your kick and lands a clean cross to the left of your jaw, fall and look up at the sky where the suns Zuúv'ah and Juah-āju are staring down at you, their heat tickling your sweat-slick skin. Pray to the Mother for strength, then get up. Continue.

3. REST.

There should be no sparring the day before G'idiidigbo. Spend the daytime alone by the river. Swim across it a dozen times.

Spend the night in your grandfather's glass and metal compound where there is a tiny opening in the ground that's linked to the network of underground caverns beneath the planet. Listen to your younger brother sing the Rakwa wa-Ya'yn. Go to your grandfather, hug him when he begins to cry. Nod confidently at Ireno'ore. Give your mother a reassuring look, repaying her for the unwavering support that persists even now.

Luxuriate in the love of your family. Listen to their echoes.

4. MAINTAIN EYE CONTACT.

Smile at Kele'leke when you cross the threshold of bright purple light that marks the pentagon-shaped arena of the silent grounds. Do not avert your gaze even when you feel the dampening of your echo, of your magic. You know why your family has chosen him of all the Yu'usara, but it's hard not to be intimidated. He's tall with lean muscles, a smooth afro, and a bloodthirsty snarl. But no one from his family looked at him when your mother issued the challenge. You must manage the distance, counter strike precisely, and be completely aligned with your family for this is the only magic allowed on the silent grounds. They will cheer, as will his family, making sounds of encouragement that neither of you will hear. But the power of the vibrations will permeate through the anechoic barrier, amplifying your abilities if you can align your echo with it.

5. BREATHE.

The purple light barrier will rise into the sky, cutting you off from the rest of the world. Suddenly, there'll be nothing but the breath of your foe and the slapping of his bare feet on the earth as he runs toward you, eyes red and full of malicious intent. Breathe. It's easy to forget to breathe when you are under pressure. When Kele'leke is close enough, use his own momentum against him. Parry. Counter. Don't get excited when he crashes to the ground. Breathe.

6. OBSERVE EVERYTHING.

Reset your stance and watch the way Kele'leke rises, the way he approaches again, more careful now. Keep your eyes on him but reach out with your echo. Search for the vibration of those who love you. When Kele'leke kicks at your calf, turn your knee out to it. It will hurt him more than it hurts you. Brace when you realize that the kick was a distraction from the incoming body punch. The pain of a cracked rib will flower on the same side your spine leans. Don't scream. Step back and pivot so that the filtered light of the twin suns is hot on your back, in his eyes. Pray to the Mother for strength.

7. RESONATE.

Remember the confidence in your mother's kohl-stained eyes. Remember the smile of pride on Ireno'ore's lips. Remember the joy in your brother's voice. Remember the rumble in your grandfather's throat when he told you stories of your ancestors going back centuries. Remember. You are an overlapping of histories. Memory is an anchor. Tether your echo to it. Find Resonance.

8. DON'T HESITATE.

When you feel the swell of strength in your arms, when the pain in your side dulls, when you see Kele'leke's movements with impossible clarity, that's the moment. Don't hesitate. Step in and deflect his attack with your shoulder then rotate your body so that your elbow crashes into the side of his head.

9. CONTINUE TO STRIKE.

Don't stop hitting him. It's when we are hurt, when our own strength fails that we rely on our family the most. You'll see the desperate look in his eyes as he finally reaches out with his echo. Hit him. You'll see the angry flare of his nose when he realizes it is too late. Hit him. There are many kinds of weakness. Hit him until his face is bloody and he falls to the ground and the light in his eyes dim and the lines of his face fall and he reaches out with a trembling hand.

"I yield." He will say.

10. SING.

The purple light-walls will fall. Sound will return to the world in a rush. You'll hear the chanting of your family. You'll see their dance, the synchronized clapping and swaying of their hips. You'll feel the vibration of the ground and the air. Join them. Dance. Sing.

WOLE TALABI IS AN ENGINEER, writer, and editor, mostly in that order. He believes the best thing in life is a clever idea. Wole is from Nigeria but now lives in Kuala Lumpur, Malaysia. Visit him online: @wtalabi on twitter or at wtalabi.wordpress.com

99

BELIEVE ME WHEN I SING THE MOON'S RETURN

SEANAN MCGUIRE

Dearest brother;

When first I took to the sea, you made me promise never to contact you. I believe your exact words, spoken as bitterly as the northern wind, were, "What belongs to the deeps should cleave to the deeps." If I went below, I was no sister of yours. If I left the land, I was none of your kin.

And for twelve long years, I have done as you requested. Acknowledge that, and read what I have written! Do not cast me aside again, because I obeyed when I was ordered, because I was in the habit of being dutiful.

The first and only time I denied your will was when I climbed to the top of the tower wall, when I clung to the bracing stones with the sea spray in my hair and said I would go. I had been called, and I would answer. You raged, then. How you raged, that I, your shameful, useless sister would be called when you were not!

But Mother knew, you see. Knew that of the two of us, only one might find contentment in the deeps, while the other would forever seethe with fury over what he'd been denied. She knew, also, that you would never forgive her, or me, for going without you; you wanted the world. You wanted both worlds. You wanted to drink the sea and swallow the moon, and believed that once you could, you'd be content. She knew then, as I know now, that you must be limited. If you were given leave to move between the realms, you would have destroyed us all.

Instead, you have only destroyed our kingdom, and yourself.

Did you think we weren't watching, brother, because we chose the deeps of the sea over the wilds of the land? Did you think we wouldn't notice the flotillas of ships which passed above us, their sails turned toward the territory of your self-proclaimed "enemies"? Most of all, did you think we wouldn't taste the ashes in our waters, the bitter brightness of blood? You have waged war against your own kind for a decade's time, slaughtering with impunity, until the bones of the defeated littered the seabed and none could sleep without hearing the moans of dead men on the tide.

And all the while, the moon was watching, and singing, as she does, to her sister, the sea. Twelve years of tragedy. Enough for the moon to take notice. Enough for the sea to listen. Enough for the two of them to decide.

When Mother wed our sire, it was to unite the lands of moon and sea, to bring a lasting peace to both halves of the world. The two of us were meant to show that balance was possible. When she returned home, as she had always told our father she would, she took me by her side, for you would remain above, to prove that the lands of men would not always empty the seas of the compassion to which all souls are heir. And yes, she saw that you were ambitious, and thought the dry lands would offer you more opportunity to whet that ambition, to sail your heart's course safe to shore.

She saw that I would be happy with an abbesses' place, and she took me by her side, to teach the daughters of the deep of the lands of man, to be one half of the equation we charted out between us on the day that we were born.

I learned peace and you waged war, and the moon shone bright and distant in your skies, a watching spirit on high, unremarkable in her constancy.

But now, brother…now all will change.

Believe me, please, I beg of you. Heed my words, and believe me. Each time the dry has made war against the world, the moon has shifted in her courses and flown closer to her sister, to offer comfort, to be comforted in her turn. And you have made war with such glorious abandon.

The moon returns, brother. She begins her descent already. Do you remember what happens when she descends to meet the sea?

The sea rises up to meet her.

Gather your people and whatever they can carry. Gather what you could stand least to lose. Gather them all, and do not look back. The moon returns. The sea will rise. The land will be reduced. This has all happened before. I hope, in the interests of those who can escape the waves, that it will not need to happen yet again.

I am sorry, brother.

I am sorry, but you were warned.

I will put this letter in a bottle, to be left in the current we played with as children, the one which carries debris so straight and true to the stream outside the palace walls. I only pray that you will read it. I only pray you will spare me, a little longer, from the ghost-songs of your bones.

With love, despite it all,
    Your sister.

Seanan McGuire is an author, TTRPG addict, and a collector of both dice and generation one My Little Ponies. She believes the best thing in life is a cold Diet Dr. Pepper in a corn field. Seanan lives in the Pacific Northwest with her extremely large, fluffy cats and one very hungry axolotl. She is also Mira Grant. Visit her online: www.seananmcguire.com.

(TRTC) addict, and a collector
Louie Pardoe. She
morn

ABOUT THE EDITOR

Jennifer Brozek is a multi-talented, award-winning author, editor, and media tie-in writer. She is the author of *Never Let Me Sleep* and *The Last Days of Salton Academy*, both of which were nominated for the Bram Stoker Award. Her *BattleTech* tie-in novel, *The Nellus Academy Incident*, won a Scribe Award. Her editing work has earned her nominations for the British Fantasy Award, the Bram Stoker Award, and the Hugo Award. She won the Australian Shadows Award for the *Grants Pass* anthology, co-edited with Amanda Pillar. Jennifer's short form work has appeared in Apex Publications, Uncanny Magazine, Daily Science Fiction, and in anthologies set in the worlds of *Valdemar*, *Shadowrun*, *V-Wars*, *Masters of Orion*, and *Predator*.

Jennifer has been a freelance author and editor for over fifteen years after leaving a high paying tech job, and she has never been happier. She keeps a tight schedule on her writing and editing projects and somehow manages to find time to volunteer for several professional writing organizations such as SFWA, HWA, and IAMTW. She shares her husband, Jeff, with several cats and often uses him as a sounding board for her story ideas. Visit Jennifer's worlds at jenniferbrozek.com.

COPYRIGHTS

Made in the USA
Middletown, DE
18 February 2024